PELICAN BOOKS

THE BLACK AMERICAN WRITER

volume II: poetry and drama

Christopher Bigsby is a lecturer in American Literature at the University of East Anglia. Bigsby received his M.A. in American Studies at Sheffield University and his Ph.D. at Nottingham. He studied for a year in this country at Kansas State University on a Fulbright Student Exchange grant, and he did part of his doctoral work while a fellow at the Salzburg American Studies Seminar in Austria. In the spring of 1968, he was a visiting professor at the University of Missouri, Kansas City, and he has recently compiled a book on his observations of the Kansas City riots in April, 1968.

Bigsby's earlier publications include, besides many articles, *Confrontation and Commitment: A Study of Contemporary American Drama 1959-1966* (1967) and *Edward Albee* (1968).

THE
BLACK
AMERICAN
WRITER

volume II:
poetry and drama

edited by
C. W. E. BIGSBY
Lecturer in American Literature
University of East Anglia

PENGUIN BOOKS INC
BALTIMORE, MARYLAND

Penguin Books Inc
7110 Ambassador Road
Baltimore, Maryland 21207

First published by Everett / Edwards, Inc. 1969
Published in Pelican Books 1971
Reprinted 1971

Printed in the United States of America by
Kingsport Press, Inc.

ACKNOWLEDGEMENTS

"Problems of a Negro Writer" by John A. Williams and Langston
Hughes, copyright 1963 Saturday Review, Inc. Reprinted by per-
mission of the Saturday Review, Harold Ober Associates, Incorpo-
rated, and John A. Williams. "The Negro Writer: Pitfalls and
Compensations" was first published in *Phylon* and is reprinted by
permission. "The Negro in American Culture" is reprinted by
permission of Pacifica Radio (WBAI-FM), "Black Orpheus" is
reprinted from *The Massachusetts Review*, ©1965, The Massachu-
setts Review, Inc. "White Standards and Negro Writing" is re-
printed by permission of *The New Republic* and Richard Gilman.
"Our Mutual Estate: The Literature of the American Negro" was
first published in the *Antioch Review* and is reprinted by permis-
sion. "Disturber of the Peace: James Baldwin" is reprinted by per-
mission of Eve Auchincloss and Nancy Lynch. "The Black Arts
Movement" was first published in *The Drama Review*, Vol. 12, No
4, Summer, 1968, T. 40. c. Copyright 1968 *The Drama Review*.
Reprinted by permission of the publishers and author. All rights
reserved. "An Interview with Ralph Ellison" is reprinted from
The Tamarack Review. "Poetry in the 'Sixties" © Paul Breman.
All rights reserved. "Contemporary Negro Fiction," by Hoyt W.
Fuller, used by permission of the author, first published in 1965,
in *Southwest Review*.

for Warren French

Contents

THE
BLACK
AMERICAN
WRITER

volume II:
poetry and drama

General Introduction

This two-volume study of the black American writer makes no claim to be completely comprehensive, certain authors of considerable merit being omitted altogether. Its aim is rather to examine the achievement of some of the major talents to emerge from the black community, to analyse and assess the difficulties facing the black writer, and to examine the problems of criticism in a field so fraught with social, cultural and political prejudices.

In recent years the white critic has found himself increasingly under attack. His motives and qualifications for the assessment of black literature have been called in question. This study consists of essays by both black and white critics and the reader will thus be in a position to judge for himself. Considerable space is devoted to this issue, and many of the general essays and interviews attempt to come to terms not merely with the achievement of the black American writer but also with the critical dilemma in an era of committed literature.

The bulk of the essays in this study were specially commissioned and appear here for the first time in print. Where articles have appeared elsewhere these are works of special significance which have not previously been published in book form. Most important among these are the symposium on "The Negro in American Culture" which appears in volume I and Sartre's seminal essay on *négritude*, "Black Orpheus" which appears in volume II. In the former James Baldwin, Langston Hughes and Lorraine Hansberry confront Nat Hentoff and Alfred Kazin in a crucial debate on the nature of the black experience and the writer's response to it. In the latter, Sartre, writing some twenty years ago, examines the concept of *negritude* and offers some profoundly significant insights into the nature of black writing. As will be apparent from the essays which appear in both volumes, *negritude* is by no means regarded with that mixture of awe and respect which it was accorded only a few years ago. Indeed a sustained attack was launched on it in the summer of 1969 at the Pan-African Cultural Festival held in Algiers. Nevertheless, Sartre's insights have played an important part in the criticism of black writing and provide a useful example of the white critic at his best.

At present the function of black writing is the subject of heated and often irrational discussion. It is appropriate, therefore, that we should choose this moment to examine the substance of Negro literary achievement and the nature of those cultural assumptions which underlie contemporary literature. It is hoped that this two-volume study by writers and critics from Great Britain and the United States will contribute materially to this examination and provide a useful tool both for the student and the general reader.

The Poet

Black Orpheus*

by Jean-Paul Sartre

W HEN YOU REMOVED the gag that was keeping these black mouths shut, what were you hoping for? That they would sing your praises? Did you think that when they raised themselves up again, you would read adoration in the eyes of these heads that our fathers had forced to bend down to the very ground? Here are black men standing, looking at us, and I hope that you — like me — will feel the shock of being seen. For three thousand years, the white man has enjoyed the privilege of seeing without being seen; he was only a look — the light from his eyes drew each thing out of the shadow of its birth; the whiteness of his skin was another look, condensed light. The white man — white because he was man, white like daylight, white like truth, white like virtue — lighted up the creation like a torch and unveiled the secret white essence of beings. Today, these black men are looking

*"Orphée Noir" appeared originally as the preface to an anthology of African and West Indian poets, edited by Leopold Sédar-Senghor (*Anthologie de la nouvelle poésie nègre et malgache de langue français,* Paris, 1948). A key document in the history of the concept of "Negritude," it has been available in English only in a difficult to come by and out-of-print issue of *Presence Africaine* (Paris, 1951). Its first American publication, in a translation by John MacCombie, was in the *Massachusetts Review.* It is this text which is reprinted here, where it appears for the first time in book form.

at us, and our gaze comes back to our own eyes; in their turn, black torches light up the world and our white heads are no more than chinese lanterns swinging in the wind. A black poet — unconcerned with us — whispers to the woman he loves:

> Naked woman, black woman
> Dressed in your color which is life . . .
> Naked woman, dark woman,
> Firm fleshed ripe fruit, somber ecstasies of black wine.

and our whiteness seems to us to be a strange livid varnish that keeps our skin from breathing — white tights, worn out at the elbows and knees, under which we would find real human flesh the color of black wine if we could remove them. We think we are essential to the world — suns of its harvests, moons of its tides; we are no more than its fauna, beasts. Not even beasts:

> These gentlemen from the city
> These proper gentlemen
> Who no longer know how to dance in the evening by moon-
>   light
> Who no longer know how to walk on the flesh of their feet
> Who no longer know how to tell tales by the fireside . . .

Formerly Europeans with divine right, we were already feeling our dignity beginning to crumble under American or Soviet looks; Europe was already no more than a geographical accident, the peninsula that Asia shoves into the Atlantic. We were hoping at least to find a bit of our greatness reflected in the domesticated eyes of the Africans. But there are no more domesticated eyes: there are wild and free looks that judge our world.

> Here is a black man wandering:
>   to the end of
>   the eternity of their endless boulevards
>   with cops . . .
> Here is another one shouting to his brothers:
>   Alas! Alas! Spidery Europe is moving its
>   fingers and its phalanxes of ships . . .
> Here is:
>   the cunning silence of Europe's night . . .
> in which

. . . there is nothing that time does not dishonor.
A Negro writes:
At times, we will haunt Montparnasse and Paris,
Europe and its endless torments, like memories
or like malaises . . .

and suddenly France seems exotic in our own eyes. She is no more than a memory, a malaise, a white mist at the bottom of sunlit souls, a back-country unfit to live in; she has drifted towards the North, she is anchored near Kamchatka: the essential thing is the sun, the sun of the tropics and the sea "lousy with islands" and the roses of Imangue and the lilies of Iarive and the volcanos of Martinique. Being [l'Etre] is black, Being is made of fire, we are accidental and far away, we have to justify our mores, our technics, our undercooked paleness of our verdigris vegetation. We are eaten away to the bones by these quiet and corrosive looks:

Listen to the white world
horribly weary of its immense effort
its rebel articulations crackling under hard stars,
its steel-blue stiffnesses piercing mystical flesh
listen to its exhibitionist victories trumpeting its defeats
listen to its wretched staggering with grandiose alibis
Have pity on our naïve omniscient conquerors.

There we are, *finished*; our victories — their bellies sticking up in the air — show their guts, our secret defeat. If we want to crack open this finitude which imprisons us, we can no longer rely on the privileges of our race, of our color, of our technics: we will not be able to become a part of the totality from which those black eyes exile us, unless we tear off our white tights in order to try simply to be men.

If these poems shame us however, they were not intended to: they were not written for us; and they will not shame any colonists or their accomplices who open this book, for these latter will think they are reading letters over someone's shoulder, letters not meant for them. These black men are addressing themselves to black men about black men; their poetry is neither satiric nor imprecatory: it is an awakening to consciousness. "So," you will say, "in what way does it interest us, if it is only a document? We cannot enter into it." I should like to show in what way we *can* gain access to this world of jet; I should like to show that this poetry — which seems racial at first — is actually a hymn by everyone for everyone. In a word, I am talking now to white men, and I should like to explain to them what black men already know: why it is necessarily through a poetic experience that the black man, in his present condition, must first become conscious of himself; and, inversely, why black poetry in the French language is, in our time, the only great revolutionary poetry.

* * *

It is not just by accident that the white proletariat rarely uses poetic language to speak about its sufferings, its anger or its pride in itself; neither do I think that workers are less gifted than our bourgeois sons: "talent" — the efficacious grace — loses all meaning when one claims that it is more widespread in one class than in another. Nor is it hard work that takes away their capacity for song: slaves used to drudge even harder and yet we know of slave hymns. It must therefore be recognized that it is the present circumstances of the class struggle that keep the worker from expressing himself poetically. Oppressed by technics, he wants to be a technician because he knows that technics will be the instrument of his liberation; he knows that it is only by gaining professional, economic and scientific know-how that he will be able someday to control business management. He now has a profound practical knowledge of what poets have called *Nature*, but it is a knowledge he has gained more through his hands than through his eyes: Nature is Matter for him — that crafty, inert adversity that he works on with his tools; Matter has no song. At the same time, the present phase of his struggle requires of him continual, positive action: political calculation, precise forecasting, discipline, organization of the masses; to dream, at this point, would be to betray. Rationalism, materialism, positivism — the great themes of his daily battle — are least propitious for the spontaneous creation of poetic myths. The last of these myths — the famous "Upheaval" — has withdrawn under the circumstances of the struggle: one must take up the matter that is most urgent, gain this and that position, raise this salary, decide on that sympathy strike or on some protest against the war in Indo-China: efficiency alone matters. And, without a doubt, the oppressed class must first find itself. This self-discovery, however, is the exact opposite of a subjective examination of oneself: rather, it is a question of recognizing — in and by action — the objective situation of the proletariat, which can be determined by the circumstances of production or of redistribution of property. Unified by an oppression which is exerted on each and every one, and reduced to a common struggle, workers are hardly acquainted with the inner contradictions that fecundate the work of art and that are harmful to the *praxis*. As far as they are concerned, to know themselves is to situate themselves within the context of the great forces that surround them; it requires them to determine both their exact position in their class and their function in the Party. The very language they use is free from the slight loosening of the screws, the constant frivolous impropriety, the game of transmissions which create the poetic Word. In their business, they use well-defined technical terms; and as for the language of revolutionary parties, Parain has shown that it is *pragmatic*: it is used to transmit orders, watch-words, information; if it loses its exactness, the Party falls apart. All of this tends more and more rigorously to eliminate the subject; poetry, however, must in some way remain subjective. The proletariat has not found a poetry that is sociological and yet finds its source in subjectivity, that is just as subjective as it is sociological, that is based on ambiguous or uncertain language and that is nevertheless as exalting and as generally understood as the most precise watchwords or as the phrase "Workers of all countries, unite" that one reads on doors in Soviet Russia. Lacking this, the poetry of the future revolution has remained in the hands of well-intentioned young bourgeois who found their inspiration in their personal psychological contradictions, in the dichotomy between their ideal and their class, in the uncertainty of the old bourgeois language.

Like the white worker, the Negro is a victim of the capitalist structure of our society. This situation reveals to him his close ties — quite apart from the color of his skin — with certain classes of Europeans who, like him, are opposed; it incites him to imagine a privilege-less society in which skin pigmentation will be considered a mere fluke. But even though oppression itself may be a mere fluke, the circumstances under which it exists vary according to history and geographic conditions: the black man is a victim of it *because he is a black man* and insofar as he is a colonized native or a deported African. And since he is oppressed within the confines of his race and because of it, he must first of all become conscious of his race. He must oblige those who have vainly tried throughout the centuries to reduce him to the status of a beast, to recognize that he is a man. On this point, there is no means of evasion, or of trickery, no "crossing line" that he can consider: a Jew — a white man among white men — can deny that he is a Jew, can declare himself a man among men. The Negro cannot deny that he is Negro, nor can he claim that he is part of some abstract colorless humanity: he is black. Thus he has his back up against the wall of authenticity: having been insulted and formerly enslaved, he picks up the word "nigger" which was thrown at him like a stone, he draws himself erect and proudly proclaims himself a black man, face to face with white men. The unity which will come eventually, bringing all oppressed peoples together in the same struggle, must be preceded in the colonies by what I shall call the moment of separation or negativity: this anti-racist racism is the only road that will lead to the abolition of racial differences. How could it be otherwise? Can black men count on a distant white proletariat — involved in its own struggles — before they are united and organized on their own soil? And furthermore, isn't there some need for a thorough work of analysis in order to realize the identity of the interests that underlie the obvious difference of conditions? The white worker benefits somewhat from colonization, in spite of himself: low as his standard of living may be, it would be even lower if there were no colonization. In any case, he is less cynically exploited than the day laborer in Dakar or Saint-Louis. The technical equipment and industrialization of the European countries make it possible for measures of socialization to be immediately applicable there; but as seen from Sénégal or the Congo, socialism seems more than anything else like a beautiful dream: before black peasants can discover that socialism is the necessary answer to their present local claims, they must learn to formulate these claims jointly; therefore, they must think of themselves as black men.

But this new self-discovery is different from that which Marxism tries to awaken in the white worker. In the European worker, class consciousness is based on the nature of profit and unearned increment, on the present conditions of the ownership of the instruments for work; in brief, it is based on the objective characteristics of the *position* of the proletariat. But since the selfish scorn that white men display for black men — and that has no equivalent in the attitude of the bourgeois towards the working class — is aimed at the deepest recesses of the heart, black men must oppose it with a more exact view of black *subjectivity;* consequently race consciousness is based first of all on the black soul, or, rather, — since the term is often used in this anthology — on a certain quality common to the thoughts and conduct of Negroes which is called *Negritude* [sic]. There are only two ways to go about forming racial concepts: either one causes certain subjective characteristics to become objective, or else one tries to interiorize objectively revealed manners of conduct; thus the black man who asserts his negritude by means of a revolutionary movement immediately places himself in the position of having to meditate, either because he wishes to recognize in himself certain objectively established traits of the African civilizations, or because he hopes to discover the Essence of blackness in the well of his heart. Thus subjectivity reappears: the relation of the self with the self; the source of all poetry, the very poetry from which the worker had to disengage himself. The black man who asks his colored brothers to "find themselves" is going to try to present to them an exemplary image of their Negritude and will look into his own soul to grasp it. He wants to be both a beacon and a mirror; the first revolutionary will be the harbinger of the black soul, the herald — half prophet and half follower — who will tear Blackness out of himself in order to offer it to the world; in brief, he will be a poet in the literal sense of "vates." Furthermore, black poetry has nothing in common with heartfelt effusions: it is functional, it answers a need which is defined in precise terms. Leaf through an anthology of contemporary white poetry: you will find a hundred different subjects, depending upon the mood and interests of the poet, depending upon his position and his country. In the anthology which I am introducing to you here, there is only one subject that all the poets attempt to treat, more or less successfully. From Haiti to Cayenne, there is a single idea: *reveal* the black soul. Black poetry is evangelic, it announces good news: Blackness has been rediscovered.

However, this negritude, which they wish to fish for in their abyssal depths, does not fall under the soul's gaze all by itself: in the soul, nothing is gratuitous. The herald of the black soul has gone through white schools, in accordance with a brazen law which forbids the oppressed man to possess any arms except those he himself has stolen from the oppressor; it is through having had some contact with white culture that his blackness has passed from the immediacy of existence to the meditative state. But at the same

time, he has more or less ceased to live his negritude. In choosing
to see what he is, he has become split, he no longer co-incides with
himself. And on the other hand, it is because he was already
exiled from himself that he discovered this need to reveal himself.
He therefore begins by exile. It is a double exile: the exile of his
body offers a magnificent image of the exile of his heart; he is in
Europe most of the time, in the cold, in the middle of gray crowds;
he dreams of Port-au-Prince, of Haiti. But in Port-au-Prince he was
already in exile; the slavers had torn his fathers out of Africa and
dispersed them. And all of the poems in this book — except those
which were written in Africa — show us the same mystical geogra-
phy. A hemisphere: in the foreground — forming the first of three
concentric circles — extends the land of exile, colorless Europe;
then comes the dazzling circle of the Islands and of childhood,
which dance the Roundelay around Africa; the last circle is Africa,
the world's navel, pole of all black poetry — dazzling Africa, burnt,
oily like a snake's skin, Africa of fire and rain, torrid and tufted;
Africa — phantom flickering like a flame, between being and
nothingness, more *real* than the "eternal boulevards with cops"
but absent, beyond attainment, disintegrating Europe with its
black but invisible rays; Africa, an *imaginary* continent. The
extraordinary good luck of black poetry lies in the fact that the
anxieties of the colonized native have their own grandiose and
obvious symbols which need only to be gone into deeply and to be
meditated upon: exile, slavery, the Africa-Europe couple and the
great Manichaeistic division of the world into black and white.
This ancestral bodily exile represents the other exile: the black
soul is an Africa from which the Negro, in the midst of the
cold buildings of white culture and technics, is exiled. And
ever-present but concealed negritude haunts him, rubs against
him; he himself rubs up against its silky wing; it palpitates and
is spread throughout him like his searching memory and his lofti-
est demands, like his shrouded, betrayed childhood, and like the
childhood of his race and the call of the earth, like the swarming
of insects and the indivisible simplicity of Nature, like the pure
legacy of his ancestors, and like the Ethics that ought to unify his
truncated life. But if he turns around to look squarely at his
negritude, it vanishes in smoke; the walls of white culture — its
silence, its words, its mores — rise up between it and him:

Give me back my black dolls, so that I may play with them
My instinct's simple games
that I may remain in the shadow of its laws
cover up my courage
my audacity
feel me as me
me renewed through what I was yesterday
    yesterday
        without complexity
         yesterday
when the uprooting hour came . . .
they have ransacked the space that was mine

However, the walls of this culture prison must be broken down; it will be necessary to return to Africa some day: thus the themes of return to the native country and of re-descent into the glaring hell of the black soul are indissolubly mixed up in the *vates* of negritude. A quest is involved here, a systematic stripping and an "ascèse"[1] accompanied by a continual effort of investigation. And I shall call this poetry "Orphic" because the Negro's tireless descent into himself makes me think of Orpheus going to claim Eurydice from Pluto. Thus, through an exceptional stroke of poetic good luck, it is by letting himself fall into trances, by rolling on the ground like a possessed man tormented by himself, by singing of his angers, his regrets or his hates, by exhibiting his wounds, his life torn between "civilization" and his old black substratum; in short, by becoming most lyrical, that the black poet is most certain of creating a great collective poetry: by speaking only of himself, he speaks for all Negroes; it is when he seems smothered by the serpents of our culture that he is the most revolutionary, for he then undertakes to ruin systematically the European knowledge he has acquired, and this spiritual destruction symbolizes the great future taking-up of arms by which black men will destroy their chains. A single example will suffice to clarify this last remark.

In the twentieth century, most ethnic minorities have passionately endeavored to resuscitate their national languages while struggling for their independence. To be able to say that one is Irish or Hungarian, one must belong to a collectivity which has the benefit of a broad economic and political autonomy; but to *be* Irish, one must also *think Irish,* which means above all: think *in*

Irish. The specific traits of a Society correspond exactly to the untranslatable locutions of its language. The fact that the prophets of negritude are forced to write their gospel *in French* means that there is a certain risk of dangerously slowing down the efforts of black men to reject our tutelege. Having been dispersed to the four corners of the earth by the slave trade, black men have no common language; in order to incite the oppressed to unite, they must necessarily rely on the words of the oppressor's language. And French is the language that will furnish the black poet with the largest audience, at least within the limits of French colonization. It is in this goose-pimply language — pale and cold like our skies, and which Mallarmé said was "the neutral language *par excellence* since our spirit demands an attenuation of variegation and of all excessively brilliant color" — in this language which is half dead for them, that Damas, Diop, Laleau, Rabéarivelo are going to pour the fire of their skies and of their hearts; it is through this language alone that they can communicate; like the sixteenth-century scholars who understood each other only in Latin, black men can meet only on that trap-covered ground that the white man has prepared for them: the colonist has arranged to be the eternal mediator between the colonized; he is there — always there — even when he is absent, even in the most secret meetings. And since words are ideas, when the Negro declares in French that he rejects French culture, he accepts with one hand what he rejects with the other; he sets up the enemy's thinking-apparatus in himself, like a crusher. This would not matter: except that this syntax and vocabulary — forged thousands of miles away in another epoch to answer other needs and to designate other objects — are unsuitable to furnish him with the means of speaking about himself, his own anxieties, his own hopes. The French language and French thought are analytical. What would happen if the black spirit were above all synthetical? The rather ugly term "negritude" is one of the few black contributions to our dictionary. But after all, if this "negritude" is a definable or at least a describable concept, it must subsume other more elementary concepts which correspond to the immediate fundamental ideas directly involved with Negro consciousness: but where are the words to describe them? How well one understands the Haitian poet's complaint:

> This obsessing heart which does not correspond
> To my language, nor to my customs,

And on which encroach, like a clinging-root,
Borrowed feelings and the customs
Of Europe, feel this suffering
And this despair — equal to no other —
Of ever taming with words from France
This heart which came to me from Sénégal.

It is not true, however, that the black man expresses himself in a "foreign" language, since he is taught French from childhood and since he is perfectly at ease when he thinks in the terms of a technician, of a scholar or of a politician. Rather, one must speak about the slight but patent difference that separates what he says from what he would like to say, whenever he speaks about himself. It seems to him that a Northern Spirit steals his ideas from him, bends them slightly to mean more or less what he wanted; that white words drink his thoughts like sand drinks blood. If he suddenly gorges himself, if he pulls himself together and takes a step backward, there are the sounds lying prostrate *in front of him* —strange: half signs and half things. He will not speak his negritude with precise, efficacious words which hit the target every time. He will not speak his negritude *in prose.* As everyone knows, every poetic experience has its origin in this feeling of frustration that one has when confronted with a language that is supposed to be a means of direct communication.

The reaction of the *speaker* frustrated by prose is in effect what Bataille calls the holocaust of words. As long as we can believe that a pre-established harmony governs the relationship between a word and Being, we use words without seeing them, with blind trust; they are sensory organs, mouths, hands, windows open on the world. As soon as we experience a first frustration, this chattering falls beyond us; we see the whole system, it is no more than an upset, out-of-order mechanism whose arms are still flailing to INDICATE EXISTENSE in emptiness; in one fell swoop we pass judgment on the foolish business of naming things; we understand that language is in essence prose, and that prose is in essence failure; Being stands erect in front of us like a tower of silence, and if we still want to catch it, we can do so only through silence: "evoke, in an intentional shadow, the object *"tu"* by allusive words, never direct, reducing themselves to the same silence."[2] No one has better stated that poetry is an incantatory attempt to suggest Being in and by the vibratory disappearance of the word: by insisting on his verbal impotence, by making words mad, the poet makes us suspect that beyond this chaos which cancels itself out, there are silent densities; since we cannot keep quiet, we must *make silence with language.* From Mallarmé to the Surrealists, the final goal of French poetry seems to me to have been this auto-destruction of language. A poem is a dark room where words are knocking themselves about, quite mad. Collisions in the air: they ignite each other with their fire and fall down in flames.

It is in this perspective that we must situate the efforts of the "black evangelists." They answer the colonist's ruse with a similar but inverse ruse: since the oppressor is present in the very language that they speak, they will speak this language in order to destroy it. The contemporary European poet tries to dehumanize words in order to give them back to nature; the black herald is going to *de-Frenchifize* them; he will crush them, break their usual associations, he will violently couple them

> with little steps of caterpillar rain
> with little steps like mouthfuls of milk
> with little steps like ball-bearings
> with little steps like seismic shocks
> Yams in the soil stride like gaps of stars[3]

Only when they have regurgitated their whiteness does he adopt them, making of this ruined language a solemn, sacred super-language, Poetry. Only through Poetry can the black men of Tenanarive and of Cayenne, the black men of Port-au-Prince and of Saint-Louis, communicate with each other in private. And since French lacks terms and concepts to define negritude, since negritude is silence, these poets will use "allusive words, never direct, reducing themselves to the same silence" in order to evoke it. Short-circuits of language: behind the flaming fall of words, we glimpse a great black mute idol. It is not only the black man's self-portrayal that seems poetic to me; it is also his personal way of utilizing the means of expression at his disposal. His position incites him to do it: even before he thinks of writing poetry, in him, the light of white words is refracted, polarized and altered. This is nowhere more manifest than in his use of two connected terms — "white-black" — that cover both the great cosmic division — "day and night" — and the human conflict between the native and the colonist. But it is a connection based on a hierarchical system: by giving the Negro this term, the teacher also gives him a hundred language habits which consecrate the white man's rights over the black man. The Negro will learn to say "white like snow" to indicate innocence, to speak of the blackness of a look, of a soul, of a deed. As soon as he opens his mouth, he accuses himself, unless he persists in upsetting the hierarchy. And if he upsets it *in French*, he is already poetizing: can you imagine the strange savor that an expression like "the blackness of innocence" or "the darkness of virtue" would have for us? That is the savor which we taste on every page of this book, when, for example, we read:

> Your round, shining, black satin breasts . . .
> this white smile
> of eyes
> in the face's shadow
> awaken in me this evening
> deaf rhythms . . .
> which intoxicate, there in Guinée,
> our sisters
> black and naked
> and inspire in me
> this evening
> black twilights heavy with sensual anxiety
> for
> the soul of the black country where the ancients
> are sleeping
> lives and speaks
> this evening
> in uneasy strength, along the small of
> your back . . .

Throughout this poem, black is color; better still, light; its soft diffuse radiance dissolves our habits; the *black* country where the ancients are sleeping is not a dark hell: it is a land of sun and fire. Then again, in another connection, the superiority of white over black does not express only the superiority that the colonist claims to have over the native: more profoundly, it expresses a universal adoration of *day* as well as our night terrors, which also are universal. In this sense, these black men are re-establishing the hierarchy they have just upset. They don't want to be poets of *night*, poets of vain revolt and despair: they give the promise of dawn; they greet the transparent dawn of a new day.

At last, the black man discovers, through the pen, his baleful sense of foreboding:

> Nigger black like misery

one of them, and then another, cries out:

> Deliver me from my blood's night

Thus the word *black* is found to contain *all Evil* and *all Good,* it covers up almost unbearable tension between two contradictory classifications: solar hierarchy and racial hierarchy. It gains thereby an extraordinary poetry, like self-destructive objects from the hands of Duchamp and the Surrealists; there is a secret blackness in white, a secret whiteness in black, a vivid flickering of Being and of Non-being which is perhaps nowhere expressed as well as in this poem of Césaire:

> My tall wounded statue, a stone in its fore-
> head; my great inattentive day flesh with
> pitiless spots, my great night flesh with
> day spots.

The poet will go even further; he writes:

> Our beautiful faces like the true operative
> power of negation.

Behind this abstract eloquence evoking Lautréamont is seen an extremely bold and subtle attempt to give some sense to black skin and to realize the poetic synthesis of the two faces of night. When David Diop says that the Negro is "black like misery," he makes black represent deprivation of light. But Césaire develops and goes into this image more deeply: night is no longer absence, it is refusal. Black is not color, it is the destruction of this borrowed clarity which falls from the white sun. The revolutionary Negro is negation because he wishes to be complete nudity: in order to build his Truth, he must first destroy others' Truth. Black faces — these night memories which haunt our days — embody the dark work of Negativity which patiently gnaws at concepts. Thus, by a reversal which curiously recalls that of the humiliated Negro — insulted and called "dirty nigger" when he asserts his rights — it is the privative aspect of darkness that establishes its value. Liberty is the color of night.

Destructions, *autodafés* of language, magic symbolism, ambivalence of concepts: all the negative aspects of modern poetry are here. But it is not a matter of some gratuitous game. The black man's position, his original "rending," the alienation that a foreign way of thinking imposes on him, all oblige him to reconquer his existential unity as a Negro — or, if you prefer, the original purity of his plan — through a gradual "ascèse," beyond the language stage. Negritude — like liberty — is a point of departure and an ultimate goal: it is a matter of making negritude pass from the immediate to the mediate, a matter of *thematicising* it. The black man must therefore find death in white culture in order to be reborn with a black soul, like the Platonic philosopher whose body embraces death in order to be reborn in truth. This dialectical and mystical return to origins necessarily implies a method. But this method is not presented as a set of rules to be used in directing the spirit. Rather, it becomes *one* with whoever applies it; it is the dialectical law of successive transformations which lead the Negro to coincidence with himself in negritude. It is not a matter of his *knowing*, nor of his ecstatically tearing himself away from himself, but rather of both discovering and becoming what he is.

There are two convergent means of arriving at this primordial simplicity of existence: one is objective, the other subjective. The poets in our anthology sometimes use one, sometimes the other, and sometimes both of them together. In effect, there exists an objective negritude that is expressed by the mores, arts, chants and dances of the African populaces. As a *spiritual exercise,* the poet will prescribe allowing himself to be fascinated by primitive rhythms, letting his thoughts run in traditional forms of black poetry. Many of the poems included here are called *tams-tams,* because they borrow from the night time tambourine players, a percussive rhythm which is sometimes sharp and regular, sometimes torrential and bounding. The poetic act, then, is a dance of the soul; the poet turns round and round like a dervish until he faints; he has established his ancestors' time in himself, he feels it flowing with its peculiar violent pulls; he hopes to "find" himself in this rhythmic pulsation; I shall say that he tries to make himself "possessed" by his people's negritude; he hopes that the echoes of his tam-tam will come to awaken timeless instincts sleeping within him. Upon leafing through this collection, one will get the impression that the *tam-tam* tends to become a *genre* of black poetry, just as the sonnet or the ode was a *genre* of our poetry. Others, like Rabemananjara, will be inspired by royal proclamations, still others will draw from the popular well of the Haintenys. The calm center of this maelstrom of rhythms, chants, shouts, is the poetry of Birago Diop, in all its majestic simplicity: it alone is at *rest* because it comes directly from Griot narratives and oral tradition. Almost all the other attempts have something contorted, taut and desperate about them because they aim at *becoming a part of* folkloric poetry rather than emanating from it. But however far he may be from "the black country where ancestors sleep," the black man is closer than we to the great period when, as Mallarmé says, "the word creates Gods." It is practically impossible for *our* poets to resume some closeness with popular traditions: ten centuries of scholarly poetry separate them from such traditions; furthermore, folkloric inspiration is drying up: at the very best, we could only imitate its simplicity from a distance. The black men of Africa, on the contrary, are still in the great period of mythical fecundity and French-language black poets are not just using their myths as a form of diversion as we use our epic poems:[4] they allow themselves to be spellbound by them so that at the end of the incantation, negritude — magnificently evoked — may surge forth. This is why I call this method of "objective poetry" *magic,* or charm.

Césaire, on the contrary, chose to backtrack into himself. Since this Eurydice will disappear in smoke if Black Orpheus turns around to look back on her, he will descend the royal road of his soul with his back turned on the bottom of the grotto; he will descend below words and meanings, — "in order to think of you, I have placed all words on the mountain-of-pity" — below daily activities and the plan of "repetition," even below the first barrier reefs of revolt, with his back turned and his eyes closed, in order finally to touch with his feet the black water of dreams and desire and to let himself drown in it.[5] Desire and dream will rise up snarling like a tidal wave; they will make words dance like flotsam and throw them pell-mell, shattered, on the shore.

Words go beyond themselves; and just as the old geography is done for, the high and the low (words) do not allow diversion either towards heaven or towards earth. . . . On the contrary, they operate on a strangely flexible range at one level: on the gaseous Level of an organism both solid and liquid, black and white day and night.[6]

One recognizes the old surrealistic *method* (automatic writing, like mysticism, is a method: it presupposes an apprenticeship, exercises, a start along the way). One must dive under the superficial crust of reality, of common sense, of reasoning reason, in order to touch the very bottom of the soul and awaken the timeless forces of desire: desire which makes of man a refusal of everything and a love of everything: desire, the radical negation of natural laws and of the possible, a call to miracles; desire which, by its mad cosmic energy, plunges man back into the seething breast of Nature and, at the same time, lifts him above Nature through the affirmation of his Right to be unsatisfied. Furthermore, Césaire is not the first Negro to take this road. Before him, Etienne Léro had founded *Légitime Défense*. "*Légitime Défense*," says Senghor, "was more a cultural movement than a review. Starting from the Marxist analysis of the society of the "Islands," it discovered, in the Antilles, descendants of African Negro slaves, who had been kept in the dulling condition of the proletarian for three centuries. It affirmed that only surrealism could deliver him from his taboos and express him in his entirety."

However, if one compares Léro with Césaire, one cannot help but be struck by their dissimilarities, and this comparison may allow us to measure the abyss that prevents a black revolutionary from utilizing white surrealism. Léro was the precursor; he invented the exploitation of surrealism as a "miraculous weapon" and an instrument for reconnaissance, a sort of radar with which one probes the depths of the abyss. But his poems are student exercises, they are mere imitations: they do not go beyond themselves; rather, they close in on each other:

> The ancient heads of hair
> Glue to the branches floors of empty seas
> Where your body is only a memory
> Where Spring trims its nails
> Helix of your smile thrown far away
> On the houses we will have nothing to do with . . .

"The helix of your smile," "the spring which trims its nails": we recognize in these the preciousness and gratuitousness of surrealistic imagery, the eternal process that consists of throwing a bridge between two extremely unrelated or separated terms and hoping — without really believing — that this "throw of the dice" will uncover some hidden aspect of Being. It does not seem to me that, either in this poem or in the others, Léro demands the liberation of the black man: at the very most he lays claim to a categorical liberation of the imagination; in this completely abstract game, no combination of words evokes Africa even remotely. If these poems were taken out of the anthology and the name of their author hidden, I would defy anyone at all, white or black, not to attribute them to a European contributor to *La Révolution Surréaliste* or *Le Minotaure*. The purpose of surrealism is to rediscover — beyond race and condition, beyond class, behind the fire of language — dazzling silent darknesses which are no longer opposed to anything, not even to day, because day and night and all opposites are blended in them and suppressed; consequently, one might speak of the impassiveness and the impersonality of the surrealist poem, just as there is a Parnassian impassiveness and impersonality.

A poem by Césaire, on the contrary, bursts and wheels around like a rocket; suns turning and exploding into new suns come out of it: it is a perpetual going-beyond. It is not a question of the poem becoming part of the calm unity of opposites; but rather of making *one* of the opposites in the "black-white" couple expand like a phallus in its opposition to the other. The density of these words thrown into the air like stones from a volcano, is found in negritude, which is defined as being *against* Europe and colonization. What Césaire destroys is not *all* culture but rather *white* culture; what he brings to light is not desire for *everything* but rather the revolutionary aspirations of the oppressed Negro; what he touches in his very depths is not the spirit but a certain specific, concrete form of humanity. With this in mind, one can speak here about *engaged* and even *directed* automatic writing, not because there is any meditative intervention but because the words and images perpetually translate the same torrid obsession. The white surrealist finds within himself the trigger; Césaire finds within himself the fixed inflexibility of demands and feeling. Léro's words are feebly organized around vague general themes through expansion and a relaxing of logical ties; Césaire's words are pressed against each other and cemented by his furious passion. Between the most daring comparisons and between the most widely separated terms, runs a secret thread of hate and hope. For example, compare "the helix of your smile thrown far away" — which is the product of a free play of the imagination as well as an invitation to revery — with

> and the radium mines buried in the abyss of my innocence
> will jump by grains
> into the feeding-trough of birds
> and the stars' stere
> will be the common name of fire-wood
> gathered from the alluvium of the singing veins of night

in which the "disjecta membra" of the vocabulary are so organized as to allow the supposition that there is a black "*Art Poétique*." Or read:

> Our beautiful faces like the true operative power of negation.

Also read:

> Seas lousy with islands cracking in the roses' fingers
> flame-thrower and my lightning-struck body intact.

Here we find the apotheosis of the fleas of black misery jumping in the water's hair, islands in a stream of light, cracking under the fingers of the celestial delouser: drawn with rose-colored fingers, the dawn of Greek and Mediterranean culture — snatched from the sacrosanct Homeric poems by a black thief — whose enslaved princess's fingernails are suddenly controlled by a Toussaint Louverture in order to crack the triumphant parasites of the black sea; the dawn, which suddenly rebels and is metamorphosed, which opens fire like that savage weapon of white men, the flame-thrower, the weapon of scientists, the weapon of executioners, strikes the tall black Titan with its white fire, and he arises intact and eternal in order to begin the assault on Europe and heaven. In Césaire, the great surrealist tradition is realized, it takes on its definitive meaning and is destroyed: surrealism — that European movement —is taken from the Europeans by a Black man who turns it against them and gives it a rigorously defined function. I have pointed out elsewhere how the whole of the proletariat completely shut itself off from the destructive poetry of Reason: in Europe, surrealism languishes and pales, rejected by those who could have given it a transfusion of their own blood. But at the very moment when it is losing contact with the Revolution, it is, in the Antilles, grafted onto another branch of the universal Revolution; it develops into an enormous somber flower. Césaire's originality lies in his having directed his powerful, concentrated anxiety as a Negro, as one oppressed, as a militant individual, into this world of the most destructive, free and metaphysical poetry at the moment when Eluard and Aragon were failing to give political content to their verse. And finally, *negritude-object* is snatched from Césaire like a cry of pain, of love and of hate. Here again he follows the surrealist tradition of *objective* poetry. Césaire's words do not describe negritude, they do not designate it, they do not copy it from the outside like a painter with a model: they *create* it; they compose it under our very eyes: henceforth it is a thing which can be observed and learned; the subjective method which he has chosen joins the objective method we spoke about earlier; he ejects the black soul from himself at the very moment when others are trying to interiorize it; the final result is the same in both cases. Negritude is the far-away tam-tam in the streets of Dakar at night; voo-doo shouts from some Haitian cellar window, sliding along level with the roadway; the Congolese mask; but it is also this poem by Césaire, this slobbery, bloody poem full of phlegm, twisting in the dust like a cut-up worm. This double spasm of absorption and excretion beats out the rhythm of the black heart on every page of this collection.

What then, at present, is this negritude, sole anxiety of these poets, sole subject of this book? It must first be stated that a white man could hardly speak about it suitably, since he has no inner experience of it and since European languages lack words to describe it. I ought then to let the reader encounter it in the pages of this collection and draw his own conclusions about it. But this introduction would be incomplete if, after having indicated that the quest for the Black Grail represented — both in its original intention and in its methods — the most authentic synthesis of revolutionary aspirations and poetic anxiety, I did not show that this complex notion is essentially pure Poetry. I shall therefore limit myself to examining these poems objectively as a cluster of testimonies and to pointing out some of their principal themes.

Senghor says: "What makes the *negritude* of a poem is less its theme than its style, the emotional warmth which gives life to words, which transmutes the word into the Word." It could not be more explicitly stated that negritude is neither a state nor a definite ensemble of vices and virtues or of intellectual and moral qualities, but rather a certain affective attitude towards the world. Since the beginning of this century, psychology has renounced its great scholastic distinctions. We no longer believe that the "facts" of the soul are divided into volitions or actions, knowledge or perceptions, sentiments or blind passiveness. We know that a feeling is a definite way of establishing our *rapport* with the world around us, that it involves a certain comprehension of this universe. It is a tension of the soul, a choice of oneself and of another, a way of going beyond the raw facts of experience; in short, a *plan* quite like the voluntary act. To use Heidegger's language, Negritude is the Negro's being-in-the-world.

Furthermore, here is what Césaire tells us about it:

> My negritude is not a stone with its deafness flung
>   out against the clamor of the day
> My negritude is not a dead speck of water on the
>   dead eye of the earth
> my negritude is neither a tower nor a cathedral
> it plunges into the red flesh of the ground
> it plunges into the ardent flesh of the sky
> it perforates the opaque pressure of its righteous patience.

Negritude is portrayed in these beautiful lines of verse more as an act than as a frame of mind. But this act is an *inner* determination: it is not a question of *taking* the goods of this world in one's hands and transforming them; it is a question of *existing* in the middle of the world. The relation with the universe remains an *adaptation*. But this adaptation is not technical. For the white man, to possess is to transform. To be sure, the white worker uses instruments which he does not possess. But at least his techniques are his own: if it is true that the personnel responsible for the major inventions of European industry comes mainly from the middle classes, at least the trades of carpenter, cabinet-maker, potter, seem to the white workers to be a true heritage, despite the fact that the orientation of great capitalist production tends to remove their "joy in work" from them. But it is not enough to say that the black worker uses instruments which are lent to him: techniques are also lent him.

Césaire refers to his black brothers as

> Those who have invented neither powder nor compass
> those who have never tamed either steam or electricity
> those who have not explored the seas and the sky . . .

But this haughty claim of non-technicalness reverses the situation: what could pass as a deficiency becomes a *positive* source of wealth. A technical *rapport* with Nature reveals Nature as simple quantity, inertia, exteriority: nature dies. By his haughty refusal to be *homo faber,* the Negro gives it life again. As if the passiveness of one of the members of the "man-nature" couple necessarily produced the other's activity. Actually, negritude is not passiveness, since it "perforates the flesh of the sky and of the earth": it is "patience," and patience appears like an active imitation of passiveness. The Negro's act is first of all an act on oneself. The black man stands erect and immobilizes himself like a bird-charmer, and things come to perch on the branches of this fake tree. A magic inveigling of the world — through silence and rest — is involved here: the white man, by acting first of all on Nature, loses himself when he loses Nature, the Negro, by acting first of all on himself, claims to win Nature while winning himself.

> Seized, they abandon themselves to the essence of
> every thing
> ignorant of the surfaces but seized by the movement
> of every thing
> heedless of counting, but playing the world's game
> truly the elder sons of the world
> porous to all the breaths of the world . . .
> flesh of the world's flesh palpitating from the very
> movement of the world.

Upon reading this, one can hardly help thinking of the famous distinction between intelligence and intuition established by Bergson. Césaire rightly calls us

> Omniscient and naïve conquerors. . . .

Because of his tools, the white man knows all. But he only scratches the surface of things; he is unaware of the duration of things, unaware of life. Negritude, on the contrary, is comprehension through instinctive congeniality. The black man's secret is that the sources of his existence and the roots of Being are identical.

If one wanted to give a sociological interpretation of this metaphysic, one would say that an agriculturist poetry is here opposed to an engineer prose. Actually, it is not true that the black man has no techniques: the *rapport* between any human group and the exterior world is always technical in one way or another. And inversely, I shall say that Césaire is imprecise: Saint Exupéry's airplane folding the earth below like a carpet is a means of disclosure. However, the black man is first of all a peasant; agricultural technique is "righteous patience"; it trusts in life; it waits. To plant is to impregnate the earth; after that, you must remain motionless and watch: "each atom of silence is a chance for ripe fruit," each instant brings forth a hundred times more than man gave, whereas the worker finds in the manufactured product only as much as he put into it; man grows along with his wheat: from minute to minute he goes beyond himself and becomes more golden; he intervenes in his watchful wait before the fragile swelling belly, only to protect. Ripe wheat is a microcosm because the cooperation of sun, wind and rains was needed for it to grow; a blade of wheat is both the most natural thing and the most improbable chance. Techniques have contaminated the white peasant, but the black peasant remains the great male of the earth, the world's sperm. His existence is great vegetal patience; his work is the yearly repetition of holy coïtus. Creating and nourished because he creates. To till, to plant, to eat, is to make love with nature. The sexual pantheism of these poets is undoubtedly what will impress us first of all: it is in this that they join the dances and the phallic rites of the Negro-Africans.

> Oho! Congo lying in your bed of forests, queen of tamed
>   Africa
> May the phalli of the mountains carry your banner high
> For, through my head, through my tongue, through my
>   belly, you are a woman,

writes Senghor. And:

> and so I shall mount again the soft belly of the dunes
> and the gleaming thighs of the day. . . .

and Rabéarivelo:

> the earth's blood, the stone's sweat and the sperm of
> the world

and Laleau:

> The conical drum laments under the sky
> And it is the very soul of the black man
> Sultry spasms of men in rut, lover's sticky sobs
> Outraging the calm of the evening.

Here, we are far from Bergson's chaste asexual intuition. It is
no longer a matter of being congenial with life, but rather of being
in love with all its forms. For the white technician, God is first
of all an engineer. Jupiter orders chaos and prescribes its laws;
the Christian God conceives the world through his understanding
and brings it into being through his will: the relation between the
created and the creator is never carnal, except for a few mystics
whom the Church looks upon with a great deal of suspicion. Even
so, erotic mysticism has nothing in common with fecundity: it is
the completely passive wait for a sterile penetration. We are
steeped in alluvium: statuettes come from the *hands* of the divine
sculptor. If the manufactured objects surrounding us could wor-
ship their ancestors, they would undoubtedly adore us as we adore
the All-powerful. For our black poets, on the contrary, Being
comes out of Nothingness like a penis becoming erect; Creation is
an enormous perpetual delivery; the world is flesh and the son of
flesh; on the sea and in the sky, on the dunes, on the rocks, in the
wind, the Negro finds the softness of human skin; he rubs himself
against the sand's belly, against the sky's loins: he is "flesh of the
flesh of this world"; he is "porous to all its breaths," to all its
pollens; he is both Nature's female and its male; and when he
makes love with a woman of his race, the sexual act seems to him
to be the celebration of the Mystery of Being. This spermatic
religion is like the tension of a soul balancing between two com-
plementary tendencies: the dynamic feeling of being an erect
phallus, and that more deaf, more patient, more feminine one of

being a growing plant. Thus negritude is basically a sort of
androgyny.

> There you are
> Upright and naked
> alluvium you are and remember yourself as having been
> but in reality you are the child of this parturient shadow
> feeding on lunar lactogen[7]
> then you slowly take the form of a bole
> on this low wall jumped over by the dreams of flowers
> and the perfume of summer at rest.
> To feel, to believe that roots are pushing your feet
> and running and twisting like thirsty serpents
> toward some subterranean spring . . .
>
> (Rabéarivelo)

And Césaire:

> Wornout mother, leafless mother, you are a flamboyant[8]
> and now wear only husks. You are a calabash tree
> and you are only a stand of *couis*. . . .[9]

This profound unity of vegetal and sexual symbols is certainly
the greatest originality of black poetry, especially in a period when,
as Michel Carrouges has shown, most of the images used by white
poets tend to mineralize the human being. Césaire, on the contrary,
"vegetalizes," "animalizes" sea, sky and stones. More precisely, his
poetry is a perpetual coupling of men and women who had been
metamorphosed into animals, vegetables, stones, with stones, plants
and beasts metamorphosed into men. Thus the Black man attests
to a natural Eros; he reveals and incarnates it; to find a point of
comparison in European poetry, one must go back to Lucretius,
the peasant poet who celebrated Venus, the mother goddess, when
Rome was not yet much more than a large agricultural market.
In our time, only Lawrence seems to me to have had a cosmic
feeling for sexuality. Even so, this feeling remains very literary in
his works.

However, although negritude seems basically to be this im-
mobile springing-forth, a unity of phallic erection and plant
growth, one could scarcely exhaust it with this single poetic theme.
There is another motif running through this collection, like a
large artery:

> Those who have invented neither powder nor compass . . .
> They know the most remote corners of the country of
>   suffering. . . .

To the absurd utilitarian agitation of the white man, the black man opposes the authenticity gained from his suffering; the black race is a chosen race because it has had the horrible privilege of touching the depths of unhappiness. And even though these poems are anti-Christian from beginning to end, one might call negritude a kind of Passion: the black man who is conscious of himself sees himself as the man who has taken the whole of human suffering upon himself and who suffers for all, even for the white man.

> On the judgment day, Armstrong's trumpet will be the
> interpreter of man's sufferings.
>
> (Paul Niger)

Let us note immediately that this in no way implies a resigned suffering. A while ago I was speaking about Bergson and Lucretius; I would be tempted now to quote that great adversary of Christianity: Nietzsche and his "Dionysianism." Like the Dionysian poet, the Negro attempts to penetrate the brilliant phantasm of the day, and encounters, a thousand feet under the Apollonian surface, the inexpiable suffering which is the universal essence of man. If one wished to systematize, one would say that the Black man blends with the whole of nature in as much as he represents sexual congeniality with Life and in as much as he claims he is Man in his Passion of rebellious suffering. One will feel the fundamental unity of this double movement if one considers the constantly tighter relationship which psychiatrists establish between anguish and sexual desire. There is only one proud upheaval which can be equally well described as a desire plunging its roots into suffering or as suffering fixed like a sword across a vast cosmic desire. This "righteous patience" that Césaire evokes is both vegetal growth and patience against suffering; it resides in the very muscles of the Negro; it sustains the black porter going a thousand miles up the Niger under a blinding sun with a fifty-pound load balanced on his head. But if in a certain sense, one can compare the fecundity of Nature to a proliferation of suffering, in another sense — and this one is also Dionysian — this fecundity, by its exuberance, goes beyond suffering, drowns it in its creative abundance which is poetry, love and dance. Perhaps, in order to understand this indissoluble unity of suffering, eros and joy, one must have seen the Black men of Harlem dance frenetically to the rhythm of "blues," which are the saddest sounds in the world. In effect, rhythm cements the multiple aspects of the black soul, communicates its Nietzschian lightness with heavy dionysian intuitions; rhythm — tam-tam, jazz, the "bounding" of these poems — represents the temporality of Negro *existence*. And when a black poet prophesies to his brothers a better future, he portrays their deliverance to them in the form of rhythm:

> What?
> rhythm
> sound wave in the night across the forests, nothing
> — or a new soul
> timbre
> intonation
> vigor
> dilation
> vibration which flows out by degrees into the marrow
> revulses[10] in its progression an old sleeping body, takes
> it by the waist
> and spins it
> and turns
> and once more vibrates in its hands, in its loins, its
> sexual member, its thighs, its vagina . . .

But one must go still further: this basic experience of suffering is ambiguous; through it, black conscience is going to become historic. In effect, whatever may be the intolerable iniquity of his present condition, it is not to that condition that the black man first refers when he proclaims that he has touched the heart of human suffering. He has the horrible benefit of having known bondage. For these poets, most of whom were born between 1900 and 1918, slavery — abolished half a century earlier — lingers on as a very real memory:

> Each of my todays looks on my yesterday
> with large eyes rolling with rancor with
> shame

Still real is my stunned condition of the past
of
blows from knotted cords of bodies calcinated
from toe to calcinated back
of dead flesh of red iron firebrands of arms
broken under the whip which is breaking loose . . .

writes Damas, a poet from Guiana. And the Haitian, Brierre:

. . . Often like me you feel stiffnesses
Awaken after murderous centuries
And old wounds bleed in your flesh . . .

During the centuries of slavery, the black man drank the cup
of bitterness to the last drop; and slavery is a past fact which
neither our authors nor their fathers have actually experienced.
But it is also a hideous nightmare from which even the youngest
of them are not yet sure of having awakened. From one end of
the earth to the other, black men — separated by languages, politics
and the history of their colonizers — have a *collective* memory in
common. This will not be surprising if one only recalls the French
peasants who, in 1789, were still aware of the panicky terrors that
went back to the Hundred Years' war. Thus when the black man
goes back to his principal experience, it is suddenly revealed to
him in two dimensions: it is both the intuitive seizure of the human
condition and the still-fresh memory of a historic past. Here, I
am thinking of Pascal who relentlessly repeated that man was an
irrational composite of metaphysics and history, his greatness
unexplainable if he comes from the alluvium, his misery unexplain-
able if he is still as God made him; that in order to understand
man, one had to go back to the simple basic fact of man's downfall.
It is in this sense that Césaire calls his race "the fallen race." And
in a certain sense I can see the *rapprochement* that can be made
between black conscience and Christian conscience: the brazen law
of slavery evokes that law of the Old Testament, which states the
consequences of the *Fault*. The abolition of slavery recalls this
other historic fact: Redemption. The white man's insipid pa-
ternalism after 1848 resembles that of the white God after the Pas-
sion. The difference being, however, that the expiable fault that
the black man discovers in the back of his memory is not his own,
it belongs to the white man; the first fact of Negro history is cer-

tainly a kind of original sin: but the black man is the innocent victim of it. This is why his concept of suffering is radically opposed to white "dolorism." If these poems are for the most part so violently anti-Christian, it is because the white man's religion is more clearly a hoax in the eyes of the Negro than in the eyes of the European proletariate: this religion wants to make him share the responsibility for a crime of which he is the victim; it wants to persuade him to see the kidnappings, the massacres, the rapes and the tortures which have covered Africa with blood, as a legitimate punishment, deserved tests. Will you say that it also proclaims equality for all men before God? *Before God*, yes. Only yesterday I was reading in *Esprit* these lines from a correspondent in Madagascar:

> I am as certain as you that the soul of a Malagasy is worth the soul of a white man. . . . Just as, before God, the soul of a child is worth the soul of his father. However, if you have an automobile, you don't let your children drive it.

One can hardly reconcile Christianity and colonialism more elegantly. In opposition to these sophisms, the black man — by a simple investigation of his memory as a former slave — affirms that suffering is man's lot and that it is no less deserved for all that. He rejects with horror Christian stagnation, melancholy sensual pleasure, masochistic humility and all the tendentious inducements to his submission; he lives the absurdity of suffering in its pure form, in its injustice and in its gratuitousness; and he discovers thereby this truth which is misunderstood or masked by Christianity: suffering carries within itself its own refusal; it is by nature *a refusal to suffer*, it is the dark side of negativity, it opens onto revolt and liberty. The black man promptly *transforms himself into history* in as much as the intuition of suffering confers on him a collective past and assigns to him a goal in the future. Only a short while ago, he was a sheer *present* surging of timeless instincts, a simple manifestation of universal and eternal fecundity. Now he calls to his colored brothers in quite another language:

> Negro pedlar of revolt
> you have known the paths of the world
> ever since you were sold in Guinée . . .

And:

> Five centuries have seen you with weapons
> in your hands
> and you have taught the exploiting races
> passion for liberty.

There is already a black Epic:[11] first the golden age of Africa, then the era of dispersion and captivity, then the awakening of conscience, the heroic and somber times of great revolts, of Toussaint Louverture and black heroes, then the *fact* of the abolition of slavery — "unforgettable metamorphosis," says Césaire — then the struggle for definitive liberation:

> You are waiting for the next call
> the inevitable mobilization
> for that war which is yours has known only truces
> for there is no land where your blood has not flowed
> no language in which your color has not been insulted
> You smile, Black Boy,
> you sing
> you dance
> you cradle generations
> which go out at all hours to the
> fronts of work and pain
> which tomorrow will assault bastilles
> onward toward the bastions of the future
> in order to write in all languages
> on the clear pages of all skies
> the declaration of your rights unrecognized
> for more than five centuries . . .

Strange and decisive turn: *race* is transmuted into *historicity*, the black Present explodes and is temporalized, negritude — with its Past and its Future — is inserted into Universal History, it is no longer a *state*, nor even an existential attitude, it is a *"Becoming"*; the black contribution to the evolution of Humanity is no longer savour, taste, rhythm, authenticity, a bouquet of primitive instincts: it is a dated enterprize, a long-suffering construction and also a future. Previously, the Black man claimed his place in the sun in the name of *ethnic* qualities; now, he establishes his right to life on his mission; and this mission, like the proletariat's, comes to him from his historic position: because he has suffered from capitalistic exploitation more than all the others, he has acquired a sense of revolt and a love of liberty more than all the others. And because he is the most oppressed, he necessarily pursues the liberation of all, when he works for his own deliverance:

> Black messenger of hope
> you know all the hymns of the world
> even those of the timeless building-works of the Nile.

But, after that, can we still believe in the interior homogeneousness of negritude? And how can one say that it exists? Sometimes it is lost innocence which had its existence in some faraway past, and sometimes hope which can be realized only within the walls of the future City. Sometimes it contracts with Nature in a moment of pantheistic fusion and sometimes it spreads itself out to coincide with the whole history of Humanity; sometimes it is an existential attitude and sometimes the objective ensemble of Negro-African traditions. It is being discovered? It is being created? After all, there are black men who "collaborate"; after all, in the prefaces he writes for the works of each poet, Senghor seems to distinguish between degrees of negritude. Does the poet who would be the Prophet for his colored brothers invite them to *become* more Negro, or does he disclose to them what they *are*, by a sort of poetic psychoanalysis? Is negritude necessity or liberty? For the authentic Negro, is it a matter of conduct deriving from essences, as consequences derive from a principle, or is one a Negro in the way that the religious faithful are believers, that is to say in fear and trembling, in anguish, in perpetual remorse for never being enough what one would like to be? Is it a given fact or a value? The object of empiric intuition or of a moral concept? Is it a conquest of meditation? Or does meditation poison it? Is it never authentic except when unmeditated and in the immediate? Is it a systematic *explanation* of the black soul, or a Platonic Archetype which one can approach indefinitely without ever attaining? Is it, for black men, like our engineer's common sense, the most widely shared thing in the world? Or do some have it, like grace; and if so, does it have its chosen ones? One will undoubtedly answer this question by saying that it is all of these at once, and still other things. And I agree: like all anthropological notions, Negritude is a shimmer of being and of needing-to-be; it makes you and you make it: both oath and passion. But there is something even more important in it: the Negro himself, we have said, creates a kind of antiracist racism. He wishes in no way to dominate the world: he desires the abolition of *all* kinds of ethnic privileges; he asserts his solidarity with the oppressed of every color. After that, the subjective, existential, ethnic notion of *negritude* "passes," as Hegel says, into that which one has of the proletariat: objective, positive and precise. Senghor says: "For Césaire, 'White' symbolizes capital, just as Negro symbolizes work. . . . When writing about the black men of his race, he is writing about the worldwide proletarian struggle." It is easy to say, not so easy to think. And it is certainly not just by accident that the most ardent cantors of Negritude are also militant Marxists. Nevertheless, the notion of race does not mix with the notion of class: the former is concrete and particular; the latter, universal and abstract; one belongs to what Jaspers calls comprehension, and the other to intellection; the first is the product of a psycho-biological syncretism, and the other is a methodic construction starting with experience. In fact, Negritude appears like the up-beat [unaccented beat] of a dialectical progression: the theoretical and practical affirmation of white supremacy is the thesis; the position of Negritude as an antithetical value is the moment of negativity. But this negative moment is not sufficient in itself, and these black men who use it know this perfectly well; they know that it aims at preparing the synthesis or realization of the human being in a raceless society. Thus Negritude is *for* destroying itself, it is a "crossing to" and not an "arrival at," a means and not an end. A poem by Jacques Roumain, a black communist, furnishes the most moving evidence of this new ambiguity:

> Africa I have held on to your memory Africa
> you are in me
> Like a thorn in a wound
> like a guardian mascot in the center of the village
> make of me the stone of your sling
> of my mouth the lips of your wound
> of my knees the broken columns of your humbling
> however
> I want to be only of your race
> peasant workers of all countries.

With what sadness he still retains for the moment what he has decided to abandon. With what pride as a *man* he will strip his pride as a Negro for other men! He who says both that Africa is in him like "a thorn in a wound" and that he *wants* to be only of the universal race of the oppressed, has not left the empire of afflicted conscious. One more step and Negritude will disappear completely: the Negro himself makes of what was the mysterious bubbling of black blood, a geographical accident, the inconsistent product of universal determinism:

> Is it all that climate extended space
> which creates clan tribe nation
> skin race gods
> our inexorable dissimilarity.[12]

But the poet does not completely have the courage to accept the responsibility for this *rationalization* of the racial concept; one sees that he limits himself to questioning; a bitter regret is visible beneath his will to unite. Strange road: humiliated and offended, black men search deep within themselves to find their most secret pride; and when they have found it at last, it challenges its own right to exist: through supreme generosity they abandon it, just as Philoctetes abandoned his bow and arrows at Neoptolemus. Thus the rebel Césaire finds the secret of his revolts in the bottom of his heart: he is of royal blood:

> it is true that there is in you something which has
> never been able to yield, an anger, a desire, a sadness,
> an impatience, in short a scorn, a violence . . . and now
> your veins carry gold, not mud; pride, not servitude.
> King you have been King in the past.

But he immediately thrusts aside this temptation:

> There is a law that I cover up with a chain unbroken
> as far as the confluence of fire which violates me
> which purifies me and burns me with my prism of amal-
> gamated gold. . . . I shall perish. But one. Whole.

It is perhaps this ultimate nudity of man that has snatched from him the white rags that were concealing his black armor, and that now destroys and rejects that very armor; it is perhaps this colorless nudity that best symbolizes Negritude: for Negritude is not a state, it is a simple going-beyond-itself, it is love. It is when negritude renounces itself that it finds itself; it is when it accepts losing that it has won: the colored man — and he alone — can be asked to renounce the pride of his color. He is the one who is walking on this ridge between past particularism — which he has just climbed — and future universalism, which will be the twilight of his negritude; he is the one who looks to the end of particularism in order to find the dawn of the universal. Undoubtedly, the white worker also becomes conscious of his class in order to deny it, since he wants the advent of a classless society: but once again, the definition of class is objective; it sums up only the conditions of the white worker's alienation; whereas it is in the bottom of his heart that the Negro finds race, and he must tear out his heart. Thus Negritude is dialectical; it is not only nor above all the blossoming of atavistic instincts; it represents "going beyond" a situation defined by free consciences. Negritude is a sad myth full of hope, born of Evil and pregnant with future Good, living like a woman who is born to die and who feels her own death even in the richest moments of her life; it is an unstable rest, an explosive fixity, a pride which renounces itself, an absolute that knows it is transitory: for whereas it is the Announcer of its birth and of its death agony, it also remains the existential attitude chosen by free men and lived *absolutely*, to the fullest. Because it is tension between a nostalgic Past into which the black man can no longer enter completely and a future in which it will be replaced by new values, Negritude adorns itself with a tragic beauty that finds expression only in poetry. Because it is the living and dialectical unity of so many opposites, because it is a Complex defying analysis, Negritude is only the multiple unity of a hymn that can reveal both it and the flashing beauty of the Poem which Breton calls *"explosante-fixe."* Because any attempt to conceptualize its various aspects would necessarily end up showing its relativity, — even though it is lived in the absolute through royal consciences — and because the poem is an absolute, it is poetry alone that will allow the unconditional aspect of this attitude to be fixed. Because it is subjectivity written in the objective, Negritude must take form in a poem, that is to say in a subjectivity-object; because it is an Archetype and a Value, it will find its most transparent symbol in aesthetic values; because it is a call and a gift, it will make itself heard and offer itself only by means of a work of art which is both a call to the spectator's liberty and absolute generosity. Negritude is the content of the poem, it is the poem like a thing of the world, mysterious and open, obscure and suggestive; it is the poet himself. One must go still further; triumph of Narcissism and Narcissus' suicide, tension of the soul beyond culture, beyond words and beyond all psychic facts, luminous night of unknowing, deliberate choice of the *impossible* and of what Bataille calls "torture" [*supplice*], intuitive acceptance of the world and refusal of the world in the name of "the law of the heart," double contradictory postulation, demanding retraction, expansion of generosity — Negritude is, in essence, Poetry. For once at least, the most authentic revolutionary plan and the most pure poetry come from the same source.

And if the sacrifice is achieved one day, what will happen then? What will happen if, casting off his negritude for the sake of the Revolution, the black man no longer wishes to consider himself only a part of the proletariat? What will happen if he then allows himself to be defined only by his objective condition? if, in order to struggle against white capitalism, he undertakes to assimilate white technics? Will the source of poetry run dry? or in spite of everything, will the great black river color the sea into which it flows? That does not matter: each era has its poetry; in each era, circumstances of history elect a nation, a race, a class to take up the torch, by creating situations that can be expressed or that can go beyond themselves only through Poetry; sometimes the poetic *élan* coincides with the revolutionary *élan* and sometimes they diverge. Let us greet today the historic chance that will permit black men to

> shout out the great Negro cry so hard that the
> world's foundations will be shaken.[13]

---

[1]*ascèse*s the ascetic's movement of *interiorization*. (translator's note)

[2]Mallarmé *Magie* (Edition de la Pléiade, p. 400).

[3]Césaire, *Les armes miraculeuses: tam-tam II.*

[4]Sartre uses "*chansons*" for what we have translated as "epic poems"; he is referring, of course, to the Medieval French epic poems, the *Chansons de Geste*. (translator's note)

[5]Sartre seems to have confused his images here, since Orpheus was instructed not to look back while he was *ascending* from Hades, *after* he had retrieved Eurydice from Pluto. (translator's note)

[6]The French "automatic writing" was so completely untranslatable that we have tried simply to give an English *approximation* of its sense. For those who care to consult the original French text, it runs as follows: "*Les mots se dépassent, c'est bien vers un ciel et une terre que le haut et le bas ne permettent pas de distraire, c'en est fait aussi de la vieille géographie. . . . Au contrare, un étagement curieusement respirable s'opère réel mais au niveau. Au Niveau gazeux de l'organisme solide et liquide, blanc et noir jour ete nuit.*"

[7]"lactogen": This is a neologism in the French text as well.

[8]*flamboyant*: a plant found in semi-tropical countries, especially in the Antilles: a *poinciana* or *peacock flower*. (translator's note)

[9]*couis*: apparently some kind of tree found in the Antilles. (translator's note)

[10]*revulses*: referring to the medical term *revulsion*: a counter-irritant. (translator's note)

[11]Epic: the French here reads "*Geste*," as in *Chanson de Geste*; Sartre is comparing the Negro Epic with the themes of Medieval French epic poetry. (translator's note)

[12]Although the poem itself and Sartre's interpretation of it suggest that there should be a question mark here, there is none in the text from which this was translated. (translator's note)

[13]Césaire, *Les armes miraculeuses*, p. 156.

The Awakening of American Negro Literature 1619-1900

by Gerald W. Haslam

DURING THEIR PROLONGED period of slavery and disenfranchisement prior to the twentieth century, Afro-Americans were too preoccupied with the demands of survival to find much time for the formal pursuit of literary art. Yet they did, from the onset of their long struggle for full citizenship, produce an informal literature in the oral tradition of their forefathers; it was oral literature — produced principally for their own satisfaction — which dominated the earliest era of American Negro literature.

In the latter half of the eighteenth century, black slaves began producing written literature — an incredible achievement in itself — and a second, more conventionally recognized tradition was begun; Lucy Terry (1746), Jupiter Hammon (1760), Briton Hammon (1760), Phillis Wheatley (1773), and Gustavus Vassa (1789) were among the first Afro-American writers. Throughout this initial literary era, Negro authors depended upon a white audience, so their work often reflected too credibly the stereotypes born of white presumptions. By the time Wheatley wrote —

'Twas not long since I left my native shore,
The land of errors and Egyptian gloom:

> Father of Mercy! 'twas thy gracious hand
> Brought me in safety from those dark abodes.[1]

—black slaves working in the older oral tradition had produced the plaintive poetry of spirituals:

> Sometimes I feel like a motherless child,
> Sometimes I feel like a motherless child,
> Sometimes I feel like a motherless child,
> A long ways from home;
> A long, long ways from my home.[2]

And the bold lyrics of seculars:

> Dis nigger run, he run his best
> Stuck his head in a hornet's nest,
> Jumped de fence and run fru de paster;
> White man run, but nigger run faster.[3]

telling fellow Negroes a very different story than Wheatley told whites.

Nonetheless, Phillis Wheatley (1753-1784) was a remarkable artist, producing poetry which, at its best, was equal to that of any American writer of her period, as "An Hymn To The Morning" demonstrates:

> Attend my lays, ye ever honour'd nine,
> Assist my labours, and my strains refine;
> In smoothest numbers pour the notes along,
> For bright Aurora now demands my song.

> Aurora hail, and all the thousand dies,
> Which deck, thy progress through the vaulted skies:
> The morn awakes, and wide extends her rays,
> On ev'ry leaf the gentle zephyr plays;
> Harmonious lays the feather'd race resume,
> Dart the bright eye, and shake the painted plume.

> Ye shady groves, your verdant gloom display
> To shield your poet from the burning day:
> Calliope awake the sacred lyre,
> While thy fair sisters fan the pleasing fire:

> The bow'rs, the gales, the variegated skies
> In all their pleasures in my bosom rise.
>
> See in the east th' illustrious king of day!
> His rising radiance drives the shades away—
> But Oh! I feel his fervid beams too strong,
> And scarce begun, concludes th' abortive song.⁴

She had been kidnapped from her native Senegal as a seven-year-old child. Purchased by the Wheatley family of Boston, who soon noted her extraordinary intelligence, she was encouraged to read and write. At thirteen she began to write poetry and, after publishing a broadside elegy in 1770 at the age of seventeen, she became a local celebrity. Three years later ill health made a sea voyage advisable, so she was manumitted and sent to Britain, where her only book, POEMS ON VARIOUS SUBJECTS, RELIGIOUS AND MORAL, was published that same year. Her return to America was followed by an unhappy marriage, poverty, the deaths of her three children, and her own death at thirty-one, her literary promise still far from fulfilled.

Phillis Wheatley's poetry was influenced by the verse of Alexander Pope, and her strongest and most commonly used form was the heroic couplet. She was in theme a proper, eighteenth-century Bostonian whose central metaphors were religious and whose form was neoclassic. Only rarely did she mention slavery in her verse, though the following lines from "To The Earl of Dartmouth" reveal something of her private pain:

> Should you, my lord, while you pursue my song,
> Wonder from whence my love of *Freedom* sprung,
> Whence flow these wishes for the common good,
> By feeling hearts alone best understood,
> I, young in life, by seeming cruel fate
> Was snatch'd from *Afric's* fancy'd happy seat:
> What pangs excruciating must molest,
> What sorrows labour in my parent's breast?
> That from a father seiz'd his babe belov'd
> Such, such my case. And can I then but pray
> Others may never feel tyrannic sway?⁵

In many ways Phillis Wheatley was the most revolutionary of all Afro-American writers for, though her overt protestations were few, the very quality of her writing made forever suspect the claim that Negroes are incapable of artistic excellence.

In 1827, the first Negro newspaper in the United States, *Freedom's Journal*, began publication and by the 1829 publication of George Moses Horton's first book of verse, *Hope of Liberty*, a more overtly militant approach to the evil of slavery was consonant with the growing wave of abolitionism. Horton (1797-1883) openly posed the seminal question of slavery in what claimed to be a democratic society:

> How long have I in bondage lain,
> And languished to be free!
> Alas! and must I still complain,
> Deprived of liberty?[6]

He was also the first Negro American writer to present something of the unique humor that was so evident in Negro folk literature, as such works as "Jeff Davis in a Tight Place" and "Creditor to His Proud Debtor" aptly demonstrate.

The abolitionist movement stimulated a great surge of Negro protest literature, spoken and written, during the desperate struggle against human bondage; Frederick Douglass (1817 - 1895), William Wells Brown (1816-1864), Samuel Ward (1817-1864), Charles Remond (1810-1873), David Ruggles (?-1849), and David Walker (1785-1830) among others emerged as effective spokesmen for their cause. While Walker's *Appeal* (1829) was very widely read, only Douglass and Brown ever became proficient writers. Douglass's autobiographies were remarkable works, while Brown's pioneering efforts made him America's first black novelist (*Clotel*; or, *The President's Daughter*, 1853) and dramatist (*The Escape*, 1858), as well as the first Afro-American to earn his living as a writer. He was also the first major Negro writer to exploit the tragic mulatto theme.

Slave memoirs were the dominant literary form during this period. The finest slave memoirs were writen by Frederick Douglass, who was born a slave in Maryland in 1817. He escaped from bondage in 1838 and, in 1841, became an important figure in the abolition movement and a close associate of William Lloyd Garrison. His autobiography, *Narrative of the Life of Frederick Douglass, an American Slave*, was published in 1845, and later revised and republished in 1855, 1881, and 1892.

One seminal scene from Douglass's *Narrative* tells of his introduction to the alphabet by his mistress, and of his master's reaction; the master tells his wife in front of the youthful Douglass:

> "If you give a nigger an inch,
> he will take an ell. A nigger
> should know nothing but to obey
> his master — to do as he is told
> to do. Learning would *spoil*
> the best nigger in the world."
> "Now," said he, "if you teach that
> nigger (speaking of myself) how
> to read, there would be no keeping
> him. It would forever unfit him
> to be a slave. He would at once
> become unmanageable, and of no
> value to his master. As to himself,
> it could do him no good, but a
> great deal of harm. It would make
> him discontented and unhappy."[7]

This episode awakened in Douglass an understanding and a drive that, ultimately, led him to become one of the great American orators of the nineteenth century, as well as a skilled and powerful writer of non-fiction prose. "These words sank deep into my heart," he wrote,

> stirred up sentiments within that
> lay slumbering, and called into
> existence an entirely new train
> of thought. . . . I now understood what
> had been to me a most perplexing
> difficulty — to wit, the white man's
> power to enslave the black man . . .
> I understood the pathway from
> slavery to freedom. . . . I set out
> with high hope, and a fixed purpose,
> at whatever cost of trouble, to
> learn how to read. The very
> decided manner with which he spoke,
> and strove to impress his wife

with the evil consequences of
giving me instruction, served to
convince me that he was deeply
sensible of the truths he was
uttering.[8]

In various journals and newspapers, and in his excellent auto-
biographies, Douglass demonstrated sensitivity and power. At the
time of his death — February 20, 1895 — he had championed
emancipation, fought disenfranchisement, worked for equality in
education and employment, endorsed women's rights, temperance
and decent treatment of the working class generally, and he had
served his country well as Recorder of Deeds in Washington, D. C.,
and as Minister Resident and Consul General to Haiti. He was
living proof of the enormous human waste of slavery and racism.

Little time was wasted on subjects other than slavery and the
white problem during the earliest period of American Negro
Literature, though by 1861 at least one writer, Frances E. W.
Harper (1825-1911), argued that black authors should concern
themselves with "feelings that are general"[9] rather than only Negro
themes. Mrs. Harper, who wrote America's first published short
story by a Negro author ("The Two Offers" in *The Anglo-African
Magazine* for September/October, 1859), attempted in both her
poetry and prose to include experiences transcending racial limita-
tions. Another writer, Martin Delany (1812-1885), broke with
melodramatic stereotypes by showing characters capable of good
or evil, no matter what their race.

But the period extending from 1619 to 1865 was principally a
time of oral literature dominated by both the folk art of slaves and
the more formal rhetoric of abolitionist spokesmen. It is, of course,
hardly surprising that the spoken word should dominate Afro-
American literature, for oratory was considered by all to be the
ultimate achievement of cultivated men, and it was an art indi-
viduals of intelligence could master without intensive academic
training.

Oratory in America has seldom served so desperate and noble
a cause as it did when Frederick Douglass remonstrated an Inde-
pendence Day audience in 1852:

Why have I been called on to speak here today?
What have I, or those I represent,

> to do with your national independence?
> Are the great principles of political
> freedom and of natural justice
> embodied in that Declaration of
> Independence extended to us?
> . . . What, to the American slave,
> is your Fourth of July? I
> answer; a day that reveals to
> him more than all other days
> in the year, the gross injustice
> and cruelty to which he is a
> constant victim.[10]

In the history of American slavery, a relatively privileged class of house servants developed. This class — often represented by the racially mixed relatives of old master — soon constituted a small, elite caste within slavery whose opportunities for literacy far outstripped those of field hands. It was house servants, in union with freedmen, who formed the core of the Negro middle-class which grew after emancipation. By the late nineteenth century enough education and stability had grown within the middle-class to stimulate literary expression: the poetry of Paul Laurence Dunbar, the short stories of Charles W. Chesnutt, and the essays and speeches of W.E.B. DuBois and Booker T. Washington represent its major achievements.

The late nineteenth century was principally a period of transition in Afro-American literature, transition best reflected in the views of Washington and DuBois. Washington (1856-1915), pragmatic and ostensibly conservative, was cast by the white public in the role of absolute Negro leadership. DuBois (1868-1963), on the other hand, appealed to a black audience with brilliant essays and editorials extolling racial consciousness and pride. Washington's statements were often printed in the national press, while DuBois was largely restricted to Negro-controlled media. Despite Washington's vital and often misunderstood contributions to black America, it was DuBois who fired the imagination of Negro intellectuals and paved the way for the emergence of the "New Negro" in the 1920s. As Saunders Redding has observed, Washington, in spite of his national reputation, did not influence any important Negro writers.[11]

A contemporary of Washington and DuBois, Paul Laurence

Dunbar, was a gifted poet whose blackness forced him into the production of verse in dialect —

> Little brown baby wif spa'klin' eyes,
> Come to yo' pappy an' set on his knee.
> What you been doin', suh — makin san' pies?
> Look at dat bib — you's ez du'ty ez me.[12]

— and it was his dialect poetry which made him contemporarily famous. White America seemed unwilling to consider any but Dunbar's minstrel rhymes, yet his own hopes for creative fulfillment rested principally with a few outstanding "standard" English poems. In one such work, "The Poet," he succinctly summarized a tragedy very like his own:

> He sang of life, serenely sweet,
> With, now and then, a deeper note.
> From some high peak, nigh yet remote,
> He voiced the world's absorbing beat.
> He sang of love when earth was young,
> And Love itself was in his lays.
> But ah, the world, it turned to praise
> A jingle in a broken tongue.[13]

That Dunbar considered Negro dialect a "broken tongue" is comment enough upon the pervasive nature of middle-class values. Ironically, much of his finest work was dialect verse. The problem was not that Negro dialect lacked the ability to become serious poetry, but that Dunbar's readers refused to give serious consideration to dialect poems.

Primarily a poet, Dunbar also wrote undistinguished novels and somewhat better short stories. He had begun writing as a schoolboy in Dayton, Ohio, where he was born in 1872; after publishing two small volumes of poems at his own expense, his work was praised by the influential William Dean Howells, who was particularly impressed with Dunbar's dialect poetry. Following the 1896 publication of *Lyrics of Lowly Life,* he became the best known black poet since Phillis Wheatley. But he was torn between the need to produce what the public wanted and his own preference for "literary" English. Dunbar died in 1906 while his ability as a poet was still growing; Sterling A. Brown has accurately summarized his position and his ability: "The wonder is that this poet, who died so tragically young and belonged to a generally denied and despised race, should have written so well."[14]

The short stories of C. W. Chesnutt demonstrated that Negro characters could be created without recourse to traditional stereotypes. Though he often used, and indeed refined, the tragic mulatto theme, many of Chesnutt's best works dealt with Negro folklore, as in his conjur tales, or with the evil of continued discrimination. "We are told," he wrote in *The Web of Circumstances,*

> When the cycle of years has rolled
> around, there is to be another
> golden age, when all men will
> dwell together in love and harmony,
> and when peace and righteousness
> shall prevail for a thousand
> years. God speed the day and
> let not the shining thread of
> hope become so enmeshed in
> the web of circumstances that
> we lose sight of it; but
> give us here and there, and now
> and then, some litle foretaste of
> this golden age, that we may the more
> patiently and hopefully
> await its coming![15]

Among the most important transitional figures in American Negro literature, Chesnutt was born in Cleveland, Ohio, in 1858. His formal education extended only through the primary grades, though he later passed the Ohio state bar examinations and worked in law until his death on November 15, 1932. His literary career began with the short story "Uncle Peter's House" in 1885. For reasons never fully explained, he ceased writing for publication in 1905.

A gifted writer of short stories, he specialized in tales free of the simplified characterization so typical of stories of Negro life by white writers such as Joel Chandler Harris and Thomas Nelson Page, and in stories of the "blue vein" mulatto society of "Groveland" (Cleveland). Of special interest was the decision of his publishers not to reveal his race, leading many readers and critics to consider his work with an objectivity normally reserved for white authors, only to find later he was a Negro and that assumptions that Negroes could not create first-rate literature were false.

Throughout the slave period oral literature dominated, and nearly all Afro-American writers worked toward gaining long-denied freedom and equality. If only Wheatley, Douglass, and the unknown bards who created the sung poetry of spirituals achieved artistic excellence, other important goals were attained and the beginning of a uniquely American literary heritage was forged. The emergence of Dunbar, and Chesnutt in the post-emancipation period moved black literature from parochial concerns and techniques into the nation's literary mainstream.

As the twentieth century dawned, the migration of Negroes from the rural South to the urban North began in earnest, and prejudice toward Afro-Americans again intensified on the heels of the "New Manifest Destiny." Yet the seeds of literary excellence had been sown: the brilliance of DuBois dominated the black intelligentsia, while in the wings were poised skilled writers such as James Weldon Johnson, Claude McKay, William Stanley Braithwaite, and Fenton Johnson, whose work would set the stage for the Negro Renaissance of the 1920's.

Black Americans had overcome staggering odds to begin their move toward the fore in American letters. They would not — did not — turn back.

FOOTNOTES

[1]Phillis Wheatley, "To The University of Cambridge, in New-England," *The Poems of Phyllis Wheatley* (Chapel Hill, 1966), edited by Julian D. Mason, Jr., p. 5.
[2]Traditional.
[3]Traditional.
[4]Wheatley, p. 26.
[5]*Ibid.*, p. 33.
[6]George Moses Horton, "On Liberty and Slavery," in *The Black Poet* (New York, 1966), by Richard Walser, p. 32.
[7]Frederick Douglass, *Narrative of the Life of Frederick Douglass, An American Slave* (New York, 1968), p. 49.
[8]*Ibid.*, pp. 49-50.
[9]Frances E. W. Harper, Letter to Thomas Hamilton, dated 1861.
[10]Douglass, speech delivered at Rochester, New York, July 5, 1852.

[11]J. Saunders Redding, *To Make A Poet Black* (Chapel Hill, 1939), p. 78.

[12]Paul Laurence Dunbar, "Little Brown Baby," *The Complete Poems of Paul Laurence Dunbar* (New York, 1913), p. 134.

[13]*Ibid.*, "The Poet," p. 191.

[14]Sterling A. Brown, *Negro Poetry and Drama* (Washington D. C., 1937), p. 49.

[15]Charles Waddell Chesnutt, "The Web of Circumstance," *The Wife of His Youth and Other Stories* (Ann Arbor, 1968), pp. 322-23.

Claude McKay and the new Negro of the 1920's

by Wayne Cooper

As used in the 1920s, the term "New Negro" referred to more than the writers then active in the Negro Renaissance. The New Negro also included the Negro masses and especially the young. "For the younger generation," Alain Locke wrote in 1925, "is vibrant with a new psychology."[1] This new spirit he described as basically a renewal of "self-respect and self-dependence."[2]

The new confidence which characterized Negroes in the twenties resulted from many forces. Prior to World War I, militant new leaders had arisen. By demanding immediately full civil liberties and an end to segregation, men such as W. E. B. DuBois had inspired a greater self-assertiveness in their people. World War I and the resulting mass migration of Negroes to the urban North further disrupted old patterns of life and created new hopes, as well as new problems. The fight for democracy abroad led to greater expectations at home. The bloody race riots of 1919 did not kill these hopes, although the remarkable popularity of Marcus Garvey and his black nationalism indicated the Negro masses could not forever contain their frustrated aspirations.[3] As the Negro people entered the twenties, the "promised land" of the old spirituals still seemed far away. But their new militancy demonstrated that the long journey down the bitter desert years of history had strengthened, not weakened, their determination to reach the good life ahead.

That sudden flowering in literature called the Negro Renaissance gave voice to the new spirit awakening in Negroes in the twenties.[4] In addition, the Negro Renaissance became a part of the general revolt by the writers of the decade against the gross materialism and outmoded moral values of America's new industrial society. Negro writers found new strength in their own folk culture. As Robert Bone has written, "The Negro Renaissance was essentially a period of self-discovery, marked by a sudden growth of interest in things Negro."[5]

Of all the Renaissance writers, Claude McKay was one of the first to express the spirit of the New Negro.[6] His first American poems appeared in 1917. Before the decade of the Negro Renaissance had begun, he was already winning recognition as an exciting new voice in Negro literature.[7] A brief examination of his early career will perhaps reveal more clearly some of the important characteristics of the New Negro of the 1920s.

Claude McKay was born September 15, 1889, on the British West Indian island of Jamaica. There he grew to manhood. In 1912, at the age of twenty-three, he came to the United States to study agriculture at Tuskegee Institute. In Jamaica, McKay had already established a local reputation as a poet, having produced before he left two volumes of dialect poetry, *Songs of Jamaica* and *Constab Ballads*.[8]

These volumes revealed McKay to be a sensitive, intelligent observer of Jamaican life. Of black peasant origin himself, he used the English dialect of rural Jamaica to record lyrically the life of his people. In evaluating McKay's Jamaican verse, Jean Wagner has recently written:

Here, we are far from the dialect of the Dunbar school, inherited from the whites, who had forged it in order to perpetuate the stereotypes of Negro inferiority, and at best fix them in their roles of buffoons charged with diverting the white race. . . .[9] All things being equal, McKay's portrait of the Jamaican peasant is in substance that of the peasant the world over. Profoundly attached to the earth, he works the soil with a knowledge gained from age long habit; although a hard worker, the Jamaican, like his counterpart the world over, is condemned to exploitation.[10]

On the eve of his departure to the United States, McKay appeared to be an ambitious, talented young man with a fine future in Jamaica. In his poetry he had closely identified himself with its people. He had also revealed a deeply sensitive, independent spirit, keenly responsive to the good and evil in both man and nature.

Like many before him, however, he was strongly attracted to the United States. Years later, he wrote that America then seemed to him, "a new land to which all people who had youth and a youthful mind turned. Surely there would be opportunity in this land, even for a Negro."[11] Although far from naïve, McKay had never experienced firsthand American racial prejudice, and he seemed to have been totally unprepared for its vicious effects.

His initiation into the realities of Negro American life must certainly have been a swift one. Landing in Charleston, South Carolina, in the summer of 1912, he proceeded to Alabama's Tuskegee Institute. In 1918, McKay recorded in *Pearson's Magazine* his first reaction to Southern racial prejudice.

> It was the first time I had ever come face to face with such manifest, implacable hate of my race, and my feelings were indescribable. At first I was horrified; my spirit revolted against the ignoble cruelty and blindness of it all. . . . Then I found myself hating in return, but this feeling could not last long for to hate is to be miserable.[12]

Accompanying this statement were several poems, which, McKay said, had been written during his first year in America. "I sent them so that you may see what my state of mind was at the time."[13] Among them was one of his most eloquent polemics — "To the White Fiends." This poem shows a personality unaccustomed to servility and murderously aroused against the brutish debasement of Southern prejudice. If the poet could not physically defeat it, he, nevertheless, could throw a revealing light on its moral inferiority.

> Think you I am not fiend and savage too?
> Think you I could not arm me with a gun

And shoot down ten of you for every one of my black
    brothers murdered, burnt by you?
Be not deceived, for every deed you do
I could match — out-match! Am I not Afric's son,
Black of that black land where black deeds are done?
But the Almighty from the darkness drew
My soul and said: Even thou shalt be a light
Awhile to burn on the benighted earth,
Thy dusky face I set among the white
For thee to prove thyself of higher worth;
Before the world is swallowed up in night,
To show thy little lamp: go forth, go forth![14]

Soon tiring of what he described as "the semi-military, machine-like existence"[15] at Tuskegee, McKay transferred to Kansas State College, where he remained until 1914. In that year he was given several thousand dollars by an English friend.[16] Having decided his future lay in writing, not agricultural science, he took the money and went to New York City.

Once there, literary success did not come quickly. In fact, during his first year in New York, little time seems to have been devoted to writing. As he described it, through "high-living" and "bad investments" he soon managed to lose all his money.[17] His marriage to a Jamaican girl shortly after his arrival in New York lasted almost as briefly as his money.[18] "My wife," McKay wrote in 1918, "wearied of the life [in New York] in six months and went back to Jamaica."[19] McKay himself made a different decision. "I hated to go back after having failed at nearly everything so I just stayed here and worked — porter . . . janitor . . . waiter — anything that came handy."[20]

He also wrote, "If I would not," he said, "graduate as a bachelor of arts, I would graduate as a poet."[21] Within two years, Waldo Frank and James Oppenheim accepted for Seven Arts Magazine two of his sonnets, "The Harlem Dancer" and "Invocation."[22] A year later he was discovered by Frank Harris, who brought him to public notice again in Pearson's Magazine. Shortly afterwards, McKay met Max Eastman and his sister, Crystal. A lifelong friendship resulted.

At the time, Max Eastman was editor of The Liberator, then America's most openly Marxist literary magazine.[23] Through the Liberator, McKay quickly became identified with the radical-bohemian set in Greenwich Village. In 1919, Eastman and his staff were eagerly praising the young communist government of Russia, violently denouncing the repressive post-war hysteria at home, and writing stories and poems that ranged from fighting proletariat propaganda to tender pieces of home and mother. Few magazines, then or now, could match the *Liberator* in enthusiasm. Despite its flamboyancy, however, it was rich in talents. "On the surface," Robert Aaron has written, "*The Liberator* reflected the aimless, pointless life of the village." Yet, as Aaron pointed out, after World War I, it displayed a "toughness and militancy in its social attitudes,"[24] which belied its bohemian character.

Into such an atmosphere McKay fitted well. Eastman has described him then as a very black, handsome, high-spirited young man, with peculiar, arched eyebrows which gave him a perpetually quizzical expression.[25] Another old radical, Joseph Freeman, remembered also in his autobiography McKay's charm and wit.[26]

If McKay was sometimes given to abandoned gaiety, in the summer of 1919 he had good reason to exhibit a greater seriousness, as well as toughness. 1919 was the year of the Great Red Scare, one desperate phase of the effort to return to pre-war "normalcy." For Negroes, the year turned into a nightmare of bloody riots and violent death.[27] From June until January there occurred no less than twenty-five riots in major urban centers throughout the country.[28] The Chicago riot of July was the worst. When it was over, authorities counted 38 Negroes and whites dead, over 520 injured, and 1,000 families homeless.[29] Like all Negroes, McKay felt the emotional effects of such battles.

In the July issue of the *Liberator*[30] there appeared, along with six other poems, his now famous "If We Must Die." Today, it is the one poem by which McKay is most widely known. "If We Must Die" was a desperate shout of defiance; almost, it seemed a statement of tragic hopelessness. At the same time, it loudly proclaimed that in Negroes the spirit of human courage remained fully alive. Here is the poem which brought McKay to the alert attention of the Negro world. If not a great poem it, nevertheless, must certainly have expressed the attitude of many Negroes in 1919.

> If we must die, let it not be like hogs
> Hunted and penned in an inglorious spot,
> While round us bark the mad and hungry dogs,

Making their mock at our accursed lot.
If we must die, O let us nobly die,
So that our precious blood may not be shed in vain;
    then even the monsters we defy
Shall be constrained to honor us though dead!

*   *   *   *   *   *   *

What though before us lies the open grave?
Like men we'll face the murderous, cowardly pack,
Pressed to the wall, dying, but fighting back!

After his appearance in *The Liberator,* McKay entered more
fully into the literary world. His career through the twenties reads,
in fact, like a romance of the decade itself. Through the generosity
of friends, he went to England in late 1919 and stayed for more
than a year, working part of the time for Sylvia Pankhurst's
socialist paper, *The Workers' Dreadnought.* While there his third
book of poems, *Spring in New Hampshire,* appeared.[31]

Upon his return to the United States in 1921, he became for
a brief time co-editor of *The Liberator* with Michael Gold. Before
leaving that job because of policy differences with Gold,[32] McKay's
first American book of poems, *Harlem Shadows,*[33] appeared. Dur-
ing this period, he also made a brief first acquaintance with many
leading Negro intellectuals, among them James W. Johnson and
W. E. B. DuBois.[34] But before the end of 1922, he was off again,
this time to Russia.

McKay was among the first Negroes to go to Russia after the
Civil War which had brought the Communists into undisputed
power. He arrived during Lenin's period of ideological retrench-
ment, when the New Economic Policy allowed a limited amount
of free enterprise and personal freedom. Because of his black com-
plexion, McKay immediately attracted the attention of people in
the street. Although not a party member, or even definitely com-
mitted to Marxist principles, McKay's popularity with the crowds
in Moscow and Leningrad helped win him favor among higher
party circles. Sen Katayama, then Japan's leading Communist, got
McKay admitted to the Fourth Congress of the Communist Inter-
national.[35] But above all, as McKay wrote James Weldon Johnson
in 1935, "It was the popular interest that irresistibly pushed me
forward."[46] His trip soon turned into one long triumph of personal
popularity.

After meeting Trotsky in Moscow, he was sent on a long and elaborate tour of Soviet army and naval bases. Besides Trotsky, he met Zinoviev and other top Communists, as well as many leading Russian literary figures.

Despite McKay's sincere attraction to the Communist Revolution, he never fully committed himself to its ideology. In the 1930s, he was viciously attacked by American Communists for going back on his principles; but, as he wrote James Weldon Johnson in 1935, he went to Russia as "a writer and free spirit"[47] and left the same. He wrote Johnson then and later repeated in his autobiography that he had desired in 1922 the title, "creative writer," and had felt it would mean more to Negroes in the long run.[38]

Throughout the twenties, and to a large extent throughout his life, McKay remained what Frederick Hoffman called the "aesthetic radical."[39] This was the artist who, typical of the twenties, stoutly affirmed the value of his non-social personality. He considered himself "the natural man," willing in an age of conformity to be only himself. That McKay shared this attitude is evident in all his writings.

Like other Negro writers of the twenties (most notably, Langston Hughes), he shared, to some degree, the same feeling of alienation that characterized Gertrude Stein's "lost generation." Thus, in 1918, McKay could write: "And now this great catastrophe [World War I] has come upon the world, proving the real hollowness of nationhood, patriotism, racial pride, and most of the things one was taught to respect and reverence."[40] His affiliation with *The Liberator* and his trip to Russia were part of a personal search for new moral and social standards.

McKay's trip to Russia marked the beginning of his long twelve-year exile in Europe. From Russia, he went briefly to Germany, then to France, where he lived for a number of years. In the late twenties, he journeyed to Spain and then to Morocco in North Africa where he remained until his return to the United States in 1934.[41]

Why did McKay spend twelve years wandering through Europe and North Africa? He never felt himself to be a typical expatriate. In his autobiography, he gave perhaps the main reason for his long expatriation.

> Color consciousness was the fundamental of my restlessness
> . . . my white fellow-expatriates could sympathize but . . .
> they could not altogether understand . . . unable to see deep
> into the profundity of blackness, some even thought . . .
> I might have preferred to be white like them . . . they
> couldn't understand the instinctive . . . pride of a black
> person resolute in being himself and yet living a simple
> civilized life like themselves.[42]

The place of Negroes in the modern world was the one great problem that obsessed McKay from his arrival in the United States until his death in 1948.[43] For a while after World War I, he undoubtedly thought that in Communism Negroes might find a great world brotherhood.

In the twenties, he turned from international communism but not from the common Negro, with whom he had always closely identified. He came to the conclusion that in Negro working people there existed an uninhibited creativity and joy in life which Europeans, including Americans, had lost. In their folk culture lay strength enough for their salvation. McKay felt Negroes should not lose sight of their own uniqueness and the value of their own creations while taking what was valuable from the larger European civilization. He laid much emphasis on the need for Negroes to develop a group spirit.[44]

Among Negro writers of the twenties, McKay was not alone in his discovery of the folk. In fact, of central importance to the Negro Renaissance was its emphasis on Negro folk culture. Jean Toomer, for example, celebrated the black peasants of Georgia, and in the following verses, associated himself with their slave past:

> O Negro slaves, dark purple ripened plums
> Squeezed, and bursting in the pine-wood air,
> Passing, before they stripped the old tree bare
> One plum was saved for me, one seed becomes
> An everlasting song, a singing tree,
> Caroling softly souls of slavery,
> What they were, and what they are to me,
> Caroling softly souls of slavery.[45]

In enthusiastic outbursts, youthful Langston Hughes was also loudly proclaiming the worth of the common folk.[46]

To a certain extent, the New Negro's emphasis on the folk was heightened by the new attitude toward Negroes exhibited by many white writers of the twenties. After World War I certain white writers such as Gertrude Stein and Waldo Frank thought they saw in Negroes beings whose naturally creative expressiveness had not been completely inhibited by the evil forces of modern civilization.[47] As the twenties progressed, Negroes and their arts enjoyed a considerable vogue. Primitive African art became popular among many intellectuals. Jazz, of course, became popular in the twenties. Negro singers found a greater public receptivity, and the blues entered American music. In many respects, American Negroes had in the twenties a favorable opportunity for a reassessment of their past accomplishments and future potentials.

The great emphasis on the primitive and the folk led however to some naïve delusions. Just as whites had previously built a stereotype of the happy, simpleminded plantation Negro, many people in the twenties stereotyped Negroes as unfettered children of nature, bubbling over with uninhibited sexual joy and child-like originality. To the extent that Negro writers accepted such an image, they limited the depth and richness of their own evaluations of American Negro life.[48]

While he was in Europe, McKay produced three novels which reflected his own interest in the Negro folk. They were *Home to Harlem* (1928),[49] *Banjo* (1929), and *Banana Bottom* (1933). He also produced a volume of short stories entitled *Gingertown* in 1932.[50] To a considerable extent, McKay's view of the Negro common folk was influenced by the newer stereotype of Negroes. *Home to Harlem,* his first novel, is the story of Jake, a Negro doughboy, and his joyful return to Harlem after World War I. Jake seems to have been McKay's ideal type — an honest, carefree worker whose existence, if a rather aimless one, is not complicated by pettiness or unnecessary worry over things that do not immediately concern him. Contrasted to Jake is Ray (McKay himself), an educated Negro, who is torn between two ways of life — Jake's and the more serious though conventional one imposed upon him by education. While the virtues of the common folk are contrasted to the doubts and confusion of the educated, McKay takes the reader on a tour of Harlem cabarets and rent parties.

His unvarnished view of Harlem night life delighted many white readers of the twenties and dismayed not a few middle-class Negroes.[51] The latter felt that an undue emphasis on the Negro lower class would damage their fight for civil rights and further delay their just battle for liberty. McKay was not the only writer of the Negro Renaissance to upset respectable Negro society.[52] One of the chief results of the Negro Renaissance was to force the Negro middle class to reevaluate their relationship to the Negro masses.

McKay's second novel, *Banjo*, told the story of the Negro beachboys of Marseilles, and further contrasted the free life of common Negroes with the frustrations of those caught in the more sophisticated web of modern civilization. In his third novel, *Banana Bottom*, he idealized the folk culture of Jamaica.

In some ways, Claude McKay differed radically from the typical New Negro writer of the twenties. For one thing, he was a Jamaican and did not become an American citizen until 1940. For another, he was older by some ten years than most writers of the Negro Renaissance; and except for a brief period, he did not live in the United States at all in the twenties.

He was also unique in the extent to which he associated with the larger literary world. Most Negro writers of the twenties had depended on Negro publications for a start. McKay's first successes were in white magazines — *Seven Arts*, *Pearson's*, and *The Liberator*. As an editor of *The Liberator* for a brief while, he was probably the only Negro writer of the time to hold such a position on an important American publication. McKay was at least partly responsible for the greater degree of communication that existed between Negro and white writers in the twenties. On the eve of his departure for Russia in 1922, James Weldon Johnson gave him a farewell party, and invited prominent writers of both races. Years later Johnson wrote to McKay concerning that event:

> We often speak of that party back in '22. . . . Do you know that was the first getting together of the black and white literati on a purely social plane. Such parties are now common in New York, but I doubt if any has been more representative. You will remember there were present Heywood Broun, Ruth Hale, F. P. Adams, John Farrar, Carl Van Doren, Freda Kirchwey, Peggy Tucker, Roy Nash — on our side you, DuBois, Walter White, Jessie Fauset, [Arthur] Schomburg, J. Rosamond Johnson — I think that party started something.[53]

Although McKay's career differed somewhat from that of the typical Negro writer of the twenties, he represented much that was characteristic of the New Negro. His movement from rural Jamaica to the big city and the literary world of the twenties is itself symbolic of the larger movement by Negro people from the rural South to the broader horizons of the urban North. His early interest in Communism was only one indication that the New Negro would no longer be unaffected by world events. World War I had ended American isolation for both Negroes and whites.

In his prose, McKay stressed the value of the common Negro and joined other Negro Renaissance writers in a rediscovery of Negro folk culture. But it is for his poetry that McKay will be longest remembered. For in his poetry, he best expressed the New Negro's determination to protect his human dignity, his cultural worth, and his right to a decent life.

[1]Alain Locke (ed.), *The New Negro* (New York, 1925), p. 3.

[2]*Ibid.*, p. 4.

[3]Two recent general discussions of the New Negro of the twenties are found in Robert A. Bone, *The Negro Novel in America* (New Haven, 1958), pp. 51-107; and Jean Wagner, *Les Poetes Negres des Etas-Unis* (Paris: Librairie Istra, 1963), pp. 161-207.

[4]Wagner, *op. cit.*, p. 161.

[5]Bone, *op. cit.*, p. 62.

[6]Wagner, *op. cit.*, p. 211.

[7]McKay first became widely known after the appearance of his poem, "If We Must Die," in *The Liberator* (July, 1919), 20-21.

[8]Claude McKay, *Songs of Jamaica* (Kingston Aston W. Gardner and Co., 1912); *Constab Ballads* (London, 1912).

[9]Wagner, *op. cit.*, p. 219.

[10]*Ibid.*, p. 220.

[11]McKay, *My Green Hills of Jamaica* (Unpublished mss. in the Schomburg Collection, New York Public Library), p. 80, written in the mid-1940s.

[12]*Pearson's Magazine* (September, 1918), 275.

[13]*Ibid.*

[14]*Ibid.*, p. 276.

[15]*Ibid.*

[16]Letter from McKay to James Weldon Johnson, March 10, 1928, in the McKay folder of Johnson Correspondence (James Weldon Johnson Collection, Yale University Library).

[17]Countee Cullen (ed.), *Caroling Dusk, An Anthology of Verse by Negro Poets* (New York, 1927), p. 82.

[18]Marriage certificate in the McKay Papers (Yale University

64

Library).

[19]*Pearson's Magazine* (September, 1918), 276.

[20]*Ibid.*

[21]McKay, *A Long Way From Home* (New York, 1937), p. 4.

[22]Wagner, *op. cit.*, p. 215.

[23]For a good discussion of *The Liberator* and its origins see, Daniel Aaron, *Writers on the Left, Episodes in American Literary Communism* (New York, 1961), pp. 5-108.

[24]*Ibid.*, p. 92.

[25]In McKay, *The Selected Poems of Claude McKay* (New York, 1953), p. 110.

[26]Joseph Freeman, *An American Testament, A Narrative of Rebels and Romantics* (New York. 1936), pp. 243, 245-46, 254.

[27]John Hope Franklin, *From Slavery to Freedom, A History of American Negroes* (New York, 1947), pp. 471-73.

[28]*Ibid.*

[29]*Ibid.*, pp. 473-74.

[30]*The Liberator* (July, 1919), 20-21.

[31]McKay, *A Long Way From Home*, pp. 59-91.

[32]*Ibid.*, pp. 138-41. See also, Aaron, *op. cit.*, p. 93.

[33]McKay, *Harlem Shadows* (New York, 1922).

[34]McKay, *A Long Way From Home*, pp. 108-15.

[35]*Ibid.*, pp. 165-66.

[36]Letters from McKay to James Weldon Johnson, May 8, 1935, in the McKay folder of the Johnson Correspondence (James Weldon Johnson Collection, Yale University Library).

[37]*Ibid.*

[38]*Ibid.*

[39]Frederick J. Hoffman, *The Twenties, American Writings in the Postwar Decade* (New York, 1955), pp. 382-84.

[40]*Pearson's Magazine* (September, 1918), 276.

[41]McKay, *A Long Way From Home*, pp. 153-341, contains an account of his travels through Europe and North Africa. A briefer account is in Wagner, *op. cit.*, pp. 215-17.

[42]McKay, *A Long Way From Home*, p. 245.

[43]For McKay's views on race toward the end of his life, his "Right Turn to Catholicism" (typewritten ms. in the Schomburg Collection, New York Public Library) is especially important.

[44]These ideas were presented by McKay in two novels, *Banjo* (New York, 1929), and *Banana Bottom* (New York, 1933). He discussed the idea of a "group soul" in *A Long Way From Home*, pp. 349-54.

[45]In Wagner, *op. cit.*, p. 292.

[46]Langston Hughes, "The Negro Artist and the Racial Mountain," *The Nation* (June 23, 1926), 694.

[47]For a general discussion of this topic, see Wagner, *op. cit.*, pp. 174-77. Also, see Hoffman, *op. cit.*, pp. 269-71.

[48]Bone, *op. cit.*, pp. 58-61.

[49]*Home to Harlem* (New York, 1928).

[50]*Gingertown* (New York, 1932).

[51]Here are two extreme views of McKay's *Home to Harlem*. The first reflects Negro middle-class opinion.

> Again, white people think we are buffoons, thugs and rotters anyway. Why should we waste so much energy to prove it? That's what Claude McKay has done. (Clipping from the *Chicago Defender*, March 17, 1928, in McKay Folder, Schomburg Collection, New York Public Library.)

Now, another view:

> [*Home to Harlem* is] . . . beaten through with the rhythm of life that is the jazz rhythm . . . the real thing in rightness. . . . It is the real stuff, the low-down on Harlem, the dope from the inside. (John R. Chamberlain, Review of *Home to Harlem, New York Times*, March 11, 1928, p. 5).

[52]Langston Hughes, *The Big Sea, An Autobiography* (New York, 1945), pp. 265-66.

[53]Letter from Johnson to McKay, August 21, 1930, in the McKay Correspondence (Yale University Library).

Poetry
in the Harlem Renaissance

by Gerald Moore

IN RECENT YEARS the Harlem Renaissance of the 1920s has been severely mauled by American critics, both white and black. Their principal target has been its lack of any clearly-defined or steadily-pursued cultural policy. Quarreling alternately with the black nationalism of Garvey and the pontifical white 'internationalism' of American Communists like Michael Gold, the writers of Harlem were left with only a narrow ground on which to stand. When this too collapsed in the Great Depression of 1929 their movement dispersed and many of them never again commanded the attention of the public. In any case, their public within America had always been largely a white one. Claude McKay, for example, sought his literary peers among the intellectual coterie of Mable Dodge in down-town Greenwich Village, where he had first found his hearing through the patronage of Frank Harris. The new black bourgeoisie, which helped to create Harlem through the deliberate penetration of this former white area in the years following 1905, largely ignored the writers and intellectuals who flourished in the first real urban environment that America had offered them. But the loss was not only that of the bourgeoisie, who sank themselves in colour-climbing, skin-lightening and hair-straightening, or in the pursuit of civil liberties of a kind useful only to the educated and articulate. The lack of an adequate black readership has dogged black American writing down to our own day and constantly threatens to turn the literary militant into an entertainer who performs at the behest of a masochistic and guilt-ridden white audience.

Harold Cruse has written one of the fairest and best-informed accounts of the period, but he too has summarized the failure of the Renaissance in these terms:

> The essentially original and native creative element
> of the 1920s was the Negro ingredient — as all the
> whites who were running to Harlem actually know.
> But the Harlem intellectuals were so overwhelmed
> at being "discovered" and courted, that they allowed
> a *bona fide* cultural movement, which issued from
> the social system as naturally as a gushing spring, to
> degenerate into a pampered and paternalized vogue.[1]

Beside this we may set the observations of a recent white critic, David Littlejohn, who sees the ultimate importance of the movement as cultural rather than artistic:

> In retrospect, the Harlem Renaissance of 1923 to
> 1933 seems far less important a literary event than
> it did to some observers at the time. There is no
> question of its importance as a progressive move-
> ment, both real and symbolic, in American Negro
> culture. The question is rather of its substantial
> worth in any other context, or its relevance to subse-
> quent generations.
> It was, in part, one more fad of the faddish twenties
> —something modish and insubstantial, and perhaps
> even a little corrupt.[2]

Although both these critics have put their fingers on points of weakness which are glaringly obvious in the militant 1960s, I believe their viewpoints suffer from an essential insularity. I want to suggest that their strictures have far more application to the plays and novels of the period than to its poetry, and that this poetry, uneven in quality though it was, has been immensely fertile in its influences throughout the Third World. It established a tradition of self-expression to which black men everywhere could react.

The worst posturing of the Renaissance, the most blatant acting-out of white expectations of Negro fecklessness, jiving and ejaculating in a timeless, free-wheeling and orgiastic world, is found in its fiction. Novels like McKay's *Home to Harlem* (1928) and *Banjo* (1929) abound in scenes of this kind, though it is fair to point out that McKay was in these years (1923-34) inhabiting a world very similar to that depicted in his novels. And it is difficult not to support the partial authenticity of his novels against the kind of frightened and reproving criticism they received in 'respectable' Negro newspapers. There is a real dilemma for the black writer who genuinely believes that his people are more spontaneous and life-loving than their white fellows, since he daren't say so without being accused of exoticism. There is no doubt that McKay was, as a person, very much like some of his own restless, hedonistic and 'wake-up' fictional heroes.

The black theatre of this period has left even fewer enduring monuments than its fiction. The title of some of its stage-musicals speak for themselves — *Hot Chocolates, Chocolate Dandies, Shuffle Along.* Ironically, it was white writers in these years who not only made fortunes out of black themes, in plays like *Black Boy, Show Boat* and *Green Pastures,* but who gave black performers their first opportunities to develop serious roles upon the stage in O'Neill's *The Emperor Jones* and *All God's Chillun' Got Wings.*

Turning to the poetry, however, we seem at once to encounter a world of real anguish and real desire struggling to find expression in an idiom which is for the most part hopelessly outmoded and literary. For in poetic terms this was not so much a Renaissance as a new and painful birth. The black man in the Americas had long developed a strong and distinctive tradition in music, song and popular speech. But for the most part the poets of Harlem left all this aside and attempted to render the pain of their lives in the idiom of the Elizabethan sonnet, the Keatsian ode and the Tennysonian ballad. Yet even those who, like McKay and Countee Cullen, never succeeded in liberating themselves from the straight-jacket of an alien and outworn style, do occasionally transfigure it with a blaze of passion and particular experience.

Let us contrast, for example, a fairly typical passage of McKay's prose with the opening lines of one of his more effective sonnets. Here is a jiving scene from *Banjo:*

> Black skin itching, black flesh warm with
> the wine of life, the love and deep
> meaning of life. Strong smell of healthy
> black bodies in a close atmosphere,
> generating sweat and waves of heat,
> Oh, shake that thing![3]

No wonder W. E. B. DuBois was shocked to his braces and Dewey Jones thundered against its "filth, obscenity and more filth" (the reader of today will look for these in vain).

Here is the McKay of a few years earlier beginning his poem "America":

> Although she feeds me bread of bitterness
> And sinks into my throat her tiger's tooth,
> Stealing my breath of life, I will confess
> I love this cultured hell that tests my youth![4]

Despite the obvious weakness of the second line, we seem at once to hear an authentic voice which is speaking for itself and of itself. The formal control so absent from McKay's fiction is widely evident in his poetry, hampered as this is by the obsolescence of its style and influences. The same quality of authentic emotion sounds in his poetry of nostalgia as in the more famous poems of anger like "Outcast" and "If We Must Die":

> I have forgotten the special, startling season
> Of the pimento's flowering and fruiting;
> What time of year the ground doves brown the fields
> And fill the noonday with their curious fluting.[5]

It is McKay too, relieved by his stranger's status from the necessity of working out a relationship to America, who is able to situate the uprooted black man in his full historical and physical isolation :

> Only a thorn-crowned Negro and no white
> Can penetrate into the Negro's ken,
> Or feel the thickness of the shroud of night
> Which hides and buries him from other men.[6]

There is a radical avowal in these lines which was not to find its equivalence for another twenty years or more. Indeed, the last two lines look directly forward to Ralph Ellison's *Invisible Man* of 1952. Despite the lulling effect of his rather dreamy pentameters, McKay frequently displays this ability to make us suddenly sit up and listen.

The poetry of his younger contemporary Countee Cullen suffers even more than McKay's from archaism. Cullen alternates between a tone of mild racial consciousness and one of literally colourless imitation of Keats. Writing in the very years when his fellow Americans Pound, Eliot and William Carlos Williams were breaking and making English poetic idiom anew, Cullen displays a blissful unawareness that anything has happened in English poetry since 1880:

> My love is dark as yours is fair,
> Yet lovelier I hold her
> Than listless maids with pallid hair
> And blood that's thin and colder.[7]

These lines display the kind of simplicity which his early admirers mistook for lyricism. Only in a few short pieces like the over-familiar poem on the childhood visit to Baltimore does this simplicity become a virtue. But in an ambitious work like "The Black Christ" it becomes an intolerable jingle, the more irritating because this guileless quality is scarcely one which befits the New Negro in the competitive jungle of twentieth century New York:

> "I have a fear," he used to say, . . .
> "Some man contemptuous of my race . . .
> Will strike me down for being black,
> But when I answer I'll pay back
> The late revenge long overdue
> A thousand of my kind and hue."

Cullen's critical position with regard to black poetry in America, though scarcely consistent, may point to one of the sources of this wilting etiolated quality in much of his own verse. In his introduction to the anthology *Caroling Dusk* (1927) he attacked the whole notion of an American Negro school of poetry and urged the importance of the Anglo-American poetic tradition upon his fellow black writers. Yet it was probably this very lack of particularity of the urgent struggle to express the quality of a certain time, place and experience, which prevented so much Harlem poetry from breaking out of its literary cocoon. Whitman did not found a new American poetic idiom by turning in to Wordsworth or Shelley, but by throwing his own words at Brooklyn Ferry and Paumonock. The black American poet needed to become just that, before he could become part of an Anglo-American tradition also.

It was precisely this lack of misplaced reverence for traditions immediately irrelevant to their condition which made the poetry of Jean Toomer and Langston Hughes so much more useful to their successors. The poetry in Toomer's one book *Cane* (1923) exhibits a totally liberated language and one which commands the nightmare sharpness and displacement of imagery that characterize surrealist art:

> Hair — braided chestnut, coiled like a lyncher's rope,
> Eyes — fagots,
> Lips — old scars, or the first red blisters,
> Breath — the last sweet scent of cane,
> And her slim body, white as the ash of black flesh
>   after flame.

The passages of prose in *Cane* display the same freedom to describe his own visions exactly as he sees them, with no dead men's fingers on the pen. The creative tension in Toomer's work springs from a certain sense of distance between himself and the life of the black poor; a distance he refuses to sentimentalize and forces to work for him:

> Through the cement floor her strong roots sink
> down. They spread under the asphalt streets. Dreaming, the streets roll over on their bellies, and suck
> their glossy health from them. Her roots sink down
> and spread under the river and disappear in blood-
> lines that waver south. . . .

Yet such is the tension of this writing that it comes as little surprise to learn that Toomer subsequently fell silent, declared himself white and vanished. Not being available to defend his example and prove its adaptability, he was probably far less influential with the coming generation of poets than the less brilliantly gifted Langston Hughes. The salient importance of Hughes was his insistence on relating the written poetry of the black American to the inexhaustible riches of his own verbal creations in blues, work-song, jazz-lyric, spiritual, sermon and everyday speech. This soil was ultimately bound to prove too thin to sustain the weight of a complex and ambitious poetic sensibility (even the greatest of the Country Blues sing much better than they read), but it was of immense value as a fertilizer. It was Hughes who finally smashed the grip of "Eng. Lit." upon black poetry and the work of later, often more important poets like Waring Cuney, Robert Hayden, Ted Joans and LeRoi Jones might have been more difficult without him. He taught the poetry of his people to respect the short line, the abrupt and jerky rhythm, the trumpet-like swoop or plunge towards a delayed rhyme. He was a man who delighted in experiment and who, significantly, remained prolific when the other Harlem poets fell virtually silent after 1930.

Like the early Cullen, Hughes alternates in his own early poetry between an insistence upon the dimension of ancestral African experience which distinguishes the Negro ("The Negro Speaks of Rivers") and an equal insistence upon his American-ness, his right to participate fully in American life ("I, too, sing America"). This is one of many characteristics which establish continuity between Hughes's work in the 'twenties and black American writing today. For if LeRoi Jones has sadly concluded his "Notes for a speech" with the lines:

> Africa
> is a foreign place. You are
> as any other sad man here
> American.

the poetry of his contemporary Paul Vesey still insists upon the vital relevance of Africa and its culture for the urban blacks of America.

Another strand of continuity stretching from the early work of Hughes is his determination to move poetry off the page and into the air. For him, a poem only exists as a text to be sung, chanted and intoned against a carefully described musical background. In later volumes like *Ask Your Mama* and *Montage of a Dream Deferred* he carried these tendencies further and was frankly writing lyrics for jazz, blues or gospel performance. But even his earlier work conveys a conviction that words-on-paper are not enough to create poetry for a people whose genius is for improvisation and the creation of a total artistic gesture embracing dance, mime, song and word:

> To fling my arms wide
> In some place of the sun,
> To whirl and to dance
> Till the bright day is done.
> Then rest at cool evening
> Beneath a tall tree
> While night comes gently
> Black like me.
> That is my dream.
> To fling my arms wide
> In the face of the sun,
> Dance; Whirl! Whirl!
> Till the quick day is done.
> Rest at pale evening,
> A tall, slim tree,
> Night coming tenderly
> Black like me.[8]

It is Langston Hughes, too, who conveys more strongly than any other poet at the time the quality of confidence and joy which suddenly filled the New Negroes of Harlem in these years. For Harlem itself, described so glowingly by James Weldon Johnson, was not yet the bitter, violent and abandoned slum it has since become. It was the first black metropolis of the modern world, the great forge for the fashioning of a new black culture in literature, music and the arts. Even in the world of politics men often found more reason to hope than to despair, despite the terrible lynchings and race riots which swept America in the years immediately following the First World War. And it was Hughes who gave a tongue to this hope:

> It's an earth song —
> And I've been waiting long for an earth song.
> It's a spring song —
> And I've been waiting long for a spring song.

Strong as the shoots of a new plant
Strong as the bursting of new buds
Strong as the coming of the first child from it's
    mother's womb.
It's an earth song,
A body-song,
A spring-song —
I have been waiting for this spring song.[9]

No sooner did this mood begin to wane in North America itself than the example of Harlem began to prove its fertility. During the middle to late 'thirties young black writers in places as far apart as Martinique, Capetown and Paris were stirred by their discovery that men like themselves had found the means to begin singing truly of their colour and condition. Most evident of this inspiration is the poetry of Léon Damas, whose *Pigments* (1937) was the first great poetic explosion heralding the arrival of *négritude*. Damas uses a sharp, slangy, tense and fast-moving technique which is new to French poetry but which is clearly derived from the example of Langston Hughes:

Alors je vous mettrai les pieds dans
le plat
ou bien tout simplement la main au collet
de tout ce qui m'emmerde
en gros caractères
colonisation
civilization
assimilation et la suite[10]

And although the stylistic influence of Hughes is less evident in the other two great triumvirs of early négritude, Aimé Cèsaire and Leopold Senghor, they themselves have testified to the liberating and fertilizing effect of the jazz, blues and poetry of Harlem to which they were exposed in the salons of Mademoiselle Nardal between 1929 and 1934 and in those of René Maran in years following 1935. The black American scholar Mercer Cook also played an important part in making known to the young students from Africa and the Caribbean the achievements of their American contemporaries. A poem like Senghor's *New York*, different as it is in style from any product of Harlem, is really inconceivable without the links forged in Paris during those years, links which found their literary expression in *La Revue du Monde Noir*.

At the far end of Africa the young coloured poet Peter Abrahams was, as he tells us in his autobiography *Tell Freedom*, awoken for the first time to the possibility of his making a distinctive mark upon the world by his discovery of the Harlem poets during a few months of working as a librarian in Capetown. From that moment, he determined to make his living as a writer, for the barriers to confidence imposed by segregation, conquest and public contempt were finally broken. Even the title of his novel *Path of Thunder* is almost certainly derived from a poem of Countee Cullen's.

Thus, though lacking real excellence as poets themselves, the Harlem writers of the twenties were a contributory cause of excellent poetry made by other men in other continents. Their influence may be found as late as the mid-fifties, in the work of the young Senegalese poet David Diop, who perished in an air-crash a few years later. It is, of course, understandable that black Americans today, turning upon their work the exigent demand of a more bitter and a more desperate hour, should find it lacking in the qualities the time seems to demand. But in terms of the black man's gradual liberation of himself during the first seventy years of this century, their achievement will be seen to have a power and an importance transcending the strict merits of the work itself.

[1]*The Crisis of the Negro Intellectual* (London, Allen, 1969), pp. 51-52.

[2]*Black on White* (New York, Grossman, 1966) p. 39.

[3]*Banjo* (New York, Harper, 1929), p. 319.

[4]*Harlem Shadows* (New York, 1922)

[5]*Ibid.*

[6]*Ibid.*

[7]*Color* (New York, Harper, 1925)

[8]"Dream Variation" in *The New Negro* ed. Alain Locke (New York, Boni, 1925) p. 143.

[9]"An earth Song," *Ibid.* p. 142

[10]"Pour Sur," *Pigments* (Paris, G.L.M. 1937)

Langston Hughes

by Allen D. Prowle

IN HIS AUTOBIOGRAPHY, *The Big Sea*, Langston Hughes describes
how he *accidentally* became a poet. When he was at grammar
school in Lincoln, Illinois, he was elected Class Poet, this position
being the only one that remained after all other elections had been
carried out. On the basis that poetry has rhythm and that all
Negroes have rhythm, he was preferred to the only other qualifying
contender. He wrote of the pride with which he returned home
and of the poem he wrote in praise of his class and teachers. He
had the most exuberant sense of humour and this account could
be read as yet another example of the comic streak that one finds
in his prose writings. But underlying this one can distinguish
also his serious concept of the poet as spokesman, and this is cer-
tainly what he was to become; but not a spokesman who was to
limit himself merely to eulogising his race. He was the first Amer-
ican Negro writer to make a living out of writing, but not through
the cautiousness which characterised the works of those black
writers of the turn of the century, who were forced to reach a com-
promise with economics and acceptability; two separate ideas
which, in reality, formed a perfect synonym.

He first started writing seriously at the time of the Negro
Renaissance of the 'twenties. The work he produced during this
period follows the general precepts laid down by the poet Sterling
Brown in his manifesto for the new Negro writer.

The first of these precepts was that the writer should try to create a sense of race pride through a rediscovery of Africa and her culture. Hughes' early poem, "The Negro Speaks of Rivers," was greeted as a fine example of what Brown was suggesting. The poem, which opens with the words "I've known rivers," goes on to evoke the antiquity and mystique of Africa through a description of the Euphrates, the Congo and the Nile. The line: "My soul has grown deep like the rivers" links the poet to this ancient past, but the poem does not remain at this level of nostalgia for Hughes wrote it as he was crossing the Mississippi, and he remembered how Abraham Lincoln had travelled by raft down this river to New Orleans to witness the barbarity of slavery. This is the last river of the poem and the reiterated "I've known rivers" takes on a bitter irony while the final line of the poem, again a reiteration, "My soul has grown deep like the rivers," adds a new intensity, ambivalent in dignity and warning. It anticipates the strong vein of protest in his work. Brown had also advocated this as a central element of the new writing, but Hughes did not need to be advised in this respect. Protest is the dominant theme of his poetry; a protest expressed in varying degrees of intensity, but which is always at the roots of his creativity. Again, like Brown, he wrote of the heroes of Black American history. His poem "October 16," from the collection *One-Way Ticket* (1949), recalls the raid on Harpers Ferry with evident pride, but also with the somewhat pessimistic feeling that the fire has gone out of the soul. The final lines of the poem

> Perhaps
> You will recall
> John Brown

express Hughes' concern at the stagnation that prevailed in the Negro conscience of the time.

In "Roland Hayes Beaten," which appeared in the same collection, Hughes uses another heroic figure as a warning of the reality that lies behind the supposedly *gentle* Southern Negro. The soft wind in the cotton fields may be part of the poetry of the South, but

> Beware the hour
> It uproots trees!

His most bitter poems are those written about the cruelty and
inhumanity of the South. In his *Collected Poems* (1961) he
assembled a number of his most violent works under the heading
of *Magnolia Flowers*. This section contains "Mulatto," which was
rewritten in dramatic form and published in 1935. Both the poem
and the play are angry testimonies to the barbarity of the South.
The play is the tragedy of the mulatto son of a white plantation
owner, Colonel Thomas Norwood, and his Negro mistress-servant.
The boy finds that the colour of his skin bars him from enjoying
the social status that should be his merely through being the
Colonel's son. Ironically, he is treated as just another coloured
servant by his father and yet he shares his father's own race preju-
dices. The situation is scarcely exaggerated, even if the impact
is somewhat dissipated by the melodramatic nature of his final
scene, which encompasses patricide, lynch violence, and suicide.

Hughes often dealt with the problem of mixed-blood. One of
his earliest poems, "Cross," centralises the dilemma. The speaker of
the poem regrets the time he had cursed his white father and black
mother, both of whom are now dead: the white father in his large,
fine house, the mother in his shack. His ambiguous situation and
his tenuous grasp on identity are thus aptly expressed in the sim-
plicity of the closing lines.

> I wonder where I'm gonna die
> Being neither white nor black?

Several of his short stories deal with this same question. "Red-
Headed Baby" from the collection, *The Ways of White Folks*
(1934), begins by describing the feelings of a white third-mate on
a tramp steamer when he is faced with the prospect of spending
some time in one of the small towns on the Florida coast. His
attitude is summed up when he curses: ". . . what the hell kind
of port's this? What the hell is there to do except get drunk and
go out and sleep with niggers? Hell!" This part of the coast is
dotted with groups of half-built houses left over from the boom.
But there is one way of making money and spending it. The
sailor has been there before and knows a house where the Negro
mother doesn't mind her daughter providing some extra money.
The last time he had been there was three years before and the
girl, then seventeen, had liked his red hair, and had been "worth
the money that time all right." When he gets there he is made

very welcome and is warming to the possibility of an entertaining evening when a red-headed baby comes into the room; a baby who looks "mighty damn white for a nigger child." The story ends with the sailor hastily paying for his liquor and forgoing any further diversions. As in "Cross," we wonder what is to become of the red-headed baby who is the product of a desperate social condition, which has forced the mother to sell herself in order to survive. Hughes does not imply any condemnation of her. He makes the child seem almost insignificant within the framework of the story; the reader is left to create his own significance. One of his great qualities as a writer is his almost Hemingway-like use of irony and understatement.

In the prose work which followed *Mulatto,* he largely avoided the temptations of melodrama as he did the theme of inter-racial violence. This was not true, however, of his poetry. In *One-Way Ticket,* a collection published in 1949, there is a section headed *Silhouettes.* Just as the title *Magnolia Flowers* had contained a macabre irony, so this title is an ironical comment on the theme of lynching in the Southern States. Poem after bitter poem catalogues the grim reality of life in the South. The first poem, "Blue Bayou," portrays the threat to a Negro whose wife has been taken from him by a white man, old Greeley. He thinks of killing him and in his anger the blue bayou seems to run red. But he hears at the back of his mind the frequently heard chant

> Put him on a rope
> And pull him higher!

The next poem, "Flight," describes the opposite situation. A Negro is being chased by a white mob for having touched a white woman. "Silhouette" is addressed directly to a Southern gentle lady. With irony, she is asked not to faint at the sight of a black man hanging from a roadside tree because it should reassure her of

> How Dixie protects
> Its white womanhood.

Many of the poems in this collection describe the way in which the Negro is tortured by fear of lynching or being beaten by the police, as in "Who But The Lord?" where the Negro sees the police coming down the street and immediately prays to the Lord to save him from being beaten to death or from being murdered by the third degree. But, as he says:

> . . . the Lord he was not quick.
> The law raised up his stick
> And beat the living hell
> Out of me!

The Lord and the law have a disturbing assonance in this poem and the "living hell" is not merely a colloquialism.

Hughes' protest is not always so directly voiced, nor is it always directed at the brutality that the coloured American can suffer. He is at his greatest when he portrays the people in their environment. This is another thing that Sterling Brown had advocated and Hughes' gift was to be able to enter the various moods and characters of Black America, to express the preoccupations and attitudes of the people, *in their own language*. This is why he was pleased with his second collection of poems, *Fine Clothes to the Jew*, for, as he says in *The Big Sea*: ". . . it was more impersonal, more about other people than myself, and because it made use of the Negro folk-song forms, and included poems about work and the problem of finding work, that are always so pressing with the Negro people." It is a curious paradox, however, that Hughes should regard this work as objective, when the tone of these and indeed of all his poems about the *people* is strongly subjective.

There is a far higher degree of objectivity, of obliqueness, of controlled irony, in the prose works. The poetic experience, however, is an intense one and Hughes was so much a poet that even though he set out in this collection to present an objective picture of life in Harlem, his personal involvement forced him to merge with the characters he describes. He may have written the poems as an observer, but the expression belongs purely to the observed. These poems were constantly dismissed by Negro critics as a return to the dialect tradition of which they were now so ashamed. Hughes, rather despairingly, writes of the way in which they took the poem, "Red Silk Stockings" as a piece of literal advice. It begins:

> Put on yo' red silk stockings
> Black gal.

> Go out and let the white boys
> Look at yo' legs.

This girl, like the one in the story "Red-Headed Baby," has no other alternative. She, too, will find that

> . . . tomorrow's chile'll
> Be a high yaller.

Hughes was regarded as an apostate to the Booker T. Washington philosophy of presenting an acceptable image of the Negro in the hope that some day equality could be achieved. In 1926, he was involved with Wallace Thurman, Zora Neale Hurston and others in the publication of *Fire,* which they described as a "Negro quarterly of the arts." The first and only issue was greeted with general abuse, Hughes himself coming in for a great deal of it. Rean Graves of the *Baltimore Afro-American* confessed to having tossed it into the fire, going on to write that "Langston Hughes displays his usual ability to saying nothing in many words." *Fine Clothes to the Jew* earned him the title of "poet lowrate of Harlem" from the critic of the Chicago *Whip.* But Hughes never accepted the validity of always presenting the Black Americans putting "their politely polished and cultural foot forward." It is typical of him that he did not feel any strong resentment at this treatment, as he was aware of the damage done in stories of the kind written by Octavas Roy Cohen and in films and Broadway plays where the Negro always emerged as a lazy, comic and permanently defeated caricature.

But his poetry is not only concerned with the degradation of the individual, for he portrays the heights and the depths of the human personality: he acknowledges despair but also recognizes the refusal to capitulate to one's circumstances. *Shakespeare in Harlem* (1942) is a collection of poems "in the blues mood," in the speech of Harlem, West Texas, Chicago and the South. There are very few light poems in this collection, and few are blues whose mood can be directly attributed to the deferment of the dream. The majority are about the universal conflict between man and woman and grow out of the awareness that,

> A human gets lonesome if there ain't two

But financial problems still play their part. In "Down and Out" the woman needs a man just to pay the credit man and the rent. She would also like a straightening comb and a glass of beer. The question of money is equally important on the male side. In "Supper Time," a husband has been deserted by his wife. He has to find a woman as a replacement or the W.P.A. will reduce his pay. The note of social criticism is deceptively more incidental here than in some of the earlier poems. Financial survival and escapism have become the foundation of human relationships. One is left to infer the dehumanization. It comes through more directly in poems such as "Evenin' Air Blues," in which a Negro has left the South to settle in the North in the belief that here was the land of untold opportunity. What he gets is hunger and the one form of escapism he can afford, dancing. He describes the essence of the blues when he says:

> But if you was to ask me
> How de blues they come to be,
> *   *   *   *   *
> Just look at me and see!

The stark simplicity of these lines also goes to the heart of Hughes' intention as a writer: to focus on the Black American, not only in order to expose the truth of his situation but also to make him aware of himself and of his potential. "Just look at me and see" is also addressed to the Negro, for Hughes sees the awareness of negritude as being fundamental to the unifying sense of pride which he felt to be lacking, thanks to the way in which every effort had been made to deprive the Negro of a real social and cultural identity. The blues lament changes to the sensual lilt of "Harlem Sweeties." The poet looks down Sugar Hill and sees the

> Brown sugar lassie,
> Caramel treat,
> Honey-gold baby
> Sweet enough to eat.

The poem is richly sensuous. This is Hughes speaking himself and he was capable of writing poetry whose imagery and warmth come as a surprise after the majority of his poems, whose prime characteristic is simplicity. Love poems such as "When Sue Wears Red" are worthy of inclusion in any anthology of love poetry, but Hughes rarely allowed himself to indulge in personal poetry.

Practically all the poems in *Shakespeare in Harlem* are written in the first person, but this persona is a fusion of Hughes and others. It is a further step in that move from simple objectivity to complete subjectivity, which was one of Hughes' greatest achievements.

In *One-Way Ticket* (1949) the moods are more varied than in *Shakespeare in Harlem*. There are blues songs, poems of anger at Southern brutality, and poems of hope. The collection opens with the superb "Madam" poems. Alberta K. Johnson is one of Hughes' finest creations and embodies the spirit of resilience created by circumstances which overwhelm others. Like Jess B. Simple of the stories Hughes wrote as a series in the weekly columns of *The Chicago Defender,* she is an ironic commentator, but more than this she is a fiercely strong individual. Both Simple and Madam are mediums for Hughes' social comment. She insists on being called Madam and even has calling cards printed. When asked whether she prefers Old English or Roman lettering she replies that she prefers American. The rent man and the census man both find her difficult to handle; the latter, not satisfied that the K stands for nothing, tries to change it to Kay, but gets nowhere with Madam. The K stands and the MRS. has to go too. As she says in "Madam's Past History":

> The Madam stands for business
> I'm smart that way.

Hughes was fundamentally an optimist and when he felt pessimistic he always struggled to cling to his faith that the wall built between the Negro and the American Dream could be smashed down "into a thousand lights of sun." *Montage of a Dream Deferred* (1951) is a picture of Harlem and is comparable to the poetry that precedes it in that it expresses the various moods and attitudes of the people in the corresponding rhythms of the songs that reflect their different emotions. But Harlem, situated between two rivers, becomes a symbol of a

> Dream within a dream
> Our dream deferred.

One feels that in *Montage* Hughes is more affected by feelings of impatience, foreboding, and impotence against which he vainly struggles. He is alarmed at what he feels will be the outcome of this impotence and frustration. He asks in *Harlem*:

> What happens to a dream deferred?
>   Does it dry up
>   like a raisin in the sun?
> *   *   *   *   *   *   *
> Or does it explode?

His forebodings have been unfortunately confirmed. It is true that he was concerned about all people for whom the dream had been deferred, but his involvement with the American Negro is so profound that when he attempted to extend this concern to others in his poetry, the expression became awkward, naïve and over-sentimental. He was involved with the Communist movement in the 'thirties and shared its ideal of a raceless society. His poem "Freedom's Plow" describes the pioneering days of America and how the seed of freedom was planted in the furrow ploughed across the fields of history by the common effort of a new nation of many races.

> From that seed a tree grew, is growing, will ever grow.
> That tree is for everybody,
> For all America, for all the world.
> May its branches spread and its shelter grow
> Until all races and all peoples know its shade.
>   KEEP YOUR HANDS ON THE PLOW!
>   HOLD ON!

It is significant, however, that the final line comes from a *Negro* song of the days of slavery. This does not mean that the universalized concern was insincere, but simply that artistically he was not able to escape his commitment to the black people of America, nor was he a polemist. The idea expressed in "Freedom's Plow" is a great ideal, but the declamatory tone is only effective in an age and a society where the poet can adopt the public manner through virtue of speaking to a converted audience. It was by remaining a Black writer that he reached the zenith of his art.

He continued to protest against the injustice suffered by the

Negro, his work becoming more ironic in its compact concentration on the various aspects of segregation, as in the Simple stories. In his last collection of poems, *Ask Your Mama: 12 Moods for Jazz* (1961), he dreams that the Negroes achieve power in the South and the whole of the history of the Southern States is inverted. The governor of Georgia is Martin Luther King, and Negro children are looked after by white mammies, such as Mammy Faubus and Mammy Eastland. But the dream ends and the present becomes even more difficult to accept. *Ask Your Mama* is a vast panorama of all the aspects of the deferred dream. It is a crystallisation of all the fragments of the dream which occur in his writing up to this point, and, in its urgent diversity, suggests the impatience that Hughes felt at a situation which had barely changed throughout his life.

He died in 1967, aged 65, leaving a vast collection of writings: 8 collections of poetry, novels, plays, short stories, 2 autobiographical works, speeches, articles and translations. From his commitment to his real concerns he was able to create a literature which, while being authentically Negro, also demonstrated what Baldwin has described as ". . . the everlasting potential, or temptation of the human race." Baldwin recognised this when he reviewed Hughes' *Collected Poems*. Baldwin had gone to Paris to avoid the pressures of social contingencies on his art but realised that it was impossible for him to cut himself off any longer from the problems of his race. Hughes immersed himself in these problems.

His terms of reference were to create a Negro literature, in which protest and self-awareness were to be combined, and to be of mutual benefit in creating its final strength and validity.

In his poem, *Note on Commercial Theatre*, he complained:

> You've taken my blues and gone;
> You sing 'em on Broadway
> And you sing 'em in Hollywood Bowl,
> And you mixed 'em up with symphonies
> And you fixed 'em
> So they don't sound like me.

He set out to change this, and the end of the poem is prophetic with regard to what he was to achieve and what is now happening in America.

But someday somebody'll
Stand up and talk about me,
And write about me —
Black and beautiful —
And sing about me,
And put on plays about me!
I reckon it'll be
Me myself!
Yes, it'll be me.

Gwendolyn Brooks:
An Appreciation
from the White Suburbs

by Dan Jaffe

NOT LONG AGO Gwendolyn Brooks appeared as part of an Afro-American week program at a small Midwestern university. She began her poetry reading by briefly discussing "black poetry." Her metaphors were earthy and appropriate. They suited the tone of the occasion, an occasion aimed at, among other things, infiltrating the academic atmosphere too long dominated by overtones of ivory rather than ebony.

Miss Brooks observed that we call the juice of oranges "orange juice" and the sauce from apples "apple sauce." It follows she said that we should call the poetry from black poets "black poetry."

Gwendolyn Brooks has dealt with the question of racial as well as personal identity from the start. She turned what for many was a psychological and practical liability, her blackness, into an asset. But she wrote about black Americans not only because she was one. Some black writers like Frank Yerby and Willard Motley have generally avoided confronting specifically black characters and situations in their work. Gwendolyn Brooks has never practiced this kind of aesthetic sublimation.

Nor has she practiced that other out so often opted for by writers with social conscience. She has not denied the demands of the Muse for the demands of the Cause. Her work reveals her dedication to craft, to the business of making. This is the test of any poet. American culture has tried for years to still the disquieting voice of the poet by insinuating that what he does has no real value. The culture seeks to undermine his faith in himself and thereby make him powerless. The black poet must find his position particularly difficult. Many of the militant voices that demand changes in the society curiously still regard the poet as a dangerous inessential. Better to have men who will man barricades rather than typewriters. The best the writer can do is utilize his talents to help the cause. The attitude is essentially the same as the establishment's. The individual, non-predictable voice is distrusted. The man sincerely concerned with the social good may feel compelled to quit his personal vocation so that he may contribute to the movement. To do so would be to deny the significance of poetry. It would really be a surrender to the establishment point of view in another guise.

Gwendolyn Brooks has managed to balance these two weights magnificiently. She has dealt with black experience honestly and expansively without becoming a sort of poetic pamphleteer. The designation "black poetry" seems to me an unfortunate one to attach to her work. The label veils her considerable achievement. I suspect the implications of the term are erroneous. The effects of such a term if widely accepted may be damaging. It may make it more difficult for other black poets to equal or improve upon Gwen Brooks' example.

True, the term "black poetry" may please those who seek to encourage black pride. Poetry is the oldest literary form, but somehow most people, even those who rarely read it, continue to regard it as the most cultivated as well as the most subversive, the most difficult as well as the most expressive, and the most sophisticated as well as the most basic form of linguistic expression. The label "black poetry" therefore calls attention to the achievement of black men.

There is of course a less insidious explanation for the label. Gwen Brooks may have had in mind the notion that poetry is the heightened expression of the personality. The poems of black poets one might presume would register the particularly "black" experiences of the poets. They would therefore be different from poems by white poets. Pride in the label "black poetry" probably implies that one of the obligations of black poets is to register those peculiar experiences that set them apart from whites.

On the surface the assumptions behind such leveling seem clearly justifiable, perhaps so self evident they hardly require discussion. But they seem to me only dubious.

The designation "black poetry" arbitrarily ignores the nature of the creative act and the creative personality and the enormous difficulty of assessing either with certainty. It also ignores what I do not mean to be a merely a facetious observation: The minority of poets is smaller and in some ways (certainly not all) more cohesive than the minority of blacks. It may be that LeRoi Jones and Robert Creeley have more in common than LeRoi Jones and Malcolm X. Nor will any protestations to the contrary by Jones alter this real possibility.

The label "black poetry" suggests that the body of poetry by black poets has certain common characteristics and that these characteristics give the poetry its literary value. If it has no *literary* value we can hardly consider it poetry. Nor can we anticipate that it will have any other lasting value.

Poets of any kind are linked by common concerns despite their differences. Foremost is the concern with language and rhythm. In addition even the most subjective poet must have imagination. This is really the capacity to put oneself into situations not actual, into skins not his own, into circumstances created and defined by emotions generated in the world of form rather than in the world of flesh. The real world is his raw material. He remakes it in his own image.

The language the poet develops emanates from the self as well as the world. It expresses his uniqueness and his magical ability to perceive in a way different from all others. The paradox is that poets are committed to step outside of themselves in order to find the special within themselves. The label "Black poetry" ignores Gwen Brooks' ability to speak as a hunchbacked girl, a male preacher, a white spokesman, in varying voices all clearly her own. It ignores Robert Frost's suggestion that the purpose of any poem is to be as different from any other poem as possible. And it forgets that though Gwen Brooks learns from Langston Hughes, she also learns from T. S. Eliot; and that she must be more than a replica of either or both.

Certainly ghetto experience has influenced the character of

Gwen Brooks' poems. Some will certainly propose that she writes
as a black spokesman. But this is half truth. How she sees and
responds reflects her training as a poet as well as the circumstances
of her life. When she functions as a poet she changes things. She
must see differently not only from whites but from blacks, and
especially from other black poets.

If what she presents seems to many of us heightened reality,
it is because it is artifice, the real fashioned and shaped to poetry.
It is both larger and smaller than that outside reality so inade-
quately reported on in the press. It is larger because Gwen Brooks
heightens our awareness of its multiplicity, textures, and signifi-
cances. It is smaller because the totality of the world of flux has
too many instances and variables for any human to fully record or
comprehend.

What I've said thus far is really a defense of any black poet
to be himself first. The label "black poetry" cheapens the achieve-
ment of Gwendolyn Brooks. It recommends that race matters
more than artistic vocation or individual voice. It would lessen
achievements by blacks by supporting a notion of caricature.

It suggests to me also that some hierarchy of blacks might best
judge the merits of black poets. I'm sure that such a committee
would finally distinguish between "black poetry" and "Negro
poetry." Eventually a poet, no matter what his pigmentation, who
did not deal with social problems in an approved way would very
likely be read out of his skin. I don't suspect Gwen Brooks of
such inclinations. I only object to "black poetry" as a useful
appellation, as much as I might object to "white poetry" or "yellow
poetry." The whole point of a poem is to avoid such easy cate-
gorizations, all of which are dangerous.

Gwen Brooks is a wise woman. It may be that her remarks
were motivated by her realization of the dangers of a programatic
appearance to poetry. Maybe she meant only to affirm her identity
as a black while retaining her individuality as an artist.

As a poet and novelist Gwen Brooks never seems to have
wondered who she was. She announced herself to the world as a
person, as a woman, as a poet, and as black. We may honor her
for her courage to be herself in the face of so many obstacles that
inhibit blacks. It may seem to some more fashionable to announce
one's blackness now. It may even seem more safe. But we should
remember that to announce the self, no matter what the time or the
social pressures, is always to become vulnerable. It may be less

difficult to make a public pronouncement of blackness now, but to be oneself is as difficult as ever, perhaps more so. Gwen Brooks has done both.

It's too soon to say anything definitive about the work of Gwendolyn Brooks. Perhaps she hasn't yet written the poems that will stand out a hundred years from now as her major ones. But she has already written some that will undoubtedly be read so long as man cares about language and his fellows.

There have been no drastic changes in the tactics and subjects she has dealt with over the years. It's doubtful if future critics will talk about the early and the late Brooks, not unless she strikes out into much different territory after 1969. What one observes is a steady development of themes and types.

Her poetry is marked by a number of central concerns: black experience; the nature of greatness; the way in which man expresses his needs, makes do, or lashes out. Ordinarily the view is one of delicate balance, that of a passionate observer. The poems strike one as distinctly those of a woman but always muscled and precise, written from the pelvis rather than the biceps. It seems only natural that a lost child should figure so importantly in "In the Mecca," the long title poem of Miss Brooks' most recent book.

In *A Street in Bronzeville,* her first book, one finds poem after poem in which the lyric voice is subordinated to a dramatic intention. It's as if she were intent on singing somebody else's blues. We get what I would call vivid snapshots, except the label snapshots is far too casual. A poem like "kitchenette building" is more than an ashcan school vignette although it contains "fried potatoes" and "garbage ripening in the hall." The subdued conclusion is more than clever though it generally evokes delighted laughter from audiences. The poem recounts the difficulty of aspiring while breathing in the onion fumes of reality. It concludes with the dramatic voice anticipating a lukewarm bath now that Number Five is out of the bathroom. It's a little anticipation substituting for a big dream symbolized by an earlier reference to an aria. The last line of the poem, "We think of lukewarm water, hope to get in it" has delicacy and thrust. The simplicity of the language, the caesura before "hope," which makes us savor with the kitchenette occupant the small pleasure waiting, the idiomatic insistency of "get in it" with its alliterative tickle, all make one feel like a renter down the hall. But what is really important remains unsaid, the enormous pathos generated by the dramatic voice's capacity to find joy in such surroundings, surroundings that provide such limited opportunities.

It's not the sociological observations that make this poem and many others such successes. It is the quiet way in which the poems invade the spirit, the technical dexterity that makes the poems into experiences rather than just ideas.

There may be some who will maintain that only a black can judge the validity of Gwen Brooks' poems, or those of any other black poet. The real judgment they may insist is not to be made by white readers and critics. It has already been made affirmatively by the black artists who fashioned the mural communicating black dignity on the wall of a Chicago slum building at 43rd and Langley, a mural that includes Gwen Brooks.

But the real question is not what Gwen Brooks has to say to those who have shared her experiences, who already know some of what she has to say. The real question is whether or not she can make the alien feel. The purpose of art is always to communicate to the uninitiated, to make contact across seemingly insurmountable barriers. Can the poet make the white feel black; the healthy, sick; the defeated, hopeful? One of the measures of a black poet's work is whether he can make a comfortable white (who has not had his sense of language and humanity thoroughly shattered) respond. This is not to say that Gwen Brooks' poetry will have no value for black readers. They may well find their own surprises.

There are a number of short folk pieces in her first book, poems like "the vacant lot," "the independent man," "when I die," and "patent leather," which unabashedly present pictures of ghetto life. This was ground mined by Langston Hughes. Like Hughes, Miss Brooks does not merely reproduce ghetto language. Neither are dialect poets. But both are attuned to the differences between black speech and white speech. They make use of the special quality of black speech when it suits their purposes. More often than not Miss Brooks suggests with just a phrase. The final lines of 'the battle' illustrates this capacity. After mentioning the whipping Moe Belle Jackson got from her husband and commenting on how differently she would have responded, the dramatic voice says sarcastically of Moe Belle:

> Most like, she shed a tear,
> And this mornin' it was probably
> "More grits, Dear?"

Like Robert Frost and William Carlos Williams, Gwen Brooks is attuned to the voicebox of the people. Far too many readers underestimate the blues and folk poetry of many black poets because they miss the special intonations that enrich the poems. It may well be that "the battle" is about the special flavor of that last line, in which the alliteration functions to help produce a voice that is both cajoling and foredefeated.

Gwen Brooks poetry is not of one texture. *A Street in Bronzeville* concludes with a sequence of remarkable sonnets, "Gay Chaps at the Bar." They don't have the characteristic literary feeling of the sonnet, the feeling that encouraged Robert Bly to comment that "The sonnet is the place where old professors go to die." In a poem like "the white troops had their orders but the Negroes looked like men" Gwen Brooks demonstrates how attitudes can change, even white attitudes. The tone of the poem changes subtly as the poem progresses, moving from overtones of stiffness and artificiality to a more natural ease.

> They had supposed their formula was fixed.
> They had obeyed instructions to devise
> A type of cold, a type of hooded gaze. . . .
>   Who really gave two figs?
> Neither the earth nor heaven ever trembled.
> And there was nothing startling in the weather.

Although these sonnets incorporate a more formal language, different from the folk pieces, they provide a sense of rising black expectations. The last sonnet, "The progress," foreshadows later poems such as "Riders to the Blood-Red Wrath."

> For even if we come out standing up
> How shall we smile, congratulate: and how
> Settle in chairs? Listen, listen. The step
> Of iron feet again. And again. wild.

It is curious that a gentle woman should have written this sequence of war poems. They are poems of dignity, skill, and empathy. If white soldiers return to civilian life strangers, black soldiers return doubly so. What we get here is the painful awakening of men to the threats of war and the threats as well as the hopes of peace, to a new idealism and a heightened cynicism. These poems may tell us as much about the time of the Vietnam debacle as they do about World War II.

Other poems in *A Street in Bronzeville* show the range of Gwen Brooks' language. "The Sundays of Satin-Legs Smith" opens with a couplet reminiscent of Wallace Stevens:

> Inamoratas, with an approbation,
> Bestowed his title. Blessed his inclination.

The tone of this opening establishes a sense of ironic contrast between the royal inclinations of the dude and the grossness of so much ghetto life. One can't help suspect that the bravura of such opulence of language and attire is a gauntlet in the face of poverty.

Gwendolyn Brooks has fashioned a style that reflects the shifting quality of the American Dream. She fuses the flavor of black dialect with rhetorical formality. She can stir the grits or stroke the rococo. Her style deals with the contradictions of American life, contradictions most apparent to blacks who must suffer through them.

When *Annie Allen* won the Pulitzer Prize for Gwendolyn Brooks in 1950, many critics and unwary readers must have been startled. Rumor has it that the telegram announcing the prize arrived at a house without electricity. *Annie Allen* makes apparent that Gwen Brooks is a student of poetry. "The Anniad" with its echoes of Robert Browning, T. S. Eliot, and W. H. Auden illustrates her technical dexterity. Unfortunately, some readers are more conscious of the language of the poem than its substance. The rhymes seem more important than the character. The often ornate diction shadows the psychological journey. But the promise of *A Street in Bronzeville* is more than amplified elsewhere. The section entitled "The Womanhood" includes some of the best poems by any contemporary American poet. I find it strange that those makers of taste, the anthologists, have seen fit to ignore poems like "the children of the poor" and "Beverly Hills, Chicago."

Both poems are rich brews of language. "The children of the poor" is a poem of statement, often startlingly direct, full of images and direct references to the ordinary stuff of the world, at the same time incorporating with extraordinary daring and precision the most elevated diction. "Beverly Hills, Chicago" is essentially dramatic. It plays rhetorical elegance, associated with the wealthy, against colloquial speech patterns, associated with the outsiders motoring through the rich suburbs. Social, emotional, and linguistic range — Gwendolyn Brooks exhibits them all. She yokes compassion and toughness, teaching by example the most important lesson, how to keep the sensitivity alive in a world that so often brutalizes or destroys.

Her next book, *The Bean Eaters*, makes one feel the whole personality trying to pull together the fragments of an often deceptive, often confusing, often unjust world. It is a world of possible and impossible dreams, personal loss, insecurity, arrogant and measured responses; a world which justifies the silken lyric, the detached and ironic observation, and the scathing file of satire. *The Bean Eaters* includes deft examples of all these types.

The opposite face of Gwen Brooks' compassion must be her hatred of hypocrisy especially that hypocritical sensitivity exhibited by the "Ladies from the Ladies Betterment League" in "The Lovers of the Poor." She describes them so:

> Keeping their scented bodies in the center
> Of the hall as they walk down the hysterical hall,
> They allow their lovely skirts to graze no wall,
> Are off at what they manage of a canter,
> And, resuming all the clues of what they were,
> Try to avoid inhaling the laden air.

Although Gwendolyn Brooks never seems hysterical, neurotic or lost, although she does not seem much like a modern antiheroine in search of her own identity, she regularly identifies, in both senses of the word. In the final poems of her *Selected Poems* and *In the Mecca* one finds portraits and biographies, moments of life and summarizations of lives, the unknowns and the famous of the world. She looks at Robert Frost ("some specialness within"), Langston Hughes ("helmsman, hatchet, headlight") and Malcolm X ("the maleness"), as well as the Blackstone Rangers. She provides us with her sense of their essentials, a clarification of their substance and meaning.

"In the Mecca," the long title poem of her most recent book, accomplishes much of the same sort of thing. Along the corridors of the decaying apartment building once a "showplace of Chicago," in a search for a lost child whose body is finally found "in dust with roaches" under a bed, we meet the contradictory faces and gestures of the ghetto. Along the way we hear songs of feeling, learn of terror and self abuse, feel ourselves in the place where "silence is a place to scream." Gwendolyn Brooks seems to be trying to pull it all together, to feel for them all at once, for the bold and the fearful, the deranged and the evasive, the fashionable and the bleak. And although "In the Mecca" may at times seem more like a collection of items than a well paced narrative in an environment of enormous pressures, it is a major attempt at synthesis.

The history of American literature it has been said is the history of a search for a definition of *American*. It seems to me that the question of race, as it is called, is at the center of that larger question. Gwen Brooks leads us to a sense of the ghetto and the black man. She leads us also to a sense of the American dilemma, one hopes towards some resolution. She has fashioned a style, developed a virtuosity, that makes it possible for her to grab big chunks of the American reality, moments of its hopefulness, portions of its resentments, and give them cohesiveness and shape.

She writes in "The Second Sermon on the Warpland,"

> This is the urgency! Live!
> and have your blooming in the noise of the whirlwind.

This is no death wish but a prideful stance reminiscent of the Old Testament it alludes to. It may stir the hearts of black militants. These words might well have been uttered at Valley Forge.

Poetry into the 'Sixties

by Paul Breman

*'for the first time in America, black people
themselves are being provided the opportunity
of deciding who their 'best' poets are'*[1]

1.

IN THE UNITED STATES, there is no such thing as 'Negro' poetry
anymore, or at least none that merits attention. There is, however,
black verse — and there are black poets. By and large, these are
the saving grace of American letters as a whole, and one is tempted
to call their position enviable. In the first place, they have some-
thing real to write about — while content has long been conspicu-
ously absent in most white American writing. Secondly, they have
a growing audience with a steadily increasing awareness of and con-
cern for what they are about.

This audience is beginning to express itself in the publication
figures of some of the poetry pamphlets, and it has long made itself
felt in the attendance at readings, concerts and festivals. It is a
city audience; little comes out of the rural South — and even less
goes into it. More and more, the city audience becomes a ghetto
one: Negroes live a bit all over the place, but black folk are herded
together in Harlems and South Sides and Wattses. Their require-
ments are simple, if complex. They have little patience with sunset
skies, budding trees, and other acquired tastes: these are not part

of their daily experience. And it is their daily experience which counts — the real, the this-I-have and that-you-took. Struggle, survival. Rats, Pigs. Smells of the alley, sounds of the tenement. Not the kind of people who in our society would read poetry, or listen to it read. But then, there is little or no resemblance between them and us — and communications have just about broken down.

Paradoxically, it is poetry which has accentuated the otherness, the second language — and it is the same poetry which may ultimately bridge the gap. We could do worse than listen, for our survival may depend on it.

2.

Black poetry has always existed, but until recently in isolated patches only. Black poets were rarer still, but even they are of long standing. It is a matter of attitude. DuBois, Dunbar (oh yes, Dunbar). Sterling Brown. Richard Wright. Margaret Walker.

Langston Hughes is a separate chapter. A Negro poet, certainly — he would not have made his living writing if he had been anything else. But a man. A natural writer, if not much of a poet perhaps. Generous to a fault, a self-appointed clearing house of information and advice, daddy of them all, providing spiritual and often physical food, revered even by the young who did not like his work. Hughes actually read the hundreds of manuscripts he received, he actually did something about the ones he thought had merit, and actually believed that the occasional spark was worth the effort. His attitude is summed up in this line: "Even in the most amateurish writing, sometimes a line, a paragraph, even a whole page would come alive, achieve a character of its own, or make vivid some element of folk culture."[2]

One of his discoveries, a t.v. mechanic called Ray Durem, can be singled out as the spearhead from which a continued pattern of what we now call 'black poetry' starts to emerge. Born 30 January 1915 in Seattle, Wash., he ran away from home at 14, joined the navy, and came of age in Spain during the civil war of 1937. He did not write a book about it — in fact, he only started writing round about 1950, and stopping again soon after. "When I was ten years old, I used my fists. When I was thirty-five, I used the pen. I hope to live to use the machine-gun."[3] He didn't, he died of cancer before he was fifty.

Since then, others have been belatedly and undeservedly promoted to being precursors of the present trends. Samuel Allen, alias Paul Vesey, comes out of the Présence Africaine and "négritude" circle, fits very snugly into the Jahn-pattern of neo-african literature, but cannot in present American terms be called a black poet. More recent and spectacular is the case of the late Melvin Beaunorus Tolson, of whom Karl Shapiro said that he "writes in Negro"[4], a true word, of which Shapiro never seems to have fathomed the true meaning: that Tolson postured for a white audience, and with an ill-concealed grin and a wicked sense of humour gave it just what it wanted: an entertaining darkey using almost comically big words as the best wasp tradition demands of its educated house-niggers.

3.

New York was the first city to have a coherent workshop of black poets. Tom Dent, who would later lead the Free Southern Theatre from a New Orleans base into deepest Dixie; Calvin Hernton, not yet preoccupied with the fact that "sex has gone to the white man's head"[5]; and David Henderson, who still holds the remnants of the group together; founded and ran "Umbra." Its weekly meetings resulted in two issues of a magazine of the same name, in 1963, and a larger 'anthology' in 1967.

"Umbra exists to provide a vehicle for those outspoken and youthful writers who present aspects of social and racial reality which may be called 'un-commercial'. . . but cannot with any honesty be considered nonessential to a whole and healthy society . . . We are not a self-deemed, radical publication: we are as racial as society demands the truth to be."[6] And Umbra consistently lived up to the most remarkable sentence in its earliest editorial: "We will not print trash, no matter how relevantly it deals with race, social issues, or anything else."

They were the first in America to print Durem, and they had Julian Bond's amusing if very occasional verse as well as the work of Sun Ra, the pianist-philosopher who now more properly belongs in the Spirit House set-up. The group itself attracted such varied talent as Ishmael Reed (probably the best black poet writing today), Oliver Pitcher, Rolland Snellings (now Askia Muhammad Touré), Lennox Raphael, Henry Dumas (shot dead by a policeman in the spring of 1968) and Gerald Jackson (one of the most promising young black painters, with William White and the Guianese Frank Bowling). James Thompson, truly 'black and beautiful' and a poet of great originality and technical powers, never quite fitted (although he was to have edited Umbra 3).

Members of the Umbra group live widely scattered through

the New York area — Harlem, the lower East Side, the Village, Brooklyn, Queens — and several of the more remote members have active community groups going or organise readings with guests from a rather wider field. Len Chandler, poet songwriter and travelling performer, lends his house for the group's continuing meetings. Lloyd Addison served on the Afro Arts Cultural Center and its festival in the Harlem streets: the movement to bring the arts into the open is gaining momentum all over, and it is encouraging to see its results for instance in the work of a group called 'the last poets' led by Gylan Kain.

4.

In Chicago, things were different. They always are. The city may be the most exciting architectural showpiece of the United States, once you are well into the South Side you might never notice it much. Coming into town over the Skyway all you notice is the visible essay in air pollution, and walking down Dearborn white and forlorn on a summer afternoon all you know is you have no place there — and how long has this been going on?

The cultural life of the black community here is dominated by two women of strong vision and very different expression. Margaret Burroughs runs her private Museum of Negro (now renamed African-American) History and Art, and the importance of this very early attempt at re-establishing the true past is too easily ignored under pressure of the outward aspects of an ill-organized over-patriotic shambles.

Gwendolyn Brooks, too, lives in Chicago — and she is steadily developing into a major influence. Her pupils are young, many, and mainly female, and the poetry prize which she herself established is beginning to attract wider attention. Moreover, Gwendolyn Brooks was quietly black way back in 1945, when it was decidedly unfashionable — even if it did win her a Pulitzer Prize. Her wards, unfortuately, have a tendency to rush into print before they have any control over their pens. Carolyn Rodgers, Jewel Latimore, Alicia Johnson, Melvyne Brown — there is a depressing same-ness about their work which bodes little good.

On another level, Chicago afforded one of the liveliest discussion groups of the middle sixties, with novelist Ronald Fair, poet Conrad Kent Rivers, journalist David Llorens (who almost managed to make Negro Digest into a magazine worth reading) and organizer Gerald McWorter. They were out to change the world, but never agreed on where to start, and eventually went their private ways without producing anything lasting — except perhaps in that they made the foundation of the Organization of Black American Culture a tangible possibility. The avoidable death of Rivers, two weeks before his last book of poetry[7] appeared, was a real loss. He was a writer with a great deal to say, on an interesting quest for ways in which to say it. Now all that actively voices the ideas of black Chicago is the until recently largely unreadable work of Don L. Lee, whose pamphlets flood the country in ever-increasing numbers. He represented a kind of all-out ranting which has become outdated more rapidly than one could have hoped. "While 'rage-poetry' has a place in the New Movement, if it is projected to represent the essence of the revolutionary new poetry — or is supposed to represent total Black feeling and experience — then it is a fraud and a stereo-type fit for the pages of some 'liberal' sociology journal, or chronicle of 'Negro protest'."[8]

5.

Detroit must, one hopes, be just about the ugliest town on earth. It isn't a city, either — it is a conglomeration of unprepossessing dormitory villages of rural character, largely of timber, and hardly any of it over two storeys high. It goes on forever, and has absolutely nothing to offer. Motown. The industrial North itself, and it isn't any better than the South, now, is it?

This curious ghetto has given birth to one of the most interesting theatre groups in the country, Concept East founded by Woodie King jnr, and to the only truly militant black bookshop in the country, Vaughn's on Dexter, which sponsored the Black Arts Conventions and was ruined during the 'riots' of 1968 (by the pigs, not the brothers, needless to say). Detroit also harbours the only consistent black poetry publishing venture inside United States territory: Broadside Press, run by Dudley Randall, librarian, translator from the Russian, craftsmanlike poet, quietly dedicated to the revolution and quietly doing something about it. In 1966 Randall started the series of single-sheet poems which gave the press its name, and now he is doing both books and tape-recordings. Margaret Danner, the doyenne of Detroit's black letters, is a close friend, and young poets like Ahmed LeGraham Almahisi, Harun Kofi Wangara, Etheridge Knight and Sonia Sanchez are looking to Randall for an outlet.

The question of outlet, black outlet, is becoming increasingly important. The issue was first raised very publicly a propos of Clarence Major's anthology "The new black poetry" which International Publishers brought out early in 1969. Ed Spriggs, a fellow New York poet, announced he would 'boycott' the book because it was handled by white publishers. It was curious that he did not boycott the LeRoi Jones & Larry Neal anthology "Black fire" brought out a few months earlier by the equally white firm of William Morrow (unless one takes the uncharitable view that Major's white wife made him a target anyway), but the ensuing discussion was valid and to the point.

The ideological stance: where we at ? writers. Black. seeking new dimensions of power. the orientation is BLACK POWER. generally, that's the stance. the image most of us present. the assumption. the writer that embraces Black Power uses that Power in a fashion that will directly (concretely) be of benefit to us all.

Dig how much mileage has been gotten out of the Malcolm legacy by Merit, et al. Whose fault it is is slightly off my point. but leRoi the terrible, baldwin the goodie gum drop, malcolm the irreplaceable, and all the rest of us git compromised just because we want to git our things out there. it's weird. black publishers and the would be ones stand in the shadows subsisting on broadsides, throwaways, rubberstamps and other trivia because black writers won't give them a decent play, but we scream 'Black Power'.

There are institutions to be built. we're young and strong enough to build but we've gotta have the vision. we have the power. if you don't believe it just ask dial, harpers, wm morrow, grove, merit, marzani and munsell or even international publishers. couldn't julian richardson, dudley randall and lafayette jamerson get into some very heavy drama if they could get just a little from our co-opted black writers? you know they could. holes in yr front because you choose not to. fatten up. writers. Black. seeking new dimensions of power. talk to me baby. we been laying back too long.[9]

6.

Newark, cowering under the Pulaski Skyway and the weight of its own factory dirt, is very much an unmentionable part of New York. Like Chicago's industrial suburb, Gary, it lies across a state line and has a predominantly black population, but unlike Gary it never got round to doing anything with or for its workers, let alone organise them politically. Consequently, its city officials are white (but all white) and the place has the healthy feel of a concrete concentration camp.

In this atmosphere operates Spirit House. Perhaps it was originally intended as an attempt to bring culture (poetry, theatre, music) to the masses of Newark and to a large extent that is just what it does. But it had to do more, and ultimately more important, things than that. Voter registration. Political persuasion. Creating a sense of participation ('togetherness', the other Americans call it), civic pride. Preparing the revolution — and keeping it in check. Nonviolence is not exactly part of everyday life, not in Newark, not if you are black.

Moving spirit of the House is Ameer Baraka, and around him gathers a changing group of the most militant new black artists: poets Yusef Iman and Ed Spriggs, musicians Pharaoh Saunders and Sun Ra, playwrights Ben Caldwell and Ed Bullins, and some of the earlier Black Arts Theatre people like Charles Patterson and Clarence Reed.

Ameer Baraka himself is one of the more interesting figures on the black arts scene, because his own development so closely represents the general trends of the last fifteen years. Comparatively young (35), he and his work are already famous both in the black community and in the world at large. In fact, it was the 'world at large' which first took him to its heart, and at that time he had very little interest in blackness, community work, or communication in general. In his early twenties, he rose to fame as LeRoi Jones, one of the 'beats', editor (with Hetty Cohen: the name is as symbolic as was the dedicatory poem to her which opened Jones's first book of poetry) of "Yugen," by far the best of the literary magazines around 1960 but very much out of the then fashionable 'universal' bag, LeRoi its only (token) black. From this starting point one can chart the spiritual quest which led from the Zen of the early days through the Yoruba craze to the Islam of 1968 — a search for self, for meaning, and for a place. The books of the middle period, 1963-4, all show the same level of involvement, whether they be plays (Dutchman), poetry (The dead lecturer) or essays (Blues people; Home). Identification, and the necessity to find a cause, are their motive force. "We are on the streets, we are somewhere in the world"[10] — collectively, that is; but for LeRoi Jones this was always tempered with the realisation that "When I walk in the streets, the streets don't yet claim me, and people look at me, knowing the strangeness of my manner, and the objective stance from which I attempt to 'love' them."[11]

The Black Arts Theatre and its workshop in Harlem provided the cause, for a while — but Harlem was never home to LeRoi Jones any more than Africa is to any afro-american. Newark is home. There are the roots. Spirit House is where it's at, and the publishing house which spread its message was called Jihad: strive against ignorance. Two violent years, with some incredibly bad writing purely as a by-product. Black was still an acquired taste, hard to learn, and it had to be screamed out every minute of the day. But this year, at last, LeRoi Jones seems to have found peace, reborn as Ameer Baraka. Perhaps he will now write good poetry, too.

7.

When Ray Durem worked in California, his family lived in Guadalajara and he commuted weekends over 1500 miles in order to give his children a chance of growing up outside the United States. To others, California dreaming still conjures up visions of paradise. It depends somewhat on whether you can avoid sitting on the dock of the bay, or living in Watts.

Watts started the true revolution in 1965. That already sounds like a phrase from a history book. Nobody shows W3 on television anymore, either. And the writers who passed through this once celebrated workshop, who were beginning to translate their acute inner frustration into words that were acutely embarassing to the outside world are never heard of anymore: nobody now sees the visionary poetry of Leumas Sirrah, the stories of Harry Dolan, the screenplays of Harley Mims, or the work of Johnie Scott "who could be the James Baldwin of 1970!"[12]

They certainly do not appear in the "Journal of black poetry" published in neighbouring San Francisco, once the capital of the "beats" whose best poet, Bob Kaufman, was also black. Still, the Journal has become the best showcase for the new writing. Run by Ruby Joe Goncalves, it has existed through four years and ten issues, and boasts a remarkably consistent and highly representative editorial board headed by LeRoi Jones, Clarence Major, Marvin Jackmon (alias Marvin X, Nazzam al Fitnah and Nazzam al Sudan) and Larry Neal. Corresponding and roving editors are Almahisi, Spriggs, Bullins and Askia Muhammad Touré. Recent issues have had "guest editors" responsible for the selection of their entire contents, and Larry Neal has managed to make number 9 of the Journal into a model anthology of the very best. It remains curious that so little native Californian talent gets exposure, though. There may not be much of a scene right now, but writers like Al Young, Jon Eckels and Marvin X, and anthologies like "From the ashes" make it plain that the local product deserves a better setting.

The Journal's black printers, Julian Richardson Associates, are now also publishing poetry books and in time may yet get into the 'very heavy drama' made possible by the 'new dimensions of power' which the Journal so ably reflects.

8.

One of the most encouraging aspects of the new poetry is the emergence, independent of local groups or trends, of a surprising number of black women writing very black and very beautiful verse, from a very specialized and very necessary point in time and consciousness.

"The black woman is hurt, confused, frustrated, angry, resentful, frightened *and* evil! Who in this hell dares suggest that she should be otherwise? These attitudes only point up her perception of the situation and her healthy rejection of same. Maybe if our women get evil enough and angry enough, they'll be moved to some action that will bring our men to their senses."[13] The assertion of self-pride and self-confidence, of awareness and concern, the true emancipation which pervades the work of the dozen or so really outstanding woman poets is perhaps their most valuable contribution to the cause.

The new awareness begins to show, in this as in all other fields, by 1960. Here, especially, Chicagoan Gwendolyn Brooks is the great forerunner. Mari Evans, in Indianapolis, born in 1923 but a late starter and therefore usually grouped with the succeeding generation, is her most immediate successor in theme, tone and technique. In New York, Audre Lorde and Sonia Sanchez write poems of very different aspect but like intent. In Chicago, Alicia Johnson and Carolyn Rodgers are the most promising new recruits for this group. From the deep South comes the lone voice of Julia Fields, while Nikki Giovanni is increasing her powers in Cincinnati. Joyce Whitsitt works in Detroit, Ridhiana Saunders in Los Angeles.

9.

As poetry takes to the streets, the sounds and rhythms of the streets grow stronger in the poem. In this technical or outward aspect, too, the black poet is deepening the gulf which separates him from the white establishment.

The process has, under various guises, been going on for years. Some of the too easily derided 'dialect' verse of the later nineteenth century was a genuine attempt at capturing certain aspects of a vanishing rural nation. The influence of 'folk' material in the work of Langston Hughes and Sterling Brown is a later variant. The most sophisticated use of black rhythm and speech patterns is found in the still undervalued poetry of Robert Hayden. The 'jazz poets' do more than illustrate LeRoi Jones's dictum that poetry is music made less abstract: Harold Carrington, who spent the whole of his very short life in the ghetto or in a jail cell, could duplicate a Cecil Taylor piece line by line in poetry and at a time when nobody bothered about Taylor (not that anyone seems to even now).

"What this has all been leading us to say is that the poet must become a performer, the way James Brown is a performer — loud, gaudy and racy. He must take his work where his people are: Harlem, Watts, Philadelphia, Chicago and the rural South. He must learn to embellish the context in which the work is executed; and, where possible, link the work to all usable aspects of the music. For the context of the work is as important as the work itself. Poets must learn to sing, dance and chant their works, tearing into the substance of their individual and collective experiences. We must make literature move people to a deeper understanding of what this thing is all about, be a kind of priest, a black magician, working juju with the word in the world."[14]

[1]Hoyt W. Fuller. Editorial in "Negro Digest" annual *Portfolio of Poetry*, September, 1968.

[2]Introduction to *An African Treasury*, 1960.

[3]*Sixes and Sevens*, p. 10. 1962.

[4]Introduction to Tolson's *Harlem Gallery*, 1965.

[5]James Weldon Johnson, *Negro Americans: What Now?* 1934.

[6]*Umbra*, Foreword, Volume 1, number 1, winter, 1963.

[7]*The Still Voice of Harlem*. London, 1968.

[8]Askia Muhammad Touré, *Journal of Black Poetry*, 1:10, fall 1968, p. 64.

[9]Ed Spriggs on the boycott. *Journal of Black Poetry*, 1:10, pps. 35-38.

[10]Introduction to David Henderson's *Felix of the Silent Forest*, 1967.

[11]From "Words," dated "Harlem 1965" and published in *Tales,* 1967, pps. 89-91.

[12]*New York Times,* August 14, 1966, pps. D 13.

[13]Abby Lincoln, "Who Will Rever the Black Woman?" in *Negro Digest,* September, 1966, p. 19.

[14]Larry Neal in his "Afterword" to *Black Fire: An Anthology of Afro-American Writing,* 1968, p. 655.

The Playwright

The Black Playwright in the Professional Theatre of the United States of America 1858-1959

by Darwin Turner

ALTHOUGH PROFESSIONAL THEATRE in the United States of America is more than two hundred years old, professional playwrights of African ancestry are relatively unknown because opportunities for black writers have been restricted far more severely in drama than in other literary fields. An African slave, Phillis Wheatley, published a collection of poems as early as 1773.[1] A fugitive slave, William Wells Brown, published an autobiography in 1847, a book of travels in 1852, and a novel in 1853.[2] But the first play by a black American was not written until 1858.[3] No Afro-American had a full-length serious drama produced in a Broadway theatre in New York City until 1925,[4] and only ten additional plays written totally or partly by Afro-Americans were produced on Broadway from 1926 until 1959, when Lorraine Hansberry's *A Raisin in the Sun* began the longest run on Broadway ever experienced by a play of Afro-American authorship.

The dearth of black playwrights cannot be attributed to a lack of literary talent among Afro-Americans. Phillis Wheatley, Frederick Douglass, William Wells Brown, W. E. B. DuBois, and Paul Laurence Dunbar earned international fame in other fields of letters before 1920. Langston Hughes, Gwendolyn Brooks, Richard Wright, Chester Himes, James Baldwin, and Ralph Ellison are only a few of the Afro-American writers who have earned international acclaim since 1920.

Instead, the shortage must be blamed on a lack of opportunity for recognition. A combination of economic, cultural, and social circumstances has restricted the black playwright.

In the United States, a reputation in drama is more expensive than in any other literary field. A poet may publish in magazines or on mimeographed sheets. He can read his work in lecture halls or on street corners. If he is heard or read by influential people, his work may be collected and published in book form at a reasonable cost. A fiction writer may publish in small literary magazines. His first novel may appear as a limited printing which does not represent a major financial gamble by a publishing house.

But a dramatist needs a cast of people and an auditorium with stage, lights, scenery, and seats. Even then, he is rarely recognized in the United States until his drama appears in one of the large theatres near Broadway Avenue in New York City, the theatrical capital of the United States. A Broadway production, needless to say, is a costly experiment which producers approach cautiously. Unwilling to lose money, they rarely gamble on new materials; instead, they revive and reshape the traditional in an effort to pander to the tastes which they presume to be characteristic of their potential audience of middle-class and upper-class white Americans.

Even daring directors and producers recognize this fact. Joe Papp, a rejected director, has earned a reputation for presenting Shakespearean plays without charging admission and for staging artistic works by little-known dramatists. Yet he has written,

> With few exceptions the large theatres in New York attract theatregoers who both have money and are settled in their attitudes. These people . . . have no desire to spend money to hear their ideals assaulted. They cannot tolerate doubts, and if they have any they certainly do not want them exposed. . . . It is perfectly human to cultivate, and cater to, the status quo. It is certainly more reasonable to

mount a production for an audience that already exists than to do shows that must find their audience (or, indeed, create it.) [1]

This combination of economic and cultural circumstances is intensified by a social fact. Since Afro-Americans represent a minority of the entire population and an even less significant percentage of the Broadway audience, Negro life is regarded as an exotic subject for the American theatre. Therefore, only a limited number of plays on Negro themes are approved. Furthermore, to please his predominantly white audience, the cautious producer wishes to have these themes developed in accordance with his customers' expectations. Too frequently, therefore, he wants the stereotypes of Negro life and character which white playwrights popularized and which many black playwrights refuse to perpetuate. For example, in the years between 1769, when the first black character appeared in a play in America, and 1923, when the first black playwright had a one-act play produced on Broadway, white playwrights established five major stereotypes: the Buffoon, a comically ignorant type; the Tragic Mulatto, the product of miscegenation who is destined to tragic exclusion from white society, which will not accept her, and black society, which she will not accept; the Christian Slave, a docile individual who worships both his mortal white master and his immortal master; the Carefree Primitive, an exotic, amoral savage; and the Black Beast, a villain who seeks equality with white people. And when white playwrights wrote of Negro life, they most frequently wrote folk comedy. By repetition, white playwrights had given reality to those stereotypes of Afro-American character and life for numerous white Americans who rarely experienced intimate personal relationships with black Americans. Therefore, producers did not seek plays written about the actual characters and lives of Afro-Americans; from black and white playwrights, they wanted dramas which would repeat the familiar.

Finally, playwrights, more than other writers, depend upon acquaintance with people who have money. Poets and novelists may submit manuscripts to publishing firms; a dramatist needs to know someone who knows a producer. In the segregated society of the United States, personal contact between black artists and wealthy producers has been very limited.

For all of these reasons, black American playwrights developed very slowly in the years between Brown in 1858 and Hansberry in 1959. The first significant efforts in dramatic writing, in fact, were not serious dramas but "coon" shows, musical variety shows. Very popular in the years between 1895 and 1905, these attracted and utilized the talents of such black writers as Paul Laurence Dunbar, one of America's most popular poets at the beginning of the twentieth century, and James Weldon Johnson, a poet and novelist who later earned a reputation as an American consul and as secretary of the National Association for the Advancement of Colored People. In these shows, which emphasized comedy, singing, and dancing rather than a story line, black poets and actors shamelessly pandered to the expectations of their white audiences. They wrote of Buffoons and Carefree Primitives. Afro-American performers put cork-black on their faces and painted red make-up around their lips to transform themselves into the grinning gargoyles popularized in the black-face minstrel shows which employed white actors. James Weldon Johnson later described the manner in which black song writers even avoided love duets for their heroes and heroines because American audiences, presuming sexual amorality to be characteristic of Negro life, refused to believe that romance could be a serious topic for Afro-Americans.

Although these all-black musical shows disappeared from Broadway for more than a decade while black writers and performers were refused opportunity, musical comedy about black people has remained popular in the American theatre. *Shuffle Along* (1921), an all-black musical, written and directed by blacks, is frequently praised as one of the works which revived American interest not only in black talent but also black culture during that decade. *Porgy and Bess* (1935), a folk opera by George Gershwin based on a play by Dubose Heyward (both white), is so highly esteemed by white Americans that, during the 1950s, the United States government selected it to be presented in Europe as the theatrical work best exemplifying American art and culture. In each decade, musical comedies about black people have extraordinary success in the theatre. The continuation of the pattern is evidenced in the present by *Golden Boy* and *Hello Dolly*, both written originally for white performers but adapted into musicals for blacks. The perennial popularity of such shows evidences both the talent of black performers and the persistence of white Americans' predilection for viewing black Americans primarily as gay, or occasionally pathetic, people continually expressing their emotions in song and dance.

In contrast to the success of musical shows is the relative failure of serious professional drama by black American playwrights, the focus of this essay.

The first to be produced on Broadway was "The Chip Woman's Fortune" (1923), a one-act play by Willis Richardson. Because of debts, Silas Green, a porter in a store, is about to lose his job and the record player he has purchased on credit. He turns for assistance to Aunt Nancy, a chip woman, who has helped him previously. But Aunt Nancy plans to give her savings to her son Jim, just released from prison after serving a term for assaulting his unfaithful sweetheart and her lover. When Jim arrives, he agrees to give Silas enough money to pay the debts. As the opener on a program which included a revival of Oscar Wilde's *Salome,* "The Chip Woman's Fortune," presented by the Ethiopian Art Players of Chicago, lasted only two weeks on Broadway.

The first full-length play, Garland Anderson's *Appearances,* first produced on October 13, 1925, treated a more serious subject — a Negro bell-hop's successful defense of himself from a false charge of rape.

Three years later, Frank Wilson, an actor, created an unusual protagonist in *Meek Mose,* which opened February 6, 1928. Most black playwrights have refused to write about docile blacks or have portrayed them as villians who must either be converted to self-respect or destroyed before the final curtain. Frank Wilson, however, not only made such a character a protagonist but even rewarded him. When white community leaders propose to move the blacks to a different section of town, peace-loving Mose, a leader of the black community, advises the blacks to agree. The blacks turn on him when disease and death result from the new living conditions, but he is rewarded for his faith when oil is discovered on the new property. Historically, of course, *Meek Mose* retells the success of some American Indians who, driven from their fertile farmland in the East, were forced to relocate in Oklahoma, where oil was later discovered. Nevertheless, it is an unusual theme for a black playwright. The play lasted only twenty-four performances.

Harlem, the final play to appear on Broadway during the 1920s, was a collaboration between Wallace Thurman, a talented, satirical black novelist, and a white playwright, William Jordan

Rapp. Thurman, who had written two novels about Harlem, blended melodrama and the exoticism of Harlem into a play which continued for ninety-three performances. The plot of *Harlem* retraces themes familiar to individuals who have read widely in literature by blacks. After migrating from South Carolina to Harlem, the Williamses find unhappiness instead of the anticipated opportunity. Impoverished, they are forced to give parties to which they charge admission so that they can pay the rent. The daughter Cordelia becomes intoxicated by the wild life of the city. After rejecting a West Indian suitor, Cordelia becomes the mistress of a Harlem gambler. When he is killed, the West Indian is suspected but acquitted. Cordelia and her family continue to search for happiness in the cold city.

Paul Laurence Dunbar had told a comparable story in *The Sport of the Gods*, 1901, when he novelized the misfortunes of Southern blacks who corrupt their souls in Harlem. In the 1920s, novelist Rudolph Fisher repeated the theme in fiction, and in the following decade Randolph Edmonds developed it in drama. Sometimes white American critics have misinterpreted this theme as evidence of the black author's willingness to perpetuate the myth that life is better for black people in the South than it is in the North. To the contrary, the black writer was often more concerned with dispelling the myth that white Americans created about Harlem — that it was a world where black people enjoyed a gay, carefree existence.

In these four Broadway productions, black playwrights worked within the framework set by white playwrights. *The Chip Woman's Fortune* tells of black peasants. *Meek Mose* presents docile blacks. While *Harlem* suggests actuality, it nevertheless perfumes the stage with exoticism and amorality, and it capitalized upon the national popularity which Harlem enjoyed during the 1920s.

In 1929, a severe economic depression hit America, and in 1930 Marc Connelly adapted Roach Bradford's *Ol' Man Adam and His Chillun* into *Green Pastures,* a comic fantasy about religion as practised by blacks. These two events motivated four dramas by black playwrights on Broadway and two in the more experimental, less costly theatres off Broadway.

Marc Connelly's play is a white man's fantasy about black people's conceptions of Biblical stories. The central character is De Lawd, a magnificent, white haired, cigar-smoking black man, excellently acted by Richard B. Harrison, a college teacher of speech who, according to Langston Hughes, required the services of a white actor who trained him to speak the "Negro" dialect which Marc Connelly had written. The heavenly fish fries and carryings-on amused white audiences but both irritated and intrigued black playwrights who capitalized upon the interest in religion as background for their works.

Staged by the Negro Theatre Guild, Augustus Smith's *Louisiana* (1933), melodramatically, but much more realistically than *Green Pastures*, depicted religious forces in a black community in Louisiana. The two most powerful community leaders are Amos Berry, minister of a Baptist church, and Aunt Hagar, who practices voodoo. When a disreputable tavern keeper attempts to force his attentions on the minister's niece, Berry and Aunt Hagar combine the powers of Christianity and voodoo to crush him.

This was not the first American drama to portray voodoo prominently. In 1822, Mary Wiborg, a white playwright, had presented *Taboo*, and within the same decade Em Jo Basshe had written *Earth*. Despite its exoticism, however, voodoo has not excited American audiences. *Taboo* barely lasted through three performances; Smith's *Louisiana* lasted only eight.

Two days after *Louisiana* opened, Hall Johnson's *Run, Little Chillun* began a more successful run of 126 performances. It too told a story of different religious forces. This time, however, there is conflict between the pagan New Day Pilgrims and the Hope Baptists. Sulamai, a New Day Pilgrim, entices married Jim Jones who is the son of the minister of the Baptist church. Finally, Christianity triumphs when Jim returns to his faith and Sulamai is stricken during a revival meeting.

Five years later, George Norford, in a theatre off Broadway, dramatized a different religious element in black life when he wrote about Father Divine, a black, self-proclaimed re-incarnation of God, who attracted a large following during the Depression.

The economic depression influenced black playwrights less directly than *Green Pastures* had. The severity of life during the 1930s prompted writers to question all aspects of life in the United States and to protest against conditions which mitigated against poor people. This concern spread even to the Broadway stages. Here again, however, black dramatists seem to have been granted opportunity to tell their stories only after paths had been prepared by white playwrights.

In 1932, white James Miller wrote *Never No More,* a protest against lynching. In 1934, white John Wexley presented *They Shall Not Die,* based on an actual incident in which nine Negro youths from Scottsboro, Alabama, were convicted of an alleged rape of two white prostitutes; and in *Stevedore,* in the same year, George Sklar and Paul Peters, white playwrights, described the manner in which a militant black youth was made to seem responsible for a crime which he did not commit.

In 1934 also, Dennis Donoghue, a black playwright with a non-black name, wrote *Legal Murder,* another version of the case of the Scottsboro boys. In Donoghue's play, the nine youths have hopped aboard a freight train to ride to Chicago to seek work as singers. Their car is invaded by two white men and two women. One white man, who is armed, orders the youths to jump from the moving train, but the youths seize the gun. At the next stop, they are arrested and falsely accused of rape. In court, they and their Jewish lawyer are ridiculed, and they are convicted.

Legal Murder lasted only seven days, but in 1935, Langston Hughes' *Mulatto* began the longest Broadway run of any play by a black dramatist before Lorraine Hansberry. Produced in 1935, but written in 1930, *Mulatto* is an emotionally engaging drama, marred by melodrama, propaganda, and crudities common to inexperienced playwrights. Developed from a short story, "Father and Son," *Mulatto* dramatizes the conflict between Colonel Norwood, a wealthy white man, and Robert, his yard child. Since the age of seven, Robert has hated his father for refusing to recognize their relationship, of which he himself has been proud. During his summer's vacation from college, Robert has strained tension to a breaking point by defying the morés of his father and of the Georgia town in which they live. Finally, on the day of Bert's scheduled return to college, the tension snaps. Incensed to learn that Bert has defied a white woman, has driven faster than a white man, and has entered the front door of the house regularly, Norwood threatens to kill him. Bert kills his father and flees; but, chased by a posse, he returns to the house, where he kills himself.

Much of the power of the play derives from the subject itself. A traditional subject in drama, father-son conflict inevitably generates excitement and frequently produces memorable characters and confrontations: Laius and Oedipus, Claudius and Hamlet, Theseus and Hippolytus are only a few. In this instance, the excitement was intensified for American audiences by the first professional dramatization of a conflict between a mulatto and his father.

The play gains strength also from Hughes' characterizations of Bert and his mother Cora. Although he is obviously modeled on the proud and noble slaves of Negro literary tradition, Bert is an interesting character. His contempt for other Negroes, his stubborn insistence that he be recognized as a man, and his arrogant defiance of custom symptomize a fatal *hubris*. In his deliberate provocation of trouble, a manifestation of what seems almost a suicidal complex, he anticipates James Baldwin's protagonist in *Blues for Mr. Charlie*, written a generation later (1964).

Cora too seems a familiar figure from American stories about the antebellum days. At first, she is merely the docile servant who, for many years, has lived with the master, nurtured him, and bore his children without concern for herself and without complaint. After Norwood's death, however, Cora assumes more significant dimensions. Revealing that love had caused her to excuse Norwood's faults and cling to him, she now repudiates him because his death threatens her son, who is even more precious to her. Unfortunately, as Hughes has written the scene, a reader is uncertain whether Cora is insane or is, for the first time, rationally aware of the manner in which she has been abused by Norwood. Regardless of the reason for her transformation, Cora appears more carefully delineated and more admirable than the male figures who dominate her life.

Even Colonel Norwood is interesting as a character. Although Hughes, writing protest drama, stereotyped him from racial bigots of his own day and slave masters of the previous century, Norwood gains reality in his final confrontation with Bert. Transcending racial identity, he becomes, like Hughes' own father, a man in conflict with his son. When Norwood cannot pull the trigger of his gun to kill Bert, Bert strangles him. Although Bert could only wonder why Norwood did not fire, a reader suspects, romantically perhaps, that, at the critical moment, Norwood realized that Bert was actually his flesh and blood, not merely a yard child whom he could ignore.

The theme of protest was continued off Broadway in Langston Hughes' *Don't You Want To Be Free?* (1937), a musical history of blacks in America, and in Theodore Ward's *Big White Fog* (1940). Although it lasted only sixty-four performances, *Big White Fog* dramatized a black man's frustrated and tragic existence more bitterly and more effectively than any play previously presented professionally in the United States.

Set in Chicago and covering a period from 1922 to 1931, the play recounts the misadventures of Victor Mason and his family. Convinced that black people cannot live profitably in the United States, Victor Mason buys stock in the Black Star liner on which Marcus Garvey, a West Indian, plans to help black people return to Africa, where they will re-establish themselves in a new community. Events intensify Mason's conviction that he must leave: His son Lester is denied a scholarship because of his race. His daughter Wanda abandons her education in hopes of earning money to purchase some of the luxuries she desires. But, despite the opposition of his wife, Mason idealistically clings to the hope that Garvey's plan will succeed. The hope collapses when Garvey is arrested and convicted of fraud.

Nine years later, the Masons have hit the bottom. Wanda has become a prostitute. Les has become a Communist. Mason's wife Ella pawns their few valuables in order to feed the family. When bailiffs come to evict the family for failure to pay rent, Victor Mason is killed attempting to stop them. The play ends with the glimmering hope that union of black and white may improve conditions in America, but one remembers more vividly Les's despairing cry: "Seems like the world ain't nothing but a big white fog, and we can't see no light no where."

Typically, in contrast to the short life of *Big White Fog* off Broadway, *Cabin in the Sky* in the same year titillated Broadway audiences for 156 performances. A comic fantasy written by whites, it repeated the familiar Negro stereotypes in a story heavily laden with primitive religious faith, comedy, and song.

The decade of protest reached its climax in Richard Wright's *Native Son* (1941), adapted for the stage by Paul Green, a white regional dramatist who had written more plays about Negroes than any other American dramatist. Written originally as a novel, *Native Son* tells the story of Bigger Thomas, a twenty-year-old black youth from Mississippi, who lives with his mother and his younger sister and brother in a rat-infested room in the slums of Chicago's black ghetto. A monster created by America's economic and social system, Bigger is characterized by envy, fear, and hatred. He envies, fears, and hates white people who control the society, own the houses and the stores in the slums, acquire education and jobs, and deny opportunity and free movement to black people.

Bigger, however, also hates Negroes because they occupy inferior positions in America. To prevent awareness of his impotence to assist his family, he even erects a wall of hate between himself and them. But, because he cannot completely conceal his impotence from himself, he also hates himself.

Hired as a chauffeur by the Daltons, white "liberals" who derive part of their fortune from slum houses such as Bigger's, Bigger is ordered to drive the Dalton's daughter, Mary, to her evening classes at the University of Chicago. Mary, however, insists that Bigger take her to an assignation with her Communist sweetheart, Jan, who attempts to enlist Bigger in the Party. At the end of the evening, Bigger assists the drunken girl to her room, where he is surprised by her blind mother. Fearing that he will be discovered and accused of rape, Bigger accidentally smothers the girl while trying to prevent her from responding to her mother's questions. After a melodramatic chase during which he rapes and kills his Negro sweetheart, Bigger is caught, tried, and executed.

As a novel, *Native Son* was a powerful and shocking indictment of America. Much of the emotional impact resulted from the subjective presentation of Bigger; readers saw the United States through his eyes, and for them also it became a world of white horror. The adaptation of the work into a drama transformed the character and the theme. Bigger was humanized and made less fearful, less brutal. In the novel, Bigger fights his black associates to prevent himself from realizing that he is too cowardly to rob a white man; in the play, his temper is the only reason for his fight. In the novel, he brutally assaults his sweetheart to prevent her betraying him to the police; in the play, she is killed by policemen. Although these character changes made Bigger a more sympathetic individual for a theater audience, they erased Wright's major thesis: that American society has shaped this Bigger and other Biggers into monsters who are brutal because they are fearful. Furthermore, in the play, a white reporter, suspecting Bigger, skillfully proves Bigger's guilt. In contrast, emphasis in the novel is placed upon the fact that, as a result of his accidental murder, Bigger, for the first time, realizes that he can outwit white people. In the novel, his guilt is discovered accidentally by reporters, who suspect him no more than Captain Delano suspected the innocent-looking black mutineers in Melville's "Benito Cereno." Finally, without the introspective examination of Bigger, *Native Son* is more a cops-and-robbers melodrama than a thesis play. Nevertheless, it ran for ninety-four performances and was even nominated for a Drama Critics Circle award for the year.

Protest did not disappear from the theater during the 1940s; but the end of World War II and the apparent triumph of democracy revived idealistic hopes for brotherhood and understanding. While white dramatists wrote pleas for integration of Negroes, black dramatists sought to educate white audiences by writing more realistically about problems of the past and the present.

In *Our Lan'* (1947), Theodore Ward described the efforts of black freedmen after the Civil War. Although the play focuses on the United States' betrayal of freed slaves, who were promised land, then forced to sign away their rights, and finally driven off by Union troops, considerable attention is given to the character of the slaves themselves and to their problems not related to land.

In 1954, in a theatre off Broadway, William Branch presented *In Splendid Error,* the story of an important episode in the life of Frederick Douglass, who, after escaping from slavery, dedicated himself to abolishing that evil from the United States. For a period of time, Douglass supported John Brown's efforts to help slaves liberate themselves by flight and by guerilla attacks upon Southern planters. When Brown, however, decided to attack federal property at Harper's Ferry, Douglass was forced to choose between unpleasant alternatives: if he accompanied Brown, he would sacrifice his life in a mission which he considered suicidal; if he refused, some would suspect him of cowardly betrayal of the cause. The play is the story of Douglass's effort to make a choice.

In 1956, off Broadway, Loften Mitchell's *A Land Beyond the River* dramatized a more recent incident in the history of black Americans. It recounted the valiant efforts of Mr. Dulane, a minister in South Carolina, to help Negro children enroll in schools reserved for white children, where facilities, supplies, and equipment promised a higher quality of education than was possible in the antiquated structures assigned to black children. Historically, Mr. Dulane succeeded; his case was one of those which persuaded the Supreme Court to rule in 1954 that all publicly supported schools must admit students without restrictions based on race or religion. Nonetheless, historically as in the play, Mr. Dulane was forced to save his life by fleeing at night from embittered white neighbors resentful of the changing conditions.

Professional drama by Afro-Americans came of age on Broadway during the 1950s. In 1953, Louis Peterson told the story, in

Take a Giant Step, of educated northern Negroes, who are neither primitive nor pathetic but who have problems. Spencer Scott, the protagonist, is a member of the only Negro family in a neighborhood in Philadelphia, Pennsylvania. When he reaches the age of sexual maturity, he becomes isolated from his former white friends, who no longer invite him to their homes or visit him. He attempts to discover companionship among members of his race, but he cannot adjust to the Negroes whom he sees in taverns. Isolated by race and by social position, he is alone except for a grandmother who loves him but cannot provide the companionship required by a teen-age youth. Peterson did not pretend to have a solution. At the end of the play, Scott remains isolated.

Take a Giant Step continued for seventy-six performances and was followed in the next year by *Mrs. Patterson,* a happier tale of the daydreams of a Negro girl. Teddy Hicks wants to be a wealthy white woman, like Mrs. Patterson, her mother's employer; but she also dreams of an exciting life with "Mr. D." from Hell. Eventually, the dreams are crushed, and Teddy faces reality. This play by Charles Sebree, black, and Greer Johnson, white, lasted for 101 performances, undoubtedly benefitting from the casting of popular Eartha Kitt as Teddy.

The trend towards verisimilitude, however, was interrupted by Langston Hughes's *Simply Heavenly* (1957), which, designed for the commercial theater, reached Broadway in a state weaker than Hughes's *Simple Takes a Wife,* the book upon which the play was based. The major sufferer in the adaptation is Jess B. Simple himself. In the tales and dialogues of the Simple books, Jess assumes the dimensions of a folk hero. Even though he drinks, cavorts with women, has difficulty paying rent, talks ungrammatically and excessively, his foibles never detract from his dignity, for, like the Greek gods and the heroes of various mythologies, he is larger than life. It may be appropriate even to say that he, like Joseph Conrad's Kurtz, is remembered primarily as a voice, in this instance a voice which utters common sense even when the speaker seems emotional and illogical. Reduced to actable dimensions, however, Simple loses his grandeur. In the play, he peeks beneath his legs to watch Joyce, his fiancée, change clothes; he turns somersaults; he is thrown from a car to land on his "sit-downer"; he is propped comically in a hospital bed with his legs in traction; sentimentally and pathetically, he tries to reform and to win Joyce. In short, Simple's reality as the embodied spirit of the Negro working class is reduced to the Harlem barfly; the Chaplinesque Comic Hero shrinks to a farcical fall guy of the model made familiar earlier by Stan Laurel and Lou Costello.

The second major injury resulting from the adaptation is suffered by the material itself. Even though incidents occur in the book, they generally serve merely as acceptable devices to generate Simple's philosophizing. Consequently, what is important is not the event itself but the reaction which it stimulates from Simple. For a Broadway show, however, Hughes needed to emphasize action and to minimize Simple's reflections. As a result, undue attention is given to Simple's unsuccessful effort to seduce Joyce, to the Watermelon Man's pursuit of Mamie, and to the domestic difficulties of Bodidilly and Arcie. The effort to please Broadway failed; the show closed after sixty-two performances.

Two years later Lorraine Hansberry achieved the kind of success which earlier black American playwrights had dreamed of. Her drama, *A Raisin in the Sun,* won the Drama Critics Circle Award as the best play for 1958-59. It continued for 530 performances in its initial run.

Appropriately, *A Raisin in the Sun* is a play about the dreams of ghetto dwellers. Descended from five generations of slaves and sharecroppers, the Youngers have moved north in the hope of realizing their dreams. In Chicago, however, their dreams are dying. Thirty-five-year old Walter Lee Younger is merely a chauffeur who cannot support his family adequately, cannot even provide a bedroom for his young son, who sleeps on a couch in the living room. Beneatha, Walter Lee's sister, wants to be a doctor even though she realizes the financial strain that her education places upon the children. Walter Lee's wife, who is pregnant, suffers with the realization that the family cannot afford another child. Walter Lee's mother wants happiness for her children and a garden for herself; but she sees weariness and sorrow in her children, and in the concrete wasteland of Chicago's ghetto, she can find space enough only for a windowbox plant for herself.

In order to earn money to support his family, Walter Lee wants to purchase a share of a liquor store with the money his mother has received from the insurance of his father, who died from overwork. His mother refuses because she believes liquor stores are immoral and because she wants to use the money to purchase a home for the family. Walter Lee steals part of the money but loses it in a swindle. The mother makes a down payment on a home, but it is in a neighborhood where black people have never lived: the exorbitant costs have prevented her buying a home in Negro neighborhoods. Despite warnings of opposition by their new neighbors, the Youngers decide to move, hoping at last to realize one dream.

Lorraine Hansberry did not idealize the Younger family. Walter Lee Younger experiences bitter frustration because no one else in his family agrees to his scheme to invest his mother's insurance money in a liquor store. Far from epitomizing nobility, he searches for pride and for maturity. As he says, "I'm thirty-five-years old; I been married eleven years and I got a boy who sleeps in the living room — and all I got to give him is stories about how rich white people live." He believes that the Negro who wishes to succeed must imitate white people.

In contrast, his sister, Beneatha (Bennie), inspired partly by racial pride and partly by the lectures of her African suitor, argues against the assimilation of the Negro race into the American culture. Whereas Walter materialistically concentrates upon acquiring money. Bennie wants to become a doctor because her desire since childhood has been to help other people.

Concerned neither with money nor with crusades, their mother desires merely to provide cleanliness and decency for her family. When she receives the insurance money left by her husband, she restrains herself from donating the ten thousand dollars to the church only because she wishes to help her children realize their dreams. She wants her children to respect themselves and to respect others.

The Youngers disagree even in their attitudes toward their race. Although Walter blames the backwardness of the race for the inferior economic status of the Negro, he responds to the rhythms of recordings of African music. Bennie recognizes the barrier which separates her from the snobbish Negroes who possess wealth; yet she considers herself a crusader for and a defender of her race. Individual in their characters and their attitudes towards life, the Youngers find unity only in their common belief in the importance of self-respect, a philosophy not unique to the Negro race.

The play also includes a wealthier Negro — well-dressed, well-educated, condescending toward lower-class blacks and ridiculed in turn by people of that lower economic class. Contrasted with him is an African, who is proud of his nationality and contemptuous of the assimilationist behavior of American blacks.

The play has been judged a comedy because it is amusing, but it remains the most perceptive presentation of Negroes in the history of American theater.

It is encouraging to observe that Afro-American dramatists of the 1950s have had the freedom to people their plays with individualized blacks rather than the stereotypes. Clearly, this indicates that the popular images are changing. Nevertheless, the Afro-American remains an exotic subject for American professional theatre. As long as this condition continues, the major opportunities for Afro-American dramatists will lie in the amateur theatrical of the colleges and in the semi-professional performances of black community groups. Despite recent awards, the black dramatist is not yet a significant force in American professional theatre.

[1]Phillis Wheatley, kidnapped from Senegal and taken to the United States at the age of seven, published *Poems* in London.

[2]Born a slave in Lexington, Kentucky, Brown escaped in 1835. He published *The Narrative of William Wells Brown* (1847), *My Three Years in Europe* (1852), and *Clotel, or the President's Daughter* (1853).

[3]*The Escape, or a Leap for Freedom* by William Wells Brown. Even though Brown gave public readings from this drama, there is no evidence that it was ever staged.

[4]Garland Anderson's *Appearances*, 1925.

[1]*New York*, II (April 21, 1962), p. 55.

On the "Emerging" Playwright

by Loften Mitchell

WHILE I WAS GROWING up in Harlem, the rising influence of the movie medium brought down the curtains on the community's three legitimate theatres—the Lincoln, the Lafayette and the Alhambra. Eventually these houses became vaudeville houses with motion pictures sandwiched between acts. Later the 125th Street Apollo began its long ascent and remains to this date one of the few "live" showhouses in the City of New York.

The changeover to movie houses proved disconcerting. The motion picture medium was then rising to its predominant position in terms of sabotaging the black image—a start it had with the insidious *Birth of a Nation*, the film which gave the Civil War to the South and painted black people as savages. The movies of the nineteen-twenties and nineteen-thirties were equally insidious. They did not reflect black life as I saw it daily in Harlem, and I found the projections of the black people much more truthfully presented at Harlem's three legitimate theatres. But, these theatres—like white theatres of the time — gave way to the onslaught of Hollywood's machinations.

I saw many of those movies along with brothers and sisters from the Harlem area. Generally, we met each Saturday and sat through the shows as long as we could. When a particular section of a film seemed untruthful, we shouted: "Man, don't bring us that jive!"

And usually we would jump up in unison, bang our seats and march out of the theatre.

One particular film that brought our wrath was about the life of George Gershwin, the man who—in the words of Langston Hughes—"wrote *Porgy and Bess* from a downtown penthouse, looking towards Harlem while the Duke was riding the A Train." Anyhow, in this film there is much discussion of Gershwin's fascination with jazz and finally Paul Whiteman—later to be called by his press agent "The King of Jazz"—declared he was going to make jazz respectable by taking it into the concert halls.

There it was! In precision we youngsters banged our chairs, marched single file up the theatre aisle and out of the theatre, screaming the Password as it has never been said before. We stood on the sidewalk in front of the theatre, urging people not to buy tickets. The manager came out of the theatre and wanted to know our objections. We let Willie, one of our crowd, tell him. And Willie told him "like it is" and like it has been for much too long. Willie said:

"Man, what are you cats trying to put down in this country? How is that man, Paul White-half-man going to make *my* music respectable? I play that music in between mopping up floors and going hungry, and it sounds respectable to me! What that man is trying to say is: "To be respectable, I got to act like him, Well, I ain't like him and I don't want to be like him!"

We did a lot more screaming, but that man didn't understand a word we said. And many years later that man still does not understand—or else he does not want to understand. Worse than that, he doesn't seem to understand that we don't care if he understands or not. The hands on the clock have ticked long past midnight and we have seen Cinderella absolutely undressed. And—if I may continue to change my metaphor—we know that she has B.O. She is funky.

She—or he—has not changed undergarments all these years. Now, being dirty and filthy is an individual matter as long as I don't have to wallow in that filth. Unfortunately, in recent years that dirty smell has been brought into my front room. I should have learned to adjust to the reality that virtually every time a Western white man opens his mouth, he insults a black man. I call attention to the 1968 American elections for verification of that statement. Here the most lawless people in the Western world campaigned for law and order. Here the hypocrite whose ancestors were the scum of Europe sing gloriously of the marauding, brutal men who committed genocide on the red man and enslaved the black man. Here the poor white man remains too ignorant to realize that he, too, was and still is a slave.

The dirty smell pervades all areas of Western life, particularly in the arts. They have been made into vehicles for lies, not truth, supported in strange, high places by so-called well-meaning people. In the nineteen-fifties television commentator and producer, David Susskind, had on his show Sidney Poitier and Harry Belafonte. The discussion concerned the black man in the American theatre. Susskind said the black theatre artist is dependent upon the development of the black playwright. He added: "There was Richard Wright and ...." And his voice trailed off, and he shrugged. I sat up in my chair, hoping Poitier would mention that he had been sitting in her house when Alice Childress wrote the play, *Florence*, I hoped, too, that he had mentioned that his Harlem barbecue shop had been a ticket agency for Ossie Davis' *Alice in Wonder* and Julian Mayfield's *The Other Foot* and *A World of Men*. I hoped, too, that Belafonte would mention that the great John Oliver Killens was on his staff, or that, as Harold G. Belafonte, he had appeared in Abram Hill's *On Striver's Row*. But, neither of these great artists were given the opportunity, so—I turned off my set.

I was less fortunate the next time the smell came my way. In March, 1957 my play, *A Land Beyond the River*, opened at New York's Greenwich Mews Theatre to unanimously good reviews. My joy over the reviews vanished when I read the columns of praise about the play being entertaining as well as enlightening. One prominent critic lauded my sense of humor and pointed out that I had *not* written a propaganda play. In fact, the critics praised me more for what I had *not* done than for what I had done. That was fair enough, too, but when one reads that I wrote about human beings who were black people, the reason for my displeasure becomes apparent. These reviews, however, brought people to the box office and I decided not to look a gift-horse in the mouth, even when it is long-eared. I had barely made this decision when my press agent scheduled a number of interviews for me. At these I met a charming group of white journalists and they wrote lovely things about me, but what troubled me was the constant reference to the "emerging black playwright."

I cautioned them against its use. For one thing, I did not feel

I had just emerged at all. I had been sitting up nights for years, writing and re-writing plays. Two of them—*The Bancroft Dynasty* and *The Cellar* had been successful on New York stages long before I wrote *A Land Beyond the River*. But, what troubled me more than my own plight was the obvious reality that black playwrights have existed longer than many people care to admit. It is obvious that labeling the black playwright as "emerging" is another way the Western world camouflages the realities of cultural trends, particularly in terms of non-white groups. The work of non-white playwrights should be known to anyone who is vaguely familiar with the Chinese and Japanese theatres. If memory serves correctly, it was a man of African ancestry—Alexandre Dumas, *fils*, author of *Camille*—who was responsible for what came to be known as the "well-made play."

In America black people have created for the theatre longer than anyone cares to realize. Sometime during the Eighteenth Century black slaves on southern plantations created the minstrel form. This form—the forerunner of the American musical comedy pattern—was designed by slaves to satirize slavemasters. Minstrelsy was a unique, fast-moving, devastating art form until whites saw it, copied it, and used that form to caricature the black man. The black man's protest was used to destroy his image.

In the Nineteenth Century, specifically in 1821, a black tragedian, James Hewlett, spearheaded the founding of the African Grove Theatre in New York City. This theatre, located at Bleeker and Grove Streets, performed the classics for free black people. It was a source of inspiration for the great Ira Aldridge. The police harassed the company, often arresting the actors in the middle of a performance. The actors returned upon their release from jail and performed again. White hoodlums also created disturbances in the theatre and the management was compelled to post a sign, asking whites to sit in the rear of the theatre because "white people do not know how to behave themselves at entertainment designed for ladies and gentlemen of color."

White hoodlums eventually wrecked the African Grove Theatre. With its destruction the great Ira Aldridge realized that America offered little to the black theatre artist. He sailed for Europe where he was acclaimed by royalty. It is significant to note that less than two years after he left these shores, the shuffling, cackling stereotype of black people was acclaimed on the New York stage—projected by a white man in "blackface."

The black playwright came into a measure of prominence long before the Civil War. William Wells Brown, a former slave, wrote *The Escape, or A Leap to Freedom*. In 1853 William Lloyd Garrison wrote in *The Liberator* of the playwright's power and eloquence.

Minstrelsy, however, remained a dominant theatrical force. After the Civil War black entertainers joined the prevalent minstrel pattern and became, in the words of James Weldon Johnson, a "caricature of a caricature." James Bland, composer of *Carry Me Back to Old Virginny* and *In the Evening By the Moonlight*, was a prominent minstrel man. However, in the latter part of the Nineteenth Century a group of black men set out to destroy the minstrel pattern by putting on musical plays. Among these were: Bert Williams, George Walker, Jesse Shipp, Alex Rogers, Bob Cole, J. Rosamond Johnson, Will Marion Cook and Paul Laurence Dunbar. In doing so they created the multi-million dollar musical comedy pattern.

The black playwright was at work. Bob Cole, along with J. Rosamond Johnson, composer of *Lift Every Voice and Sing*, wrote the operas, *The Red Moon* and *The Shoofly Regiment*. In April, 1898 Mr. Cole was represented by a vehicle known as *A Trip to Coontown*, produced at the Third Avenue Theatre. This multi-talented young man died at an early age and brought despair to black theatre lovers.

Two other outstanding writers for the stage were Paul Laurence Dunbar and Will Marion Cook. Their *Clorindy—the Origin of the Cakewalk* was particularly well received. During this era, too, Jesse Shipp and Alex Rogers were creating works for Bert Williams and George Walker. The Williams and Walker Company, after a number of "road vehicles," crashed Broadway with an original musical called *In Dahomey*. This work went on to London where it played for a year. It was presented at a command performance at Buckingham Palace in the year 1903.

Williams and Walker's next musical, *In Abyssinia*, had a book by Jesse Shipp and Alex Rogers. This musical, incidentally, was called by a New York critic "a little too high brow for a darky show." The work opened with Will Marion Cook's soaring number, *Song of Reverence to the Setting Sun*. The story told of George Walker obtaining some money and taking Bert Williams and some friends to Abyssinia. There the comic, ragged Bert wandered in and out of royal African settings, beautifully contrasting the conditions of the Afro-Americans to those of the Africans.

Williams and Walker's next show, *Bandanna Land*, made even more acid comments about black-white relationships in the United States. This work produced in 1908, told of a group of black people who wanted to get rich quick. They bought up land in a white section of a city and then proceeded to sell it back to the whites at twice the amount they paid for it. If this were not an attack upon the Negro-scare racket, one does not exist.

George Walker became ill during the run of *Bandanna Land*. This led to his retirement and Bert Williams went alone into *Mr. Lode of Kole*. After that, at the invitation of Abraham Erlanger, he went into the *Follies*.

To this writer's knowledge, Bert Williams was the only black artist who worked in the downtown theatre between the years 1910 and 1917. Black people were excluded from Broadway as performers and patrons. Nor was this an accident. It was a product of the sabotaging of the Reconstruction Era, of the same type of backlash faced by black people today in America. The United States Supreme Court was then an oracle for the rights of white people and rampant racism, highlighted by its *Plesey vs. Ferguson* decision in which it upheld the separate-but-equal doctrine. The American power structure had placed a "badge" on color and it became fashionable to attack black people in the press, the pulpit and in public places. Jimcrow laws appeared on the statute books of Southern states and lynch mobs rode the night. Race riots flared in cities as the rape of the black American continued.

Big business assumed control of the American theatre. A powerful group known as the Theatrical Trust Syndicate took control of all bookings, hirings and firings. They punished prominent white stars who failed to cooperate with them, forcing the great Sarah Bernhardt and Mrs. Dwight Fiske to appear in second-rate theatres. This, then, was the tone of the nation of the "Robber Barons."

The attack on black people in New York City was merciless. White hoodlums went into black people's homes and beat women and children. Black men coming home from work had to meet other black men on street corners and walk together. It was this type of terror that made many black people welcome the development of the community known as Harlem.

From 1910 through 1917 black theatrical artists worked primarily in the Harlem area. In 1909 writer-actor-producer Eddie Hunter produced shows at the Crescent Theatre on the site of Lenox Terrace apartments today. Mr. Hunter wrote many of the shows produced at the Crescent, notably, *Going to the Races* and *The Battle of Who Run.* In addition, there were other vehicles presented at the Crescent, among them an opera by Harry Lawrence Freeman called *An African Kraal.* And down the street near Lenox Avenue stood the Lincoln Theatre where Henry Kramer and S. H. Dudley had their plays produced with notable success.

White Americans are strange people. Despite the fact that they want black people off to themselves, whites have a chronic need to race off to black places. And so the whites followed blacks to Harlem to see their shows and sit in their nightclubs. In 1913 when J. Leubrie Hill's *Darktown Follies* opened at the Lafayette Theatre, 132 Street and Seventh Avenue, one critic wrote that "it looked like a Broadway opening." Florenz Ziegfeld bought the Finale of that show for his *Follies.* Another Lafayette show, *Darkydom* by Aubrey Lyles and Flournoy Miller, saw many of its sketches sold to Broadway.

In 1921 there came *Shuffle Along* by Aubrey Lyles and Flournoy Miller, with music and lyrics by Noble Sissle and Eubie Blake. It was a smash hit and it launched the period that came to be known as the Black Renaissance. Several editions of the show followed as well as *Blackbirds.* In 1923 Eddie Hunter's *How Come?* was seen on Broadway with that great jazz musician, Sidney Bechet.

Other black playwrights during the Nineteen-Twenties included Willis Richardson, author of *The Chipwoman's Fortune,* Garland Anderson, who wrote *Appearances* and Wallace Thurman, co-author of *Harlem.* And there was work by Eulalie Spence and prolific Randolph Edmonds, author of forty-nine plays.

The *so-called* emerging black playwright *emerged* a long time ago.

The Nineteen-Thirties saw too many fine black writers to be dealt with here. Langston Hughes' *Mulatto* had a long, long Broadway run. Hall Johnson's beautiful *Run, Little Children,* was seen on Broadway and in Harlem. And there was J. Augustus Smith's *Turpentine,* Rudolph Fisher's *The Conjure Man Dies,* and the plays of George Norford, Abram Hill, William Ashley and Ferdinand Voteur, produced by Dick Campbell and the Rose McClendon Players. And the American Negro Theatre produced the plays of Abram Hill, Theodore Browne, Owen Dodson and other black writers. It is said that veteran actor John Proctor practically wrote *Anna Lucasta* for the American Negro Theatre.

In the Nineteen-Fifties there were William Branch's *A Medal for Willie* and *In Splendid Error*, Alice Childress' *Just a Little Simple, Gold Through the Trees* and *Trouble in Mind*, and Theodore Ward's *Our Lan'*. Louis Peterson penned *Take A Giant Step*; Sidney Easton, *Miss Trudie Fair*; Sallie Howard, *The Jackal*; as well as plays by Virgil Richardson, Gertrude Jeanette, Oliver Pitcher, Harold Hollifield, Julian Mayfield, Ossie Davis and this writer.

Broadway saw Charles Sebree's *Mrs. Patterson*, and there were Lorraine Hansberry's two fine plays. And James Baldwin's. And Off Broadway saw LeRoi Jones and Douglas Turner Ward. And C. Bernard Jackson. And this summer I saw the fine work of Ted Shine. And Ed Bullins. And every time I look around I see another black writer—Sara Fabio.

What kind of "emerging" are these folks digging?

I am reminded of an incident during the writing of my book, *Black Drama.* I returned home after a day of research and my wife asked me how things were going. I told of the day's work — of documenting the land owned by black people when New York City was called New Amsterdam in the 17th Century. I spoke of the black people who had owned land around City Hall Park, along 23rd Street, on Pell Street and in other areas.

I spoke too, of the artisans and doctors who had been in New Amsterdam. She looked at me and asked: "Where do folks get this nonsense that all black people were slaves?" I snapped at her: "The white folks wrote those history books! And they've been writing plays about us and getting them on while we have to sweat and strain to be heard!"

We had a big argument. Then suddenly we stopped and laughed. We both knew the real enemy had made us argue. It was funny, but it was deadly serious. — It was, in short, America's style of genocide.

Three Black Playwrights: Loften Mitchell, Ossie Davis, Douglas Turner Ward

by C. W. E. Bigsby

I

THE NAMES OF black playwrights such as Lorraine Hansberry, James Baldwin and LeRoi Jones are reasonably well known to the American theatre-goer and literary critic alike. Broadway success and political militancy have conferred a fame which, though deserved, was largely denied their predecessors. As Loften Mitchell points out in his essay, white recognition of the black playwright has been more than a little belated. The reason for this has had less to do with simple perversity than with the mainly poor quality of Negro drama until comparatively recent times and the economic exigencies of Broadway production which have successfully kept the Negro writer and actor out of the limelight. Nevertheless it is a fact that while writers like Jack Gelber, Arthur Kopit and Jack Richardson gained a quick and largely undeserved reputation, black playwrights seemed to exist only on the periphery of white critical awareness. Today this situation is being in some degree rectified as appreciative gestures are made in the direction of the

Negro Ensemble Company and the more powerful products of the revolutionary black theatre. It remains true, however, that virtually a whole generation of Negro playwrights has failed to secure the kind of critical attention which their work deserves. Writers like Loften Mitchell, Ossie Davis and Douglas Turner Ward have produced plays of considerable merit, winning Mitchell a Guggenheim Award and Ward two off-Broadway prizes. If they are not, for the most part, innovators nor to be compared to LeRoi Jones or Lorraine Hansberry at their best, they have played a significant role in moulding a theatre rooted in the black experience, while, with the exception of Mitchell's *A Land Beyond the River*, they have avoided the melodramatic implications of the racial situation which had undermined plays like Eugene O'Neill's *All God's Chillun Got Wings* and even Langston Hughes's *Mulatto*.

II

Although he had written sketches for a drama group while still in high school, Loften Mitchell, like Ossie Davis, really started his theatrical life as an actor with the Rose McClendon Players. It was a short-lived career. After receiving poor notices for his performance in Dennis Donaghue's *The Black Messiah* (1939) he relinquished his acting ambitions, and went first to Telladega College in Alabama and then into the navy. Having completed his naval service he moved to Columbia University where, under John Gassner, he began work on a history of the Negro in the American theatre which was subsequently published in 1967 under the title *Black Drama*. At the same time he returned to playwrighting, producing *The Bancroft Dynasty, Shame of a Nation, The Cellar* and *Land Beyond the River*.

Shame of a Nation, which took as its theme the case of the Trenton Six, was produced by the Harlem Showcase in the mid 40s and the same group was responsible for his first modest success when it produced *The Cellar* in November 1952. This was concerned with a Negro blues singer whose detective fiancé destroys what Mitchell calls a "fugitive from southern injustice." Paradoxically, given the play's title, the performance was staged in a loft theatre. Although performed only at weekends it nevertheless enjoyed a considerable run.

Despite the moderate popularity of this work it was another five years before he scored his greatest success with *A Land Beyond the River* which opened at the Greenwich Mews Theatre in March

1957. Scheduled for a ten week run it eventually continued, with a brief break, for a year. After its New York success it was sent on tour, one performance being given at Mitchell's old college at Talladega. In 1958 he was the recipient of a Guggenheim Award for creative writing in the drama.

A Land Beyond the River[1] tells the story of a small South Carolina community which played a part in the process which finally led to the Supreme Court desegregation decision of 1954. The Negroes of Clarendon County, led by the Rev. Dr. Joseph DeLaine, decided to press for buses to transport their children to remote rural schools. Thurgood Marshall, then head of the legal division of the NAACP, took up the case and encouraged them to extend their demands to include separate but equal schools. This in turn gave way to an onslaught on the principle of segregation itself. The play takes the story up to the point at which the State Supreme Court had ruled in favour of the old separate but equal doctrine.

Mitchell's interest was stimulated when Ossie Davis used the material for a concert reading. With Davis's encouragement he met Dr. DeLaine and started work on the play. DeLaine himself had been forced to leave Clarendon County after his house had been burnt down and eventually had been driven out of the south altogether. Those who stayed behind were subject to economic harassment. Thus the play which Mitchell now started writing quickly assumed the nature of a testament to their courage and a polemical denunciation of white injustice. Appropriately enough the work was subsequently sponsored by the Automobile Workers as a means of raising funds for the people of Clarendon County. From the proceeds a harvester was actually dispatched to those who had been suffering such hardships since the events which Mitchell details in his play.

As the play opens the black community is facing a minor crisis. The floor of the school house has collapsed. Suddenly their campaign to secure buses seems pitifully ironical since the school itself is demonstrably so inadequate. Nevertheless even this campaign has served to highlight the divisions within the Negro community and the real nature of the hostility between black and white.

In so far as the Negro community is concerned the conflict is embodied in the antagonism between Dr. Layne and a school principal, Philip Turnham, who is described as a "humorless, fair complexioned Negro." Turnham is an Uncle Tom. As one of the characters puts it, "he's colored all right, but sometimes he don't know it." (p. 22). Thus the debate is not really about schools but about the attitude which the Negro should adopt towards white authority. Turnham's family history is the history of the Negro middle class, which had originally grown out of the caste divisions between the house slave off-spring of white slave owners and the black children of the field slaves. Turnham's family had taken pride in its white blood and he himself identifies with the white world. Yet his sycophancy is reflected in some degree by the determined passivity which has characterized the black community up to this moment. Rather than combine against white injustice they have fought amongst themselves. They now realize that they are faced with a straight choice between passivity and activism.

While the white world, as represented by the school superintendent, Rev. Mr. Cloud, is prepared to discuss the possibility of securing transportation, as soon as the demands are increased and go, indeed, to the heart of the issue, all pretence of liberality is dropped. Dr. Layne is dismissed and intimidation, legal and illegal, is applied. Cloud is presented as a sanctimonious hypocrite. While seeing it as "our Christian duty" to "lead the colored people forward" (p. 18) he stops short of anything which might provoke any kind of opposition. He even has the effrontery to tell Layne that he does not "know what it is to be a Negro down here." (p. 19) Yet his dislike of Layne does not prevent him from cynically offering to bribe him with a principalship for both himself and his wife. The episode epitomises Mitchell's analysis of black/white relations in the South. The black leader is first assured of white benevolence, then made the victim of persecution and finally, when he has demonstrated the reality of his leadership, he is bribed. Thus Layne's fight stands as the epitome of the whole fight for justice in the South.

Mitchell does create a white character who is bereft of prejudice. Dr. Willis has learnt by experience that irrational hatred and fear are finally self-defeating. He urges Layne and his wife to withdraw from the fight but does so because of his genuine regard for their well-being. The fact remains, however, that he feels no real commitment to their cause. He stands on the sidelines, offering moral support but unwilling to translate this into concrete action. Thus the white community is presented as consisting simply of pathologically violent tear-aways, hypocrites and ineffectuals. Whatever the justice of this assessment of small town white southerners the effect, in terms of the play, is to underscore the melodramatic tone of Mitchell's homily. For just as the whites are without exception either wilfully perverse and destructive or simply weak and vaccilating so the blacks, with the single exception of Turnham, are the epitome of courage, tenacity, wit and dogged determination. If they are tempted to settle for considerably less than total victory this serves merely to underline their passionate commitment to life rather than to the techniques and strategies of social skirmishes. Mitchell is as much a Calvinist as are the whites who for so long had used religion as their justification. He is in danger of replacing one form of elitism with another. The elect are now black where formerly they were white.

Mitchell himself has admitted that *A Land Beyond the River* "is far from the well-made play" and that "sometimes the dramaturgy is coarse." He also claims, however, that "This is, in a sense, deliberate, for the emphasis of the work is on character illumination."[2] Despite his sensitive treatment of Joseph Layne's personal doubts and frustrations his treatment of the other characters scarcely bears out his claim. He has said that he was glad of the opportunity to bring to the stage a group of "simple" human beings. The phrase, unfortunately, is more revealing than it should have been. They are "simple" not because they are pleasantly unsophisticated, bereft of the self-justifying formulas of the intellectual faced with a moral or social dilemma, but because they are one dimensional. *A Land Beyond the River* is a morality play in which vice and virtue are personified and the victory of the latter over the former an accepted assumption.

To serve the cause of Mitchell's didactic purpose characters tend to be reduced to essential components. Turnham is the Uncle Tom, Cloud, the hypocritical white man, Duff Waters, the convert won over from passivity to proud rebellion and Mrs. Simms, the wise old woman who knows a thing or two about life. The action itself, although based on actual events is melodramatic in the extreme. Joseph Layne's house is burnt to the ground and his wife drops dead from a heart attack as the white fire brigade refuse to help.

Where characters are not simply elements in Mitchell's homily all too often their complexity is sacrificed to his symbolic purpose. A minor subplot, which involves the emancipation of Philip Turnham's daughter, Laura, remains shadowy and ineffectual. Laura had originally opposed the campaign for buses, sharing her father's fear of antagonising the white authorities. She had even taken this as far as precipitating a break with her lover, Ben Ellis, an attractive and intelligent young lawyer. Her conversion is potentially very significant as one of 'Uncle Tom's children' is won over to the need for activism. Yet the entire episode lacks credibility, never becoming anything more than a symbolic redemption. Ellis is an undeveloped figure who appears only briefly at the beginning and end of the play. His skill and authority remain untested and when he presumes to act as Layne's conscience, insisting on the need to continue the fight, we have no reason to feel that this is anything more than bombast. We have seen Layne suffer for his cause; Ellis's exhortations remain only an intellectual commitment. Yet Mitchell clearly intends us to take Ellis as a valid and wise counsellor.

His involvement with Laura is similarly insubstantial and seems little more than a contrivance, useful for its symbolic overtones. Laura herself seems from the very beginning too much of a humanitarian ever to have accepted her father's reactionary views. Her break with him at the end of the play thus tends to seem an artificial climax owing more to the exigencies of the plot than to the apparent truth of her character and her relationship to her father.

It is no longer possible to view this play without an overpowering sense of irony. When it was written and first produced the fact of the Supreme Court desegregation decision of 1954 stood as an unstated reality against which the stuggle could be viewed. It was a comment on the folly of those whites who opposed Negro agitation. The temporary set-backs of the Negro cause could be looked at in the light of the known achievement which would inevitably follow. The stage directions actually indicate that the stage should be dominated by the courthouse, with a flag flying from the top—a visual reminder of the ultimate success of their efforts and the attainability of justice.

By the late 60s the failure of the 1954 decision had become self-evident. The decay of the inner cities together with population movements now meant that for many areas, particularly in the North, segregation was worse than it had been prior to the Supreme Court's decision. Anyone viewing the play now could not help but be affected by the irony. The play has become something of a period piece. At the same time of course the nature of the civil rights struggle itself has changed radically. Integration, the great goal of the 50s and early 60s, is now increasingly rejected as a strategy and a target. The assumption that Negroes should be assimilated by white society is dismissed as Caucasian arrogance. Hence, for a modern black audience the whole ethos of Mitchell's play is liable to seem increasingly alien as are the virtues of Joseph Layne, steadfastly working through the law and placing his faith in the integrity and effectiveness of democratic institutions. The fact that he now seems painfully naive is an expression not of Mitchell's sense of ambiguity but of the pace of social change. The passage of time has served both to reveal the weakness of his approach and to give an added historical dimension to the play itself.

Layne's determined pacifism is an accurate reflection of civil rights' strategy but it is not without its ambiguities. When he declares that "if a white man walked into this church and stuck a gun in my face, I'd have to go down on my knees and pray for him" (p. 60) one looks in vain for a sense of irony to deflate the pretentious tone. By the end of the play, with his wife dead and his home in ruins his stoical acceptance seems, perhaps admirable, but also a little excessive. Nor is it totally devoid of a self-justifying pride. As he declares, "The Voice of God has roared in my ears, testing my faith—by letting them burn up my house, by letting them crucify my beloved wife—testing me as Job was tested." (p. 82) And yet one is never entirely convinced that this irony is a product of Michell's sensitive objectivity. Ambiguity seems rather to be a product of our changed perspective. To a modern audience there seems to be more than an element of the masochist in Layne. At times he seems little more than a would-be martyr. As he says at one stage "God Almighty, you're calling me to have the guts to let people kill me." (p. 60) .

Yet while Mitchell occasionally permits his characters a self-indulgent rhetoric the play is not without a saving humour which explains his bitterness at those critics who later hailed *Purlie Victorious* as a refreshing revival of humour in Negro drama. One character, for example, tries in vain to reconcile the south's determined advocacy of segregation with its liberal willingness to "integrate" his tax dollars. For all its faults, then, the play is both moving and powerful. Part of its effectiveness undeniably stems from the emotive nature of the central theme but Mitchell's ability to capture the essence of the courage and somewhat facile optimism of the 50s shows his skill as a writer. If the simplistic approach to character and theme suggest his limitations as a playwright it also says something about the nature of a period in the civil rights campaign which seems in many senses a whole world removed from the present.

Following the success of *A Land Beyond the River* Mitchell returned to his critical work, producing, among other things, an article on the Negro in the American theatre for the *Oxford Companion to the Theatre*. In the course of researching this article he met Bert Williams, the old Negro entertainer. *Star of the Morning*, the story of Bert Williams, was the result of this meeting. This was followed by *Ballad for Bimshire*, a musical which Mitchell wrote with Irving Burgess. It was, in Mitchell's own words, "a throwback to the days when Negroes wrote, produced, directed and managed their own shows."[3] Despite the support of largely Negro audiences the play had only a short run and closed in mid December, 1963. This in turn was followed by *Ballad of the Winter Soldiers* which Mitchell wrote with John O. Killens and which took as its subject what he called "freedom fighters throughout history." Finally, he again collaborated on a musical play when he and W. F. Lucas wrote *Ballad of a Blackbird* which is based on the life of Florence Mills who had starred in *Shuffle Along*, the famous Negro revue which had marked the beginning of the 20s Renaissance. The play owed its title to the name of the show in which she was appearing at the time of her death.

III

Ossie Davis, who came from Waycross, Georgia and was educated at Howard University, has contributed to the American theatre as actor, stage manager, promoter and playwright. On coming to New York he joined the Rose McClendon Players in the late 30s and was in the Famous Production of *On Strivers Row*. Later he joined the American Negro Theatre which, like the Rose McClendon Players in its latter stages, tried to establish a purely Negro repertory group performing, where possible, plays by Negro playwrights. Ironically, its greatest success was Philip Yordan's *Anna Lucasta*, a play originally about a Polish family and only adapted to suit the ANT. When this transferred to Broadway Ossie Davis went with it, as did his wife, actress Ruby Dee, and such other famous Negro actors as Canada Lee and Sidney Poitier. Davis continued his acting career, appearing in many plays, including Lorraine Hansberry's *A Raisin in the Sun* (1959), Loften

Mitchell's *Ballad for Bimshire* (1963) and Howard DaSilva and Felix Leon's *The Zulu and the Zayda*.

His first play was produced in 1952 at the Elks Community Theatre. *Alice in Wonder* was one of three plays which appeared under the same generic title; the other two being by Julian Mayfield. Davis's contribution was concerned with the pressures exerted on a Negro artist by a television company which wishes him to testify before a Washington committee. Although it had only a short run Davis was encouraged to expand it into a full-length play and in its new form it opened as *The Big Deal* in 1953. Davis's greatest success, however, came in 1961 with the Cort Theatre production of *Purlie Victorious*[4] in which he and his wife played the two main roles, and which was subsequently made into a film under the title *Gone are the Days*.

The Negro has always been the victim of those who would make him into a stereotype. Davis's achievement in *Purlie Victorious* is to take precisely those stereotypes and manipulate them for his own purposes. The Uncle Tom, the Afro-American nationalist, the race leader, the civil rights worker are all gently mocked but at the same time they achieve a symbolic victory over the forces of white oppression. It is this subtle mixture of self-irony and biting satire which gives the play its special tone and which makes of Purlie himself a picaresque hero capable of exposing the faults of black and white alike. As Davis realized, only a Negro could dare to present such stereotypes on stage in the 1960s. He himself pointed out that things "which would be offensive in the hands of a white writer, might become, in the hands of a Negro writer a totally unexpected revelation of the true substance of Negro wit and humour."[5]

The play is set in South Georgia, in a community dominated by the scatologically named Ol' Cap'n Cotchipee, the white cotton boss. The black community crosses swords with him in its attempt to get him to part with five hundred dollars which they intend to use to buy the Big Bethel church. The money is a legacy payable to Cousin Bee who has inconvenienced them by dying. Rather than see the money lost Purlie Victorious Judson thoughtfully provides a substitute in the person of an ex-maid, Lutiebelle Gussie Mae Jenkins, whose name Purlie calls "an insult to the Negro people." Purlie is confident that the ploy will succeed since "white folks can't tell one of us from another." Unfortunately, although attractive, Lutiebelle is not really qualified to imitate the college-educated Cousin Bee. Thus, when asked to sign a receipt for the money which they have acquired she uses her own distinctive name.

Subtlety having failed they turn to more direct methods and work through the Cap'n's liberal-minded son, Charlie, who, to the Cap'n's dismay, has recently shown a tendency to "get nonviolent." He steals the money and gives it to Purlie while securing the deeds to the church in Purlie's name rather than his father's. Shocked by this act of treachery by a true Caucasian the Ol' Cap'n literally dies on his feet and is buried in the same position—out of respect.

Purlie Victorious presents a series of satirical portraits which *in toto* constitutes a vivid parody of the racial situation. Lutiebelle is a gullible if amusing dupe, but despite the wild humour of the scene in which she tries desperately to imitate the educated Cousin Bee, Davis cannot resist making a serious point in his stage directions. He says of her that she is "like thousands of Negro girls . . . keenly in search for life and for love . . . but afraid to take the final leap: because no one has ever told her it is no longer necessary to be white in order to be virtuous, charming or beautiful." (pp. 6-7). But Lutiebelle is not only intimidated by the white world she is also a gullible disciple to any leader with the right blend of personal attractiveness and glib conviction. Her admiration for Purlie has less to do with his emotive appeals for freedom and justice than his personal magnetism which puts her in mind of marriage.

Purlie himself is the would-be Negro leader whose rhetoric outreaches his possibility for action. One of the highlights of the play, indeed, is its skillful deflation of demagogic language. The mixture of bombast, religious appeal and meaningless rhetorical devices is seen at its painful worst in the oration which Purlie delivers at the Cap'n's funeral and in which he calls upon his followers to "stifle the rifle of conflict, shatter the scatter of discord, smuggle the struggle, tickle the pickle, and grapple the apple of peace." (p.81.)

Purlie's heart is obviously in the right place. Wanting to show solidarity with the Montgomery bus boycotters but balked by the lack of buses he boycotts mules instead since they are the cotton patch equivalent. But while voicing the 'correct' sentiments his very exuberance becomes an element in Davis's satiric method. When he hails Lutiebelle as "This Ibo prize—this Zulu Pearl—This long lost lily of the black Mandingo—Kikuyu maid, beneath whose brown embrace Hot sons of Africa are burning still" (p. 15) his inflated language serves to undermine the poetic assumptions of the "Negro Renaissance," for the lyrical references to Africa can scarcely survive the determined plebianism of Gussie Mae Jenkins. When he goes on to denounce her name as the mark of a "previous condition of servitude, a badge of inferiority" (p. 15) this commonplace of nationalist jargon is made to seem pitifully excessive. At the same time his resounding insistence on the need for race pride is met with Lutiebelle's unanswerable confession that, as a house maid, black pride is something of a luxury. His proud enumeration of the languages of Africa and his attempt to link his wide-eyed disciple to his fanciful "ten thousand Queens of Sheba" (p. 16) is thus inevitably deflated by the mundane reality of the cotton patch. Try as he will he cannot make reality match up to the ideas of racial glory to which he has pledged his allegiance. Posing at one moment as a professor of Negro Philosophy and another as a minister he struggles to destroy the racial mores of the South with his own stock of black mythology. His eventual success, thanks to the cooperation of the Cap'n's white son, is thus a sign of his determination rather than his cunning but it is also an expression of Davis's personal conviction that Purlie's tenacity must eventually prove victorious, given the help of at least a section of the white community. Charlie, however, is the only available white ally. The incompetent sheriff and his deputy have a marked tendency to arrest and beat Negroes on sight while the Cap'n clings tenaciously to an outdated vision of black/white relations. Since he is as determined as Purlie to reshape reality to fit his own philosophy he sees only what he wants to see. The black community has long since capitalised on this fact and Purlie is particularly skillful in playing on his need for flattery and reassurance, even persuading him that he has been elected Great White Father by his grateful darkies. Since the Cap'n, for his own peace of mind, has to believe that "the old-fashioned, solid, hard-earned, Uncle Tom type Negro" (p. 35) still exists he is easily taken in by this.

The submissive Negro is, of course, not entirely a figment of the Cap'n's imagination, and Davis is at his best in his portrait of a man whose respect for the white man is so profound and unreasoning that he is mortified when he drops a cotton bole because "cotton is white" and "We must maintain respect." (p. 12) Gitlow, the appropriately named Uncle Tom, is gloriously obsequious, indulging only in the occasional irony. He is so pliable that he is accepted by the white world as a spokesman for the black community, even being conferred with the ambiguous title 'Deputy-for-the-Colored,' surely a comment on the Negro spokesman whose real loyalty lies with his white masters.

Thus we have two examples of black leaders, the one appointed by the white community to reflect its own prejudices and the other self-appointed, determined to "preach freedom in the cotton patch" to those whose ambition is "Freedom—and a little something left over." The cotton patch thus contains the wider scene in microcosm and the battle over Cousin Bee's inheritance is a wild parody of another, more significant, struggle for justice. As Davis himself has said, *"Purlie Victorious* is, in essence, the adventures of Negro manhood in search of itself in a world for white folks only."[6]

Purlie Victorious is, I suppose, what Harold Cruse would call an integrationist drama in that it sees integration as a desirable objective and satirises the old attitudes on the assumption that things are changing for the better in the South. Ol' Cap'n Cotchipee has had his day; the future lies with his son Charlie and if his name still contains a satirical comment on the white world (Mr. Charlie) there is no mistaking the integrity of his liberal motives. Thus, when he asks to be accepted as a member of the Big Bethel church this is a natural outcome of the play's action and a logical result of his dogged humanity. The central target of the play is clearly segregation. In the words of "Purlie's I.O.U." which prefaces the play, "our Theatre will say segregation is ridiculous because it makes perfectly wonderful people, white and black, do ridiculous things." (p. 4) Segregation produces not merely the white bigot but also the Uncle Tom, the Afro-American nationalist and the civil rights worker and despite Davis's personal commitments he satirises all their excesses with striking impartiality. Indeed, he has more than a sneaking admiration for the unashamed Uncle Tom whose charm lies precisely in his determined passivity.

Predictably, there are those who have regretted the play's "integrationist" tone. Adam Miller, of the San Francisco Aldridge Players/West, points out that "Young white Cotchipee . . . becomes the first member of Big Bethel. . . . He is happy to join, they are happy to have him." To Miller's mind this shows that Davis is falling into the trap of "either catering to the good will of a white audience or of making statements irrelevant to the Negroes."[7] This might seem a strange accusation to level at a man who had been a member of both the Rose McClendon Players and the ANT yet

Davis's involvement with Broadway and his equivocal attitude with regard to the black writer's responsibilities towards the Negro community, had cast doubt on his *bona fides.* After the success of *Purlie Victorious,* however, he made his position clear. He admitted that the play had itself brought about a complete change in his outlook. As he subsequently explained, "the act of writing became my long moment of truth; it took me five years to adjust my eyesight, to be able to look squarely at the world, and at myself, through Negro-colored glasses." He now came to feel that "my *manhood* was hidden within by Negroness,"[8] and in 1962 he announced that the Negro writer must learn to create for his own people and that he should write from "a black position."[9] It is difficult to appreciate precisely what this means in concrete terms. Is *Purlie Victorious* itself written from a "black position?" Davis himself has denied it, saying that since oppression, and the resistance of oppression, are universal themes, "If Purlie speaks at all he speaks to everybody—black and white." Certainly the play would appear to offer a comfortable feeling of well-being to a white audience. The setting is purely southern and bigotry is demonstrably on its last legs. The new generation seems generously prepared to embrace the black community even in its more bizarre manifestations. But this is a rather tendentious way of looking at a play whose purpose is not so much to analyse America's radical problem as to deflate the pretensions of black and white alike. Davis's commitment to black culture came after and not before the production of his play, and perhaps it is just as well since it relies so heavily for its effectiveness on his willingness to parody black zealots as well as white bigots. This is the source of much of the play's humor.

Even when an underlying seriousness threatens to break through, the context largely serves to undermine the bitterness. Thus, when Purlie exclaims that his mother had "died outdoors on a dirty sheet cause the hospital doors said—'For White Folks Only' " (p. 72) Davis is not trying to repeat the point of Albee's *The Death of Bessie Smith.* The claim is part of Purlie's desperate attempt to divert attention from his own cowardice. Nevertheless, the reference is not entirely de-fused. It hangs in the background, like an earlier reference to white brutality, as an oblique comment on the play's farcical tone and a reminder of the bitterness which lies only just beneath the surface.

The play was well reviewed but attracted poor audiences, and it was only the support of Negro theatregoers which guaranteed it a reasonable success. This fact played an important part in Davis's conversion. He now came to feel that "if we can, in fact, create for our own people; work for our own people; belong to our own people we will no longer be forced into artistic prostitution . . . it is time for us . . . to rejoin the people from which we came. . . . Only then can we begin to take a truly independent position within the confines of American culture."[10]

IV

Douglas Turner Ward began his career as a writer but when the market showed signs of drying up he turned to acting. Under the name of Douglas Turner he understudied Robert Earl Jones in Jose Quintero's famous Circle-in-the-Square production of *The Iceman Cometh*, and later appeared in Mitchell's *A Land Beyond the River* and Lorraine Hansberry's *A Raisin in the Sun*.

In 1960, according to Loften Mitchell's account, attempts were made to raise money to finance a production of two one-act plays which Ward had written. The attempt was a failure and it was not until 1964 that actor/producer Robert Hooks acquired an option on the two plays and after further difficulty staged them in November, 1965. Philip Meister, who had desperately tried to find financial support five years before, now directed the plays. Douglas Turner Ward, under his stage name, himself worked as an actor in the production, as did Robert Hooks.

Even now there was more trouble in store. A subway strike reduced audiences considerably. Nevertheless, in spite of this catalogue of disasters, the plays enjoyed a fourteen-month run and in the spring of 1966 Douglas Turner Ward achieved the remarkable distinction of receiving an Obie award for his acting and a Vernon Rice award for his writing.

Both *Happy Ending* and *Day of Absence*[11] are in a sense plays for a black theatre not merely because they utilise Negro actors but because they derive much of their humour from the ironical reversal of stereotypes. Where white audiences had been amused by minstrel shows in which whites performed in blackface, Ward, in *Day of Absence*, reverses the process. The humour of both plays is largely at the expense of a white community which is seen as insipid and stupid, unconsciously manipulated by a Negro world which it holds in contempt. These are plays primarily for a black audience but which are by no means limited in their appeal to such an ethnic audience. Neither do they resort to the bitter and humourless denunciation of whites which has become a commonplace of the revolutionary black arts movement. As he has said, "I've always felt that those Black plays which seem to be so clenched-fist-and-teeth, almost shrill, in their attack against Whitey emerge out of the Black writer's knowledge that he's talking to white people who don't hear him, don't understand him. He's got to sock it—scream."[12] Despite the ambiguity created by the Negro Ensemble's initially white-dominated audience it is clear that the subtle satire of his own one-act plays owes more than a little to the nature of his audience. This is not black theatre for its own sake. The fact that the cast is a black one is itself the origin of many of the play's complex ironies.

Happy Ending, like its companion piece, is based on a simple anecdote. Ellie and Vi are Negro domestics who work for a rich and self-indulgent white couple, Mr. and Mrs. Harrison. At the beginning of the play they are in tears over the prospect of the imminent break up of the Harrison marriage after the husband has caught his wife in the arms of her lover. When their nephew, Junie, a young black militant, sees the distress which their employers' trouble inspires, he is horrified. They seem to conform to precisely those stereotypes which he is anxious to forget. "Maybe *Gone with the Wind* was accurate! Maybe we jist can't help "Mis Scarrrrrrlet-ing" and "Oh Lawdying" every time mistress gets a splinter in her pinky." (p. 12) The reason for his aunts' depression, however, has nothing to do with racial humility. They are simply distraught at the loss of their meal ticket. The Harrisons have long financed the entire household, paying for Junie's food and clothes, for the furniture and even for his mother's air-fare on her regular yearly visit. When Junie finally understands the real reason for their dismay he becomes equally depressed and news that the Harrisons have become reconciled is greeted with enthusiasm by the whole household.

In *Happy Ending* Ward is creating an image of Negro/white relations. The whites seem to have the monopoly of wealth and power but are in fact manipulated and exploited by a cunning black community which, if it cannot secure justice directly, can at least drain off some of the surplus money as a result of its knowledge of the working of white society. As Ellie points out, "after cutting cane, picking rice and shucking corn befo' we could braid our hair in pigtails" we "figure we just getting back what's owed us." (p. 18) But while they recognise that "waiting for the Harrisons to voluntarily *donate* their Christian charity is one sure way of landing head-first in the poor-house dungeon" (p. 17) they avoid the effusions of the black militants. In fact Ward satirises Junie's nationalist ardour. His rhetorical appeal to black pride is shown not only to be out of all proportion to the ostensible pretext but also to be built on a naive perception of the reality of black/white relations. His description of "Africa rising to its place in the sun wit' prime ministers and other dignitaries taking seats around the conference table" and "us here fighting for our rights like never before, changing the whole image, dumping stereotypes behind us and replacing 'em wit' new images of dignity and dimension" is merely a prelude to his attack on his aunts for "DROWNING themselves in tears jist 'cause bos man is gonna kick bosslady out on her nose." (p. 12) His black pride is also in contrast to his studied indolence as he lives contentedly on relief and the charity which his aunts are able to offer thanks to their white connections.

The ending is 'happy' for everyone. The white community is happy with its illusions of power and superiority while the black community is content to foster those illusions so long as there is a percentage in it for them. In the words of the toast which Junie offers at the end of the play, "To the victors and the vanquished, top-dog and bottom dog! Sometimes it's hard to tell which is which." (p.22).

Yet beneath the humor the play might seem to endorse the status quo and even to reinforce those stereotypes against which Junie had rebelled. For Ward is drawing on the old tradition of the light-fingered black house servant and the bemused and deceived white master. It is scarcely surprising that Ward should have found himself under attack for his ambivalent attitude both in this play and *Day of Absence*. Thus Junie's comment that "if some gray cat was peeping in on you, he'da sprinted home and wrote five Uncle Tom's Cabins and ten Old Black Joes" (p. 13) is not entirely without its ironical implications for a writer who seems to feel that the mutual deceptions of a racial stand-off do indeed constitute a happy ending.

Day of Absence is what Douglas Turner Ward has called "a reverse minstrel show done in white-face." (p. 29) Again the basic idea is an extremely simple one. All the black inhabitants of a southern town simply vanish from the scene leaving the whites to realize the consequences of life without Negroes. By degrees the town grinds to a halt as essential services collapse under the impact of this basic assault on the economy.

The disappearance of the Negroes also serves to throw a new light on the racial pretensions of some of the whites. Not only does it expose the weaknesses of white society, it also reveals the precarious nature of ethnic purity for along with the domestics, the chauffeurs and general menials, various prominent citizens, including the chairlady of the Daughters of the Confederate Rebellion, simply disappear. The streets are then patrolled by distraught and surprised relatives carrying signs reading "WHY DIDN'T YOU TELL US—YOUR DEFILED WIFE AND TWO ABSENT MONGRELS." (p. 45)

Ward also attempts a side-swipe at white welfare arrangements. In the person of the significantly named Mrs. Aide, he presents a savage satire of schemes whose ostensible aim is that of finding "meaningful work" for the "Nigras." These turn out to be no more meaningful than careers as "maids, cooks, butlers, and breast-feeders, cess-pool-diggers, wash-basin maintainers, shoe shine boys, and so on." (p. 48) Mrs. Aide's motto, "Work or Starve," is thus not altogether inappropriate either to the exaggerated world of this southern town "on a somnolent cracker morning" or even to the realities of southern ADC payments which are as bizzare as anything Ward could create.

The whites themselves are presented as simple incompetents or dedicated sycophants desperate to embrace the American dream even if this means simultaneously embracing "the boss' left rump." They rely on the black community for everything from rearing their children to serving their coffee and in the construction of their mechanical Eden are prepared not only to exploit the Negroes but even to justify their actions by reference to a pliable religion. The Reverend Reb Pious appeals to them to fulfill their usual passive role, quoting in the process a fraudulent line from Booker T. Washington, whom he predictably calls "one of your greatest prophets." When they refuse to fall in line with their usual alacrity an air of panic seizes the town and its mayor, appropriately named Henry R. E. Lee, appears on television in a frantic and unsuccessful attempt to lure back lost Negroes. Having tried persuasion and intimidation he finally resorts to abject contrition, being thereafter beaten by a white mob for his pains. The play ends as the Negroes reappear. It is apparent, though, that things can never again function in the same old way. The whites have learnt that they are dependent on the blacks; the blacks have discovered the reality of their power.

The real strength of the play rests in its humour. The unabashed caricatures of the white world are obviously designed for Negro consumption yet they are drawn with such vigour and presented with such panache that *Day of Absence* can be almost as effective with a white audience. The use of Negroes in white-face, a device repeated by Ray McIver in *God is a Guess What*, permits Ward not merely to create a series of ironical comments on white pretentions but also to claim a freedom in revealing white contempt for Negroes which would have been impossible for a white writer. White abuse is thus adroitly turned back on itself.

Ward's theme in *Day of Absence* is basically that of *Happy Ending* and it is scarcely surprising to find Adam Miller attacking the play for its racial conservatism. In his own words, "In Douglas Turner Ward's *Day of Absence*, we see a black audience laughing at the whites in their helplessness at the loss of their Negroes for a day. Look, they say, the white folks need us. Ha, ha. One must ask if this is something Negroes need to be told. The image of the black woman who raises Miss Ann's children at the sacrifice of her own is one all too familiar to Negroes. What Negroes need to know is not that they are needed by whites but that they are needed by one another. They need to be shown by their playwrights how to reach out to each other across this need."[13] While this kind of dogmatism is a dubious basis for criticism and particularly so when leveled at a play whose comic purpose perhaps precludes such profound racial objectives, there is an undeniable undertone of self-justification which might indeed antagonise the ethnic separatist. More recently, however, Ward has made the real nature of his own commitment abundantly clear.

In August, 1966 he was approached by the *New York Times* and asked to write an article on the role of the Negro in the American theatre. In this article he called for the establishment of a black oriented theatre on the basis that, "If any hope, outside of chance individual fortune, exists for Negro playwrights as a group—or, for that matter, Negro actors and other theatre craftsmen—the most immediate, pressing, practical, absolutely minimally essential active first step is the development of a permanent Negro repertory company." This was to be a "theatre concentrat-

25

ing primarily on themes of Negro life, but also resilient enough to incorporate and interpret the best of world drama."[14] Together with Robert Hooks and Gerald Krone he had already participated in a modest venture along these lines. The Group Theatre Workshop had established a training programme and a production group. Now, with the aid of a substantial grant from the Ford Foundation, he was instrumental in founding the Negro Ensemble Company of which he became artistic director. With this company apparently firmly established perhaps we need no longer fear that writers of the calibre of Loften Mitchell, Ossie Davis and Douglas Turner Ward will go unnoticed by critics for whom the Negro playwright was formerly an unknown quantity.

[1]Loften Mitchell, *A Land Beyond the River* (Cody, 1963).

[2]Loften Mitchell, *Black Drama: The Story of the American Negro in the Theatre* (New York, 1967), p. 180.

[3]*Black Drama*, p. 197.

[4]Ossie Davis. *Purlie Victorious* (New York, n.d.).

[5]Ossie Davis, "Purlie Told Me!" in *Harlem, U.S.A.* ed. John Henrik Clarke, p. 155.

[6]"Purlie Told Me!" p. 152.

[7]Adam David Miller, "It's a Long Way to St. Louis," *The Drama Review*, XII, IV (Summer, 1968), pp. 149-150.

[8]"Purlie Told Me!" pp. 152-153.

[9]*Op. cit.*, p. 156.

[10]*Ibid.*

[11]Douglas Turner Ward, *Happy Ending, Day of Absence* (New York, 1966).

[12]Quoted in the Negro Ensemble Company's Programme for the World Theatre Season at the Aldwych Theatre London, May 1969.

[13]"It's a Long Way to St. Louis," p. 150.

[14]Douglas Turner Ward, "American Theatre: For Whites Only?" *New York Times*, Aug. 14, 1966. Section II, pp. D1, D3.

Lorraine Hansberry

by Jordan Y. Miller

AT ONE TIME in the not so distant past, along about 1959 for instance, it would have been a comparatively routine task to discuss the position of Lorraine Hansberry as a contemporary American dramatist, and to evaluate *A Raisin in the Sun* as a highly significant and inevitable step in the assimilation of the Negro artist into the contemporary theatre. The progress made since Eugene O'Neill's historic departures from established stage stereotypes in the sensational *Emperor Jones*, or the less successful but equally important *All God's Chillun Got Wings*, had been tremendous, if not phenomenal. Had not the authorities in 1924 attempted to close down the latter play on the grounds of the indecent gesture performed by the white actress who, in her affection for her black stage husband, had dared to kiss his hand? Indeed they had, and was it not, at that time, a revelation to discover that such an outrageous act had not brought the universe to an end nor even caused the moral collapse of contemporary society as it was then known? Yes, the Negro throughout the 1930s and 40s was increasingly demonstrated to have dramatic "significance"; it was becoming increasingly possible to admit that he could experience "problems," and that he had, as well, of all things, human emotions and sensitivities which could attract the play-going public and achieve a certain amount of financial return. By 1941 the social indictments of *Native Son*, with its killing of a white girl by its black protagonist, were positive indications that black writers and black subjects had broken many a former barrier protecting what was supposed to be commercially and artistically acceptable around that limited geographical and mostly mythical area called Broadway. Negro talent in writing and performing was actually in modest demand, and the list of plays continued to grow. The sympathetic portrayal in 1944 of a Negro prostitute in *Anna Lucasta,* an early day exploration of the entrance of a Negro family into an exclusive white community in *On Whitman Avenue* in 1946, and the case of the Negro adolescent in *Take a Giant Step* in 1953 accumulated among themselves nearly 1200 performances.

Of course, the one obvious fact remained: the Negro as a dramatic subject, even when being created by a black playwright, was aimed at an audience virtually 100% white. While O'Neill had created a wholly sympathetic character in *All God's Chillun* in Jim Harris, and had dared present interracial love and marriage as potentially tragic material, those who came and witnessed remained, as the theatre audience had always been, almost pure white and, comparatively speaking, upper class. *In Abraham's Bosom* in 1926 showed that Paul Green could, to be sure, stage with forceful impact the pitiful story of a black son of a prosperous Southern white father, and could win a Pulitzer Prize, and that Marc Connelly, winning the same award, could achieve one of the American theatre's most brilliant coups in *The Green Pastures* of 1930. But these were plays by whites for whites. It had to be admitted, however, that, coupled with the later messages of a Richard Wright or Louis Peterson, all of these did seem to indicate that there was slowly developing an important body of "Negro" drama, but a Negro theatre in the true sense of the term was not yet here.

By the time Lorraine Hansberry arrived the social changes which would place her in a logical but unique position as a dramatic artist were being wrought with astonishing speed. Whereas it had taken perhaps 150 years to get society to the place where O'Neill could make his protagonist black,* and a further thirty

---

*Dion Boucicault some 60 years earlier did make Zoe, the one-eighth Negro beauty, the heroine of *The Octoroon,* but she was technically a slave and "blackness" in the sense we speak of it here was not the issue. Not until O'Neill did the American theatre introduce a contemporary Negro character as a full fledged protagonist.

years to crack the separate but equal hypocrisy, now, within months and, often, from day to day, the pattern visibly changed. As Doris Abramson has pointed out in her study of Negro playwrights in America, the late fifties were the years when "imminent integration" seemed likely. As the courts struck down archaic and discriminating laws one after another, the Negro was soon to take his place in the "mainstream" of American life that had been denied him so long. Who, then, could protest? Who, then, would need to use the stage to point the accusing finger at the wrongs of centuries, so rapidly being eliminated? No longer need one rail against the sins of legislated prejudice. Why should any writer, black or white, waste his time arguing causes, when law and the courts were so quickly dissipating them? Emphasis, so it appeared, must now turn from the perpetual black-white conflict and show, instead, the struggles within the racial groups themselves, reflecting the universal human problems of daily life, while relegating the social or ethnic ills to secondary and supporting rank.

This, you see, is why I make my opening statement. The time is appropriate, the circumstances propitious. Enter center stage the young black dramatist with a play so well fitted to the rapidly changing times that its significance almost slips by unnoticed. It is so much a part of the progress of things that one says (in terms of 1959, don't forget) that it is only natural. But to stop and raise the question of just how long the subject matter of *A Raisin in the Sun* has been so "natural" can give more than momentary pause. Consider: A play by a Negro about a contemporary Negro family called the Youngers, though introducing various problems complicated or even caused by the existence of their blackness, causes no more sensation than, say, the play about the Bergers who happened to be Jewish and happened to live during a crippling economic depression whom Clifford Odets wrote about in *Awake and Sing* some twenty-five years earlier. Stepin Fetchit and the minstrels of Amos 'n' Andy are far behind. American audiences stand ready to welcome and to understand the "inside" problem, the "inside" joke, regardless of race, creed, or color. It is the rather heady time of universal appreciation of the monologues of the brilliant Dick Gregory, abandoning the patronizing crudities of what once stood for racial "humor" in the tradition of The Two Black Crows or pre-war radio's Molasses and January. To watch the frailties and failings, the tragedies and conflicts of Lena Younger and her family in an artistic world that ignores the color line, "natural" as it may appear, shows the distance from 1924 to 1959 to be vast indeed.

No longer, of course, is it all this easy. Brown *vs.* Board of Education did not remake the world in quite the fashion once expected. All deliberate speed became agonizingly prolonged rearguard action. In the midst of the rise of the factionalism of the 1960s, the position of Lorraine Hansberry abruptly changes. To explain, a decade after the fact, to a college class in American drama how neatly *A Raisin in the Sun* fits into a logical evolution within the theatre, to justify its dramatic viewpoint, and to praise its creator for her skill in writing a black (we find it increasingly difficult to say Negro, now so widely pejorative) play without "blackness," remaining all the while a black writer who refuses to call attention to the fact, will raise instant challenges. The accusations are many. Is not Lorraine Hansberry an Uncle (Aunt?) Tom? Is not *A Raisin in the Sun* a sellout to the white power structure? Are not the Youngers really betraying themselves and their own? Is not their attempt to assimilate themselves into the white society, and to force themselves, however peacefully, into the neighborhood where they are so obviously unwanted, simply a gratuitous attempt to become white? Will not the material world of the white man force them to subject themselves to even more debasing servility in order to maintain a mere token economic level within it? Therefore, to discuss, to attempt to teach the plays of Lorraine Hansberry in terms of the "colorless" world in which she at one time seemed to belong becomes a greatly complicated matter. To justify what once was regarded as part of a highly favorable development in the commercial theatre now raises spectres of pandering to the white viewpoint, avoiding the inevitable and necessary confrontation. Miss Hansberry, in this light, becomes the progenitor of television's *Julia* or the cinema's *Guess Who's Coming to Dinner,* both anathema to the militant black and white alike. The teacher or critic, particularly if he is white, is faced with a dilemma, for regardless of his views of *A Raisin in the Sun* as drama *per se,* he faces serious questions concerning the position of the black writer in contemporary literature. He is forced into a recognition that, with the plays of LeRoi Jones and those who share his outlook, other values have intruded, and whatever stand he takes regarding the plays of Lorraine Hansberry, it must be stated and defended with care.

At this point, then, we take the following stand. We refuse

to discuss the merits of Miss Hansberry's two plays on the basis of any form of racial consciousness. We are going to avoid any temptation to place them in any niche of "social signficance." In short, we take no sides, and we maintain the right, indeed the critical obligation, to judge them as exceptional pieces of dramatic literature quite apart from any other factors. *A Raisin in the Sun* and *The Sign in Sidney Brustein's Window* are two excellent contemporary plays. They have dramatic appeal and theatrical viability. They introduce attractive characters, and they develop important conflicts. They resolve, and leave unresolved, problems eternally old and eternally new. They are, in short, superior drama. We must express our great admiration for the unique abilities of Miss Hansberry which permit her, as a black writer, to present both a "black" and a "white" play with equal skill, remaining herself permanently in the background. Her human beings and their very human problems speak for themselves. In this way, we maintain, they are socially significant, and we will let it go at that.

And now to the plays themselves.

Structurally, Lorraine Hansberry remains essentially within the bounds of the conventional realistic well-made play, something almost anachronistic amidst the styles of the 1960s. The term "well-made" can be misleading because of its unfortunate connotations with the emptiness of nineteenth century tradition, but we need only look at the plays of a modern dramatist such as Lillian Hellman to recognize that orderly development of plot and a neatly planned series of expository scenes, complications, and climaxes can greatly assist in thematic and character development of a superior nature. Plot in Miss Hansberry's plays is of secondary importance, for it is not her main dramatic purpose. Nonetheless, because the audience has considerable interest in *what* is happening as well as *to whom,* both *A Raisin in the Sun* and *The Sign in Sidney Brustein's Window* are thoroughly enhanced by well-ordered revelation of the events which are so important in the lives of the characters. The straightforward telling of a story remains a thoroughly honorable literary accomplishment, and Miss Hansberry has practiced this ancient dramatic art with eminent respectability. Moreover, the scene, incident, and dialogue are almost Ibsenesque, avoiding overt stylization for its own sake and performed within the standard "box" set that progressively becomes more rare.

To one like myself who welcomes theatrical innovation and will tolerate a lot of nonsense if it has some underlying legitimacy in valid experimentation, it is still a pleasure to experience a play constructed in Miss Hansberry's style, watching fairly "normal" people confront themselves with those around them on the basis not of social revolt and upheaval, nor because of excessive emotional hangups, but on the basis of their fundamental human decency, expressed in commensurately decent language. Those who enter Miss Hansberry's scene may be tarnished as Gloria, corrupt as Wally, irresponsible as Walter Lee, sexually aberrant as David, or exotic as Asagai, but not a single one of them is a case history nor a living symbol of any particular human ill. These are very little people, performing in a world of other little people, and their confusion and their anger have solid basis in their irritations at the refusal of the world to behave the way it should. They never become sentimentally maudlin, for they are not by any means the charmingly impossible nice folk of a Saroyan fantasy. Nor are they in the tradition of Grover's Corners, and they make no happy journeys to Trenton or Camden. On the other hand, inhabiting an essentially sane if not always rational world, they never become the puzzled but game little people of Thurber's wacky universe. They are, in short, attractively and convincingly real people, for whom no excuses are made and none sought.

Lorraine Hansberry's success with her characters is, I think, accomplished through her ability to make us become very very interested in every one of them from the beginning, and as each assumes his identity the interest is consistently maintained. The author's dramatic techniques show up best in the ensemble portrayal of the members of the Younger household and the beneficiaries of the Brustein's open door policy. Each person is clearly individualized and none are able to dominate the others. From the first act awakening of the Younger household to the moment when Walter Lee assumes command of the family move, and from the entrance of the indefatigably optimistic Sidney lugging his cases of restaurant glasses until he and Iris sit numbed and lonely to weep over their sorrow, we have walked closely and in fascination with real people.

John Braine's observation in his Foreword to the Signet edition of *Sidney Brustein* is pertinent in this regard and applies almost equally to *A Raisin in the Sun*. One of the reasons for the restrained critical response to the former, he explains, could well

be the fact that nobody in the entire *dramatis personae* is a super-
numerary; nobody carries the spear or dusts the parlor, each and
every person emerging as a character in his own right, wholly
involved in the events at hand. The critic, says Braine, is bothered
by this aspect and, finding too much evenness and too little indi-
vidual brilliance, he sees nothing to take hold of. Braine is right,
of course, in what he observes, even though one can seriously ques-
tion it as the explanation of a tepid critical reaction. Ensemble
playing, as far back as the days of the Group Theatre, was a source
of consistent critical praise, and it hardly seems likely that ensemble
writing, if that is the term, would cause a lack of enthusiasm. On
the contrary, the beautifully executed patterns of interrelationships
evidenced in both plays are major factors in their attractiveness.
The absence of a hero or a heroine is no flaw, as Chekhov so well
demonstrated. Thus in *Raisin* Hansberry offers us in equal por-
tions Lena, Walter, Ruth, and Beneatha, and though comparatively
undeveloped but hardly of less importance, George Murchison,
Asagai, and of course Linder the white intruder. Nobody in *Sidney
Brustein* remains peripheral. Although Sidney and Iris are on
stage almost continually and it is "their" play, they simply do not
emerge as any more important than the next person. Nobody is
their foil and what they are and what they become are parts of
what Mavis, Alton, David and Gloria are. We must listen to Sid-
ney's ideas more because he talks more, but his affirmation of some
of the more old fashioned values is no more significant in the
play's development than David's revolt against Ibsen or Gloria's
pitiful race toward her own destruction. Who, in either play, has
the most to say? Lena in her nearly shattered dream of better
things for her family? Sidney with his mirage of Appalachian
spring, among other dreams? To whom does the playwright
prefer we listen? Beneatha with her visions of redemption in
Africa? Mavis with her illusion that she can "save" her little
sister? The critics, Braine feels, found it impossible to determine,
and so *A Raisin in the Sun*, as some would have it, is dismissed
as merely a latter day black *Awake and Sing!* and *The Sign in Sid-
ney Brustein's Window* fails in its lack of protagonist.

Miss Hansberry provides ample possibilities to satisfy such
critical reaction. How easy it would be to place, for instance, the
predicament of Walter Lee above all else. Here could so readily
be proclaimed the Cause of the Emasculated Negro, the Plight of
the Matriarch Conditioned Non-Man, forced into modern slavery

behind the wheel of Mr. Whitey's Cadillac. Or how very easy to place Lena Younger in dominant position as the Matriarch Herself. She is full of boundless love, long suffering and enduring, beautiful in soul as well as face, the Uniting Family Force, Strength Personified. Or the long-suffering Ruth, faced with an unwanted increase in family, forced to give her children a home that is a mockery of the word, while holding her husband's family together through the force of her own will, cursing the drudgery of her life as Mrs. Whitey's maid. And above all, why not assign the whole emphasis to the pitiful Case of the Clybourne Park Improvement Association? Here is the heart of the Issue, here the Real Cause. But the playwright will not have it so, for she is far more concerned with the commitment of her characters to finding themselves as individuals and as a family, rather than to the Absolute and Ultimate Confrontation which is so quickly and shockingly brought to their door. The Big Scene is not to be allowed. The helpless Kurt Linder, confounded by Walter's sudden switch, must return empty handed and report, offstage, the failure of his mission. "They" are coming; "they" for some inexplicable reason cannot be bought. "They" are committed and that is all we need to know. The confrontation comes after, and the Youngers will not be those who seek it. It is now up to the Clybourne Park Improvement Association, and we are not permitted to remain to watch. The curtain, instead, has come down.*

The Sign in Sidney Brustein's Window, on the other hand, while lacking the opportunity for the melodramatic moment provided because of the racial theme in *A Raisin in the Sun,* tosses together as separately articulated a group of dramatic "types" as one could want, places them in Greenwich Village where anything can happen and generally does, and proceeds, once more, to blend all together with such evenness that nobody is permitted the privilege of major emphasis. The abrasive and therapeutic action of each upon the other, countered by their abilities, upon occasion, to settle each other's ruffled feathers, keeps the balance and, in Braine's view, the critics disturbed. Miss Hansberry mixes everyone into a potentially explosive collage of characters, but try as one may, one cannot cite a single one of the many fine scenes

---

*See the chapter on Lorraine Hansberry in C. W. E. Bigsby's *Confrontation and Commitment* (Univ. of Missouri Press, 1968) which discusses the two plays in terms of this aspect of commitment.

as better than another. Sidney's justified reprimand of David for insisting that only his own kind are the beautiful sufferers is truly a highlight, but equally so is Alton's shocked discovery of Gloria's profession and the revelation of his own reverse prejudices. Then there is Mavis' horribly confused moment when she recognizes the sinister meaning of her feelings that it is better for Gloria to continue on the streets than to bring into the family an in-law who is black. Surely one should note the charming, touching idyll when Iris and Sidney play out their hopeless romantic fantasy as dawn illuminates the Brustein front stoop, or Sidney's embarrassingly tasteless attempt to bribe David into writing a part for Iris in return for favorable reviews. And finally, as Sidney, like Walter Lee in facing Linder, turns on Wally perhaps we have The Big Scene, but is not the chilling display of Sidney's sodden disinterest in Gloria's desperate plea for help just as "Big"?

If this form of dramatic structure is so seriously flawed as to bother the viewers of *Sidney Brustein,* I fail to see it. There are high points as well as low, and the uniformity of emphasis on character does not by any means prevent the development of a satisfactory dramatic rhythm. This sort of writing, like the appeal of Chekhov or some of Odets, may not exactly be everybody's cup of tea, but it meets the author's requirements for what the plays are designed to do. Of course, *A Raisin in the Sun,* as has been noted, is not quite the same, with the lesser characters such as Asagai comparatively undeveloped. But Asagai serves to provide Beneatha a dream as important in its way as Walter Lee's liquor store, and he remains absorbed in his own idealism regarding his homeland, standing considerably outside the Younger family's immediate preoccupations.

If any segment of Hansberry's well-made play technique is open to question it could well be the *deus ex machina* of the $10,000 insurance check in *A Raisin in the Sun.* The inclination to cringe at the thought of fortunes that turn up in old socks or discarded coats, or arrive from long lost relatives is natural; even the better playmakers of hardly half a century back relied too heavily upon such tricks. The situation here, however, is saved by the expedient of setting all the action after the fact, so that to condemn the insurance check is, to all intents and purposes, to condemn the entire play. The insurance money is expected and cannot under any circumstance serve as the sudden reverser of fortune which the routine 19th century meller would demand. This god has descended from his vehicle *before* the opening curtain. He appears as no last act messenger from the king, but instead arrives with ample warning and departs to leave his beneficiaries to work out how wisely they may now make use of their modest wealth. Oh, I suppose it's true that a case might be made against the money's introduction in this manner. A more challenging dramatic situation involving the rise of the Youngers from slum to suburb might be imagined were the action to center on something less reminiscent of the good fairy's offer of three wishes, all grossly misused as the moral is made of human inability to react sensibly to good fortune. This seems a specious argument when the situation is more carefully considered. Husbands do die and insurance checks do arrive. Since this is not a play denouncing the debilitating effects of the husbandless-fatherless Negro household, there is no reason to assume but that Big Walter had, at one time, been the head of the house. His income had been sufficient to maintain a policy of this size, a rather substantial amount of protection given the conditions in which the Younger family have always lived. Their dreams of leaving the Southside had been long deferred, but it had been a decent life, and the family is still together in relatively good shape. So why *not* a $10,000 policy?

Maybe the argument should be against the method of disposal. Why did not Lena choose another option, a guaranteed monthly income, for instance, instead of $10,000 cash? Knowing what that amount of hard cash in hand can do to end the dream's deferment at once, when wisely used, why should she? Once in hand, the money's disposition also falls within the prerogative, an admittedly arbitrary prerogative at that, of the playwright, who now comes face to face with the dilemma that confronts any dramatist who chooses a situation like this; namely, that whatever choice is made, it will be open to serious question as a dramatically sound step. There are two fundamental choices to make, once an item as large and important as this amount of money has been introduced on stage. It is like the pistol in the first act. We know it is there. We have seen it, and we anticipate its use. To what end it will be put remains to be seen, but we know that it must enter into the action in one of two ways. It will be fired by the good guys, or it will be fired by the bad guys. It can't, because of its highly theatrical nature, do anything else, and however it is used will affect the outcome of the play. Willy, nilly, the author will be accused of plot manipulation. So we know that either the money will be wisely used, or it will not; and thereby either it will bring the Youngers an opportunity to accomplish things their color and economic status have previously denied them, or it will not. Lena has not chosen a monthly income, and we know it won't be put back in the bank merely to be looked at. It will act, and it becomes one of the most powerful objects on stage. Which way shall the dramatist go?

Back to the previous analogy of the gun, we can say the gun misfires. It serves its purpose, yet it fails. The hero is held at bay, but his life is saved when the bullet does not go off, or, on the other hand, the villain is temporarily checked, only to leap with renewed violence into the struggle when the hammer merely clicks. In any event, no matter what the result, the gun did not remain quiescent in the drawer. What it did to those encountering it depended entirely on the author's wishes, and however arbitrary the choice, the question to be answered is how well justified it ultimately stands revealed.

Like the misfired pistol, the misuse of the money results in compromise between the two possible extremes, but still retains much of the impact. Lena has had the good sense to make the down payment on the house first, but in full keeping with her character, she turns the rest over to her son. Misguided, but a trust that must be shown if Walter Lee is ever to climb out of his personal impasse. Walter Lee, then, in a second series of choices, will do right, or he will do wrong. In his desperation to become the bread-winner and to achieve some of the status of his father, his childish and bullheaded monomania about the liquor store is dramatically valid, placing the instant loss of the remaining $6,500 in believable perspective. Keeping the thief himself permanently offstage, the author makes use of the disaster to assist Walter in his assumption of his new dignity. Unable to blame anyone but himself for what he has done (society, economics, The Man, cannot be accused in the face of the repeated warnings given), he can now scorn Mr. Lindner and his Improvement friends in an entirely fitting climatic scene. Though each member of the household is probably faced with even increased drudgery and humiliation, for the real struggle to survive in Clybourne Park is yet to come, the important factor is that the dream is no longer deferred, and now, in its greatly weakened form, must be more vigorously defended than ever. To the stunned Youngers, there is no doubt it will be worth it.

The great miracle of *A Raisin in the Sun* is, I firmly believe, that Lorraine Hansberry has presented one of the most volatile of our society's problems, telling it precisely "like it is," within the most conventional of dramatic frameworks, without rancor and without violence. The play *is* a problem play, and the problem is blackness in a white society. The underlying humanity of the characters, however, and the decency of their struggle because and in spite of their blackness, will prevent the dream from drying up. The heavy load has not, as yet, been dropped, and as the Youngers move into Clybourne Park it will become heavier still. But that is another play entirely.

In 1964 with *The Sign in Sidney Brustein's Window* Lorraine Hansberry became more than a black playwright in the American theatre. She stood apart as an important American playwright who happened to be black. This play, even more than *A Raisin in the Sun*, would also place her completely outside the world of racial dogma and protest, for it had even less of a social bone to pick than her first. Because of her most untimely death at 34, one can only speculate to what distances she might have gone. This second play had shown plainly that *A Raisin in the Sun* was not an accident and that she was a dramatist of considerable skill whose sense of theatre, notwithstanding race, ethnic identification or social background, was superb.

The Sign in Sidney Brustein's Window did not succeed in the commercial sense, and short of extended revival it must remain as one of those *successes* d'estimes which earn little or no royalties and constantly frustrate their creators as well as those who seek and support a theatre of high artistic integrity. It is a charming, delightful, and touching play, and furthermore, it is a very moral play. In its straightforward old-fashioned way, *Sidney Brustein* goes somewhere, says something, and arrives at a conclusion, all of which seems, in the midst of the turmoil of the 1960s, a mighty good way to have it.

The play fits very comfortably into the category I like to call the Comedy of Sensibility, an invention, I believe, more or less my own but which I find more suitable to plays of this sort than "social drama," "thesis play" or even that self-contradictory if highly pedigreed "tragi-comedy." To use the word "tragedy" in the definition of a play that happens to turn into comedy by means of a happy ending always struck me as a little foolish. Instead, I prefer to point to plays like *The Sign in Sidney Brustein's Window*, a fundamentally comic play with the most serious of overtones, as a very special kind of drama called the comedy of sensibility.

Comedy in all forms is based upon the continual reminder that human beings are ridiculously fallible creatures, far from the gods which they all too often aspire to become. Thus the comic character is never quite what he hopes to be, and he is constantly brought emphatically back to his basic humanity by becoming aware of his gravitational and emotional instability through the devices of everything from crude pratfalls to the most sophisticated of wit. There is no doubt but that the characters of *Sidney Brustein* are comic, for they are human, they are attractive, and they are constantly made aware of their human shortcomings. Furthermore, their comic nature keeps us from becoming sentimentally involved with them, while at the same time our emotional response to them is directed toward a refined sensitiveness, with especial attention to their pathetic nature — in short, they arouse our sensibilities. There is complete lack of contrivance for emotional effect, for in a comedy of this type, a product of modern realism, we are dealing with factors of reality which may include, as does this play, intense discomfort and even death. The tears that are shed are tears of compassion, but all is underlain with the awareness of the goodness of the characters, their very ordinary humanity and, thereby, their truly comic nature.

The comedy of sensibility, then, becomes a play of character far more than one of plot or theme. It favors, almost always, those little, ordinary people that inhabit Lorraine Hansberry's play. Except for David's momentary public attention as a promising playwright, and Wally's victory, soon to be swallowed up by the devouring political machine, the effects of the forces moving around these people are back page news. That gross and inappropriate, and finally bitterly ironic sign that disfigures the Brustein's front window no doubt had little effect on anybody, and will soon be forgotten.

Since those who walk so freely in and out of the Brustein's attractively cluttered apartment are of little significance in the way the world turns (how right is Sidney's pointed observation to David in this regard) they are going to have to be made significant to those who watch if the play is to have any meaning at all. What we have, I think, is a significant look at ourselves. Most of us regard ourselves as pretty decent people, and so do those in Sidney Brustein's house. Most of us have rather firm beliefs that our ways of looking at things are probably better than anybody else's, though, of course, we are candid enough to know we cannot deny that we are willing to learn. That act of learning, however, as we ourselves know and as we witness in Sidney's friends and family, can be a bothersome and disturbing business. Unhappily it just may force us to look a lot closer at ourselves than we might like to admit is necessary. It will take for many of us a blow as severe as Wally's defection to crack our idealistic views about ourselves, to bring us down to a realization that signs and slogans won't change the world. Sidney Brustein does not, of course, "deserve" this blow any more than any of us nice people would deserve it. And for the Irises in us, perhaps more tolerance, less offense at such harmless habits as Sidney's infatuation with his wife's long hair. Cutting it off, painting our faces, buying the favors of the lecherous casting director won't help either the Irises or the Sidneys. Thoughout the play runs that constant plea to make the important and painful elements of others' lives a bit more important to ourselves, with the companion warning that there is considerably more to life than our own narrow visions. It's all been said many times before, and Miss Hansberry discovers absolutely nothing new, but her ability to make use of the varied group of individuals she pulls together to say it makes the renewal well worth the effort.

"Let's forget we *absolutely love mankind*," says Sidney in his opening dialogue with Alton. "Don't venerate, don't celebrate, don't hallow what you take to be — the human spirit. . . . Presume no commitment, disavow all engagement, mock all great expectations." By the final curtain, Sidney has come to know how wrong this outlook is. He and Iris together then realize, too late, that no defeat is so important that the Glorias in our lives are allowed to die in the bathroom while we weep in our beer for the hurt somebody did us.

Two plays only, the total product of Lorraine Hansberry, playwright.* We owe her a great deal, for she demonstrated that a good old fashioned play is worth having around. She showed us that good people are worth knowing on the stage, and that the struggles to live with pride and dignity are worth it. If the world of art — the world itself — is to survive as a going concern, it is going to have to take people for what they are and the polarization of clichés and slogans, color and economic status will have to give way. Lorraine Hansberry has shown a good direction to follow.

---

*With the exception of her posthumous work, *Les Blancs*.

James Baldwin's "Agony Way"

by Walter Meserve

DURING A YOUTH which held little pleasure, James Baldwin found that writing was one means for self-satisfaction. As a writer, for example, he could be racially anonymous. Except as the writer chose to reveal himself, his readers could not tell the color of his skin. It was also a kind of consolation for a sensitive and imaginative person. Alone and full of fear for the world he saw, writing for James Baldwin, as he looked back at his youth, became a way to live, an attempt to be loved. He summed up his life at this early time as "the agony way," and he liked that phrase so well that he scribbled it wherever he went — on paper, on walls, in the air. Because he has mainly written about himself, the thought permeates his work; and today he still seems self-branded as one who sees both his life and his work as "the agony way."

Pointedly ambitious in his desire to be a writer, Baldwin worked hard to be successful when neither his education, which was inadequate, nor his "accident of birth" into real poverty would have led one to suspect his career. Yet those who knew him in childhood expected him to be a writer. When still in high school, he observed: "If I am to be a playwright, I should try to improve a troubled world, and try to be numbered among the great artists of my race." The fact that he equated playwriting with improving a troubled world explains his theory of drama quite clearly. It may also explain why he is not a better playwright and why he has not written more plays. While the theatre brings the most immediate response for the propagandist; it also brings adverse criticism which has always been painful for Baldwin. Although his playwriting ranged over ten or twelve years, his experiences in the professional theatre were limited to two years (1964-65), and he has not returned. It is perhaps vital to note that although he used similar theses and argued the same points in his fiction and in his plays, he used different major characters in his plays which essentially remove Baldwin, his own model-hero, from the center of the work. For some reason the drama forces him to change his attitude toward his material.

Considering his career in *Notes of a Native Son*, Baldwin wrote: "I wanted to be an honest man and a good writer." He has, however, had his problems. The idea that "nobody cares" showed both his sense of betrayal and the absence of love which were his "agony way" while "Nobody Knows My Name" became his *cri de coeur*. His response was to describe his own problems in life and to suggest an attitude of responsibility so effectively that he became, in the words of Langston Hughes, "the white-haired black boy of America." Considered both a gifted writer and a spokesman for his race, Baldwin found himself with an international reputation. But that articulately rebellious spirit which rose from fear and loneliness to bring him success could not escape certain fears. Although emphasizing the Negro cause and his own outrage, he still remained a human being who did not love all Blacks and hate all Whites. He wanted to be honest, and he wanted to be loved, but his writings could not do both for him. Consequently, his life has remained an "agony way." Because one can be more personal in a narrative and more distant from critics, fiction will probably remain his major interest.

Whether he is writing fiction or drama, however, Baldwin has parlayed a youthful "agony" into a philosophic view of life. Whatever form he uses, certain attitudes and ideas relative to the "agony way" are dominant. Religion was basic in his first novel, *Go Tell It on the Mountain*, and in his first play, *The Amen Corner*. In the opening scene of the play Sister Margaret, the evangelistic leader of her flock, is fervently preaching: "Set thine house in order, for thou shalt die and not live." Then the action of the play reveals her own problems as her son, David, leaves to go out into the world, the husband that she deserted returns to die and bring confusion to her religious life, and her flock reads her out of the church. At the end of the play, it is as an understanding and loving person that she excels rather than as a religious leader. Religion in the form which overwhelmed Baldwin's youth and even made him a preacher does not hold the answers for Margaret or for David. It is also significant that the victim-hero of *Blues for Mister Charlie* is, like Baldwin, the son of a preacher. Although Meridian, the minister-father, speaks as forcefully as he can, he recognizes only too clearly an impotence which Baldwin felt in his own family. Instead of supplying the answers that the youthful Baldwin was led to admire and to expect, the church can only ask questions and hold out to man the agony of Christian suffering.

Baldwin's attitude toward his own father is reflected throughout his art, but perhaps it can be shown most successfully with reference to *Blues for Mister Charlie*. During the rehearsal period Baldwin had some difficulty getting the cast to reach the exact meaning which he found in the play, and one result was his fourteen page written analysis of his work. The play, of course, was based on the Emmett Till case. Richard, the son of the Negro minister, returns to his home town after several years up North, rebels at the attitude of the Southerners concerning Negroes and particularly at the flagrant denial of justice when his mother was "accidentally" killed some years past. Offensive in his relationship with white people, Richard is killed. In the subsequent trial of the known murderer various voices for race problems are presented, but the liberal white is defeated, the killer exonerated, justice denied. In his analysis Baldwin clarified Richard's character in one statement: "His father has betrayed him." Certainly, Baldwin seemed to feel this way about his own father. Although the plea from the father, Luke, in *The Amen Corner* is meaningful, his son, David, also feels betrayed.

The major problem in the "agony way" is one of identity. A variety of critics have pointed this out in studies of Baldwin and his work, and Baldwin himself has been very much aware of his problem ever since he wrote his early "Paris Letter" for the *Partisan Review,* July, 1954: "A Question of Identity." In this charming and somewhat innocent essay Baldwin was concerned with himself not so much as a Negro or even as an American but as a man. As numerous others did after World War II, even though he did not participate in it, he went to Europe looking for that affirmation which comes from self-questioning and eventually brings individual maturity. From the vantage point of Europe he discovered something of his own personality. But this was only a beginning to his own search which, he suggests in his latest work (*Tell Me How Long the Train's Been Gone*, 1968), is still continuing: "and so found myself [Leo Proudhammer], presently, standing in the wings again, waiting for my cue."

The significance of his continuing search for an identity or for a certain meaning in life may be clearly seen in the major themes of his works as well as his own numerous activities. He is clearly a man of great sensitivity who wants to be loved for what he is and for what he says. This is obvious from his early comments on the "agony way" and his stated objective as a writer. All of his heroes show this need for love from John in *Go Tell It on the Mountain* to David in *The Amen Corner*, Richard in *Blues for Mister Charlie*, Rufus in *Another Country* or Leo Proudhammer. In a story published in *Cornhill, Spring*, 1961, "This Morning, This Evening, So Soon," Baldwin, masquerading as an internationally successful movie star, reflects on his own discovery of "who I am" and agrees on the goodness of one who believes in love. Richard in *Blues* has also ironically found himself just before he is killed, and the love he feels for Juanita is largely responsible. Sister Margaret in *The Amen Corner* finally learns that "to love the Lord is to love all His children — all of them, everyone!" The first line that Baldwin wrote for her was: "It's an awful thing to think about, the way love never dies!" "How can you live if you can't love?" asks Vivaldo in *Another Country;* "and how can you live if you do?" Love was a paradox for Baldwin, and it was also the major answer he found for his "troubled world." It is one of the few "positive affirmations" which his characters discover. Hope is another, but it is a hope for love. Meridian in *Blues* shows this. A belief in the value of suffering is a third possibility for a Baldwin sensitive hero. Cass in *Another Country* confesses that she is "beginning to think that growing just means learning more and more and more about anguish;" Vivaldo declares, hopefully, that "suffering doesn't *have* a color." The triumph that Sister Margaret finally reaches is an acceptance through suffering of the loss of her old, fiery but false self and the revelation of her new selfless love. Juanita in *Blues* asks, "Must we always suffer so?" and Meridian can only answer that they must all bear their burdens. For Baldwin the revelation of Christian suffering and an idealized personal love are necessary human affirmations? He believes in love as an individual, in art and life; through it he finds an identity.

Unfortunately, such a simplistic approach to life does not always brings him the response that he himself needs in contemporary life. And there are other reasons why Baldwin lacks complete personal satisfaction. Because he is honest, he feels that he must also say unpleasant things. *Blues for Mister Charlie* was written, he has said, to shock people and upset them. Because he passionately believes what he writes and what he says in lectures, he is extremely sensitive to criticism. His statement that he does not hate all Whites infuriates the Black Militants whom he both fears and respects. Yet quite honestly he sees the disaster that hatred brings to man and has vowed "to keep my own heart free of hatred and despair." At the same time and because he senses betrayal in his own attitudes he fears writing what may be interpreted as a betrayal of his own race. One important result of the agony which Baldwin feels in his position as an artist and spokesman for his race is a strong ambivalence in his writing. In his very recent (1968) introduction to *The Amen Corner* he makes his duality very clear. Sister Margaret needs both "human affirmation" and vengeance; she finds love at the mercy of terror.

Ambivalence is perhaps a logical retreat for an insecure person, but it is a very revealing artistic device throughout Baldwin's writing. Although Baldwin admits to a definite commitment toward preaching during his early youth, he became less certain about life in his late teens and twenties. His quest for an identity began and in some ways was satisfied during his time in Europe, but, as his writings have appeared, he seems to have become progressively less certain, more ambivalent in his life as well as his art. As a member of the Establishment and a respected writer, he remains something of a mercurial person. In *The Furious Passage of James Baldwin* Fern Eckman describes him as a sulphurous person, still pursuing life, both remorseful and exultant, insecure in his work as well as his everyday life, difficult to pin down, paranoid under pressure. Tired of writing about social issues, he seems unable to look in any other direction. Counseling peace, he suggests violence. Frequently, he talks about his fears ("I've always been afraid."), but he can also be arrogantly defensive. Although the feeling of religious betrayal (institutional and father determined) is obvious in much of his work, there is also a strong dependence on religion and the church, particularly in his plays. As an artist he finds a dilemma because he is essentially a humanitarian poet, concerned with man rather than race. Forced, however, by society as well as his own subject matter to be a spokesman for his race, he feels a compunction to do battle for the Negro. Yet he wants mainly to be treated as a man, as do the heroes in his plays and stories, and to be an honest writer. Many critics point out Baldwin's fusion of race and sex, both treated in his works with considerable violence. Perhaps race and sex most effectively illustrate that ambivalence toward life which becomes more dominant as he writes. The Negro, as Baldwin presents him (and lived himself) is used ambivalently in both race and sex. Rufus was used by men and women; Richard, too; and Leo Proudhammer explains that he is "bisexual." Racially, also, Baldwin sees himself ambivalently — as both Black and White.

Although less successful artistically and financially as a dramatist than as a writer of stories, Baldwin still lives and writes the "agony way." Using race, sex, violence, and his own perceptive understanding of human nature, he has attempted to use the drama for his own purposes. In fact, one of his strong attitudes since his youth is that he wants to do things, but on his own terms. Unfortunately, his relationship with theatre has not always been a happy one because there he was forced to work with people equally certain that their terms were best. The result has been frustrating for Baldwin who enjoys the feeling that he would make a fine actor and in *Tell Me How Long the Train's Been Gone* presents his self-hero (Leo Proudhammer) as a successful actor. Baldwin's attitude toward acting, however, is one reason why he writes the kind of plays he does. The preacher and the actor, he feels, are extremely close, and it is certainly true that Baldwin tries to use the theatre as a pulpit for his ideas. Mainly his plays are thesis plays — talky, over-written, and cliché dialogue and some stereotypes, preachy, and argumentative. Essentially, Baldwin is not particularly dramatic, but he can be extremely eloquent, compelling, and sometimes irritating as a playwright committed to his approach to life.

With both of his published plays — *The Amen Corner* and *Blues for Mister Charlie* — Baldwin had great difficulty getting his work onto the professional stage or keeping it there. Written in 1954 and first performed at Howard University, *The Amen Corner* was not produced professionally until 1964 when Frank Silvera produced it in Los Angeles where it ran for nearly a year. There

Nat King Cole saw the play and began arrangements for a Broadway production which were completed by Mrs. Cole after the great and much-loved singer's death by cancer. It was then 1965. *Blues for Mister Charlie* had opened on April 23, 1964, at the ANTA theatre, and been kept open after a month only through a $10,000 gift by the Rockefeller sisters, closing finally on August 29, 1964. Part of the problem with *Blues* was Baldwin, part the play. With an eye to playwriting since a young age, Baldwin was further stimulated to work in the theatre by his friendship with Marlon Brando and a quick dramatization of his novel, *Giovanni's Room*, which was done by the Actor's Studio Workshop. Then in late 1958 he gathered more theatre experience by following Elia Kazan through his direction of Archibald MacLeish's *J.B.* and Tennessee Williams' *Sweet Bird of Youth*. By the time *Blues for Mister Charlie* went into rehearsal, Baldwin had many ideas about the theatre which he proudly asserted. He quarrelled with Lee Strasberg, scrapped with the Actors' Studio Theatre, didn't like the "method," changed directors to Burgess Meredith, insisted on casting his brother David, wrote his fourteen page analysis of the play, and generally haunted the theatre. It was a long play, but Baldwin felt that if O'Neill could get away with great length, so could he. When the flashbacks were criticized as confusing, Baldwin remained adamant, relenting only after the play was in production and never seeing the play in chronological order. He seems to have been as determined an experimenter as he was a preacher, and neither has been easily accepted in the theatre.

Critical reaction to both plays was reserved. Reviewers saw Baldwin's eloquence and his potential. They commented favorably on his ability to electrify his audience with *Blues,* his originality in *The Amen Corner,* and his familiarity with his material. But the critics also showed their disappointment with certain clichés of character and language which Baldwin used and in his inability to raise his polemic to the level of universal art. With all criticism in mind, however, one could conclude that Baldwin was certainly encouraged as a playwright, although the production run was not sufficient to make him much of a reputation as a playwright. Essentially, he remains a journalist and a writer of fiction who has made two rather widely spaced ventures into the theatre.

Although Baldwin's plays remain largely thesis or propaganda plays with eloquently preached theses and controlled views of Negro society, they are still plays with the structure and devices of the theatre. Baldwin is certainly not ignorant of the art of the theatre, but neither is he always effective in creating theatrical excitement, probably because he accepts too readily the idea of playwright as polemicist. Too often, he looks at his actors as preachers and presents little action on the stage. His major characters have inner conflicts which he has as much difficulty externalizing as he does making their inner struggles meaningful. He is, however, very clearly concerned with the visual scene on the stage and the various means by which he can achieve an emotional effect upon his audience through both eye and ear. In *The Amen Corner*, for example, the stage is divided. Stage right is the church, dominated by the pulpit and the open Bible; stage left shows Sister Margaret's apartment kitchen and the small bedroom in which Luke dies. It is a divided life for Margaret and the other major characters who must live in both the church of their creation and the world that faces them otherwise. The set for *Blues for Mister Charlie* exhibits another division; but whereas the set of *The Amen Corner* showed a personal conflict, this set indicates public and racial conflict. Here the stage is both a Negro church (acts one and two) and a courthouse (act three) divided by a southern street which also functions as an aisle of the church and the division between Whitetown and Blacktown. Throughout the first two acts of this play one must always be conscious of the courthouse dome and its American flag as ironic symbols of justice and national unity, while in act three the steeple of the church with its cross suggests another hope. This use of contrasting scenes effectively supports the themes in his play and suggests something of Baldwin's potential in the theatre.

The devices by which Baldwin excites emotion in his audience also deserve comment. His command of language has always been clear from his fiction, but his use of dialogue has been memorable mainly for its violence. Chiefly he has relied upon brief dialogue, vivid exposition, and narrative monologues. Monologues, of course, are not generally effective in drama, but with the exception of sermons in each play, he has avoided them. His dialogue on the other hand, tends either to be argumentative or polemical rather than dramatically related to action. A major problem, however, is his limited ability to fuse meaningful action and dialogue with developing character. Instead, he tries to keep things moving with numerous brief scenes, many of which are flashbacks to previous action, and a scattering of songs. Although the use of songs in *The Amen Corner* is overdone, the idea for creating the proper emotional feeling is a good one. In *Blues* Baldwin used a choral effect for Whitetown and Blacktown during the courtroom scene that added to the creation of the desired emotional reaction. In these and other ways Baldwin shows some natural talent for the theatre in spite of his limited experience with some of the more demanding aspects of the drama.

Although Baldwin has been criticized for creating stereotypes, his major characters are the most successful and memorable aspects of his plays. People are important to Baldwin, and their problems, generally embedded in their agonizing souls, stimulate him to write plays. A humanitarian, sensitive to the needs and struggles of man, he writes of inner turmoil, spiritual disruption, the consequence upon people of the burdens of the world, both White and Black. Action is shown to be less important in his plays than thought. The murder of Richard in *Blues* is accomplished very quickly and immediately as a stimulating force for the developing problems in the play. Even in the climactic scene the flashback to the murder is very brief. It is not the central issue in the play. Other opportunities for violence in the fight between Lyle and Richard are passed over quickly; other violence in the past is narrated — which may be less effective in the theatre but shows clearly Baldwin's interests. The same is true for *The Amen Corner*. Confrontation between Sister Moore and Sister Margaret when the former assumes control of the flock is handled briefly and effectively. Luke dies without great agony; David leaves in a scene of inner rather than outward turmoil. With Baldwin, the playwright, people are his major concern.

In Baldwin's novels and plays the characters which represent his own position are always young — aspects of his own youthful past: John in *Go Tell It on the Mountain*, David in *The Amen Corner*, Rufus in *Another Country*, Richard in *Blues for Mister Charlie*, Leo Proudhammer in *Tell Me How Long the Train's Been Gone*. Even though Leo in the last mentioned work is a mature man in the present scene of the novel, most of the action described is from his past, and nowhere is the distinction between ambitious past and frustrating present more dramatically presented than in this work. All of those youthful heroes are rebels; and, as Baldwin presents them, they feel their betrayal, they leave home to go into the world, they commit suicide, they are murdered, or they live to a fearful and frustrating middle age. In the agonizing life that Baldwin sees, each hero presents an aspect of his own past. Even the careers that each covets — preacher, pianist, writer, actor — show his own passion for artistry that is personally creative.

It is interesting, however, that the characters which suggest the youthful rebellion in society, Negro society — those young heroes in whom one sees Baldwin expressing his own past — are not the main characters in his plays. David is not the central character in *The Amen Corner*; it is his mother, Sister Margaret, who forces life, makes a discovery, and becomes a better person. David simply reacted to the stimuli around him, sensed the truth in his father's words, and left. The audience knows relatively little about him, and he functions in the play to show the necessity of going into the world, of being a man. His decision to leave simply prepares the audience for Sister Margaret's more significant discovery and decision at the climax. But the play belongs to the mother, the older person with greater problems. The same is true in *Blues for Mister Charlie*. Although the play is based on the Emmett Till murder, the major character is not the rebellious Richard Henry, the Emmett Till figure. Instead, Richard becomes a catalyst for making both Whites and Blacks aware of a horrible situation. His part is substantial, and he does make a discovery before he is killed, in which love and understanding are involved. But this is minor in the play, although most significant to a hopeful Baldwin; and Richard has neither the problems nor the suffering of the older people in the play. Presented much more fully are Parnell, the White liberal, and Meridian, Richard's father. At the end of the play Meridian has developed most significantly, made the crucial discovery of his life, and is determined toward a direction in which there is hope. For Baldwin, the playwright, youth seems to provide the stimulus necessary to move the older generation to action, but in his plays it is this older generation which has the problems and must devise solutions and face consequences. Baldwin, the novelist, gives major emphasis to youthful characters.

The importance of religious and father figures in these plays and Baldwin's understanding mastery in their creation shows Baldwin's ironic dependence upon Christian love as a solution as well as his insistent hope for the Black man's ability to discover who he is and what he must do. Modeled after Mother Horn, an evangelist whom Baldwin knew in his youth, Sister Margaret is a finely drawn character who recognizes her dilemma and triumphs in her discovery. The thesis of the play is set with the subject of her sermon in the first act: set thine house in order! With zeal born of a fiery evangelist, Sister Margaret is certain of herself, while others in the flock are not as convinced, particularly Sister Moore whose virginity makes her pure compared with Margaret whose husband left her. Margaret's limited and biased view of life appears when she advises a distressed woman to leave her husband. Another factor pointing toward a disturbance in the house is David's secretive attitude about his whereabouts the previous night. Then Luke, the husband who has been gone many years, appears, worn out and sick. Unable to avoid him, Sister Margaret is forced to admit that she left him, rather than the opposite which she has always maintained. Even though his drinking and other activities drove her to the action, she has now faced one truth about herself. In act two Luke tells David the one thing that Baldwin believes: man needs someone to love him. That the church does not provide this is clearly shown by the gossiping and politicking members of Sister Margaret's flock. Left together, Luke and Margaret reveal their separate reasons for their actions and their need for love. Here Luke is the strongest. He sees the need for David to live and the weakness of Margaret's religion. Essentially, she must change in her beliefs, and the basis for this change is accomplished in this act. Unfortunately for Margaret's character development, Luke's strength and her weakness in this act make her decision and change less dramatically effective in the final act of the play.

Act three is Margaret's act and comparatively strong in spite of the fact that she has had only one night to think over her past. She can't say "Amen" anymore, the word which means "Thy will be done"; and all of the action prepared for in acts one and two collapses upon her. The woman whom she advised to leave her husband returns to revile her advice. David appears and voices her fears: "I want to be a man. It's time you let me be a man. You got to let me go." The opposition in her church has taken her pulpit. Going to Luke, she declares her love just before he dies, and then she faces the congregation. Now, however, this defeat means very little because she has discovered that one must love, and suffer, and rejoice and never count the cost. She removes her white robe, the symbol of her pure office, and goes to the bedroom where she falls on the bed beside Luke. Although the compression of time for her discovery is as artificial as Luke's ghostly arrival and death and David's rather immediate decision and departure, Sister Margaret has the potential for a moving and complete woman. Essentially she reveals a basic Baldwin belief, but she does so with a certain eloquence and poignancy.

Meridian (whose name shows his philosophical position) and Parnell in *Blues for Mister Charlie* are also well-drawn individuals showing Baldwin's commitment. Both are pathetic, both represent agonizing positions in the modern world; but both share the meaningful struggles that such people must face. Meridian is a Christian who wants the murderer to know that what he did was evil; he wants "this town to be forced to face the evil that it countenances and to turn from evil and do good." But Meridian also recognizes his social impotence. At Richard's funeral at the end of act two he can only plead: "Let not our suffering endure forever." At the trial in act three he shows the same difficulty with Christianity that Richard had, but he still talks of freedom for both races, "a people so free in themselves that they will have no need to fear." By the end of the play, he has a gun in his pulpit, under the Bible, like the Pilgrims. Sister Margaret asked to be able to begin again. Meridian keeps the strength of his religion and tries to relate it to the situation. Parnell is the humanitarian liberal who loves both Black and White. Caught in a position where he must deny his entire culture by testifying that the wife of a close friend, Lyle, the murderer, has lied, he fails. Lyle is acquitted, and Parnell could have brought true justice. Many times Baldwin has suggested that at the root of the Negro problem is the necessity of the White man to find a way of living with the Negro in order to live with himself. Parnell symbolizes this situation of the White man "sick with a disease only white man can catch, Blackness." Although in speeches Baldwin has called the white liberal the *affliction* of the Negro, for Parnell he allows grace and pathos. As the Negroes move toward their church at the end of the play, Parnell asks Juanita, the Negro who loved Richard and whom he also loves: "Can I walk with you?" And she answers symbolically: "Well, we can walk in the same direction, Parnell. Come. Don't look like that. Let's go on."

Unlike *The Amen Corner* where the entire thesis of the play is lodged in one character, *Blues* has no single character, no strong single action which determines the climax. A man is killed; a murderer is freed; life goes on. The lack of a strong discovery suggests something of the weak structure of the play whose climax comes with a scatter gun effect and propaganda interest. Richard wants to live, and his murder, repeated in a flashback in the final moments of the play, could have been more effective had Richard not become a stereotype at this moment and reverted to Baldwin's often repeated cliché of the superiority of black women to white women in his last accusation of Lyle. Lyle also stands on a stereotype: "I had to kill him then. I'm a white man!" All that remains is a minister with a gun, a pathetic white liberal, and a forward-looking Negro girl. People are still the most important aspect of a play for Baldwin who split his climax among several in the play.

With only two plays to judge, it is perhaps presumptuous to draw conclusions about a dramatist's art. From the existing evidence, however, one may say that Baldwin emphasizes character and inner conflict more than external conflict, uses argument in language rather than deed, and shows little interest in suspense or surprise. A well-built plot is not a strong point of Baldwin's art either in the drama or the novel. There is, however, a certain inevitability in his plays as they build to a climax in a manner which stops and fills. Because Baldwin is primarily concerned with ideas, emotionally projected, his characters have long speeches and arguments which slow the action. Avoiding crowds, his strongest scenes are those with two people facing an issue together and reaching some conclusion. Undoubtedly feeling his deficiency in creating meaningful action, he tries to add to the drama by changing scenes frequently, using flashbacks, and inserting music. All have their effect, but they do not compensate for other weaknesses. For lack of plot, intrigue, action, and suspense, there develop very few crises in Baldwin's plays. He has meaningful curtains in terms of his pleading messages, but they lack dramatic effect in that no surprise, no suspense, no crisis is introduced or anticipated. Instead, his curtains reveal a character's point of view or a thought that relates to the play's message. Although the comment is frequently charged with emotion, his only strong dramatic climax comes at the final curtain of *The Amen Corner*.

Structurely, Baldwin's two plays are very different — which makes it even more difficult to draw meaningful conclusions about his art. Of the two, however, *The Amen Corner* is more successful as drama. In the first act he carefully presents the character of Sister Margaret from her sermon, her actions, and the comments of others before he sets up all of the forces which will make her see herself as a person. Beneath the vigorous, self-satisfied, and definite preacher of truth there is the worried and uncertain woman who feels betrayed. Her own house is obviously not in order, while her presumption (like all of the others) is sacrilegious. If the love the congregation sings about in the first act is to be taken seriously, Sister Margaret must recognize what it means. In a manner which suggests the inevitability of Baldwin's thesis the play moves forward as each action foreshadowed in act one is accomplished. There is no surprise. The intrigue of the sister who usurps Sister Margaret's pulpit takes place off stage and is simply presented as a *fait accompli*. In act two Baldwin presents his argument for personal love through Luke who dies only to make Margaret's triumph more pathetic. Meanwhile the political gossiping of the flock is a light touch which provides a good change of pace to Margaret's great inner conflict. So is the concern for Margaret's new Frigidaire. David's drunken confrontation with his mother who slaps him provides a brief drama, but the resulting revelation by Margaret that "love never dies" sentimentally overwhelms that situation. The ending of the play brings all the pieces together in a fine scene for Sister Margaret who learns the way of sacrificial and suffering love that Baldwin had in mind. The play develops in a straight line—a single thesis structure.

Blues for Mister Charlie is no less a thesis drama but much more complicated in structure. The scene is Plaguetown, U.S.A. Richard is murdered by the white store-owner, Lyle Britten. Meridian and a group of Negro students practice reviling each other, as the Whites do the Blacks, so they can hate more easily; they have been demonstrating against Richard's murder. Parnell enters to tell them that Lyle will be arrested. In his house Lyle plays with his infant son, complains that the Negroes have boycotted his store, and hears from Parnell that he will be arrested. Parnell tries to suggest the Negro problem, but Lyle has the stereotyped Southern attitude and refuses to take anything seriously. In the Blacktown church the Negroes talk about Richard who then appears in a flashback as he talks to his father and Mother Henry just after returning from New York. He is belligerent, full of hatred for the white who killed his mother, and he has a gun. Juanita appears; the scene shifts to Papa D's joint where the group of Negroes dance and sing as Richard brags of his white sexual conquests in New York. Lyle comes in, meets Richard. The scene shifts to the church where Pete and Juanita talk of Richard. Then Mother Henry enters to tell of two white men who have been seen under a Negro's porch fooling around with the gas pipes. A flashback again as Richard and his father talk of Juanita. Back at the church the young people are still worried about prowlers as Parnell and Meridian argue about Christianity and practical living in this town. There is going to be a struggle and Mr. Charlie (all white men) had better change. Both Meridian and Parnell know that Lyle killed Richard, but that in the courtroom he will lie. Meridian wants Parnell to get the truth, to ask Lyle to say he did it, but Parnell balks: "I don't know if I can do it for you." And the act ends as Meridian wishes that he had died for Richard.

Obviously, the structure is over complicated. Act two provides the white reaction to the murder, shows that Parnell once loved a Negro girl, that Lyle killed another Negro, and that Jo, his wife, suspects that he killed Richard. But Lyle never admits the truth, and the act ends with Meridian's funeral sermon and a scene between Parnell and Juanita that suggests their love. Act three in the courtroom is structured with flashbacks as each witness — Papa D., Juanita, Jo, Meridian, Parnell — tells what he knows about the murder and reveals his own problems. Intermittently Blacktown and Whitetown talk about the prosecution. Meridian makes his plea, Jo lies on the stand, and Parnell will not contradict her. As the courtroom empties, Lyle, Parnell, and Meridian face each other. Goaded by Meridian, Lyle finally explains what happened in a flashback, and confesses in a single but very dramatic speech. It is over for the whites, and there is only hope for everyone: Lyle is found not guilty. The flashbacks are more effective here than in act one but the pace of the play drags with the weight of the message — no suspense, no crisis. The people are interesting — most of them are stereotypes — if scantly portrayed; some, such as Jo and Parnell, evoke sympathy. But there is little relief from the posturing and the preaching. The choral response in the trial provides some; the scene changes others. One could not call it a very good play dramatically, which does not mean that its message is not meaningful.

Baldwin is a very serious writer, and this is particularly evident in a play where a good change of pace or a bit of humor could be used to advantage. Instead, Baldwin sticks to his thesis with a deadly conviction, presents his main characters well but is more interested in argument than action. Few critics, however, would contend that he does not have something worth saying, although that fact does not make his plays good drama. Obviously, Baldwin is concerned with the Negro as a man — both David and Richard rebelled to this purpose. He also sees religion as important in man's life but not as it is now practiced. In fact, the people who do develop in his plays — Sister Margaret and Meridian — do so because they have found something beyond the church as institution. A humanitarian, Baldwin shows in *Blues* that he does not hate all white men; Parnell is clearly accepted for the direction he takes. In both plays Baldwin's serious answer for all human problems, Black or White, is love through suffering. It is a thesis which goes through most of his work and for which within the new Black movement he receives little sympathy.

Throughout his artistic life James Baldwin has taken advantage, although in part unconsciously, of a crucial situation. This was particularly evident in *Blues for Mister Charlies*. As time has passed, however, that situation has changed, and the eloquent and passionate plea that Baldwin has made is less acceptable as an argument than it once was. One result is a diminishing of his reputation, not as an artist but as a spokesman for his race. And perhaps this is good! That part of his reputation had made him live a role which he does not seem to enjoy, as he sees himself as a tragic figure and talks of martyrdom. Like Ida in *Another Country* he feels that he pays his dues to be a man and should be allowed freedom. As a free creative artist, in whatever form he chooses, Baldwin is most effective as a spokesman for mankind in a troubled world. Certainly Baldwin's instincts are with man, and if his life is "the agony way," he best illustrates his most repeated idea by travelling the same road he advocates for all others.

The Black Arts Movement

by Larry Neal

THE BLACK ARTS MOVEMENT is radically opposed to any concept of the artist that alienates him from his community. Black Art is the aesthetic and spiritual sister of the Black Power concept. As such, it envisions an art that speaks directly to the needs and aspirations of Black America. In order to perform this task, the Black Arts Movement proposes a radical reordering of the western cultural aesthetic. It proposes a separate symbolism, mythology, critique, and iconology. The Black Arts and the Black Power concept both relate broadly to the Afro-American's desire for self-determination and nationhood. Both concepts are nationalistic. One is concerned with the relationship between art and politics; the other with the art of politics.

Recently, these two movements have begun to merge: the political values inherent in the Black Power concept are now finding concrete expression in the aesthetics of Afro-American dramatists, poets, choreographers, musicians, and novelists. A main tenet of Black Power is the necessity for Black people to define the world in their own terms. The Black artist has made the same point in the context of aesthetics. The two movements postulate that there are in fact and in spirit two Americas — one black, one white. The Black artist takes this to mean that his primary duty is to speak to the spiritual and cultural needs of Black people. Therefore, the main thrust of this new breed of contemporary writers is to confront the contradictions arising out of the Black man's experience in the racist West. Currently, these writers are re-evaluating western aesthetics, the traditional role of the writer, and the social function of art. Implicit in this re-evaluation is the need to develop a "black aesthetic." It is the opinion of many Black writers, I among them, that the Western aesthetic has run its course: it is impossible to construct anything meaningful within its decaying structure. We advocate a cultural revolution in art and ideas. The cultural values inherent in western history must either be radicalized or destroyed, and we will probably find that even radicalization is impossible. In fact, what is needed is a whole new system of ideas. Poet Don L. Lee expresses it:

> . . . We must destroy Faulkner, dick, jane, and other perpetuators of evil. It's time for DuBois, Nat Turner, and Kwame Nkrumah. As Frantz Fanon points out: destroy the culture and you destroy the people. This must not happen. Black artists are culture stabilizers; bringing back old values, and introducing new ones. Black Art will talk to the people and with the will of the people stop impending "protective custody."

The Black Arts Movement eschews "protest" literature. It speaks directly to Black people. Implicit in the concept of "protest" literature, as Brother Knight has made clear, is an appeal to white morality:

> Now any Black man who masters the technique of his particular art form, who adheres to the white aesthetic, and who directs his work toward a white audience is, in one sense, protesting. And implicit in the act of protest is the belief that a change will be forthcoming once the masters are aware of the protestor's "grievance" (the very word connotes begging, supplications to the gods). Only when that belief has faded and protesting ends, will Black art begin.

Brother Knight also has some interesting statements about the development of a "Black aesthetic":

Unless the Black artist establishes a "Black aesthetic" he will have no future at all. To accept the white aesthetic is to accept and validate a society that will not allow him to live. The Black artist must create new forms and new values, sing new songs (or purify old ones) ; and along with other Black authorities, he must create a new history, new symbols, myths and legends (and purify old ones by fire). And the Black artist, in creating his own aesthetic, must be accountable for it only to the Black people. Further, he must hasten his own dissolution as an individual (in the Western sense) — painful though the process may be, having been breast-fed the poison of "individual experience."

When we speak of a "Black aesthetic" several things are meant, First, we assume that there is already in existence the basis for such an aesthetic. Essentially, it consists of an African-American cultural tradition. But this aesthetic is finally, by implication, broader than that tradition. It encompasses most of the usable elements of Third World culture. The motive behind the Black aesthetic is the destruction of the white thing, the destruction of white ideas, and white ways of looking at the world. The new aesthetic is mostly predicated on an Ethics which asks the question: whose vision of the world is finally more meaningful, ours or the white oppressors'? What is truth? Or more precisely, whose truth shall we express, that of the oppressed or of the oppressor? These are basic questions. Black intellectuals of previous decades failed to ask them. Further, national and international affairs demand that we appraise the world in terms of our own interests. It is clear that the question of human survival is at the core of contemporary experience. The Black artist must address himself to this reality in the strongest terms possible. In a context of world upheaval, ethics and aesthetics must interact positively and be consistent with the demands for a more spiritual world. Consequently, the Black Arts Movement is an ethical movement. Ethical, that is, from the viewpoint of the oppressed. And much of the oppression confronting the Third World and Black America is directly traceable to the Euro-American cultural sensibility. This sensibility, anti-human in nature, has, until recently, dominated the psyches of most Black artists and intellectuals; it must be destroyed before the Black creative artist can have a meaningful role in the transformation of society.

It is this natural reaction to an alien sensibility that informs

the cultural attitudes of the Black Arts and the Black Power move-
ment. It is a profound ethical sense that makes a Black artist ques-
tion a society in which art is one thing and the actions of men
another. The Black Arts Movement believes that your ethics and
your aesthetics are one. That the contradictions between ethics
and aesthetics in western society is [sic] symptomatic of a dying
culture.

The term "Black Arts" is of ancient origin, but it was first used
in a positive sense by LeRoi Jones:

> We are unfair
> And unfair
> We are black magicians
> Black arts we make
> in black labs of the heart
>
> The fair are fair
> and deathly white
>
> The day will not save them
> And we own the night

There is also a section of the poem "Black Dada Nihilismus"
that carries the same motif. But a fuller amplification of the nature
of the new aesthetics appears in the poem "Black Art":

> Poems are bullshit unless they are
> teeth or trees or lemons piled
> on a step. Or black ladies dying
> of men leaving nickel hearts
> beating them down. Fuck poems
> and they are useful, would they shoot
> come at you, love what you are,
> breathe like wrestlers, or shudder
> strangely after peeing. We want live
> words of the hip world, live flesh &
> coursing blood. Hearts and Brains
> Souls splintering fire. We want poems
> like fists beating niggers out of Jocks
> or dagger poems in the slimy bellies
> of the owner-jews . . .

Poetry is a concrete function, an action. No more abstractions. Poems are physical entities: fists, daggers, airplane poems, and poems that shoot guns. Poems are transformed from physical objects into personal forces:

> . . . Put it on him poem. Strip him naked
> to the world. Another bad poem cracking
> steel knuckles in a jewlady's mouth
> Poem scream poison gas on breasts in green berets . . .

Then the poem affirms the integral relationship between Black Art and Black people:

> . . . Let Black people understand
> that they are the lovers and the sons
> of lovers and warriors and sons
> of warriors Are poems & poets &
> all the loveliness here in the world

It ends with the following lines, a central assertion in both the Black Arts Movement and the philosophy of Black Power:

> We want a black poem. And a
> Black World.
> Let the world be a Black Poem
> And let All Black People Speak This Poem
> Silently
> Or LOUD

The poem comes to stand for the collective conscious and unconscious of Black America — the real impulse in back of the Black Power movement, which is the will toward self-determination and nationhood, a radical reordering of the nature and function of both art and the artist.

2.

In the spring of 1964, LeRoi Jones, Charles Patterson, William Patterson, Clarence Reed, Johnny Moore, and a number of other Black artists opened the Black Arts Repertoire Theatre School. They produced a number of plays including Jones' *Experimental Death Unit No. One, Black Mass, Jello,* and *Dutchman.* They also initiated a series of poetry readings and concerts. These activities represented the most advanced tendencies in the movement and were of excellent artistic quality. The Black Arts School came under immediate attack by the New York power structure. The Establishment, fearing Black creativity, did exactly what it was expected to do — it attacked the theatre and all of its values. In the meantime, the school was granted funds by OES through HARYOU-ACT. Lacking a cultural program itself, HARYOU turned to the only organization which addressed itself to the needs of the community. In keeping with its "revolutionary" cultural ideas, the Black Arts Theatre took its programs into the streets of Harlem. For three months, the theatre presented plays, concerts, and poetry readings to the people of the community. Plays that shattered the illusions of the American body politic, and awakened Black people to the meaning of their lives.

Then the hawks from the OEO moved in and chopped off the funds. Again, this should have been expected. The Black Arts Theatre stood in radical opposition to the feeble attitudes about culture of the "War On Poverty" bureaucrats. And later, because of internal problems, the theatre was forced to close. But the Black Arts group proved that the community could be served by a valid and dynamic art. It also proved that there was a definite need for a cultural revolution in the Black community.

With the closing of the Black Arts Theatre, the implications of what Brother Jones and his colleagues were trying to do took on even more significance. Black Art groups sprang up on the West Coast and the idea spread to Detroit, Philadelphia, Jersey City, New Orleans, and Washington, D. C. Black Arts movements began on the campuses of San Francisco State College, Fisk University, Lincoln University, Hunter College in the Bronx, Columbia University, and Oberlin College. In Watts, after the rebellion, Maulana Karenga welded the Blacks Arts Movement into a cohesive ideology which owed much to the work of LeRoi Jones. Karenga sees culture as the most important element in the struggle for self-determination:

> Culture is the basis of all ideas, images and actions. To move is to move culturally, i.e. by a set of values given to you by your culture.

> Without a culture Negroes are only a set of reactions to white people.

> The seven criteria for culture are:

1. Mythology
2. History
3. Social Organization
4. Political Organization
5. Economic Organization
6. Creative Motif
7. Ethos

In drama, LeRoi Jones represents the most advanced aspects of the movement. He is its prime mover and chief designer. In a poetic essay entitled "The Revolutionary Theatre," he outlines the iconology of the movement:

> The Revolutionary Theatre should force change: it should be change. (All their faces turned into the lights and you work on them black nigger magic, and cleanse them at having seen the ugliness. And if the beautiful see themselves, they will love themselves.) We are preaching virtue again, but by that to mean NOW, toward what seems the most constructive use of the word.

The theatre that Jones proposes is inextricably linked to the Afro-American political dynamic. And such a link is perfectly consistent with Black America's contemporary demands. For theatre is potentially the most social of all of the arts. It is an integral part of the socializing process. It exists in direct relationship to the audience it claims to serve. The decadence and inanity of the contemporary American theatre is an accurate reflection of the state of American society. Albee's *Who's Afraid of Virginia Woolf?* is very American: sick white lives in a homosexual hell hole. The theatre of white America is escapist, refusing to confront concrete reality. Into this cultural emptiness come the musicals, an up tempo version of the same stale lives. And the use of Negroes in such plays as *Hello Dolly* and *Hallelujah Baby* does not alter their nature, it compounds the problem. These plays are simply hipper versions of the minstrel show. They present Negroes acting out the hang-ups of middle-class white America. Consequently, the American theatre is a palliative prescribed to bourgeois patients who refuse to see the world as it is. Or, more crucially, as the world sees them. It is no accident, therefore, that the most "important" plays come from Europe — Brecht, Weiss, and Ghelderode. And even these have begun to run dry.

The Black Arts theatre, the theatre of LeRoi Jones, is a radical alternative to the sterility of the American theatre. It is primarily a theatre of the Spirit, confronting the Black man in his interaction with his brothers and with the white thing.

> Our theatre will show victims so that their brothers in the audience will be better able to understand that they are the brothers of victims, and that they themselves are blood brothers. And what we show must cause the blood to rush, so that pre-revolutionary temperaments will be bathed in this blood, and it will cause their deepest souls to move, and they will find themselves tensed and clenched, even ready to die, at what the soul has been taught. We will scream and cry, murder, run through the streets in agony, if it means some soul will be moved, moved to actual life understanding of what the world is, and what it ought to be. We are preaching virtue and feeling, and a natural sense of the self in the world. All men live in the world, and the world ought to be a place for them to live.

The victims of the world of Jones' early plays are Clay, murdered by the white bitch-goddess in *Dutchman,* and Walker Vessels, the revolutionary in *The Slave*. Both of these plays present Black men in transition. Clay, the middle-class Negro trying to get himself a little action from Lula, digs himself and his own truth only to get murdered after telling her like it really is:

> Just let me bleed you, you loud whore, and one poem vanished. A whole people of neurotics, struggling to keep from being sane. And the only thing that would cure the neurosis would be your murder. Simple as that. I mean if I murdered you, then other white people would begin to understand me. You understand? No. I guess not. If Bessie Smith had killed some white people she wouldn't have needed that music. She could have talked very straight and plain about the world. . . . Just straight two and two are four. Money. Power. Luxury. Like that. All of them. Crazy niggers turning their back on sanity. When all it needs is that simple act. Murder. Just murder. Would make us all sane.

But Lula understands, and she kills Clay first. In a perverse way it is Clay's nascent knowledge of himself that threatens the existence of Lula's idea of the world. Symbolically, and in fact, the relationship between Clay (Black America) and Lula (white America) is rooted in the historical castration of black manhood. And in the twisted psyche of white America, the Black man is both an object of love and hate. Analogous attitudes exist in most Black Americans, but for decidedly different reasons. Clay is doomed when he allows himself to participate in Lula's "fantasy" in the first place. It is the fantasy to which Frantz Fanon alludes in *The Wretched Of The Earth* and *Black Skins, White Masks*: the native's belief that he can acquire the oppressor's power by acquiring his symbols, one of which is the white woman. When Clay finally digs himself it is too late.

Walker Vessels, in *The Slave*, is Clay reincarnated as the revolutionary confronting problems inherited from his contact with white culture. He returns to the home of his ex-wife, a white woman, and her husband, a literary critic. The play is essentially about Walker's attempt to destroy his white past. For it is the past, with all of its painful memories, that is really the enemy of the revolutionary. It is impossible to move until history is either recreated or comprehended. Unlike Todd, in Ralph Ellison's *Invisible Man*, Walker cannot fall outside history. Instead, Walker demands a confrontation with history, a final shattering of bullshit illusions. His only salvation lies in confronting the physical and psychological forces that have made him and his people powerless. Therefore, he comes to understand that the world must be restructured along spiritual imperatives. But in the interim it is basically a question of *who* has power:

EASLEY. You're so wrong about everything. So terribly, sickeningly wrong. What can you change? What do you hope to change? Do you think Negroes are better people than whites . . . that they can govern a society *better* than whites? That they'll be more judicious or more tolerant? Do you think they'll make fewer mistakes? I mean really, if the Western white man has proved one thing . . . it's the futility of modern society. So the have-not people become the haves. Even so, will that change the essential functions of the world? Will there be more love or beauty in the world . . . more knowledge . . . because of it?

WALKER. Probably. Probably there will be more
. . . if more people have a chance to understand what it is.
But that's not even the point. It comes down to baser hu-
man endeavor than any social-political thinking. What
does it matter if there's more love or beauty? Who the fuck
cares? Is that what the Western ofay thought while he was
ruling . . . that his rule somehow brought more love and
beauty into the world? Oh, he might have thought that
concomitantly, while sipping a gin rickey and scratching
his ass . . . but that was not ever the point. Not even on the
Crusades. The point is that you had your chance, darling,
now these other folks have theirs. *Quietly.* Now they have
theirs.

EASLEY. God, what an ugly idea.

This confrontation between the black radical and the white
liberal is symbolic of larger confrontations occurring between the
Third World and Western society. It is a confrontation between
the colonizer and the colonized, the slavemaster and the slave.
Implicit in Easley's remarks is the belief that the white man is
culturally and politically superior to the Black Man. Even though
Western society has been traditionally violent in its relation with
the Third World, it sanctimoniously deplores violence or self-
assertion on the part of the enslaved. And the Western mind, with
clever rationalizations, equates the violence of the oppressed with
the violence of the oppressor. So that when the native preaches
self-determination, the Western white man cleverly misconstrues
it to mean hate of *all* white men. When the Black political radical
warns his people not to trust white politicians of the left and the
right, but instead to organize separately on the basis of power,
the white man cries: "racism in reverse." Or he will say, as many
of them do today: "We deplore both white and black racism." As
if the two could be equated.

There is a minor element in *The Slave* which assumes great
importance in a later play entitled *Jello.* Here I refer to the
emblem of Walker's army: a red-mouthed grinning field slave.
The revolutionary army has taken one of the most hated symbols
of the Afro-American past and radically altered its meaning.* This

*In Jones' study of Afro-American music, *Blues People,* we find
the following observation: ". . . Even the adjective *funky,* which

is the supreme act of freedom, available only to those who have liberated themselves psychically. Jones amplifies this inversion of emblem and symbol in *Jello* by making Rochester (Ratfester) of the old Jack Benny (Penny) program into a revolutionary nationalist. Ratfester, ordinarily the supreme embodiment of the Uncle Tom Clown, surprises Jack Penny by turning on the other side of the nature of the Black man. He skillfully, and with an evasive black humor, robs Penny of all of his money. But Ratfester's actions are "moral." That is to say, Ratfester is getting his back pay; payment of a long over-due debt to the Black man. Ratfester's sensibilities are different from Walker's. He is *blues people* smiling and shuffling while trying to figure out how to destroy the white thing. And like the blues man, he is the master of the understatement. Or in the Afro-American folk tradition, he is the Signifying Monkey, Shine, and Stagolee all rolled into one. There are no stereotypes any more. History has killed Uncle Tom. Because even Uncle Tom has a breaking point beyond which he will not be pushed. Cut deeply enough into the most docile Negro, and you will find a conscious murderer. Behind the lyrics of the blues and the shuffling porter loom visions of white throats being cut and cities burning.

Jones' particular power as a playwright does not rest solely on his revolutionary vision, but is instead derived from his deep lyricism and spiritual outlook. In many ways, he is fundamentally more a poet than a playwright. And it is his lyricism that gives body to his plays. Two important plays in this regard are *Black Mass* and *Slave Ship*. *Black Mass* is based on the Muslim myth of Yacub. According to this myth, Yacub, a Black scientist, developed the means of grafting different colors of the Original Black Nation until a White Devil was created. In *Black Mass*, Yacub's experiments produced a raving White Beast who is condemned to the coldest regions of the North. The other magicians implore

---

once meant to many Negroes merely a stink (usually associated with sex), was used to qualify the music as meaningful (the word became fashionable and is now almost useless). The social implication, then, was that even the old stereotype of a distinctive Negro smell that white America subscribed to could be turned against white America. For this smell now, real or not, was made a valuable characteristic of 'Negro-ness.' And 'Negro-ness,' by the fifties, for many Negroes (and whites) was the only strength left to American culture."

Yacub to cease his experiments. But he insists on claiming the primacy of scientific knowledge over spiritual knowledge. The sensibility of the White Devil is alien, informed by lust and sensuality. The Beast is the consummate embodiment of evil, the beginning of the historical subjugation of the spiritual world.

Black Mass takes place in some pre-historic time. In fact, the concept of time, we learn, is the creation of an alien sensibility, that of the Beast. This is a deeply weighted play, a colloquy on the nature of man, and the relationship between legitimate spiritual knowledge and scientific knowledge. It is LeRoi Jones' most important play mainly because it is informed by a mythology that is wholly the creation of the Afro-American sensibility.

Further, Yacub's creation is not merely a scientific exercise. More fundamentally, it is the aesthetic impulse gone astray. The Beast is created merely for the sake of creation. Some artists assert a similar claim about the nature of art. They argue that art need not have a function. It is against this decadent attitude toward art — ramified throughout most of Western society — that the play militates. Yacub's real crime, therefore, is the introduction of a meaningless evil into a harmonious universe. The evil of the Beast is pervasive, corrupting everything and everyone it touches. What was beautiful is twisted into an ugly screaming thing. The play ends with destruction of the holy place of the Black Magicians. Now the Beast and his descendants roam the earth. An off-stage voice chants a call for the Jihad to begin. It is then that myth merges into legitimate history, and we, the audience, come to understand that all history is merely someone's version of mythology.

Slave Ship presents a more immediate confrontation with history. In a series of expressionistic tableaux it depicts the horrors and the madness of the Middle Passage. It then moves through the period of slavery, early attempts at revolt, tendencies toward Uncle Tom-like reconciliation and betrayal, and the final act of liberation. There is no definite plot (LeRoi calls it a pageant), just a continuous rush of sound, groans, screams, and souls wailing for freedom and relief from suffering. This work has special affinities with the New Music of Sun Ra, John Coltrane, Albert Ayler, and Ornette Coleman. Events are blurred, rising and falling in a stream of sound. Almost cinematically, the images flicker and fade against a heavy backdrop of rhythm. The language is spare, stripped to the essential. It is a play which almost totally eliminates the need for a text. It functions on the basis of movement and energy — the dramatic equivalent of the New Music.

3.

LeRoi Jones is the best known and the most advanced play-wright of the movement, but he is not alone. There are other excellent playwrights who express the general mood of the Black Arts ideology. Among them are Ron Milner, Ed Bullins, Ben Caldwell, Jimmy Stewart, Joe White, Charles Patterson, Charles Fuller, Aisha Hughes, Carol Freeman, and Jimmy Garrett.

Ron Milner's *Who's Got His Own* is of particular importance. It strips bare the clashing attitudes of a contemporary Afro-American family. Milner's concern is with legitimate manhood and morality. The family in *Who's Got His Own* is in search of its conscience, or more precisely its own definition of life. On the day of his father's death, Tim and his family are forced to examine the inner fabric of their lives: the lies, self-deceits, and sense of powerlessness in a white world. The basic conflict, however, is internal. It is rooted in the historical search for black manhood. Tim's mother is representative of a generation of Christian Black women who have implicitly understood the brooding violence lurking in their men. And with this understanding, they have interposed themselves between their men and the object of that violence — the white man. Thus unable to direct his violence against the oppressor, the Black man becomes more frustrated and the sense of powerlessness deepens. Lacking the strength to be a man in the white world, he turns against his family. So the op-pressed, as Fanon explains, constantly dreams violence against his oppressor, while killing his brother on fast weekends.

Tim's sister represents the Negro woman's attempt to acquire what Eldridge Cleaver calls "ultrafemininity." That is, the attrib-utes of her white upper-class counterpart. Involved here is a rejec-tion of the body-oriented life of the working class Black man, symbolized by the mother's traditional religion. The sister has an affair with a white upper-class liberal, ending in abortion. There are hints of lesbianism, i.e. a further rejection of the body. The sister's life is a pivotal factor in the play. Much of the stripping away of falsehood initiated by Tim is directed at her life, which they have carefully kept hidden from the mother.

Tim is the product of the new Afro-American sensibility, in-formed by the psychological revolution now operative within Black America. He is a combination ghetto soul brother and militant intellectual, very hip and slightly flawed himself. He would change the world, but without comprehending the particular history that produced his "tyrannical" father. And he cannot be the man his father was — not until he truly understands his father. He must understand why his father allowed himself to be insulted daily by the "honky" types on the job; why he took a demeaning job in the "shit-house"; and why he spent on his family the violence that he should have directed against the white man. In short, Tim must confront the history of his family. And that is exactly what happens. Each character tells his story, exposing his falsehood to the other until a balance is reached.

Who's Got His Own is not the work of an alienated mind. Milner's main thrust is directed toward unifying the family around basic moral principles, toward bridging the "generation gap." Other Black playwrights, Jimmy Garrett for example, see the gap as unbridgeable.

Garret's *We Own the Night* (see TDR, Summer, 1968, pp. 62-69) takes place during an armed insurrection. As the play opens we see the central characters defending a section of the city against attacks by white police. Johnny, the protagonist, is wounded. Some of his Brothers intermittently fire at attacking forces, while others look for medical help. A doctor arrives, forced at gun point. The wounded boy's mother also comes. She is a female Uncle Tom who berates the Brothers and their cause. She tries to get Johnny to leave. She is hysterical. The whole idea of Black people fighting white people is totally outside of her orientation. Johnny begins a vicious attack on his mother, accusing her of emasculating his father — a recurring theme in the sociology of the Black community. In Afro-American literature of previous decades the strong Black mother was the object of awe and respect. But in the new literature her status is ambivalent and laced with tension. Historically, Afro-American women have had to be the economic mainstays of the family. The oppressor allowed them to have jobs while at the same time limiting the economic mobility of the Black man. Very often, therefore, the woman's aspirations and values are closely tied to those of the white power structure and not to those of her man. Since he cannot provide for his family the way white men do, she despises his weakness, tearing into him at every opportunity until, very often, there is nothing left but a shell.

The only way out of this dilemma is through revolution. It

either must be an actual blood revolution, or one that psychically redirects the energy of the oppressed. Milner is fundamentally concerned with the latter and Garrett with the former. Communication between Johnny and his mother breaks down. The revolutionary imperative demands that men step outside the legal framework. It is a question of erecting *another* morality. The old constructs do not hold up, because adhering to them means consigning oneself to the oppressive reality. Johnny's mother is involved in the old constructs. Manliness is equated with white morality. And even though she claims to love her family (her men), the overall design of her ideas are [sic] against black manhood. In Garrett's play the mother's morality manifests itself in a deep-seated hatred of Black men; while in Milner's work the mother understands, but holds her men back.

The mothers that Garrett and Milner see represent the Old Spirituality — the Faith of the Fathers of which DuBois spoke. Johnny and Tim represent the New Spirituality. They appear to be a type produced by the upheavals of the colonial world of which Black America is a part. Johnny's assertion that he is a criminal is remarkably similar to the rebel's comments in Aimé Césaire's play, *Les Armes Miraculeuses (The Miraculous Weapons)*. In that play the rebel, speaking to his mother, proclaims: "My name — an offense, my Christian name — humiliation; by status — a rebel; my age — the stone age." To which the mother replies: "My race — the human race. My religion — brotherhood." The Old Spirituality is generalized. It seeks to recognize Universal Humanity. The New Spirituality is specific. It begins by seeing the world from the concise point-of-view of the colonialized. Where the Old Spirituality would live with oppression while ascribing to the oppressors an innate goodness, the New Spirituality demands a radical shift in point-of-view. The colonialized native, the oppressed must, of necessity, subscribe to a *separate* morality. One that will liberate him and his people.

The assault against the Old Spirituality can sometimes be humorous. In Ben Caldwell's play, *The Militant Preacher,* a burglar is seen slipping into the home of a wealthy minister. The preacher comes in and the burglar ducks behind a large chair. The preacher, acting out the role of the supplicant minister begins to moan, praying to De Lawd for understanding.

In the context of today's politics, the minister is an Uncle Tom mouthing platitudes against self-defense. The preacher drones in a self-pitying monologue about the folly of protecting oneself against brutal policeman. Then the burglar begins to speak. The preacher is startled, taking the burglar's voice for the voice of God. The burgler begins to play on the preacher's old time religion. He *becomes* the voice of God insulting and goading the preacher on until the preacher's attitudes about protective violence change. The next day the preacher emerges militant, gun in hand, sounding like Reverend Cleage in Detroit. He now preaches a new gospel — the gospel of the gun, an eye for an eye. The gospel is preached in the rhythmic cadences of the old Black church. But the content is radical. Just as Jones inverted the symbols of *Jello,* Caldwell twists the rhythms of the Uncle Tom preacher into the language of the new militancy.

These plays are directed at problems within Black America. They begin with the premise that there is a well defined Afro-American audience. An audience that must see itself and the world in terms of its own interests. These plays, along with many others, constitute the basis for a viable movement in the theatre — a movement which takes as its task a profound re-evaluation of the Black man's presence in America. The Black Arts Movement represents the flowering of a cultural nationalism that has been suppressed since the 1920s. I mean the "Harlem Renaissance" — which was essentially a failure. It did not address itself to the mythology and the life-styles of the Black community. It failed to take roots, to link itself concretely to the struggles of that community, to become its voice and spirit. Implicit in the Black Arts Movement is the idea that Black people, however dispersed, constitute a *nation* within the belly of white America. This is not a new idea. Garvey said it and the Honorable Elijah Muhammad says it now. And it is on this idea that the concept of Black Power is predicated.

Afro-American life and history is full of creative possibilities, and the movement is just beginning to perceive them. Just beginning to understand that the most meaningful statements about the nature of Western society must come from the Third World of which Black America is a part. The thematic material is broad, ranging from folk heroes like Shine and Stagolee to historical figures like Marcus Garvey and Malcolm X. And then there is the struggle for Black survival, the coming confrontation between white America and Black America. If art is the harbinger of future possibilities, what does the future of Black America portend?

LeRoi Jones and
Contemporary Black Drama

by Louis Phillips

"The Black Arts movement is radically opposed to
any concept of the artist that alienates him from his
community. Black Art is the aesthetic and spiritual
sister of the Black Power concept. As such, it en-
visions an art that speaks directly to the needs and
aspirations of Black America. In order to perform
this task, the Black Arts movement proposes a radi-
cal reordering of the western cultural aesthetic. It
proposes a separate symbolism, mythology, critique,
and iconology."

    LARRY NEAL in "The Black Arts Movement,"
The Drama Review (Summer, 1968).

THE TRUTH OF the matter is that it has been a white man's
theatre, a theatre in which the most oft produced plays about the
black, the Negro, the Afro-American, have been written by whites,
all the way from Harriet Beecher Stowe's *Uncle Tom's Cabin*,
through Eugene O'Neill's *The Dreamy Kid, The Emperor Jones,
All God's Chillun Got Wings*, through the work of Paul Green,
down to the vastly over-rated *The Great White Hope*. Thus, when

the artistic director of Harlem's New Lafayette Theatre states (as Robert Macbeth did in 1968) that he hasn't seen "a real Negro onstage in years,"[1] he means it, he really means it.

The American theatre is a theatre in which the audience is predominantly white, the critics white, the producers white. As Loften Mitchell, the black playwright of *Land Beyond the River*, puts it, "Theatre in America remains a middle class luxury wherein the playwright speaks, cajoles, seduces, and lies to an expense-account audience."[2] It would be grand and eloquent to say that color is invisible in the theatre, that it has no bearing on the making of a successful play, but tell it to the angry young playwright whose works are artistically hedged in by the failure of white producers and white critics to comprehend them. It is a sobering thought to remember that the first play by a black playwright to reach Broadway didn't reach the Great *White* way until 1925 (Garland Anderson's *Appearances*), and that "prior to 1945 only three Broadway houses sold seats to Negroes that were not on the aisle. This practice was based on the belief that whites did not want Negroes climbing all over them."[3]

In Joseph Dolan Tuotti's *Big Time Buck White*, Buck White asks rhetorically, "Did you ever hear a black man say 'Our Army' Did you ever hear a black man say 'Our President?' " The question can be extended. Have you ever heard a black man say 'Our Theatre'? From the very beginning of the black American plays, from William Wells Brown's *The Escape, or a Leap For Freedom: A Drama in Five Acts* (1858) — perhaps the first play written by an American Negro[4] — to the recent *Reckoning* by Douglas Turner Ward, the black man has recognized at least two over-riding needs in the theatre: the need to be his own playwright and the need to speak to an audience of other Negroes. Douglas Turner Ward, whose two short plays *Happy Ending* and *Day of Absence* were recipients of Obie awards, speaks out strongly on both of these needs:

> Even the most emphatic white artist can only comprehend the black experience as a second hand observer. This is not to suggest that blackness can be expressed only through isolation or separatism. Black experience can be a profoundly fertile expression without isolation.[5]

. . . . .

But for a Negro playwright committed to examining the

contours, contexts, and depths of his experience from an unfettered, imaginative Negro angle of vision, the screaming need is for a sufficient audience of *other Negroes,* better informed through commonly shared experience to readily understand, debate, confirm, or reject the truth or falsity of his creative explorations.[6]

These then are two of the premises upon which the younger black playwrights, playwrights such as Ward, Adrienne Kennedy, Ed Bullins, Ron Milner, Ben Caldwell, Charles Patterson, Herbert Stokes, and LeRoi Jones have begun to build. Some like LeRoi Jones and Ed Bullins demand a revolutionary theatre, a theatre of social change, a theatre of victims, a militant theatre, a theatre devoted to the Black Arts. Others like Douglas Turner Ward and Ben Caldwell use more conventional approaches to theatre but infuse their concepts and criticisms with biting satire or fable-like qualities. *Day of Absence,* for example, concerns itself with a small southern town where the blacks mysteriously disappear, leaving the whites to do their own chores. The whites soon find themselves completely helpless and begin a desperate search to recover their "Nigras." Ward himself calls his play a satirical fantasy. An unlabelled satirical fantasy is Ben Caldwell's *Riot Sale or the Dollar Psyche Fake Out,* for in that short play the playwright turns his anger against his fellow blacks who surrender their revolutionary zeal for money. During a riot in Harlem, the police disperse the crowd by firing huge sums of money out of a cannon:

And the cannon's missiles can be seen clearly. Money! Money flying high in the air, and in all directions. Paper money. No one has been injured by the blast. MONEY! Apparently millions of dollars; Fives, tens! Twenties! Millions; Again the cannon roars, belching forth more money. Utter chaos as the blacks scatter-scramble for the loot. Those few still bent on revolution are now easily subdued by the police, as their fellow 'freedom fighters' now fight among themselves over the loot.[7]

Yet no matter the militancy of the playwright, one principle is shared: a black man talking to other black men, not talking simply to an audience of middle-class, credit-card-carrying whites.

No one shares that principle as profoundly as LeRoi Jones does, for if he is not the best of the contemporary black playwrights, he is at least the most militant, the most revolutionary, the most explosive, and the most controversial playwright on the American scene. He is also frequently the most maligned, especially by those white critics who are threatened and shocked by Jones' obscenities and outrages, for when LeRoi Jones uses the phrase "Our Theatre" he means a theatre where victims will be prominently displayed, a theatre that "will show victims so that their brothers will be better able to understand that they are the brothers of victims, and that they themselves are blood brothers."[8] Jones' idea of the victim is probably best shown in his three short plays, *The Slave*, *Black Mass*, and *Dutchman*, but it is present in his other plays as well.

The Slave, for example, takes place during a race war (Jones believes that a war between whites and blacks is inevitable) when the whites are being shot and dynamited by an army of blacks led by Walker Vessels. During the battle, Vessels, a tall thin Negro of forty years of age, breaks into the house of a white couple, Bradford and Grace Easely. Bradford Easely is a university Professor, completely furnished with the standard liberal views, and was once Vessels' friend. Bradford's wife Grace was formerly married to Vessels and had two children by him. Vessels claims that he is returning for his daughters, but, in reality, he has already killed them. Vessels shoots Bradford, and Grace is crushed under a falling beam when a bomb explodes near the house, so by the end of the play the spectator is presented with a variety of victims.

The guerrilla warfare between Blacks and Whites, and the play's senseless violence has caused Jones to become the target of angry criticism. George Dennison, writing for *Commentary* magazine, went so far as to identify the play as part of the "rot" eating away at America:

> Like every demagogue, he (Jones) speaks to the private and fragmentary wishes of individuals, and like every demagogue he assures the fragmentary person that he is in reality a thundering herd. His *taking of a position is analogous* to the Stalinist maneuvering of the 30's, and in fact he has been quoted as saying, 'My ideas revolve around the rotting and destruction of America, so I can't really expect anyone who is part of that to accept my ideas' — as

if he himself stood outside history, I would like to identify these plays, especially *The Slave,* as part of the rot of America, particularly the racist rot that flickers back and forth, north and south, east and west.[9]

But every good playwright speaks to the private and fragmentary wishes of individuals so that each individual realizes that many of his ideas and feelings are shared by others. Violence is at the very core of life in America ("As American as cherry pie"), the fear of the outsider, the struggle between the exploited and the exploiter, and if Jones sets this forth in a play does this necessarily add to the "rot" or does it allow us to see what is there, what is within us? Dennison's response to *The Slave* is perhaps typical of the response of the middle-class white playgoers, who would prefer the ideal of nonviolence to the reality of the violence that is present within us.

Perhaps the best clue to an understanding of *The Slave* and other plays by Black militants can be found in Jones' own essay, "What Does Nonviolence Mean?" for in that essay Jones explodes the myth that non-violence can accomplish anything for the black man in America:

> Nonviolence, as a theory of social and political demeanor concerning American Negroes, means simply a continuation of the *status quo.* As this "theory" is applied to define specific terms of personal conduct Negroes are supposed to utilize, it assumes, again, the nature of that mysterious moral commitment Negro leaders say the black man must make to participate as a privileged class among the oppressed. Nonviolence on this personal (moral) level is the most sinister application of the Western method of confusing and subjugating peoples by convincing these peoples that the white West knows what is best for them.[10]

The logic of *The Slave,* however, if it is a logic, is not that Negroes, once they use violence to gain their ends, will govern society better than the Whites, or that they will be more judicious and more tolerant and will make fewer mistakes, but that it is simply someone else's turn. Violence by blacks is no more correct (morally) than is violence by Whites; it is simply the blacks' turn to wield the power:

WALKER: . . . What does it matter if there's more love
or beauty? Who the fuck cares? Is that what the Western
ofay thought while he was ruling . . . that his rule somehow
brought more love and beauty into the world? Oh, he
might have thought that concomitantly, while sipping a gin
rickey and scratching his ass . . . but that was not even the
point. Not even on the Crusades. The point is that you
had your chance, darling, now these other folks have theirs.
(Quietly)
Now they have theirs.
EASELY: God, what an ugly idea.
WALKER: (Head in hands) I know. I know.

The fact that Walker himself admits that the taking of turns is
ugly, that grasping for power for the sake of power (as in *1984*) is
ugly — the fact that he admits it is significant for it shows that he
and his followers, like their white counterparts, are still enslaved
by certain ideas and forces they do not understand.

The idea of the Negro doing certain things simply because
it is his turn finds its most ironic moment in the theories of Mr.
Yacub, the "big-head scientist" who is seen as a character in LeRoi
Jones' *Black Mass* and whose theory of the radical superiority
of the Negro is briefly noted in *The Autobiography of Malcolm X*:

From his studies, the big-head scientist knew that black
men contained two germs, black and brown. He knew that
the brown germ stayed dormant as, being the lighter of the
two germs, it was weaker. Mr. Yacub, to upset the law of
nature, conceived the idea of employing what we today
know as the recessive genes structure, to separate from each
other the two germs, black and brown, and then grafting
the brown germs to progressively lighter, weaker stages.
The humans resulting, he knew, would be, as they became
lighter, and weaker, progressively also more susceptible to
wickedness and evil. And in this way finally he would
achieve the intended bleached out white race of devils.[11]

Just as the whites formulated their reasons for racial superiority
(leading to the inevitable conclusion that it was morally right for
the white man to sleep with a black woman since it is the mating
of a "higher" animal with a "lower" one, but never correct for a

black man to have coitus with a white woman, for it is never justified that a "lower" animal should mate with a "higher" one), the blacks have created their own theories of race. In *Black Mass,* for example, Jones extends Yacub's theories and dramatizes them, showing that white men and women are simply horrible mutations, beasts that must be tracked down and killed. Again, as in the racist theories of the whites, say the formulas of the KKK, what is at stake is not scientific accuracy but a political position. Hence, it is easy to see how certain white critics are prone to lament Jones' artistic failures and to complain that he has taken refuge in black propaganda. Gerald Weales, who has been drama critic for *Commonweal,* has stated that "it is clear in everything that Jones writes and says that the off-white poet has finally become the black revolutionary. There is more to regret here than the loss of a potentially good playwright."[12] The adjective *off-white* is a particularly unfortunate choice of words and indicates quite graphically the failure of the white critic to comprehend black revolutionary theatre.

Again, to show how poorly much recent criticism has come to grips with Jones' work, let me quote further from George Dennison's article:

> It is hard to know whom Jones is speaking for: 'Guerrilla warfare is inevitable in the North and South' — so he is quoted in a recent interview. 'Every black is a potential revolutionist. . . . You can't use nuclear weapons against us when we kill cops . . . there is no way of saving America.'
>
> Is he, in fact, offering *anyone* anything to do? Or anything *to be*? He is only freezing the lines of conflict, sacrificing change for passivity, and real emotion for a kind of frenetic anger, born in the first place of being bottled up.[13]

First, it is easy to know for whom Jones is speaking. He is speaking for all militant blacks who wish to bring about a revolution in America, for all those who are concerned with the idea of *liberation.* Liberation, as opposed to token integration, is the watch-word. Jones, in fact, has publicly stated that he believes Harlem should be recognized as a separate nation, complete with its own ambassadors and treaties.[14] Now a moderate, conservative, or liberal white may not want Jones to speak for that group, but it is the group he does speak for. Is he offering anything to do?

This should be irrelevant to drama criticism, but, in fact, Jones does offer someone something to do. He offers the action of a bloody insurrection, an action that certainly does not sacrifice change for passivity. But the real misreading of *The Slave* and of much contemporary black drama can be found in the assumption that there is a difference between *real* emotion and frenetic anger. Anger is a real emotion, even frenetic anger, and the anger that the black man feels toward the white, and the anger that the white feels toward the black, is one of the very real emotions present in America. How much longer must we cling to the heresy that evil is an illusion or that "negative" feelings aren't real feelings, that anger is not as real as love and joy? LeRoi Jones is a very angry man, but he is a very real man, and when he says "I don't see anything wrong with hating white people. Harlem must be taken from the beast and gain its sovereignty as a black nation,"[15] he is expressing something that must be paid attention to. His feeling is no illusion, no matter how many whites close their eyes to it, the frenetic anger will not go away.

As for accusing Jones' play *The Slave* of freezing the lines of conflict, the charge is nonsense. The lines of conflict were frozen long before Jones ever picked up a pen. The lines of conflict were frozen the first time a white man chained a black man and sold him. The black man lost his identity on the slave ships to America, and since then the black man has had no real identity of his own, lost somewhere between two continents. In *The Slave,* Walker Vessels is reduced to saying that all he knows about himself is what he can use, and his most useful tool is violence against the slave-owners:

> GRACE: There are so many bulbs and screams shooting off inside you, Walker. So many lies you have to pump full of yourself. You're split so many ways . . . your feelings are cut up into skinny horrible strips . . . like umbrella struts holding up whatever bizarre black cloth you're using this performance as your self's image. I don't even think you know who you are any more. No, I don't think you ever knew.
>
> WALKER: I know what I can use.
>
> GRACE: No, you never even found out who you were until you sold the last of your loves and emotions down the

river . . . until you killed your last old friend . . . and found out *what* you were. My God, it must be hard being you, Walker Vessels. It must be a sick task keeping so many lying separate uglinesses together . . . and pretending they're something you made and understand.

WALKER: What I can use, madam . . . what I can use. I move now trying to be certain of that.

The black man moves trying to be certain of what he can use. But can he use the white man's educational institutions? Can he use the white man's Christianity? Can he use any of the white man's legal and military establishments? Many people, including blacks, would say yes. LeRoi Jones emphatically says no. Jones contends that "There is no way the black man can be heard or seen clearly in the existing system,"[16] and that the present system will reduce the Negro to "a drab lower middle-class buffoon who has no more political power or cultural significance than his social interment petty ambition allows."[17] The black man's search for an identity within the present social structure can be keenly felt in Jones' plays *Dutchman* and *The Toilet*.

In *Dutchman*, Clay, a twenty-year old Negro is picked up on the subway by Lula, a thirty-year old white woman. During the course of their conversation they exchange sexual advances and verbal attacks, until Lula stabs him. The rest of the passengers toss Clay's body off the train, and, at the play's conclusion, Lula is about to begin the same process all over again with another black boy. *Dutchman* is probably Jones' most successful and coherent play, for in it the inevitable violence between black and white, and the sexual tension between the black man and the white woman (a tension honestly discussed in Eldridge Cleaver's *Soul on Ice*) are brought sharply into focus. In a long speech near the end of the play, Clay makes it clear to Lula that he cannot be understood by any white person, and that all attempts at verbal communication by the blacks are merely camouflage for the need to commit violence:

I mean if I murdered you, then the other white people would begin to understand me. You understand? No, I guess not. If Bessie Smith had killed some white people she wouldn't have needed that music. She could have talked very straight and plain about the world. No metaphors.

No grunts. No wiggles in the dark of her soul. Just straight two and two are four. Money. Power. Luxury. Like that. All of them. Crazy niggers turning their backs on sanity. When all it needs is that simple act. Murder! Just murder! Would make us all sane.

The dramatic irony, of course, is provided by the fact that Clay talks about murder, but, because of his upbringing and middle-class background, he cannot perform the act which he claims will free him and make him sane. Lula, on the other hand, calmly plunges the knife into Clay's chest. Jones himself, in discussing *Dutchman*, has stated that

> The boy senses the basic delusions in middle class Negro life; the girl is still a product of the establishment, of the great white power structure. So the pressures get to them too, causing friction, baring murderous instincts.
>
> They say essentially true things to each other (mixing racial barbs — 'Remember, boy, your grandfather was a slave' — into the sex chatter). But honesty is useless as long as the guilt is still there. The truth appears like an accusation. We must learn to accept truth as fact rather than accusation.[18]

Lula mocks Clay and accuses him of being an Uncle Tom, an "Ol Thomas Woolly-Head," whereas Clay would like to see himself as a black revolutionary. The truth, however, is that he is neither one nor the other, and, hence, feels a real lack of identity.

In *The Toilet*, the black adolescent's search for identity is clearly shown when a group of black high school students gather in the school's bathroom to beat up a white boy who has supposedly written a 'love' note to one of their members. At the end of the play, however, Ray Foots, the black who allegedly received the note but who may have written the note himself, returns to the bathroom to cradle the beaten white boy in his arms. The play's blistering obscenities have offended many theatre-goers, but it uncompromisingly tackles the sexual identity of the young black man. Gerald Weales believes that "Jones is obviously using homosexuality to represent something else in this play. Acceptance in the white world, perhaps,"[19] but the black man doesn't want acceptance into the white world as much as he wishes to escape the traditional matriarchy of the black community. Throughout the history of the Negro in America, it has been the woman who was able to find work, either as a servant or as a cook, and it has been the woman who has been the ruler and center of the family, hence the black man sometimes turns to homosexual relationships to escape the stranglehold of the black woman. According to Larry Neal,

> In Afro-American literature of previous decades the strong black mother was the object of awe and respect. But in the new literature her status is ambivalent and laced with tension. Historically, Afro-American women have had to be the economic mainstays of the family. The oppressor allowed them to have jobs while at the same time limiting the economic mobility of the black man. Very often, therefore, the woman's aspirations and values are closely tied to the white power structure and not to those of her man. Since he cannot provide for his family the way white men do, she despises his weakness, tearing into him at every opportunity until, very often, there is nothing left but a shell.[20]

Homosexuality is a prominent theme in Jones' *The Baptism,* also, but the play is primarily an attack on the failure of Christianity to help the black man achieve a sense of selfhood. In that play, which is essentially an allegory, a 15 year old homosexual invades a Christian church, where he is followed by a chorus of women who sexually desire him. At the conclusion of the play, the boy kills the church's minister and the chorus of women, and a messenger arrives on a motorcycle to carry the boy away. The play is a confusing one, but it displays a variety of themes that Jones is fundamentally concerned with, for disgust with the church establishment can be seen right from the opening where a plaque that says WHBI radio appears right under the inscription IHS on the altar. In recent years much has been made of the black man's anti-semitism, a hatred of the Black directed against the Jews who owned and maintained business establishments in Harlem and other black communities, but very little anti-semitism is seen (as yet) in contemporary black drama. What is far more prevalent is the Negro's disgust at the failure of Christianity to provide the black man with viable solutions to his problems. In *The Baptism*

or James Baldwin's *Blues For Mister Charlie,* and in segments of
Loften Mitchell's *Land Beyond the River,* and in Ben Caldwell's
Mission Accomplished, disappointment and disgust about church
leadership is keenly felt. In many ways, Christianity in America
can be viewed as a force used by the white man to further the
cause of slavery, and oftentimes whites appealed to the Bible as
proof of white supremacy. Furthermore, Christianity preached non-
violence, and hence a slave-owner would theoretically have less to
fear from his Christian slaves than his non-Christian ones. Also
Christianity, with its commandments against suicide, kept the slaves
alive to do their masters' bidding. Those who felt it was better
to be dead than to be a slave were morally prevented from killing
themselves. In addition, Christianity directed the black man's
attention to the rewards of the next life since they were very
unlikely to get many rewards in this one. The white man brought
Christianity to the Negro, not because he was concerned with sav-
ing the black man's soul, but because the white man wanted to
save his own skin. No wonder then that the failure of the Christian
religion is coupled with homosexuality in some of the contemporary
plays, most prominently in *The Baptism.*

These then are a few of the themes that Jones concerns himself
with in his plays: the inevitability of violence between blacks and
whites, the emphasis on the black "taking his turn," the black
man's hang-up over the white woman, the problem of adolescent
homosexuality, and the failure of Christianity, coupled with the
failure of the diabolism of all the white man's institutions. Jones'
contention that "There is no way the black man can be heard or
seen clearly in the existing system" is, of course, one of the reasons
for his revolutionary theatre. How wide-spread are Jones' ideas
about a theatre of victims? It is still far too early to tell, for most
of the black plays being produced off Broadway are being produced
for and by whites. Very few of the contemporary playwrights
whose plays are being staged now are as incendiary as Jones, but
it is likely that other playwrights of Jones' ilk will be arriving on
the scene. Some measure of Jones' influence can already be seen
in the theatre concepts of Ed Bullins, author of *In The Wine Time*
and *Clara's Old Man.* Bullins' nonsense drama *How Do You Do*
is prefaced with a quote from Jones, and, in an essay entitled "The
So-Called Western Avant Garde Drama," Bullins maintains that

(If the media is the message, we black artists have been far ahead of anything the white man has conceived.)

For the white man there are no new stories, or plots, or characters; and somehow, by the time they filter down to present theatre, there are *no* really new ideas in his culture. His sense of reality cannot extend far enough to encompass what is not merely himself, or to perceive what is really happening, i.e. *Black*.[21]

But as long as societies change, and the times change, there will always be new characters and stories. Unfortunately the establishment theatre, like prime time on television, is always years behind in perceiving what is really happening. And so usually are the critics and the academic taste-makers. What is happening in theatre today provides the potential for a revolution — a revolution in attitudes toward drugs, nudity, and race relations, a profound upheaval of the establishment's lack of honesty and vision — and this potential for revolution is being felt throughout a new generation of playwrights, directors, and actors. What is happening is that *black playwrights are beginning to express their own experiences and feelings to an audience of other blacks.* No one can dare prophesy what this means for the future of theatre in our country, but it might mean that the traditional white man's theatre will become an American theatre, a theatre of many voices and many audiences, a theatre where anger can be recognized as a real emotion.

NOTES

[1]"Robert Macbeth and the New Lafayette Theatre," *Theatre Today* (Fall, 1968), p. 13.

[2]"The Negro Theatre and the Harlem Community," in *Black Expression*, edited by Addison Gayle, Jr. (New York, Weybright and Talley, 1969), p. 158.

[3]*Ibid*, p. 155.

[4]Doris M. Abramson, "William Wells Brown: America's First Negro Playwright," *Educational Theatre Journal*, XX (October, 1968), pp. 370-375.

[5]*New York Times*, February 2, 1969.

[6]*New York Times*, August 14, 1966.

[7]Ben Caldwell, *Riot Sale or the Dollar Psyche Fake Out*, in *The Drama Review* (Summer, 1968). Ben Caldwell is also editor of *Black Theatre Magazine*.

[8]Quoted in Larry Neal's "The Black Arts Movement," *The Drama Review* (Summer, 1968).

[9]George Dennison, "Demagogy of LeRoi Jones," *Commentary*, 39 (February, 1965), p. 68.

[10]LeRoi Jones, "What Does Nonviolence Mean" in *Crisis: Contemporary Reader*, edited by Peter Collier (New York, Harcourt, Brace & World, Inc., 1969), p. 81.

[11]*The Autobiography of Malcolm X* (New York, Grove Press, 1965), p. 165.

[12]Gerald Weales, *The Jumping-Off Place: American Drama in the 1960's* (London, Collier-Macmillan Limited, 1969), p. 147.

[13]Dennison, p. 70.

[14]Alfonson Narvaez, "Playwright's Demand: Harlem Its Own Nation," *New York Herald Tribune*, October 26, 1965.

[15]Hollie West, "Harlem Actors Play at Hating Whites," *New York World-Telegram and Sun*, November 30, 1965.

[16]"What Does Nonviolence Mean," p. 77.

[17]*Ibid.*, p. 71.

[18]Gene Palatsky, "Seeing the Lie," *Newark Evening News*, March 30, 1964.

[19]Weales, p. 141.

[20]Neal, p. 38.

[21]*Black Expression*, p. 145.

SELECTED LIST OF PLAYS BY CONTEMPORARY
BLACK AMERICAN PLAYWRIGHTS

BALDWIN, JAMES. *Amen Corner, Blues For Mister Charlie.*

BULLINS, ED. *In The Wine Time, The Corner, How Do You Do, It Has No Chance, The Game of Adam and Eve, Clara's Old Man, The Gentleman Caller, A Son, Come Home; The Electronic Nigger.*

CALDWELL, BEN. *Militant Preacher, Riot Sale or Dollar Psyche Fake Out, The Job, Mission Accomplished.*

ERROL, JOHN. *Moon on a Rainbow Shawl.*

GORDONE, CHARLES. *No Place To Be Somebody.*

HANSBERRY, LORRAINE. *A Raisin In the Sun, The Sign in Sidney Brustein's Window.*

IMAN, JUSAF. *Praise the Lord, But Pass the Ammunition.*

JONES, LEROI. *Dutchman, Baptism, The Slave, The Toilet, Slave Ship, Black Mass, The Great Goodness of Life* (a 'Coon' Show), *Arm Yourself or Harm Yourself, The Eighth Ditch.*

KENNEDY, ADRIENNE. *The Owl Answers, Funny House of the Negro, A Lesson In a Dead Language, A Rat's Mess, A Beast's Story.*

MILNER, RONALD. *Who's Got His Own, Life Agony, The Warning — a Theme for Linda.*

MITCHELL, LOFTEN. *Land Beyond the River.*

SHEPP, ARCHIE. *Junebug Graduates Tonight.*

WARD, DOUGLAS TURNER. *Reckoning, Happy Ending, Day of Absence.*

WARD, THEODORE. *Our Lan'.*

WILLIAMS, ELLWOODSON. *Voice of the Gene.*

Lonne Elder III:
An Interview

THE NEGRO ENSEMBLE COMPANY was founded in the summer of 1967 as a successor to the Group Theatre Workshop. It was financed by the Ford Foundation to the extent of $1,200,000. The first production, in January, 1968, was Peter Weiss's *Song of the Lusitanian Bogey* and in April, 1969, the Company received a 'Tony' award for the development of new talent and audiences.

The NEC's most successful production by a Negro playwright is Lonnie Elder's *Ceremonies in Dark Old Men* which opened on February 4, 1969, and was hailed by Richard Watts of the New York Post as the "best American play of the season."

The following interview was conducted in England where the NEC was appearing in the Royal Shakespeare Company's World Theatre Season at the Aldwych Theatre. The interview itself took place in the Strand Palace Hotel on May 8, 1969.

BIGSBY: How did you begin your writing career?

ELDER: I first started writing short stories and poetry in about 1953-4 when I went to live in Harlem. Before that I had lived in Jersey City. It was in Harlem that I met Turner Ward who was primarily interested in writing for the theatre and through my association with him I became interested in writing for the theatre as well. To me at that time it seemed something very very far away, something that was almost unattainable, something that you go after.

BIGSBY: Before you started writing for the theatre what kind of work were you producing and where were you living?

ELDER: No place. I was just a young stupid kid who was trying to write. Some of it was very infantile. Meanwhile I was doing whatever I could. I was living. At one time when I was about 19 or 20 I was a professional gambler. I used to be a dealer in an after hours joint, for about six months.

BIGSBY: How did you meet Douglas Turner Ward?

ELDER: We were both involved in the black civil rights movement in Harlem so that it was inevitable that we would meet. We actually met in an office in Harlem and became good friends. He was writing and I was writing and we decided that we would study acting because we figured that it would be easier for us to get jobs as actors than it would be as writers, even though the jobs for actors were so scarce. But we were lucky in a couple of instances whereby we managed to become involved in two long-running shows, *A Raisin in the Sun* and Douglas Turner Ward's two one-acters. It was during that time that I did a great deal of writing.

BIGSBY: When did you start work on *Ceremonies*?

ELDER: I worked on *Ceremonies* over a period of two years from 1963 to 1965, although I suppose the actual writing time was about six months. Nobody wanted to produce it. It had been optioned once.

BIGSBY: Is this because of the lack of companies like the Negro Ensemble?

ELDER: Yes, that is one of the reasons. The New York theatre, both on and off Broadway grabs anything that is fashionable. It is terribly commercial and conventional.

BIGSBY: And yet your play was greeted as a conventional play.

ELDER: Yes. The interesting thing about the play is that it won quite a few awards. Before it was produced I'd earned about $8000 off it. It won the Stanley Drama Award, the Yale, Joseph E. Levine Award and the Bishop K. Hamilton Award. As for the critics saying it was conventional, the interesting thing about that is that what they found conventional is mainly because I took the time, the care, put a lot of energy into it to make it workable, from moment to moment, from scene to scene. It's written in long scenes. The play also depends a great deal on its language, on the tone, innuendo and rhythm of its language. But there's one very interesting thing. I had a producer tell me in 1966 that there were too many obscenities. He said that that was fine and good but that the New York stage just wasn't ready for it at least not for this kind of blunt, direct and casual introduction of obscenity which doesn't emerge from a dramatic confrontation. It becomes a casual pattern of communication and the casual exchange between characters. I mentioned to him the Jones plays but he said that that was a question of direct conflict and communication that could grow out of a certain anger in people. I said "Well that's bullshit. If you're dealing with these kinds of characters it's inescapable because it's one of the areas of communication."

BIGSBY: The critics seem to have suggested that your play was totally naturalistic. Is that how you regard it?

ELDER: The critics said it was naturalism. It's naturalism to them mainly because they're unacquainted with the flow and the various colours of life in the black ghetto. It's just like one stupid left-wing critic who writes for the Free Press made the stupid comment that one character says to another character that "I was born about six blocks from here but by the time I was ten I didn't know how to cry." He said that no black person in Harlem would find it necessary to tell another black person his predicament. That just shows you his ignorance. That's bullshit. The thing is that the terror and the brutality of racism in the black community is not always evident in the natural behaviour of the people. But the thing is that the only way that myself as a writer can bring it forth is to exalt it in some way, to give it a certain shape, a certain form.

BIGSBY Like a caricaturist?

ELDER: That's what happens if you rely too much on the natural modes and habits of your characters and people. That's what it really becomes. It becomes a caricature.

I definitely disagree with some of the critics who say that the play was naturalistic in the traditional or conventional sense of the word. It is naturalistic out of necessity in areas where it had to be. I would call it more akin to exalted realism.

BIGSBY: Who exactly were you writing this play for? Is it aimed at a specifically black audience?

ELDER: No. I can't possibly do that. If I do that I think I'm crippling myself in terms of what I am and what I can do with the material before me. I write out of the black frame of reference, which is different from saying that I am writing for all black people. I'm writing out of a black frame of reference because of my personal situation — I'm black. My experience has been black and my frame of reference is black. That frame of reference automatically and inevitably moves in the direction of a black audience. It has to. You no longer try to appease a theatre-going audience which is basically white. If you write for the theatre you've got to be writing for a white audience. I'm writing for an audience which at this time doesn't really exist. Thanks to the Negro Ensemble and the black theatre movement in America this audience is being cultivated.

I can't segregate myself. For instance a lot of the white people who come to the Negro Ensemble Company fail to understand everything, a lot of the things escape them.

BIGSBY: Do you go along with those who say that the white critic should accept that the time has come for him to admit that he is not qualified to judge material by black writers?

ELDER: White critics often make asinine mistakes. Some of them are openly racist in their reaction to black material. Walter Kerr, for example. Too often it becomes not criticism but a personal attack on the substance of his material. There are a lot of white critics who simply make asses of themselves. But of course there are white critics who are astute. The critics did catch one thing. The play really is based on the daily ritual of survival in the black community, which does not necessarily have anything to do with black/white confrontation or any clenched fist anger. They caught this. Clive Barnes for example. Clive Barnes is white. I don't deny this. Just because a man is black doesn't mean that he's possessed of any special gifts of critical evaluation.

BIGSBY: In *The Crisis of the Negro Intellectual* Harold Cruse has attacked Lorraine Hansberry for trying to ape the white world. Do you agree?

ELDER: No. Quite definitely. My opinion of Lorraine Hansberry is this. I think that she was one of the finest dramatists in the world at the time of her death. I thought she was one of the most informed, one of the most astute, gifted and talented writers of this particular time. The only way I can judge anything that any writer has done is to judge it on the end result.

BIGSBY: Cruse has said that in *The Sign in Sidney Brustein's Window,* which only has one black character, Lorraine Hansberry is more concerned with elevating the Jewish image than with the plight of her own people.

ELDER: I think that's stupid because Lorraine Hansberry or

any other black writer can write about anything she wants to write about. The only thing I can do is look at the end result of it. A lot of people knock Adrienne Kennedy. I say Adrienne Kennedy can write about anything she wants to write about. The only thing I can do is judge on the end result and if its short of excellence then that's what it is. You can't do any more than that. You can't tell a writer that he has to write about blacks, or the black movement, or black anger. That's stupid. It just so happens that I'm hung up on my experience as a black man living in America. I'm hung up on it.

BIGSBY I don't want to belabour Cruse but he has raised some interesting issues which have a direct bearing on your work and on the NEC. For example, he has said that from his point of view the Negro playwright can only operate within an ethnic theatre. How do you react to that?

ELDER: Well, what can you say to that? It's crude, it's ludicrous, it's unreal and its unbelievable. I'm sick and tired of people telling other people what they can do and what they cannot do. That's ridiculous. I would allow anyone to be an ass if that's what they want to be. I've grown past saying what people can or can't do. I can only judge by the end result. A person may say all kinds of things that I disagree with. I think, basically, of say Ed Bullins whose politics and philosophy I'm certainly not in complete agreement with. I'm a great admirer of his plays. And that's what makes the remarks of someone like Harold Cruse stupid.

BIGSBY: Are you tempted to take theatre out onto the streets as Bullins and Jones have done?

ELDER: I don't know. It may come to that.

BIGSBY: Do you think, perhaps, that involvement of this kind is in fact counter-productive as far as writers are concerned? Do you think that the more you become involved in the fighting the less time you have for writing and the narrower the perspective?

ELDER: It is counter-productive. For example, my involvement with the Negro Ensemble Company — Douglas Turner Ward can vouch for that — when you become actually involved in the creation of a theatre, of an organisation. But a determination is made about those things in terms of what you yourself feel that you must do. I've always been involved to a lesser or greater degree. My basic involvement is what I am in terms of the creation of the Negro Ensemble. I've realised that the NEC is a very important thing as far as a theatre is concerned, relating to black life and black people. I'm doing whatever I can to make it bigger and better.

BIGSBY: But of course that doesn't only draw on black writers; it draws on white dramatists as well. Is that something you would like to see discontinued?

ELDER: I don't know. I would like to see the NEC being an exclusive place for black writers. That's not a problem. One of the things about it is that I look at it from this standpoint, that Peter Weiss can have his play done anywhere he wants, but the average young black writer really doesn't have anywhere to go to. I'm not against the production of Peter Weiss's play. I think that his play has been a greater contribution to us as an organisation than we have been to Peter Weiss. The trouble with where we are now is that we have to be exclusive. This season all the plays we have done have been plays by black writers.

BIGSBY: There have been experiments of this kind in the past but they have never lasted very long.

ELDER: But they've never been on this level and it was not at this time.

BIGSBY: But can you see the same thing being repeated? Is this merely the American Negro Theatre over again?

ELDER: No. This is an entirely different kind of operation. For example, the American Negro Theatre didn't really have a guiding force. It was a theatre that, when it did come up with something, a big hit, the first impulse was to dissolve themselves into the general commercial theatre.

BIGSBY: *Anna Lucasta.*

ELDER: Yes. *Anna Lucasta* being an example. This is totally different thinking from the NEC.

BIGSBY: You can't see it happening again?

ELDER: This happened with *Ceremonies,* which was the first instance that this happened. The kind of money that was offered ran into the millions. My first reaction was, no. If that had happened the NEC would have crumbled at the expense of us running off to Broadway. I think this is the difference. The NEC is not a step towards the great commercial theatre.

BIGSBY: Would a success of this kind really kill it?

ELDER: Well we're not really set up for it. They wanted to transfer the members of the cast. They wanted the whole package. The NEC allowed a producer to pick up the rights for an off-Broadway production. But these were the only rights he had, just for the off-Broadway production. And in the midst of the rehearsal period, which was with an entirely different cast outside of the NEC, a producer came and gave us a great offer, a theatre-owning producer, at fantastic personal prices for myself. And I told him, no. Mainly because, as I told him, I can't reach my audience at $9 a seat. I can't do it.

BIGSBY: The money for the NEC comes from a white foundation.

ELDER: Well I don't care what colour the money is. But the thing about that is that the NEC will have to become self-support-ing. That's my feeling. When you get something like *Ceremonies*, they will have to use it to their best advantage, in terms of becoming self-supporting because those kind of chances don't come too often. They own the rights to the play and will be doing future projects with the play itself on a national scale, which I'm hopeful will bring in some money.

BIGSBY: Do you pay much attention to the critics?

ELDER: I read them all.

BIGSBY: Are they any use to you?

ELDER: Yes. It causes me to think. For example, one of the things they said was that the play was long. I knew it was long but it wasn't long in terms of time. It was long in terms of the fact that the last act is very long. What happened is that the second act should really be another act but that in terms of what I was doing, the movement of the play, the rhythm, the move from one irony to another, I knew that if I made this another act, the last scene, the third act, it would kill what had gone before it. There wouldn't be that connecting element. So I had to keep it there because the whole last scene is total irony, it's completely against what has gone before. If I broke it up and made that the third act it wouldn't be effective. So that is why they said it was too long. So what I did, when I sold it to the other producer, I did some pruning because I knew it was too long. Whenever I stood there in the theatre I kept saying 'they're right. It's too long, it's too long.' But I could not make it a third act. If I did it would kill the play.

BIGSBY: Which version is being published?

ELDER: The NEC version, the longer version.

BIGSBY: What exactly is your role with the NEC?

ELDER: My title is Playwrights/Directors Co-ordinator. The most important thing I do is, I am the director of the Playwrights/

Directors division workshop of the Negro Ensemble. That workshop consists of directors and playwrights meeting twice a week in the workshop and experimenting with their material and holding a polemic on each other's work. This particular workshop has a Monday night series. We present plays on Monday nights which we have worked on in the workshop. We do versions of these plays on Monday nights, utilising some of the actors in our other workshops, our acting workshops. This has been very successful. Also, while we're in Europe, we have a May festival. We have all of the workshop's productions going on every week. We are doing a series of about six plays that will be running. This is what we call a bonus on our subscribers list, and they come to see, these are basically students who are participating in it and the writers and directors in the workshop.

BIGSBY: What are you working on now?

ELDER: I've had one guy who wants to pay me $2000 for the rights of my next play that I haven't even written yet. It's a weird existence. I'm not going to do another play for at least a year and a half. I run out of time.

BIGSBY: You're not doing any other writing?

ELDER: Occasionally I write a poem for my wife.

Harold Cruse: An Interview

The following interview with Harold Cruse
was recorded at the University College of
Wales, Aberystwyth, on 18th June, 1969.

BIGSBY: You say in your book, *The Crisis of the Negro Intellectual,* that the criticism of Negro writing is mainly the Negro's responsibility. Does this mean that in some way you feel that the white critic is disqualified from approaching black literature, that the criteria which he would bring to bear are no longer relevant? Or is this simply a cry for the emergence of black critics who so far haven't put in much of an appearance?

CRUSE: Well, the answer to that is both. There are two answers to the questions. The white critic is not disqualified by my saying that. The white critic is necessary, but usually the white critic approaches black literature out of another kind of social context and very often he is unfamiliar with what the black writer is usually trying to describe or write about. He describes black writing from another critical criterion, which attempts to compare either the best or the worst of black writing usually with the best of white writing, which in many ways is unfair. On the other hand his role is one which discourages, very often minimises, the importance of black criticism which is practically absent from the literary scene in America and has been for many years, and if the white critic continues to co-opt the role of the emergent black critic, black criticism will hardly ever emerge to any level of literary importance.

BIGSBY: On the other hand if there are at the moment no black critics on the horizon isn't it better that some white critics should pay attention to black writing rather . . .

CRUSE: It can't be any other way given the circumstances, it's a pattern of literary creativity in America, I think. It has to be altered — the relationship between the black writer and his public. It has to be altered and to alter for the better one must expect black critics to emerge on the scene.

BIGSBY: But you are saying, then, that you think that white critics are simply not competent to deal with black literature.

CRUSE: In most cases no, not really. They are not competent to deal with the implications of black literature; let us put it that way. The white critic is very competent when it comes to dealing with literary competence — whether it is good writing or bad writing and so on and so forth. But sociologically, that is in so far as black literature is an expression of black experience, or what that experience really amounts to — I don't think that the average white critic is really competent to deal with that question or to deal with it from a constructive point of view, because the white critic has a tendency to encourage the black writer not to be a black writer at all, but to be what he calls a universal writer — the definition of which escapes me. I'm still in the dark as to what constitutes universality of literary expression.

BIGSBY: In fact that leads us on to something else that you have said — that the job of the black writer is to concern himself with what constitutes the black experience.

CRUSE: In the main I should say that should be his role, his natural role. It's not to attempt to impose anything on any writer, black or white, so let's understand that. Individually, I admit that it is a writer's prerogative to deal with any aspect of life that appeals to him, regardless of race, creed, colour, national origin or whatever.

BIGSBY: But on the other hand you have said that you would like to see Negro film makers make films about Harlem and . . .

CRUSE: Yes, I'd like to see that.

BIGSBY: But you've taken this so far as to say that those black writers who don't concern themselves with the black experience are not Negro writers.

CRUSE: No, they really aren't, they really aren't.

BIGSBY: So what is your definition of a Negro writer?

CRUSE: The definition of a Negro writer is one that is

predicated on the definition of a white writer because our conception of a white writer historically is one who concerns himself with the white experience.

BIGSBY: Does this mean that you would agree with those critics who attacked William Styron's *Nat Turner* on the basis, fundamentally, that he shouldn't concern himself with the black experience — it wasn't his business to do so?

CRUSE: I wouldn't agree thoroughly with that. Styron is a peculiar kind of American literary product. In American Negro history there has been a collaboration going on between the black and white literary scene and the whites have been predominant, have been the ones that set the tone for writing about Negroes. This has influenced the black writer's perception of what the black experience is, because craftwise, formwise, he has imitated the white writer's imitation of himself and this has worked, I think, to the detriment of the black writer. This has very little to do now with the writer's right to write about what he wants to write about. In America it has a peculiar connotation which is not experienced in other cultures, where, because of the role of the Styrons, historically, it has worked to the detriment of the black writer. That's why it is of peculiar and unique importance to discuss this question in terms of the black writer's responsibility. The reason these critics find themselves in the position of having to attack Styron for writing about Nat Turner is because they haven't done it themselves, and this only bolsters my argument. If they had been carrying out their literary and social responsibility with regard to Nat Turner or any other historical hero, then I don't think they would have the grounds to deal with Styron in this fashion and I don't think Styron would have bothered to write about it the way he did. Styron did it because nobody else had done it, including the black writers.

Another question is posed here. The black writer is usually anti-historical. He will not use historical figures. He has been led to believe that a writer's function is to deal with the present — that's one of his deficiencies.

BIGSBY: How do you react, in fact, to the book of critical reviews of *Nat Turner* published by ten black writers?

CRUSE: Frankly, I didn't read it. I knew what it was going to say. I glanced through it but it didn't move me that much.

BIGSBY: Although you said a little while ago that you don't feel that you are determining for a Negro writer what he should write about, that a writer should be free to write about whatever he wants to write about, the fact remains that in your book you have attacked both Lorraine Hansberry and James Baldwin for writing the kind of works which you don't think a black writer should be writing.

CRUSE: Well, that's my way of expressing what I call some standard of black criticism. You don't have to accept it. You don't have to accept my standard of criticism, but it is a form of criticism.

BIGSBY: But it's a rather claustrophobic idea that the black writer should only write about the black experience.

CRUSE: I agree, but the black writer is under too many different kinds of compulsions, don't you see. I raised the question about what Baldwin writes about and what Hansberry writes about, based on my own personal experience of when I was attacked for the same reasons and became very defensive about it, and took the position — all right then, let's have some critical discussion about this problem, about what the black writer should write about. But these writers don't indulge in any kind of criticism in public about this role. So I felt that, all right, if this is the case I'll jump in and get my feet wet on this question and let them respond because I don't mean for my personal criticism to be taken as a transcendent truth. We've got to have some kind of consensus on this problem because if we don't have this then what are we talking about. Each writer can go his own way and then no one has any loyalties, or any connection with any kind of philosophy or movement or trend, because the writer is an individual. He has no social responsibilities at all but he is constantly being told by the movement's leaders, 'You have a responsibility to the movement.' But if that is true then what is my responsibility?

BIGSBY: But can a Negro writer not renounce his position as spokesman? In fact doesn't the position of many Negro writers as spokesmen for the cause in fact work to the detriment of their art — James Baldwin being a case in point?

CRUSE: It does. This is just my point, the point I'm trying to bring out for discussion. I want some consensus on this. I want the people involved to take a position and let us argue this question out. It is important that the question be argued out now, because it has been bandied about for too many years without any conclusion about what is the black writer's role.

BIGSBY: But in your criticism of Lorraine Hansberry and

particularly in reference to *The Sign in Sidney Brustein's Window* you accuse her in your book of bending over backwards to glorify the Jewish image in the face of the rising tide of colour. Now is this a specific argument levelled at this specific play or is this part of a general movement in the Negro community?

CRUSE: It's part of a general movement that I see developing in the black community. Now this is the case and this movement says that black writers should be identified with this movement and Lorraine Hansberry has assumed a certain spokesmanship role about what the black experience is all about. Taking her at her own word, then I say well if that is the case young lady then what are you doing writing about a group which has arrived on the American scene? They don't need any support from the likes of you.

BIGSBY: But on the other hand that play is about, among other things, the nature of commitment. Now, isn't that in itself relevant to the black experience, to the black situation at this moment?

CRUSE: Not from the Jewish point of view. Because he is not committed to being involved in any Jewish movement.

BIGSBY: But to what extent in *The Sign in Sidney Brustein's Window* is the Jewishness a real element? Why Jewish as opposed to just white?

CRUSE: She makes the point herself. He is a Jewish hero. She makes it very explicit in the play, that he's a Jewish hero. Now what relevance is a Jewish hero involved in a reform movement, which is what he was involved in, in a Village reform movement which never really had any connection with the black struggle, with the black community? What relevance has this to the content of the black movement which according to her and others is not merely a reform movement; it is a movement for basic social changes, fundamental social changes in this country. The movement which Brustein comes out of, or the movement which he functions in in her play, is a liberal reform movement. It has no relevance at all to black commitment because black commitment long ago put down reformism as being luke-warm and irrelevant to the black situation.

BIGSBY: Now Hansberry, among other black playwrights, has moved outside of the sphere of the ethnic theatre, and you say elsewhere in your book that the black playwright can only come to fruition within the context of an ethnic theatre.

CRUSE: I think so.

BIGSBY: But at the moment, if we take one example of the ethnic theatre, namely LeRoi Jones's Black Arts theatre and the theatres which have followed it in Newark and other places, doesn't this seem to indicate the reverse, that in fact there is a kind of new dogmatism laid down by this theatre which is counter-productive to the artist.

CRUSE: Well, you could say that. On the other hand you have to admit that any new trend based on any kind of ethnicity goes through these kinds of phases, where they limit their focus and attempt to become propagandistic because the movement itself demands this kind of cut-and-dried, black and white characterisation or polarisation of issues in order to make the so-called message clear. The black critics themselves influence the writer, Jones in this instance, to write this way. I personally don't feel that the writer should bend wholeheartedly to this. I feel that the black community is big enough and broad enough and multi-faceted enough not to have to be dogmatic about one's message. But this again is one of the weaknesses in the black writer. He's never had the wherewithall to develop any kind of perspective on his material.

BIGSBY: Wasn't LeRoi Jones in fact a better writer before he became involved in this kind of movement? *Dutchman* and *The Slave* . . .

CRUSE: I think so, I think so.

BIGSBY: Why?

CRUSE: Why? Because it is inevitable that when a writer attempts to project ideology in his writings he tends to be narrow, he tends toward anti-creativity.

BIGSBY: But aren't you yourself being ideological when you say that the black writer should concern himself with the black experience?

CRUSE: Yes, but I'm being ideological on another level. I don't mean narrow political ideology, because I think that the black experience is extensive enough to allow this. My argument is that the black writer has not handled his material wholeheartedly. He's avoided so many areas of black life, for some subjective reason of his own. And I wonder why. I wonder why the black writer avoids the black middle-class, because most of them come out of the black middle-class themselves. Why is it that LeRoi Jones, for example, in his essays castigates the black bourgeoisie, but he never satirises them.

BIGSBY: Well, I suppose he does to an extent in *Dutchman*.

CRUSE: Yes, but that's a very personal kind of thing. It's based on his personal individualised experience in the white world. That's all right. But I look for something much more sophisticated than that.

BIGSBY: Is it not legitimate for a Negro writer to write about whites?

CRUSE: It is very legitimate, I'd say. But I think that the expertise that the black writer could develop in dealing with whites would be enhanced if he approached his own materials more completely. I think that his views on the whites are pretty limited. And I think that the reason his views are so shallow on whites is because his views on black life are so shallow.

BIGSBY: Do you think there's a danger that in calling for the establishment of what amounts I suppose to a new tradition in black writing that you are going to betray youself into the position of denigrating other traditions?

CRUSE: What other traditions?

BIGSBY: Well, for example you have some fairly nasty things to say about T. S. Eliot in your book. If I can remind you what you say, you say that what bothered Eliot in America was that "the cultural status of his ethnic group was wide open for invasion by other culturally impure ethnic groups such as niggers, Jews, wops, Polacks and bohunks." Now isn't that really overstating the situation with regard to Eliot?

CRUSE: I don't think so. I think that Eliot personally was a class snob.

BIGSBY: Does it follow therefore that he's against all these ethnic groups?

CRUSE: I think that it's implied as part of the whole literary tradition, the genteel literary tradition coming out of England as it has been exemplified in the United States by certain writers who have adhered to this tradition, that anyone who is not a white anglo-saxon protestant is of a lower order and that their whole way of life is not really worthy of much serious attention by writers.

BIGSBY: But does this reflect on Eliot as a writer?

CRUSE: Well what about some of the references to Jews in some of his poetry?

BIGSBY: Well it's interesting that you should say that because in a sense if Eliot is anti-Semitic . . .

CRUSE: I didn't say he was . . .

BIGSBY: If there are elements in his poems which can be interpreted in that way . . .

CRUSE: I'm not saying so . . .

BIGSBY: Then it could also be said of some of the things which you have said.

CRUSE: I know it.

BIGSBY: Now, what is your attitude towards the Jews as an ethnic group in America?

CRUSE: The Jews as an ethnic group in America need no defence by anyone. They are very capable of defending their own cultural, social, economic and political position and they have done it very successfully. They don't need anybody's defence. But, on the other hand, as a black writer, Jews have been very much involved in setting literary standards, critical standards and creative standards for black writers, which I thoroughly resent on the part of a group which itself is constantly arguing against the anti-Jewish stereotype and who are fighting constantly for the maintainance of *their* unique cultural image. But they are either intentionally or unconsciously, whatever the case may be, working to the detriment of the Negro as an important ethnic group establishing *their* own national group image just as the Jews had done. And for that reason I have a lot of critical things to say about Jews and their participation in this whole literary development.

BIGSBY: And you don't restrict this in fact to the literary world as I gather. You feel that this is true even of music for example.

CRUSE: I certainly do.

BIGSBY: How?

CRUSE: Well, if you examine the cultural role of Jewish artists in America as a whole you'll find that much of the exploitative activities going on in the cultural world are done by Jews, as well as other groups.

BIGSBY: Exploitation in what sense?

CRUSE: Exploitation in the musical field; exploitation in the theatrical field; exploitation in the literary field; in the critical field; in the writing field and practically every cultural and creative endeavour the Jew is involved in.

BIGSBY: You say in your book that the truly original strain in America rests fundamentally on the black aesthetic, that this is the source of American originality.

CRUSE: Yes, it definitely is. Everything else, for the most part, is an imitation of European standards.

BIGSBY: An imitation or a development?

CRUSE, Well, call it an imitative devolopment. I'll put it that way.

BIGSBY: Is there no American originality in, for example, the novel?

CRUSE: Well, the novel? Yes, there is. But you see the novel is not an American creative form. It's an adapted form. When I speak of cultural creative originality I'm speaking of cultural and artistic ingredients in forms which are native to the American cultural development. In the theatre, in the novel, in poetry, with the exception let us say of Whitman, there has been no innovation on the American scene at all. This is an extension of European creative standards. But in other areas such as music and dance America has had ingredients and forms which are peculiarly American in their originality and their origins and the Americans have not developed this because of racism and a racial attitude towards the origins of these ingredients.

BIGSBY: Do you mean that they consciously shun those elements which are Negro?

CRUSE: That's right.

BIGSBY: That's a conscious action?

CRUSE: It's a conscous action on their part to denigrate anything that smacks of black originality on the American scene.

BIGSBY: Can you think of any examples?

CRUSE: I can think of music and I can think of theatre and I can think of dance.

BIGSBY: In the. theatre who are you particularly thinking of? Which major black American playwrights have failed to secure the kind of recognition which is their desert?

CRUSE: It isn't a question of individual playwrights or musicians, although that does explain the situation. I'm speaking of the development of form. For example, in the theatre America has made one original contribution to world theatre, that is in the minstrel show, which was a slave creation and which in the nineteenth century was the main popular theatrical form long before the 1890 producers and managers went to Europe to import Shaw and Ibsen in the attempt to establish an American theatre. In the 1890s the Negroes broke with this black-face minstrel pattern which was considered a stereotype of their theatrical function.

But that calls for an explanation of how the minstrels started. The minstrel was the original American theatrical form, as you know. It was a slave creation which was taken over by the whites in the South who imitated Negroes by blacking their faces and creating the American minstrel. The Negroes coming out of slavery re-adapted the minstrel form by also adopting the black-face imitation of themselves and from 1865 or thereabouts down to the 1890s this minstrel show form was the original native American contribution to the theatre. You see elements of this minstrel pattern still lingering in the American musical, which by the way is the American contribution to the theatre, not drama. That's European. But the native thing they have stereotyped, caricatured. Why? Because it was black. And the blacks in turn rejected it because it's a stereotype. In the 1890s the blacks in the theatre attempted to develop the minstrel pattern into another musical form. In reality the Negro theatrical form is really not a dramatic form. It's a musical form. That's the real native American Negro form. These playwrights you see coming up, they're writing black plays but they've adapted a European form.

BIGSBY: But doesn't this make it unlikely that there's going to be a realisation of your desire for black creativity in the field of the novel, for example, or the drama in that these forms are essentially European in origin?

CRUSE: I have some questions about how far black writers can go in these forms, particularly in the theatre because the black experience, in my estimation, cannot be limited or be held in the vise of a restricted European dramatic form which is not part of their heritage anyway. It's an adapted thing in which they have taken a European form, specifically a Greek form, and they have attempted to put the black experience into this limited theatrical mold, which I think is an unnatural fit.

BIGSBY: Where is this black originality to come from then, except in the sphere of music?

CRUSE: The black originality will come, I think, when the blacks in America attempt to reclaim their musical tradition in terms of pantomime, music, movement, dance, in a theatrical form, which is more natural to them because for many years the Negro's chief form in the theatre was a musical form. He didn't adapt the dramatic form seriously until the 1920s. There are no Negro dramatists coming out of the 19th century.

BIGSBY: So that in fact you don't have much hope for an organisation such as the Negro Ensemble Company.

CRUSE: Well I will have to reserve opinion on that until I see where it leads. I'm not going to be dogmatic about this form question. I have thoughts about it. But historically in the area of artistic forms the black writers and the black creators are still functioning in European derived forms of expression which immediately limits their range because they are not calling on the full play of the black experience to begin with.

BIGSBY: How important do you think these cultural issues are to the wider social and political questions?

CRUSE: They are of supreme importance. In America I consider the black situation has three important sides, a political side, an economic side and a cultural side. And each aspect calls for specific kinds of approaches. And I think that unless sufficient attention is paid by movements to the cultural aspects of the question, of the struggle in America, if there is a laxity on this front, there's going to be a concomitant laxity on the political and economic fronts because we are dealing here with the question of a group's identity in the American context. The identity has been besmirched and denigrated in the historical process to the extent that the average Negro in America is ashamed of his own background, his own cultural background. Even the most militant of black militants has some of this in them. A lot of them are embarassed by certain aspects of their cultural history, particularly in the American context. A lot of them talk about . . . they like jazz, yes, but how many actually know or are aware of the history of the jazz development. Very few. A lot of them are very much involved in the Negro dance rhythms, the Negro bodily movements and rhythms but a lot of them at the same time consider black dancing a form of Uncle Tomism, the shuffling, buck 'n wing kind of dance. As a result very little attention, if any, is paid to the development of black dance in America because a lot of the militants consider it a part of a submissive social role that was played by many Negroes, particularly in the dance field. Dance was cultivated for the entertainment of whites but this was overlooking the fact that dance has aesthetic possibilities in its own right, which they should pay attention to.

BIGSBY: But I still don't quite see what the connection is between this ethnic culture and the broader problems. For example, you say in your book that a lack of interest in ethnic culture goes hand in hand with a lack of real sympathy for the social problems of people in ghettos and how such problems can best be tackled. Isn't that rather an extreme position to adopt to say that if people are not interested in culture then they aren't interested in the social aspects?

CRUSE: No, that's not a far-fetched statement at all. Because if you consider why did it take so long for black leadership to consider black community control of institutions of education, why was that not considered important twenty or thirty years ago and what does this movement for black community control of schools actually imply? It implies that what was being taught in these schools has not been relevant to the intellectual development of black children, because the black past was not emphasised in previous educational institutions inside the black community. The schools were not giving black children the kind of education that would enhance their respect for their own image and their own development in their society. They were given education on purely white terms. So, therefore, it stands to reason then that if a group does not have any knowledge of or respect for its own cultural background and its own cultural contribution to the society as a whole then how can this group be expected to be mobilised in any definitive way on any other front to fight for their equality? They have no concept of self to bolster any other kind of demand that they could make on society. The integrationists themselves ran out of steam precisely because of this question. The integration leadership never concerned itself with the black community control of anything, because their objective was the obliteration of the black community as a community, the dispersion of Negroes into the body politic to the point at which they said there would be no black problem for anybody to be worried about. This was a utopian idea.

BIGSBY: Lastly, how do you see the situation at the moment with regard to the black writer? How do you see him developing? Is he moving along the line of ethnic culture?

CRUSE: He certainly is. Whether I say so or not. If you examine what has happened on the literary and theatrical scene. In fact some of my young critics in Harlem accuse me of not admitting in my book that such things as I was calling for were already in the process of developing. Like the black theatre and the new black poets and novelists.

BIGSBY: These people exist but what is the value, the quality of their work?

CRUSE: That's another question.

BIGSBY: But it's an important question.

CRUSE: It's an important question but we're now discussing craft problems rather than problems of content. I have been emphasising the necessity for developing a new black content, hoping that the questions of form and craft will take care of themselves.

BIGSBY: But presumably you're not calling for bad black writing.

CRUSE: No.

BIGSBY: Well at the moment what kind of hopes do you have with regard to the quality of this black literature?

CRUSE: I think it will improve as time goes on. It's got to improve. And black critics have a role to play there.

BIGSBY: Is there anything to be gained from adopting the position which you do in your book and which Richard Gilman does, that there should be a kind of white critical withdrawal?

CRUSE: I would agree with that. If they look at the situation and say that 'Well look, we have played this preponderant critical role all of those years. We have been the arbiters really, the judges of what black writers write and I think that it is time that we stepped aside and allowed them the leeway to develop their own standards.' I think that that would be very beneficial to American culture as a whole.

BIGSBY: On the other hand if these black critics don't emerge you are liable to find yourself in the situation where there is a critical vacuum.

CRUSE: I doubt it. If you examine *Negro Digest* you'll see that there's a whole crew of younger critics emerging who are taking up in very sharp terms evaluation of black writers. It's happening right now.

About the Contributors

MICHAEL ALLEN is a lecturer in English at Queen's University, Belfast and has visited Yale as an ACLS Fellow and taught at Smith College. He is the author of articles on various American writers and has published a study of *Poe and the British Magazine tradition* (O. U. P., New York, 1969).

JAMES BALDWIN was born in New York City in 1924 and is the author of four novels: *Go Tell it on the Mountain, Giovanni's Room, Another Country* and *Tell Me How Long the Train's Been Gone.* He has also published two plays, *The Amen Corner* and *Blues for Mr. Charlie,* and three volumes of essays, *Notes of a Native Son, Nobody Knows My Name* and *The Fire Next Time.*

PAUL BREMAN is an antiquarian bookseller born in Holland in 1931, whose hobby is publishing the work of afro-American poets. His privately printed series, 'Heritage', started in 1962 with Robert Hayden's book, *A Ballad of Remembrance* (which won the Grand Prix de la Poésie at the Dakar Festival of Negro Arts in 1966). Breman is also the author of a book on *Blues and Other Secular Folk Songs* (1961) and editor of several anthologies including *Sixes and Sevens* (1962), the first anthology of the 'new black poets', and the forthcoming *You Better Believe It: The Penguin Book of Black Verse.*

WAYNE COOPER At the time of writing this essay Cooper was a
graduate student in American History at Tulane University,
New Orleans, Louisiana.

HAROLD CRUSE was born in Virginia but raised in New York. He
has worked as a free-lance magazine writer and social critic
and was for a time a community organiser in Harlem col-
laborating with LeRoi Jones in the Black Arts Theatre. He
is presently the director of the black studies programme
at the University of Michigan. He is the author of *The
Crisis of the Negro Intellectual* and *Rebellion or Revolution.*

LONNE ELDER spent his youth in Jersey City and then moved to
Harlem where he made his living for a time in various after-
hours joints. He wrote poems and short stories and, after
meeting Douglas Turner Ward, turned to the theatre. His
first play, *Ceremonies in Dark Old Men* was eventually pro-
duced by the Negro Ensemble Company, of which he is now
an active member.

RALPH ELLISON was born in Oklahoma in 1914 and studied at
Tuskegee Institute. In 1936 he went to New York where he
met Richard Wright and thereafter began to write. Since
1939 his work has appeared in national magazines and
anthologies. His first novel, *Invisible Man,* published in 1952,
received the National Book Award and the Russwurm
Award. From 1955 to 1957 he was a fellow of the American
Academy in Rome. He has served as Visiting Professor of
Writing at Rutgers University. Much of his work has been
collected in *Shadow and Act.*

ROBERT FARNSWORTH is a professor of English at the University of
Missouri at Kansas City. He is a founder member of the
local chapter of CORE and in addition to publishing num-
erous articles in academic journals has prepared an edition
of Charles Chesnutt's *The Marrow of Tradition* and written
an introduction to the same author's *The Conjure Woman.*

WARREN FRENCH is presently chairman of the English Department
at the University of Missouri at Kansas City. He has also
taught at the universities of Mississippi and Kentucky as

well as Stetson and Kansas State. Professor French is the author of *The Social Novel at the end of an Era* as well as books on Frank Norris, John Steinbeck and J. D. Salinger. He is also the editor of a series of books on American literature and is a regular reviewer for the *Kansas City Star*. A collection of his reviews was recently published by the University of Missouri Press.

HOYT FULLER is Managing Editor of *Negro Digest,* has taught writing at several universities, and has contributed widely to important journals and magazines. He has been published often in anthologies and is a frequent contributor to *Collier's Encyclopedia.*

RICHARD GILMAN was formerly the drama editor of *Newsweek* magazine and literary editor of *The New Republic.* He lectures at Columbia University and has been on the faculty of the Salzburg Seminar.

THEODORE GROSS is Associate Professor of English at City College. He has published in the *Yale Review, The South Atlantic Quarterly, Georgia Review, Colorado Quarterly, Bucknell Review* and *Critique.* He is the co-editor of *Dark Symphony*: *Negro Literature in America* and author of studies of Albion W. Tourgée and Thomas Nelson Page. He is presently Visiting Professor of American literature at the University of Nancy.

LORRAINE HANSBERRY was born in Chicago in 1930. Her first play, *A Raisin in the Sun* was produced on Broadway in 1959. It was awarded the New York Drama Critics Circle Award. Her second play *The Sign in Sidney Brustein's Window,* was staged in 1964 and closed with the author's death in January, 1965. She left behind a third play, *Les Blancs,* which in some degree was intended as a response to Genet's *Les Noires.*

GERALD HASLAM was born in 1937 and is an assistant professor at Sonoma State College. He has published many articles on American literature in academic journals. He has two books pending: *The Forgotten Pages of American Literature* and *Black and Beautiful*: *The Literature of Afro-Americans from Slavery to the Present.*

LANGSTON HUGHES, who died in 1967, was the author of many volumes of poetry from *The Weary Blues* (1926) to a collection published in the year of his death. Hughes wrote a number of plays, including the highly successful *Mulatto* (1935) and was justly famous for his stories and novels about Jesse B. Simple. He also wrote two autobiographical works; *The Big Sea* and *I Wonder as I Wander*.

DAN JAFFE is a professor of English at the University of Missouri at Kansas City where he teaches creative writing. He is a recipient of a Hopwood Award for poetry and is the author of *Dan Freeman* (1967). His poems and reviews have appeared in many national publications. He has also collaborated with Herb Six on the production of an opera, *Without Memorial Banners*.

BRIAN LEE is presently tutor in American studies at the University of Nottingham. He has taught at Kings College, London, and at Antioch and was an ACLS fellow at Harvard. He has published articles in academic journals, specialising in Henry James and D. H. Lawrence. He has published an edition of Byron and is currently working on a book on Henry James.

WALTER MESERVE is presently Professor of Speech and Drama at Indiana University. He is associate editor of *Modern Drama* and has published a number of articles in academic journals. His edition of *The Complete Plays of W. D. Howells* appeared in 1960. He has also edited and contributed to *Discussions of Modern Drama* and is the author of *An Outline History of American Drama*.

JORDAN MILLER is chairman of the department of English at the University of Rhode Island. In addition to articles published in academic journals he is the author of *American Dramatic Literature, Eugene O'Neill and the American Critic* and *Playwright's Progress: O'Neill and the Critics*. He is also the author of a forthcoming biography of Elmer Rice and the editor of a collection of essays on *A Streetcar Named Desire*.

LOFTEN MITCHELL is a native of Harlem and a well-known playwright. He performed with the Rose McClendon Players and studied at Talledega College and Columbia University. His plays include *A Land Beyond the River, Ballad of the Winter Soldiers* and *Star of the Morning.* He held a Guggenheim fellowship grant in 1958-9 for playwriting. He is also the author of *Black Drama: The Story of the American Negro in the Theatre.*

GERALD MOORE was born in London in 1924 and educated at Cambridge University. In 1953 he went to Nigeria to work as an extra-mural lecturer and subsequently directed the extra-mural department at Makerere College in Uganda. He is a member of the Committee of *Black Orpheus,* the Journal of African and Afro-Asian Literature. Together with Ulli Beier he has edited a collection of *Modern Poetry from Africa* and is the author of *Seven African Writers.* He is a lecturer in African literature at the University of Sussex.

LARRY NEAL is a poet and essayist. He has been associated with LeRoi Jones and the Black Arts movement for several years, publishing in *Soulbook, Black Dialogue, Negro Digest* and *Liberator.* With Jones he is the editor of an anthology of black writing called *Black Fire.*

LOUIS PHILLIPS is a young poet, critic, and photographer who lives in New York City and teaches English at the U. S. Maritime Academy. He has been widely published in journals and magazines and has published several volumes of poetry.

ALLEN PROWLE is a graduate of Sheffield University and is presently teaching French in Lincolnshire. He is editor of *Lincolnshire Writers* and his poems are to be published in a forthcoming book. He is the recipient of several awards for poetry.

WILSON RECORD received his Ph.D. in sociology from the University of California at Berkeley. He has published in excess of seventy-five articles and has written four books on Negrowhite relations in the United States, the latest being *Race and Radicalism.* He is also the author of the definitive study *The Negro and the Communist Party.* Wilson Record is white and has been concerned with the applied as well as the academic aspects of race relations.

JEAN-PAUL SARTRE, the French writer and philosopher, is the author of several novels, including *La Nausée* and the trilogy, *L'Age de Raison, Le Sursis* and *La Mort dans L'Ame*. His plays, which frequently embody his philosophical ideas, include *Les Mouches, Huis Clos* and *Les Mains Sales*. As well as a series of literary and political essays he has published a number of complex and important philosophical studies, the most important being *L'Etre et le Néant* and *L'Existentialisme est un Humanisme*.

WILLIAM GARDNER SMITH published his first book, *Last of the Conquerors*, at the age of 20 and followed this three years later with *Anger at Innocence*. He went to Paris in 1951 and wrote his third novel, *South Street*. He subsequently married a French *lycée* teacher and decided to stay in France. He has two children, one born in Paris and the other in Africa. A fourth book, *The Stone Face*, was published in 1963.

MIKE THELWELL is a native of the West Indies. He was educated at Howard University and the University of Massachusetts. At present he is assistant professor of English at that institution and is in charge of establishing a department of Afro-American Studies there. An activist in the black liberation struggle in the United States and the Third World, Thelwell has worked in Mississippi and the Deep South for the Student Nonviolent Coordinating Committee and the Mississippi Freedom Democratic Party. He has served as a consultant to the National Endowment for the Humanities, is a Fellow of the Society for the Humanities of Cornell University and has recently been awarded a writing fellowship from the Rockefeller Foundation. His work has appeared in *Negro Digest, Freedomways, The Partisan Review, The Massachusetts Review, Presence Africaine, Short Story International, Ramparts Magazine* and such anthologies as *The American Literary Anthology 1968, Story Magazine Prize Stories 1968* (First Prize) and William Styron's *Nat Turner: Ten Black Writers Respond*, Beacon Press 1968. Thelwell is presently working on two novels, one of which concerns the slave rebellion led by Nat Turner in 1830.

DARWIN TURNER is Dean of the Graduate School at North Carolina Agricultural and Technical State University. He has published a book of poems and numerous articles and reviews on literature by Negroes.

JAMES TUTTLETON received his Ph.D. from the University of North Carolina and taught for a while at the University of Wisconsin. He is presently assistant professor at New York University. He has published many articles in learned journals and is the editor of Washington Irving's *Voyages and Discoveries of the Companions of Columbus* and the author of forthcoming books on Edith Wharton and *The Novel of Manners in America*.

JOHN A. WILLIAMS is a Negro novelist. His books include *Journey Out of Anger* and *The Men Who Cried I Am*.

Index